Other Books by Jack Vance

Novels:
(1953)
oid (1953)
(1956)
)
u (1958)
of Pao (1958)
Cage (1960)
sters (1963)
(1964)
szm (1964)
nces (1964–1981,
ibus 1997)
65)
(1966)
arth (1966)
(1967)
dventure
, Tor Omnibus,

)
73)
Men (1973)
978, Tor Omnibus

74)
e (1974)
d (1975)
(1976)
996)
:
Earth (1950)
of the Overworld

a (1983)
Marvelous (1984)

arden (1983)
Pearl (1985)
989)

The Cadwal Chronicles:
 Araminta Station (1987)
 Ecce and Old Earth (1991)
 Throy (1992)

Short Stories:
Future Tense (1964)
The World Between (1965)
Eight Fantasms and Magics (1969)
The Worlds of Jack Vance (1973)
The Best of Jack Vance (1976)
Green Magic (1979)
Galactic Effectuator (1980)
Lost Moons (1982)
The Narrow Land (1982)
The Complete Magnus Ridolph
 (1984)
Light from a Lone Star (1985)
The Dark Side of the Moon
 (1986)
The Augmented Agent (1986)
Chateau d'If and Other Stories
 (1990)
When the Five Moons Rise (1992)

Mystery Novels:
Take My Face (1957)
Isle of Peril (1959)
The Man in the Cage (1960)
The Four Johns (1964)
A Room to Die In (1965)
The Madman Theory (1966)
The Fox Valley Murders (1966)
The Pleasant Grove Murders
 (1967)
The Deadly Isles (1969)
Bad Ronald (1973)
The House on Lilly Street (1979)
Strange Notions (1985)
The Dark Ocean (1985)

PORTS
& LUR

Jack Vance

Ports of Call & Lurulu

SCIENCE
FICTION

PORTS OF CALL   Copyright © 1998 by Jack Vance
    Publication History: Tor hardcover, April 1998
                          Tor paperback, March 1999
LURULU   Copyright © 2004 by Jack Vance
    Publication History: Tor hardcover, December 2004

First SFBC Science Fiction Printing: December 2004

Published by arrangement with:
Tom Doherty Associates, Inc.
175 Fifth Avenue
New York, NY 10010

Visit The SFBC online at http://www.sfbc.com

ISBN # 0-7394-4999-0

Printed in the United States of America.

CONTENTS

PORTS OF CALL

To

John and Tammy
Ryan and Alison

PREFACE

During the first expansion of the Gaean Reach, when every adventurous youth yearned to become a locator, thousands of worlds in remote places had been explored. The most benign of these worlds attracted immigrants; there seemed no end to the sects, factions, societies, cults, or simple groups of free-thinkers who fared bravely off as pioneers to live their lives on worlds of their own. Sometimes they survived or even prospered; more often the alien environment defeated the Gaean soul; the settlements decayed; the folk departed, sometimes leaving behind odd little clots of humanity which by one means or another came to terms with the surroundings. Some of these worlds, seldom visited and remote from public notice, provided substance for Thom Hartmann's haunting work *Lost Worlds and Forgotten Peoples*.

Gaean philosophers recognized that a variety of social forces operated between the worlds, which could be classified by several systems: isolationist versus collectivist; centrifugal versus centripetal; homogenizing versus differentiating.

In the absence of a central government, order was maintained by the IPCC, originally the Interworld Police Coordinating Company, an organization dedicated to legality, order, and the curbing of crime, with attendant punishment of criminals, pirates, miscellaneous sociopaths—a program which it performed with convincing efficiency. In the end, the IPCC became a de facto administrative agency which controlled the smooth functioning of the Gaean Reach and everywhere projected an awareness of Gaean identity.

Incidental note: The unit of Gaean currency, the sol, has approximately the value of ten contemporary dollars.

ONE

1

As a boy Myron Tany had immersed himself in the lore of space exploration. In his imagination he wandered the far places of the Gaean Reach, thrilling to the exploits of star-dusters and locators; of pirates and slavers; of the IPCC and its brave agents.

By contrast his home in the bucolic village of Lilling on the pleasant world Vermazen seemed to encompass everything easy, tranquil, and soporific. Despite Myron's daydreams, his parents persisted in stressing the practicalities. "Most important is your education, if you are to become a financial analyst like your father," Myron was told. "After you finish your course at the Institute, that will be the time to flutter your wings for a bit before taking a post at the Exchange."

Myron, mild and dutiful by temperament, pushed the intoxicating images to the back of his mind, and enrolled at the College of Definable Excellences at the Varley Institute, across the continent at Salou Sain. His parents, who well understood his casual disposition, sent him off with a set of stern injunctions. He must concentrate with full diligence upon his studies. Scholastic achievement was highly important when a person prepared for a career.

Myron agreed to do his best, but found himself waylaid by indecision when it came time to propose a schedule of studies. Despite his best intentions, he could not put aside images of majestic space-packets sliding through the void, of cities redolent with strange smells, of taverns open to the warm winds where dusky maidens in purple skirts served foaming toddy in carved wooden beakers.

In the end Myron fixed upon a set of courses which, in his opinion, represented a compromise. The list included statistical mathematics, economic patterns of the Gaean Reach, general cosmology, the elementary theory of space propulsion, and Gaean anthropology. The program, so he assured his parents, was known as "Economic Flux-ions," and provided a solid foundation upon which a good general edu-cation might be based. Myron's parents were not convinced. They knew that Myron's decorous manner, though at times a trifle absent-minded, concealed a streak of irrational intransigence against which no argument could prevail. They would say no more; Myron must dis-cover his mistakes for himself.

Myron could not dismiss the foreboding which his father's glum pre-dictions had induced. As a consequence he attacked his work more vigor-ously than ever, and in due course he was matriculated with high honors.

His father suggested that, despite Myron's odd yearnings and un-conventional course of studies, he might still qualify for a place in the lower echelons of the Exchange, from which he could launch his ca-reer. But now an unforeseen factor disturbed the flow of Myron's life. The disruptive influence was Myron's great-aunt, Dame Hester Lajoie, who had inherited great wealth from her first husband. Dame Hester maintained her splendid residence, Sarbiter House, on Dingle Terrace, at the southern edge of Salou Sain. During Myron's last term at Varley Institute, Dame Hester noticed that Myron was no longer a slender stripling with a vague and—as she put it—moony expression, but had become a distinctly good-looking young man, still slender, but of good physical proportions, with sleek blond hair and sea-blue eyes. Dame Hester enjoyed the presence of nice-looking young men: They acted, so she imagined, as a foil or, perhaps better to say, a setting, for the pre-cious gem which was herself. For whatever reason, during Myron's last term, he resided at Sarbiter House with his great-aunt: an education in itself, so it turned out. Myron was not allowed to address her as "great-aunt," nor did she care for "Aunt Hester." She preferred "Dear Lady," or the soubriquet "Schutzel," as he chose.

Dame Hester fitted no familiar patterns or categories of Gaean womanhood. She was tall and gaunt, though she insisted upon the word "slim." She walked with long strides, head thrust forward, like a rapacious animal on the prowl. Her wild mass of mahogany-red hair framed a pale hollow-cheeked face. Her black eyes were surrounded by small creases and folds of skin, like parrot's eyes, and her long high-bridged nose terminated in a notable hook. It was a striking face, the mouth jerking and grimacing, the parrot's eyes snapping, her expres-sion shifting to the flux of emotions. Her tempestuous moods, whims, quirks, and fancies were notorious. One day, at a garden party, a gen-tleman artlessly urged Dame Hester to write her memoirs. The fervor of her response caused him shock and dismay. "Ludicrous! Graceless!

Stupid! A beastly idea! How can I write memoirs now, when I have scarcely started to live?"

The gentleman bowed. "I see my mistake; it shall never be repeated!"

An hour later the gentleman had recovered his aplomb sufficiently that he was able to describe the incident to a friend who, so he discovered, had also excited Dame Hester's wrath. After looking over his shoulder, the friend muttered, "I suspect the woman has forged a pact with the Devil!"

"Wrong!" muttered the more recent victim. "She is herself the Devil!"

"Hmm," said his friend. "You may be right; we must take care not to annoy her."

"That is impossible!"

"Well, then, let us consider the matter over another gill of this excellent malt."

For a fact Dame Hester was not always discreet. She conceived herself a creature of voluptuous charm for whom time had no meaning. Undeniably she made a gorgeous spectacle as she whirled about the haut monde, clad in remarkable garments of magenta, plum, lime-green, vermilion and black.

Dame Hester had recently won a judgment of slander against Gower Hatchkey, a wealthy member of the Gadroon Society. In satisfaction of the judgment she had accepted the space-yacht *Glodwyn*.

Initially Dame Hester thought of the *Glodwyn* only as proof that whoever chose to call her a "bald old harridan in a red fright-wig" must pay well for the privilege. She showed no interest in the vessel, and rather than inviting her friends to join her for a cruise, she prohibited them from so much as setting foot aboard the vessel. "Amazing!" she told Myron with a sardonic chuckle. "Suddenly I have dozens of new friends, all bright-eyed and cheerful as larks. They declare that, no matter what their personal inconvenience, they would never refuse to join me on an extended cruise."

"Nor would I!" said Myron wistfully. "It is an exciting prospect."

Dame Hester ignored him. She went on. "They'll drift away when they find that I am planning no cruises whatever."

Myron looked at her incredulously. "No cruises—ever?"

"Of course not!" snapped Dame Hester. "Spaceflight is a weird and unnatural ambition! I, for one, have neither time nor inclination to go hurtling through space in an oversize coffin. That is sheer lunacy and a mortification of both body and spirit. I shall probably put the vessel up for sale."

Myron had nothing to say.

Dame Hester watched him closely, parrot's eyes snapping. "I see that you are perplexed; you think me timid and orthodox. That is incorrect! I pay no heed to convention, and why is this? Because a youthful spirit defies the years! So you dismiss me as an eccentric madcap! What then? It is the price I pay for retaining the verve of youth, and it is the secret of my vivid beauty!"

"Ah yes, of course," said Myron. He added thoughtfully, "Still, it is a sad waste of a beautiful ship."

The remark irritated Dame Hester. "Myron, be practical! Why should I gad through empty space or trudge through dirty back alleys, testing out strange smells? I lack time for my normal pursuits here at home. At this very moment I have a dozen invitations in prospect; they cannot be ignored. I am in demand everywhere! The Golliwog Gala is upon us, and I am on the committee. If I could get away, I'd spend a week at Lulchion's Mountain Resort. The fresh air is like balm for my nerves. You must realize that I am constantly on the qui vive!"

"No doubt about that," said Myron.

2

One morning Dame Hester found herself at loose ends and on sudden whim decided to inspect the *Glodwyn*. She summoned Myron and the two rode in her big black float-car to the spaceport and around to the storage yard. Halfway along a line of miscellaneous spacecraft, they found the *Glodwyn*: a ship of moderate size, enameled in shades of gold and green, with trim and sensor bosses picked out in plum red. Dame Hester was favorably impressed by the glossy exterior surfaces, the vessel's size and solidity, and its interior appointments, which she found unexpectedly luxurious. "It is a handsome craft," she told Myron. "The saloon is quite commodious and the fittings seem of good quality. Nor could I complain of the decor; it is quaint but in good taste. I am surprised that anything connected with a blatant brute like Gower Hatchkey could be anything other than slovenly. His remarks concerning my person were truly beyond the pale!"

Myron nodded thoughtfully. "Someday I will calculate what his statement cost him per syllable. A really exorbitant amount, when you think of it. After all, a syllable when spoken by itself conveys no meaning. If Hatchkey had separated his comment into syllables, then had read the list to the judge from bottom to top, the judge would have found no offense, and might have let Hatchkey off with only a warning."

Dame Hester became restive. "Let us take the subject no farther. Your ideas are absurd. Come; it is time to leave. I will mention the vessel to Dauncy; he is highly knowledgeable in this regard."

Myron forebore comment.

Dauncy Covarth had become a frequent caller at Sarbiter House. He was a hearty gentleman, bluff and dashing, with a crisp mustache, sandy-brown hair which he wore clipped short, in the so-called "Regimental" style. Myron could not accurately gauge the degree of intimacy existing between Dame Hester and Covarth, but at the moment he seemed to be her favorite chum. With cynical disapproval Myron noted how, under the spell of Dauncy's gallantries, Dame Hester simpered and gushed like a smitten schoolgirl.

A few days after her visit to the spaceport, Dame Hester let fall a casual remark to the effect that, perhaps someday, when her social calendar had eased, she might consider a short cruise aboard the *Glodwyn*— perhaps to the nearby world Derard, where a cycle of bucolic festivals was said to be entertaining, what with the high-kicking peasant dances and outdoor banquets beside firepits where entire wild boars sizzled on spits and a wine keg with six spigots graced every table. Myron endorsed the project, but Dame Hester paid him no great heed. "Yes, Myron, I am aware of your enthusiasm; at heart you are an unmitigated vagabond! But that is no surprise! Suddenly I find myself with a great entourage of new friends, each of which, when the *Glodwyn* is mentioned, describes himself or herself as a natural spacefarer, with the lust for adventure bred into his or her bones, and each expects to be invited aboard the *Glodwyn* for a luxurious vacation. I have assured everyone that there will be no languid idlers aboard the *Glodwyn* if I were to undertake a cruise."

"A sound idea!" declared Myron. "I am particularly well qualified; as you know, I took my degree in the College of Cosmology."

"Tchah!" Dame Hester gave her fingers a contemptuous flutter. "It is all classwork and cookypushing, of no practical use whatever."

"Not so!" cried Myron. "I studied space dynamics, in all its phases, Gaean economics, the mathematical basis of transdimensional propulsion. I am familiar with *Handbook to the Planets* and *Gaean Cosmography*. In short, I am not just another dilettante! I am anxious to apply my knowledge to useful purposes."

"Correct and proper," said Dame Hester. "Perhaps someday you shall have the opportunity." She spoke somewhat absently. "By the way, since your studies have been so exhaustive, what do you know of the world Kodaira?"

" 'Kodaira'? I don't come up with anything definite. In fact, nothing at all."

"So much for your expensive education," said Dame Hester with a sniff.

"There are thousands of worlds, some inhabited, some not. I can't remember them all. Even if I could, I would not trouble to do so, since the information changes every year. It is why the *Handbook* goes through so many editions."

Myron went to the bookshelf and found a relatively recent copy of the standard reference. He looked through the index. "Nothing here by that name."

"Odd."

Myron shrugged. "Sometimes a world has several names, not all listed in the *Handbook*. Why are you interested?"

Dame Hester indicated the magazine she had been reading. "This journal is edited and published here in Salou Sain. It has a wide readership among the upper intellectual strata and must be considered a magazine of prestige. This is the current edition. I have just read a pair of articles, both dealing with an important subject. The articles are of unequal weight, the first being rather flippant. The second article was written by someone using a pseudonym, and is far more significant than the first, though both are thought provoking."

Dame Hester took up the journal. The title, so Myron saw, was *Innovative Salubrity*.

"The first article," said Dame Hester, "is called, 'The Fountains of Youth: Fact or Fancy?' The author, I am sorry to say, has given sensational treatment to a serious subject. Still, it provides items of information, which might otherwise be overlooked. His topic is rejuvenation and revitalization of aging tissue, a matter of concern to everyone."

"True enough," said Myron. "What have you learned?"

Dame Hester glanced down at the journal. "Much of the material is of no great value and is also marred by the author's unfortunate attempts at whimsy. There is, first, a historical survey, then a discussion of faith healers, religious mania, and, of course, fraudulent practitioners. The author ends the piece with a waggish anecdote regarding the Eternal Hope Fellowship. He reports that the treatment is so expensive and prolonged that many of the patients die of old age before they are rejuvenated. The concept is poignant and, once again, facetiousness is not appropriate."

"What about the second article?"

"It is different, in both tone and content, and certainly more consequential. Unfortunately, explicit details are carefully guarded. The author, who uses the pseudonym 'Serena,' seems to be a woman native to the area. She describes some very advanced research conducted on a remote world she calls 'Kodaira.' The thrust of the work is entirely therapeutic. The goal is to repair or reverse the effects of aging; there is no tinkering with the genes. The editor's foreword to the article is inspiring. It reads:

" 'Kodaira is known as the "World of Laughing Joy" and the "Place of Resurgent Youth." The source of this wonderful ambience is the unique fountain known as Exxil Waters, where a scientist called Doctor Maximus (not his real name) first studied the remarkable power of the water and eventually evolved the science of metachronics. The author knows the world Kodaira intimately, and uses the pseudonym "Serena" to safeguard her privacy. Originally a scientist in her own right, Serena now resides in the vicinity of Salou Sain, where she devotes her time to writing articles based upon her experience as a comparative botanist. The editorial staff considers the following article to be one of the most important ever published on Vermazen.' "

Dame Hester looked sidewise to assure herself that Myron was paying attention. She asked, "What do you think of that?"

"I think that now I understand your interest in the world Kodaira."

Dame Hester spoke with muted annoyance, "Sometimes, Myron, your apathy becomes dreadfully tiresome."

"Sorry."

Dame Hester thrust the journal at him. "Read for yourself."

Myron politely accepted the journal and fixed his attention upon the article. It bore the title: "For the Select Few: A Regeneration." Myron started to read: at first languidly, then with increasing interest. Serena described Doctor Maximus: "He is a tireless little man of enormous zest, who bounces, rather than walks, from place to place. He is impatient with prejudice, stupidity, and cant, and rejects both social acclaim and social censure, and most of all the sheer weight of society. This is one reason why he continues to work on the remote world we shall call Kodaira. The second and more important reason is the fountain known as Exxil Waters."

Serena went on to describe what she called the real Fountain of Youth. "The water arises in a volcanic spring from deep within the world, where it encounters a variety of complex minerals. It seeps through a dense jungle, absorbing virtue from herbs, molds and deep decaying humus. Finally it flows, pale green and faintly effervescent, into Exxil Pool. Doctor Maximus, a biologist by training, became interested in the unique newt-like creatures which inhabit the mud surrounding the pool. He noticed their hardihood and longevity, which far exceeded that of similar individuals elsewhere. After tests and analyses, he threw caution aside and drank the water. The results were encouraging. In the end he developed a therapeutic regimen, which initially was tested by volunteers. Finally, Doctor Maximus organized the New Age Clinic and began to treat clients who could pay the not inconsiderable fee.

"Serena, with her husband, came to Kodaira in order to conduct botanical research. Serena chanced upon the clinic and applied for regenerative therapy. She undertook the regimen. The results were entirely to her satisfaction.

"Doctor Maximus meanwhile continues his research, hoping to improve the program and discover the basic processes involved in the therapy. At the moment he believes that a variety of factors cooperate to synergistic effect, and he wants to optimize active factors and reduce the sometimes irksome aspects of the regimen. He is aware that the therapy is not yet perfected and suspects that it may never be so, owing to the complexity of the systems involved. Meanwhile, he insists that the location of the clinic be kept secret, in order to avert a pell-mell onrush of the lame, halt, and moribund. By the same token, he refuses to theorize as to whether his work, in the end, will benefit society, or the reverse."

Myron put the journal aside. Dame Hester asked tartly, "Are you tongue-tied? What is your opinion?"

"Interesting, but vague and mysterious. Also highly expensive."

Dame Hester stared at him incredulously. " 'Expensive'? What else is money good for? Doctor Maximus sells youth and life and vivacity! How can a price be set on such commodities?"

Myron reflected. "I expect that Doctor Maximus charges whatever the traffic will bear."

Dame Hester made a sound of disgust and went back to her reading. After a time she looked up. "Tomorrow you can put your expensive education to some practical use. Go early to the Cosmological Library and systematically explore its resources. Consult all the indexes, trace down every reference, give your intuition full scope. For once in your life show a modicum of persistence. Achieve results! Find Kodaira!"

3

Two days passed. Myron, responding to his great-aunt's instructions, had searched the voluminous files of the Cosmological Library without result. He had become convinced that "Kodaira" was a name improvised for the occasion, and he so informed Dame Hester. She accepted the judgment without surprise. "It is as I suspected. Well, no matter. Tomorrow we will attend Sir Regis Glaxen's garden party. Dauncy Covarth has kindly agreed to be my escort of course, but there may be persons present whom I will want you to meet."

"Why me? Let them meet your chum Dauncy."

"Not another word, if you please. Be sure to dress appropriately; this will be a notable occasion."

"Oh well; just as you like," Myron grumbled. "I still can't understand any of this."

"You will, in due course. It is truly important, and I may well need your most active and alert intelligence."

Myron had no further remark to make, and on the following day he accompanied Dauncy Covarth and Dame Hester to Sir Regis Glaxen's garden party. Dame Hester had chosen to appear in an exciting ensemble, consisting of a burnt orange blouse, deeply cleft, and a full lime-green skirt with a slit up the left side. The slit from time to time revealed a goodly length of left leg, which was encased in a yellow silk stocking. The leg was long and thin, the knee was knobby, but Dame Hester felt certain that pulses quickened and hormones raced whenever the slit allowed a glimpse of the lank member.

Sir Regis Glaxen's occasion was, as usual, notable for the perfect verdure of his trees, and flowers, the sweep of his lawns, the opulence of the buffet, and the éclat of his guests. Dame Hester's standards, however, were extraordinarily rigid. As she entered the garden, she halted and appraised the company with a darting sweep of her sharp black eyes. It was, so she decided, a mixed bag, and included a number of persons with whom she was not prepared to associate. Meanwhile, the persons whom she especially wished to see were not in evidence. Restraining her annoyance, she allowed Dauncy Covarth to lead her to a table at the side of the lawn, in the shade of a great flowering hyssop tree. Dauncy seated her with punctilious gallantry. Myron thought the display, which had included a clicking of the heels, somewhat excessive, but Dame Hester accepted the attention with complacence. A waiter approached and Dauncy, with an air of wise expertise, ordered Pingaree Punch for all.

Sir Regis Glaxen appeared: a round-faced gentleman of middle-age, plump, pink, and cheerful. He bent and kissed Dame Hester's cheek. "You'll find this very strange," he told her. "I could not see your face because that hyssop branch hung in the way. What I saw was a lovely yellow leg, and instantly I said to myself: 'Dear me! Surely I recognize that leg! It is the property of Hester Lajoie, the most ravishing of women!' The yellow leg told me all I needed to know. In my haste to join you I tripped over a petunia, but suffered nothing and here I am."

"Ah, flattery!" cried Dame Hester. "I like to hear it, even when it's a transparent lie. I never want it to stop."

"This is an enchanted garden, where nothing begins and nothing ends," declared Sir Regis stoutly. "Eschatology is a dangerous lore!"

Dame Hester knit her brows. "I scarcely know how to spell the word, let alone comment upon its vagaries."

Sir Regis seated himself. "There is no past and no future; only the twinkling flicker of an instant which is the present. Tell me this, my dear Hester! Have you ever thought to measure the exact duration of that instant? I have tried, but I know less now than ever. Is it a tenth of a second? A full second? Or the hundredth part of a second? The more you ponder, the more confused you become. The idea is diaphanous, and cannot be grasped!"

"Yes, all very interesting. I will think about it, or perhaps I shall have Myron do a calculation. Meanwhile, you may tell me who will be on hand today."

Sir Regis looked with rueful skepticism around the garden. "I'm not sure that I know. Sometimes I think I am entertaining half the riff-raff of Salou Sain, none of whom I have invited. Still, they are often quite amusing, and they drink my best wines with truly flattering gusto."

"You mentioned that you were inviting a certain publisher in whom I had an interest."

"So I did. You refer, I believe, to Jonas Chay, who—with a straight face, mind you—disseminates the *Vegetarian Herald*."

Dame Hester spoke with dignity: "I prefer to associate him with *Innovative Salubrity*, which is a more serious work."

"It may well be. Still, I fear I cannot supply Jonas Chay, who apparently has better things to do." Sir Regis looked around the garden and pointed. "Notice that tall gentleman yonder with the face of a herring. That is Chay's assistant editor; will he serve as an acceptable substitute?"

Dame Hester surveyed the gentleman in question, who wore a black suit, a brown cravat, and long pointed yellow-brown shoes.

"He may be more debonair than he looks," said Dame Hester. "I would be pleased if you would introduce him to me."

Sir Regis dutifully went off and brought back the tall gentleman. "This is Ostvold Socroy, who assists Jonas Chay with *Innovative Salubrity*; and here Dame Hester Lajoie, a notable bon vivant and the new proprietress of a fine space-yacht, the *Glodwyn*."

"I am pleased to meet you," said Dame Hester. "Sit down, if you please, and tell me about yourself."

Ostvold Socroy complied with the request. "There is little to tell. I work in the realm of ideas. I think, I judge, I communicate, I redirect."

Dame Hester listened patiently, making an occasional comment, smiling graciously from time to time, even though there was little about Socroy to charm her. He was thin and bony, with a long pale face, a black beard, and a high forehead. Dame Hester might have forgiven him his appearance, had it not been for his manner, which was smilingly tolerant, as if he found Dame Hester's foibles amusing but of no great interest. She was further prejudiced by his refusal to ingest anything other than herbal tea, which protected him from the antics induced by strong drink.

Socroy said at last, "But surely that is enough of me and my concerns. Tell me something about your space-yacht!"

"There is little to tell," said Dame Hester politely. "It is a new acquisition."

"That is truly exciting!" declared Socroy. "I'm sure that you are enthralled by the possibilities which are now open to you?"

Dame Hester spoke in a reedy voice. "I am not the intrepid space-farer you assume me to be. For a fact, I have seen the vessel only once. I am told that it is quite sturdy. The hull is nicely enameled in pleasing colors. The internal appointments appear to be comfortable. My friends want me to undertake a cruise, but my social calendar will not permit it. Still, perhaps someday—who knows?"

Ostvold Socroy laughed graciously. "When that time comes, I hope that you will consider placing me on your guest list. I know several card tricks and I play chansons on the lute. I fancy that I can make myself both amusing and entertaining."

"That is good to know," said Dame Hester. "I will make a memorandum of what you have told me." Dame Hester brought a slip of paper from her hand pouch and wrote upon it. "I suppose you can always be reached at your offices."

"Of course! Call me any time you like!"

Dame Hester nodded. "What with your knowledge of the publishing business, you should make a valuable addition to such a cruise. I suppose that you determine which articles appear in, let us say, *Innovative Salubrity*?"

"Well yes, to a certain extent."

"Did you arrange for the two articles on the subject of revitalization?"

"Oh indeed! In fact, I wrote the first article myself, to serve as an introduction to the second, more circumstantial, piece."

"Ah yes; most amusing and well-balanced. What of the second article? I am rather curious about this 'Serena.' I suppose you came to know her well?"

Socroy pursed his lips. "Not really. Jonas Chay was principally involved with her."

"But you must have formed some opinion as to her integrity?"

Socroy gave an uncomfortable shrug. "Not really. It was not suggested that I do so."

"She is a local woman, I believe. It's quite possible that I know her. In strict confidence, what is her name?"

Socroy gave a tolerant laugh. "You must ask me something else, my dear lady. We never divulge such a fact; it is against our rules."

Dame Hester nodded slowly. "I see." She took up the memorandum on which she had noted Socroy's name and looked at it thoughtfully. Her nose twitched. With her keen black parrot's eyes, she studied Socroy. He had been watching her intently.

"Naturally I would not want you to betray your trust," said Dame Hester. "Still, there is something you may tell me without straying an iota from your rules, and it will quite satisfy me. Who is the scientist whom the author accompanied on the expedition to Kodaira?"

Socroy grimaced. He looked down at the memorandum, then back up at Dame Hester. "This particular fact is extraneous to the rules and I can speak without qualm."

Dame Hester gave an approving nod. "Your logic is sound! You are a valuable asset to your company! What is the gentleman's name?"

Socroy looked up into the branches of the hyssop tree, formed his lips into a prim little rosebud, then said, "It is, or, rather, he was Professor Andrey Ontwill; on that trip he suffered a fatal accident in the Kodaira jungle. His work was sponsored by the College of Botanical Sciences at the Institute."

"My curiosity is satisfied," declared Dame Hester. "I never met the unfortunate Professor Ontwill and probably will never meet his widow. Already I have forgotten our conversation." She picked up the memorandum and carefully tucked it into her handbag.

Socroy spoke casually, "And when do you think you might be going off on a cruise? I ask so that if I were in fact invited, I might arrange for a suitable leave of absence."

Dame Hester nodded. "At the moment I can announce no definite departure date. There are a dozen demands upon my time, and I must simply wait for favorable circumstances."

"Hmm," said Socroy. "The third of Baron Bodissey's Ten Succinct Apothegms is 'Sooner is better than later.' My own favorite dictum is: 'Do it now!'"

"All very well," said Dame Hester. "However, a cruise cannot simply be ordained. It must be planned and organized."

Dauncy Covarth leaned forward, smiling in whimsical apology at Dame Hester. "Experience, my dear lady, has taught me a sad truth: time flows in one direction only! As the days pass none of us grows younger. Sometimes we postpone glorious schemes only to discover in the end that they never have materialized! Procrastination is the thief of life!"

Dame Hester, who liked to think of herself as ageless, was not pleased by Dauncy's references to mortality. "So it may be! Still I reject such dismal precepts! I shall maintain my thirst for life and love and every wonderful excitement for an indefinite period—forever, if my élan will carry me so far! I reject all contrary views!"

Ostvold Socroy inclined his head. "The concept does you credit!"

"Thank you," said Dame Hester. She looked up and down the length of the garden. "There is really no one here to interest me. Myron? Dauncy? I am ready to go."

Dauncy sprang to his feet and assisted Dame Hester from her chair. Ostvold Socroy also rose to his feet. He bowed. "I am pleased to have made your acquaintance, and I hope that we shall soon meet again."

"I shall look forward to the occasion," said Dame Hester. Taking Dauncy Covarth's arm she set off across the lawn toward Sir Regis, who stood by the marble portal welcoming a pair of late-arriving guests. Dame Hester paused and inspected the newcomers. "Dauncy, who are those people?"

Dauncy studied the two, and pulled at his mustache. "I'm afraid I don't know."

Dame Hester muttered, half to herself, "Somewhere I have seen the gentleman. He is quite distinguished, don't you think? And the woman seems rather dashing, though her gown is not in the best taste."

Myron glanced sidewise at Dame Hester's own carnival attire, but made no comment. The newcomers were apparently persons of consequence. The gentleman was white-haired, tall, erect, with strong decisive features. He seemed considerably older than his companion, whom Myron thought quite attractive. Her age was not immediately obvious; she looked, he thought, both innocent and wise, to intriguing effect. Blond curls were caught up in a mesh at the back of her head. Her skin, smooth tawny-gold, glowed with health and happy activity outdoors in the sunlight. The white gown which had excited Dame Hester's comment was notable mainly for its simplicity and the manner in which it molded to her elegant figure.

Dame Hester snapped, "Myron, try to control yourself. You are absolutely pawing the ground with your hooves!"

"Sorry."

Dame Hester, having induced contrition in Myron, turned back to the new guests. She mused: "I wonder who they are. The gentleman seems of some consequence; yet, he fawns over her in a most fatuous manner. It is what happens when a pretty girl chances to look twice at an elderly man! I hope, Myron, that when you become senile, you will try to behave with more dignity."

"Absolutely," said Myron. "I would never dream of anything else, unless I thought the chances were good."

Dame Hester only sniffed and said, "Come! Let us find out what is what."

The three proceeded to the portal and halted. Dame Hester said, "Regis, we must be leaving, though your party is most delightful! We thank you very much."

"Charmed that you were able to make an appearance!" declared Sir Regis. "By the way, allow me to present Jonas Chay, who publishes *Innovative Salubrity*, and this is Dame Betka Ontwill, one of his staff writers. This is Dame Hester Lajoie, and Myron Tany and Dauncy Covarth."

"I'm happy to meet you," said Jonas Chay.

"And I as well," said Dame Hester.

4

Dame Hester telephoned Betka Ontwill at her villa on the edge of Angwyn Heath, in the countryside five miles south of Salou Sain. The two appraised each other's images, then Dame Hester said brightly: "Perhaps you will remember me; Regis Glaxen introduced us as you were arriving at his party. I am Hester Lajoie."

"Yes. I remember you well, the lady with the red hair and the yellow stockings."

"Something of the sort," said Dame Hester graciously. "Your own frock, as I recall, was of a very tasteful simplicity, and truly charming."

"Thank you. That is nice to hear, coming from a celebrity."

"A celebrity?" Dame Hester gave a mischievous chuckle. "I wonder why? Could it be—"

Dame Betka said placidly, "Sir Regis mentioned that you own a spaceyacht; it must give you a wonderful feeling of freedom."

"Oh, the spaceyacht. I suppose you are right. The vessel came to me as part of a legal settlement, so I cannot claim to be a keen space-farer. I called, however, to comment upon your article in Jonas Chay's journal: the piece on revitalization! It is a topic in which I myself am interested."

There was a pause of several seconds. Then Dame Betka said carefully, "I am aware of this article. If you recall, it was signed by a certain 'Serena.' Evidently she wishes to remain anonymous."

"Yes, all this is clear. Nevertheless, I would like you to join me for dinner tomorrow night. I will send my car for you, and I can promise you an excellent meal. Further, the identity of 'Serena' will not be publicized, and your privacy will be assured."

There was another short pause. Then Dame Betka spoke in a voice now cold: "My name is Betka Ontwill; you are making some very shaky and even intrusive assumptions."

"Am I?" Dame Hester chuckled. "If so, and my assumptions are incorrect, the circumstances are even more uncanny than they now appear."

"This is totally preposterous," said Dame Betka. "I have nothing more to say. And now, if you will excuse me—"

"Just a moment. Your husband was Andrey Ontwill. The College of Botany register lists an Andrey Ontwill whose wife, some thirty-five years ago, was Betka Ontwill. Most extraordinary!"

Dame Betka said drily. "Yes; quite."

Dame Hester went on. "You are a striking woman, and you wear your clothes with panache. Your posture is erect, you look strong and capable, and your age is not instantly obvious! Could there be two un-related Betka Ontwills? Could both Betkas have married scientists named 'Andrey' and gone off on jungle expeditions? Could both husbands be similarly dead? Very strange. Coincidence cannot be carried so far—especially just after a certain 'Serena' has published an article describing her revitalization on the world Kodaira. I am confused—but, even more, I am curious."

Dame Betka's voice was brittle. "You have no right to be curious."

"Incorrect! Your articles put you in the way of public attention and you are now the legitimate object of curiosity."

Dame Betka retorted: "Not when I take pains to use a pseudonym!" She compressed her lips, realizing that she had admitted considerably more than she had intended to this sly old creature.

"Be calm," said Dame Hester. "No matter what I learn, it will not be trumpeted abroad. I want information for my personal use alone. I am entitled to it, and you have no cause for complaint, since you chose to tantalize us with your hints and concealments. You are like a girl who teases a boy into a state of erotic frenzy, then primly cries out: 'How dare you!'"

"That is not what I had in mind. I wrote the article only because Jonas Chay offered me a large sum of money, which I badly needed."

"That is irrelevant. The effect is the same, and I have a right to pursue my inquiries. I am growing no younger, and the time is coming when I must peer behind the veil, so to speak. I will postpone this moment by all practical means, including those cited by 'Serena.'"

Dame Betka laughed without humor. "You are not alone in your yearnings."

"That is as may be! But I am quite alone in being Hester Lajoie! I strike my own personal path through the wilderness of life, and I intend to resist dissolution tooth and nail!"

"Perhaps so, but I have a commitment to secrecy, and I prefer not to discuss the circumstances."

Dame Hester nodded. "Certainly not over the telephone. We will talk tomorrow evening at Sarbiter House."

"I can make no such commitment."

"Come now!" coaxed Dame Hester. "We will enjoy a splendid meal, and you shall taste my best wines! A quiet affair, of course! And then there need be none of the sensation and publicity surrounding the mysterious 'Serena' that there would most certainly be otherwise."

Dame Betka stared grimly at Dame Hester. "Are you trying to blackmail me?"

"Yes," said Dame Hester. "You have fixed upon what is known as the *mot juste*. But it is a relatively painless process, and I will see that you enjoy an excellent dinner."

In a strained voice Dame Betka said, "I see that you lack all compunction."

"Not so! You do me a frightful wrong! I would never serve a Spanzenheimer hock with deviled oxtails, nor yet Romany bull's blood with whitebait."

"I am encouraged on that score, at least." Dame Betka wavered, torn between conflicting emotions.

"Just so," said Dame Hester confidently. "I will send my car to pick you up at about six."

5

Dame Hester's long black car called for Dame Betka at the hour specified, and transported her to Sarbiter House. She was met by Dame

Hester and escorted into the pleasant gray and green drawing room, where the butler served aperitifs, and where they presently were joined by Myron. Dame Hester told him, "As you know, Dame Betka is a veteran of several expeditions to far-off worlds. Unfortunately, her husband was killed on the last of these expeditions." She looked aside at Dame Betka. "Perhaps I am tactless! Does it pain you to talk of the tragedy?"

Dame Betka gave her head a smiling shake. "By this time the pain has drained away. I don't mind telling you what happened. Andrey had ventured a mile into the jungle and was taking samples of sap from an iron tree. A creature called a bottle-bird settled into a cluster of pods at the top of the tree. A twenty-pound pod, mostly iron, fell a hundred feet and killed poor Andrey instantly. I'm sure that he never knew what struck him."

"Not the worst way to go," observed Dame Hester. "Putting aside this terrible event, you have lived a remarkable life, and I'm sure that you have a thousand wonderful memories! Where, for instance, did you go on your last expedition?"

Dame Betka shook her head. "It's not important, and it's something I prefer not to dwell on."

"Of course not!" said Dame Hester.

Myron watched as the ladies went on to discuss other matters in which he took no interest. He fixed his attention upon the agreeable image projected by Dame Betka. Tonight she wore a demure suit of soft blue-gray which went nicely with her complexion and from which Dame Hester could draw no unfavorable conclusions. Initially Myron had thought of her as an attractive young matron not a great deal older than himself. Her golden curls were tucked up into a bundle at the nape of her neck, with a pair of golden tendrils trailing down at right and left to her shoulders. Her skin was as smooth as still cream, lightly tanned by the light of distant suns. However, without actively searching, Myron began to notice certain small signs which jarred against his first impressions. Her body was something less than youthfully flexible. When the three had walked in to the dining room, Myron, bringing up the rear, observed that the articulation of her hips, knees and ankles seemed rather stiff, so that she walked carefully, without elasticity or bounce. She was definitely a pleasant lady, thought Myron, but not the spring chicken she had originally seemed.

As Dame Hester had promised, dinner was a splendid affair of ten courses and nine wines, indicating that Dame Hester intended to induce in her guest a state of semi-inebriated satiety, to such a degree that the guest would grant Dame Hester whatever favor Dame Hester might suggest. Myron had seen the ploy in action before.

Over dessert Dame Hester begged Dame Betka to describe one of her more interesting expeditions.

Dame Betka smilingly shook her head. "I'm afraid I would bore you. Our work, for the most part, was quite routine: the collecting of samples, the gathering of specimens, the struggle of setting up camp in wild places, which was seldom entertaining, since many of the environments were far from hospitable. Still, we were dedicated to the work and never fretted at hardships. Andrey was a talented scientist and a fine man; it was a great tragedy to lose him."

"I'm sure of it!" intoned Dame Hester. "Were you far from civilization when it happened?"

Dame Betka smiled bitterly. "I was not there at all. At the time I was undertaking a course of treatment at a local clinic and a week passed before Andrey's second in command informed me of the accident."

"How dreadful! Then what did you do?"

Dame Betka shrugged. "We buried Andrey locally and I continued treatment at the clinic; it would have been pointless to do otherwise." She turned Dame Hester another smiling glance. "I tell you this because it is all implicit in the article."

Dame Hester's mouth twitched, but she made no comment.

"In the end, I gathered our gear and all our records and returned to Vermazen—to rest, and take stock of myself and consider the future, which is what I am doing now. In a way, I'm sorry I wrote that article for Jonas. I think it might well have been an indiscretion, but the fee was hard to refuse, since it allowed me to clear up all our debts."

Dame Hester seemed to hesitate, then put on a coy smile. "I know you don't care to talk too much of your treatment—but tell me this. How does one gain admittance to the program at the clinic?"

"I don't really know. The doctor is capricious, to say the least, and his methods are unusual."

"Does the clinic take applications?"

Dame Betka began to fidget with the stem of her wineglass. "I don't think I want to discuss the subject any further."

"Answer me this, at least: Could you recommend new patients to the clinic?"

"No."

Dame Hester studied Dame Betka with somber calculation. "I am not one to intrude upon another's secrets, so I will ask you no further questions."

"I am glad to hear this," said Dame Betka. "You would only find my responses exasperating."

The dinner party came to an end and Dame Betka was driven back to her home on Angwyn Heath.

6

The black car had departed, carrying Dame Betka home. Myron started for his room, but Dame Hester called him back. Myron reluctantly dropped into an armchair and waited, while Dame Hester paced back and forth on long bent-kneed strides. She had run her fingers through her mop of roan-red hair to create a disorganized tangle. Finally she halted, and swung around to face Myron. "Well then, what is your opinion?"

Myron looked at her blankly. "As to what?"

"You heard the wretched woman! She is as devious as an oiled snake! She came here intending to tell me nothing; she devoured her dinner with both hands, and when she had gulped down the last of the wine, she belched three times for the sake of formality, then departed, leaving me no better informed than before. She gave me smirks, deceit and evasion; surely you must have noticed!"

"I was paying no great attention."

Dame Hester stared down at him. "Sometimes, Myron, you are utterly obtuse! Do you realize that she is older than I?"

Myron shrugged and frowned. "I thought that she might be a bit long in the tooth."

"In this regard, at least, you are correct. She married Andrey Ontwill thirty-five years ago."

"Amazing how she keeps her looks! Do you think that she is the 'Serena' who wrote that article?"

"Of course! She admits as much!"

Myron nodded judiciously. "The therapy seems to have helped her. She looks to be a young woman; at least, that is the semblance she projects."

"What of my own poor semblance?" cried Dame Hester passionately. "Everyone tells me that I radiate an invincible fervor that defies time! I feel within myself the essence of youth; it is inherent in every atom of my being: my bones, my spirit, my deepest yearnings! Dauncy Covarth tells me that I dance through life like a nymph through the eternal springtime of my own imagination!"

"Dauncy has a silver tongue."

Dame Hester resumed her pacing. After a few moments Myron yawned and rose to his feet. "I think the time has come—"

"Be good enough to sit down," snapped Dame Hester. "When the time comes, I will let you know. Meanwhile, there is more to be said! Whatever the secret, I am entitled to know the truth! Why should I not participate in this miracle? No reason whatever, and I intend to do so!"

Myron sat in uneasy silence, watching Dame Hester stride back and forth.

She halted, turned to face him. "You are a student of Cosmology; now is the time to put this expensive training to practical use. I want you to locate 'Kodaira.'"

Myron laughed and drew his fingers through his sleek blond hair. "My dear lady, 'Kodaira' is a fiction! It's a figment of the woman's mind! It doesn't exist!"

"Nonsense! We've proved only that Dame Betka invented the name 'Kodaira.' I want you to identify and locate this world."

"That is easy to say, but I haven't a clue!"

"You have dozens of clues! Professor Ontwill was a botanist; go to the Institute, learn the facts regarding his last expedition—specifically, his itinerary and where he died. Surely these facts will be on record; am I correct in this regard?"

"Very likely. What happens next?"

Dame Hester gave a laugh of girlish excitement. "Can't you guess, when the *Glodwyn* is at my disposal? I shall attempt a voyage."

Myron was not surprised. "That is not a trivial project."

"Of course not! But in this regard I can rely upon Dauncy Covarth; he is knowledgeable in such matters."

"So am I, so far as that goes."

"That may be so. But your knowledge is theoretical. Dauncy's experience is practical."

"I see."

Dame Hester looked off across the room. She spoke pensively: "You may have noticed that Dauncy and I have been much together recently. I am a bit older than he, but what of that? A remarkable harmony joins our souls; Dauncy tells me that never before has he felt such a unity of purpose! He says that it is altogether inspiring. He brushes aside all considerations of age; he insists that mutual interests and generous hearts are more important than a few brief years."

"A few brief decades, more likely," thought Myron, but did not put the idea into words. He asked tentatively, "Are you making a serious commitment to this fellow?"

Dame Hester gave another gay little trill of laughter. "He is a distinguished gentleman, handsome and sophisticated. His manners are perfect; he wears his clothes with the ease of a true cosmopolitan. If he makes a proposal, I shall give it serious thought."

Interesting, thought Myron, in view of other information which he had chanced upon.

Myron rose to his feet. "Time I was in bed. Tomorrow I'll look into the Ontwill expeditions."

At dinner of the day following, Dame Hester asked Myron, "Have you made any progress?"

"I'm starting to put the pieces together."

"And you will have definite information?"

"I believe so."

Dame Hester gave a nod of approval. "I have good news, as well! Dauncy has put himself totally at my disposal. He will hire a crew of seasoned professionals, who will work the *Glodwyn* with expert competence. The crew will be minimal. We shall carry neither passengers nor dilettantes of any sort. Dauncy will serve as captain and navigator; I will be what Dauncy humorously calls 'the Grand Poo-Bah,' with ultimate authority. Dauncy insists upon this arrangement, and together we shall work the ship with spartan efficiency."

"All very well," grumbled Myron, "but I hope that your ban on passengers does not apply to me."

Dame Hester compressed her lips. "My dear Myron, this voyage is not a pleasure trip. It is dedicated to a single goal: therapy for my poor body, which has served me so well, but probably can use a 'minor tune-up,' so to speak. Dauncy and I are agreed that there shall be no deviation from the rule."

Myron said, "Still and all, there must be some sort of slot into which I can fit! I am neither physically nor mentally deficient."

Dame Hester laughed. "Quite true! You are a nice-looking lad and you are trained in the field of cosmological studies. Still, the matter rests with Dauncy, who is assembling the crew."

Footsteps approached the drawing room; Dame Hester turned her head to listen. "He is arriving at this moment. Take him aside and put your case to him."

"I shall do so at once." Myron left the room and accosted Dauncy Covarth in the foyer. "I understand that you are hiring a crew for the *Glodwyn*."

Dauncy paused in the act of hanging up his cloak, and glanced down at Myron, fine military mustache bristling. "That is so."

"Dame Hester tells me that if I want a place aboard I must apply to you. I'm sure you know that I have specialized in cosmological studies at the Institute."

Dauncy smilingly shook his head. "It's no good, my dear fellow. I've already filled all the billets with qualified personnel, and there is simply no place open. Sorry and all that, but that's how it is."

Dame Hester had come to stand in the doorway. Dauncy looked over his shoulder. "So there you are, my dear. I have just explained to Myron that the *Glodwyn* is fully staffed with experienced personnel." He turned back to Myron. "We think of this trip as a working expedition and are not prepared to entertain passengers."

Dame Hester spoke kindly to Myron, "Perhaps another time, on a less serious voyage."

"Quite so," said Myron. "The world goes on."

Dame Hester appraised Myron keenly. "You are nonchalant. I hope that you are still looking into that Ontwill matter."

"Yes, of course. I've already collected most of the significant information. As a matter of fact, I've been caught up in a fascinating side issue."

"Truly, Myron, I am not interested in side issues. Please, at this moment, let me have a summary of what you have learned."

"Not just yet. One or two of the facts are still uncertain." Myron turned toward the door.

Dame Hester called out sharply: "Where are you going?"

Myron made a vague gesture. "Oh—just here and there. Nowhere in particular."

Myron departed Sarbiter house, leaving Dame Hester frowning after him. "Myron is acting strangely," she told Dauncy. "Have you noticed?"

Dauncy gave a brusque laugh. "I am barely aware of Myron. No doubt he is a nice lad, but I find him just a bit of a milksop."

"Hm. I'm not so sure. Myron mystifies me. He often seems insipid and rather moony, but he is demonstrably intelligent."

"Perhaps so." Dauncy dismissed Myron from his attention. "The news is good. The crew has been engaged: a top-notch set of veterans. In two or three days they will be on hand and ready to go."

"I will want to meet them, as soon as possible. Can you bring them here, to Sarbiter House?"

"Of course; I will make the arrangements and let you know."

"That will do very nicely."

Two days passed, during which Myron avoided Sarbiter House, and Dame Hester began to fret. This sort of evasiveness was really too bad of Myron! He knew how urgently she required full information, if only to soothe her restlessness. It was wicked for him to keep her on tenterhooks while he went his way, flighty as a will-o'-the-wisp. Providence be thanked for Dauncy Covarth, who was a safe harbor in a storm. He was stalwart and bold, a true gentleman, oblivious to the difference in their ages. Dauncy used a keen sensitivity to plumb to the inner essence of a person: that spirit which yearned for true understanding as well as the transports of more immediate joys! Dauncy was a jewel, a treasure, a rock of faith! In Dauncy she could and would trust.

7

On the morning of the third day Myron telephoned Sarbiter House. Dame Hester could hardly speak for vexation. "Well, Myron?" she managed to say. "You have kept us agog with suspense! Important events are in progress, while you keep me in a vacuum of information! Where are you? I must speak with you at once, since tonight I will meet the full *Glodwyn* crew. If I cannot so much as hint of our destination I will feel a fool."

"Oh, don't worry on that account! The destination exists; in fact, I've had the information well in hand for some time now."

Dame Hester's voice cracked as she tried to speak evenly. "Then why have you not done your duty and brought this information to me?"

"Today we will meet for lunch and everything will become clear."

"Stuff and nonsense!" barked Dame Hester. "At this moment, if you please, I want to hear what you have learned!"

"Sorry; there is no time just now. Do you know Floiry Place, north of the Old Market?"

Dame Hester pulled a haughty face. "It is not a part of town I like to visit."

"Today you must make an exception. I will meet you at noon precisely, under the Banjer Tower clock."

Dame Hester made an energetic protest. "This is a great nuisance! I cannot imagine your motives!"

"I will explain in detail when I meet you."

"Myron, please don't be tiresome! It is an unsavoury district, which I prefer to avoid! Why do you insist upon such foolishness?"

"It's quite simple. I have reserved a table at a nearby restaurant."

"Very well; as you like. Please be prompt."

Myron arrived at the rendezvous ten minutes early, to find Dame Hester already on hand, pacing back and forth under the clock. For the occasion she had selected one of her more striking ensembles: a green cape, flaring wide at the hips; voluminous pantaloons striped green, blue, and black, tucked into ankle boots of magenta leather. A hat of silver mesh controlled her mop of roan-red hair and anchored a tall green plume which bobbed and waved as she marched back and forth. At Myron's approach, she stopped short and greeted him with a raucous cry: "There you are, at last! Do you know how long I have waited?"

"Not long. It is still five minutes short of the hour."

"No matter! It's all an absurdity. This is a disreputable neighborhood. I see no restaurant of quality! I see a theater of the nude; I see a dog-barber; yonder is a shop selling exotic herbs and vegetarian pellets. And what is that place?"

"That is the Club Kit-Kat, a cellar cabaret. It is quite fashionable among the avant-garde. But come; they will not hold our table forever."

Myron escorted Dame Hester across Floiry Place and into a narrow lane which led down to the riverside docks. Dame Hester complained at once. "Where are you taking me? I do not care for ultra-quaint! Or even squalid establishments."

Myron pointed to an overhead sign, which read:

ZAMSKI'S BOHEMIAN GRILL

"That is our destination. It is quite a decent place, though the clientele includes a variety of unconventional types, like yourself."

Dame Hester was pleased by Myron's description of herself. "Well, yes," she conceded. "I cannot deny my occasional recklessness. I am a woman who loves life! I suppose that a few old woohaws consider me unconventional. In a sense, it is a compliment! I fear that you, with your almost morbid rectitude, will never qualify."

Myron shrugged. "It is a matter of preference."

The two entered the restaurant and found themselves in a noisy dining room, high-ceilinged and decorated with theatrical posters. A waiter led them out upon an open terrace overlooking the river Chaim, and seated them at a table to the side, in the shade of a lucanthus tree. Myron glanced across the terrace and noted that a table beside the railing was occupied as usual by a couple taking an early lunch.

In general, Dame Hester was favorably impressed by what she saw. The tables were spread with gay cloths checked either red, green, or blue, and fresh flowers appeared on every table. Grudgingly she admitted that the restaurant seemed, at least superficially, attractive. "Still, why are we sitting over here, crammed into a corner under a plant? Are no other tables available? Remember: I am a creature of the sun! I crave light and air and open space! Surely you must know my foibles by this time!"

"This table is the best I could get on short notice. The others are reserved for regulars. Are you hungry? Here is the menu. The deviled mandrake is a house specialty. The goulash is quite good, as is the stuffed cuttlefish."

Dame Hester tossed the menu aside. "I shall have a salad, poached eel, and a bit of toast. You may order a flagon of good wine."

The waiter took their orders. Myron looked across the terrace, to the table by the railing, where the man and woman were finishing their lunch.

"Now then," said Dame Hester. "My patience has run its course! Tell me what you have learned of the Ontwill expedition."

"Very well. I visited the botanical library and looked through the records. I read the proposal for Professor Ontwill's final expedition, which detailed his itinerary and his destination. I saw the report describing how he had met his death. He had been killed when a twenty-pound ironwood pod dropped from a height of a hundred feet to crush his skull."

Myron again glanced across the terrace. The man and the woman, now drinking tea, were still engrossed in conversation. The man's back was turned and his face could not be seen. The woman was somewhat older than Myron. She wore a dark gray jacket buttoned close up to her neck with tight trousers of a soft rose-pink stuff which clung to her slender legs. Fine tawny-brown hair hung past delicate features; dark eyelashes hooded her eyes. She sat relaxed and languid in the sunlight, her mouth curving in a smile, as if every aspect of life were happy and amusing. The man reached forward, took her hands, and made an earnest remark. The woman tilted back her head and laughed; apparently the world had become more amusing than ever.

Dame Hester said, "Please continue, Myron. You need not draw out your story for dramatic effect."

"As you like. Professor Ontwill died on the world Naharius in Virgo GGP 922; Dame Betka seems to have undertaken her therapy at a local clinic."

"Hmmf. That is circumstantial enough. What keeps attracting your attention?" Dame Hester looked over her shoulder and followed Myron's gaze. The man at the table across the terrace raised the woman's hand to his lips and kissed her fingers with tender emotion. The woman bent her head forward and spoke a few words. The man sighed and glanced at his watch; it was time to leave. He bent his head and gave her wrist a playful little nip. The woman laughed, jerked away her arm, fluttered her napkin in his face. He seized her hand, began to gnaw at the knuckles. She jumped to her feet, dropped the napkin, and the game was over; regretfully he joined her and the two slowly threaded their way through the tables. Now it could be seen that the man, his mustache bristling, his face complacent, was Dauncy Covarth.

Dame Hester made an inarticulate sound, half-gasp, half-croak. Her jaw sagged. She tried to call out, but she had lost her power of speech. The words, catching in her throat, seemed almost to strangle her.

Dauncy Covarth and the woman departed the terrace.

Dame Hester at last said, "That was Dauncy! Go after him; bring him back here!"

Myron shook his head. "That would not be tactful. Dauncy and his friend are busy with their private affairs."

"Go after them!" croaked Dame Hester. "Find out the name of that woman!"

"No need," said Myron. "Her name is Vita Palas; at least, that is the name she uses when she performs at the cabaret. I refer to the Club Kit-Kat, of course, out on the Place Foiry. The cabaret, incidentally, is where Dauncy met the lady, while she was acting in the comic burlesque: *Captain Dog's-body and the Pirate Queen*. This perhaps is where Dauncy learned to be a spaceship captain."

Dame Hester glared at Myron. "How long have you known of this travesty? Is this why you brought me here?"

Myron thought a moment. "I have another explanation which I would rather have you believe."

"And what is that?"

"Since Dauncy and his ladyfriend were coming here day after day, I assumed that it must be a restaurant of quality which you would enjoy."

"Yes, the visit here was most enjoyable," said Dame Hester savagely. "Are you ready to go?"

"Not yet. I have not finished my pickerel, and I have ordered rum pudding for us both."

"Never mind your pickerel! Tonight Dauncy will bring the ship's crew to Sarbiter House. I want you on hand, in the event that he feigns innocence. Never before has my trust been so abused! He is a monster of perfidy!"

Myron and Dame Hester took an early dinner in an alcove beside a tall
window overlooking the landscape to the west, where a bank of low
clouds reflected a dozen somber colors from the setting sun, including
the opalescent greens and blues that were peculiar to the world Vermazen and for which the meteorologists had no explanation.

The meal was consumed in silence. Dame Hester trifled with a
peach and a truffled sausage, and stared out the window to watch dusk
drift across the land. Myron dined more substantially on mixed grill
and a risotto with pine nuts and saffron.

Dame Hester waved away dessert and sat with hands clenching her
teacup, while Myron stolidly partook of apricot tart. Beyond the window, the sky grew dark and the constellation known locally as the Uni-
corn rose in the east.

Dame Hester threw down her napkin. "Come. In ten minutes we
will meet the *Glodwyn*'s crew, along with that Covarth person."

But she hesitated before rising.

"I feel no shame. He is a personable fellow and quite persuasive.
He will be rife with abject explanations, of course. But I see him now
for what he is: a poseur with a blatant mustache. Still, what of me? If he
is truly abject and truly penitent, how can I not forgive him? I am sorry
to say that I am as naive as a schoolgirl, who never learned to say 'no.'
Ah well, we shall see. I am intensely vulnerable to honest shame. I find
it easy to blame, but even more easy to forgive. At heart, I am pure
woman, generous and chronically susceptible to a kindly gesture. And
yet, and yet: how could he waste a single instant on that vacuous trollop
when he could share the rich intimacy of soul and spirit with me, Hester Lajoie? It is beyond comprehension!"

Myron put on a dubious expression. He started to speak, but
changed his mind.

Dame Hester, despite her distrait condition, was as keenly observant as ever. "You were about to speak, Myron? I am curious to learn
your views."

Myron raised his eyebrows and looked toward the ceiling. "I was
about to say that your instincts will guide you through this jungle of
emotion."

"Bah!" muttered Dame Hester. "I can never take comfort in your
ambiguities." She rose to her feet. "You may wait in the drawing room,
if you please. I will join you shortly, after I refresh myself." She
paused. "Dauncy and the crew will arrive in a few moments. Ask Harry

to serve them what they wish to drink. I must have a moment or two of tranquility."

Myron went pensively to the drawing room. He poured himself a tot of the best Frugola Brandy, then went to stand by the fire.

Five minutes passed. Henry appeared in the doorway. He spoke formally, with only a nasal overtone to hide his distaste for the proceedings. "Master Covarth has arrived with a party of friends. He says they are expected."

"It can't be helped. Show them in, then serve them what they want to drink—from the ordinary bottles, of course."

"Of course, sir."

Dauncy entered the drawing room, followed by six persons, all dressed in the casual garments used by spacemen, from one end of the Gaean Reach to the other. Dauncy, however, wore the uniform affected by the officers of luxury passenger packets: a trim dark blue jacket, with brass buttons, gray trousers, and a loose white cap. He looked around the room. "Where is Dame Hester?"

"She will be with us presently. Henry will serve you whatever you would like to drink."

Henry fulfilled the orders. Dauncy said to Myron, "Here is the crew: a top-notch group. Yonder stands the chief mate, beside him the chief engineer, then the chef and the chief steward, along with a pair of technicians and a pair of understewards. More than adequate for the *Glodwyn*, or so I believe."

Myron politely acknowledged the introductions. He spoke to the crew: "Dame Hester will want to examine your references. You carry them with you, I hope?"

Dauncy spoke with asperity: "You need not concern yourself. I have taken care of every detail."

Myron chuckled and Dauncy glanced at him narrowly, but before he could speak, Myron turned away to pour himself more brandy.

Minutes passed. Dame Hester at last appeared. She had changed into a short-sleeved dark red jacket over a swirling gown, striped yellow, red, and black, with a dark red bandeau controlling her hair.

Dauncy stepped forward and gallantly doffed his cap. "Ah, my dear lady, you appear at last; you are absolutely stunning in that marvelous dress!"

Dame Hester stood rigid as a post, looking from face to face. She darted a glance toward Myron, who merely made a wry grimace.

Dauncy spoke on. "Here is our crew: all professionals of the highest competence. Let me introduce Chief Mate Atwyn and Chief Engineer Furth. Alois deGrassi our chef and beside him is our Chief Steward Vita Palas. Next—"

Dame Hester spoke in a low voice thick with emotion. "Dauncy, I cannot find words to express my feelings. You are a horrid insect which hides by day under a damp rock. You have attempted to smuggle your trollop aboard my ship, under my very nose. The act is so sublimely insulting as to cause me first to laugh, then to retch! You are so vile that you pollute the air with the stink of your miserable soul!"

Dauncy pretended bewilderment. "I fail to understand this—"

"Silence!" Dame Hester turned to appraise Vita Palas, who had dressed with scrupulous care in a demure gray skirt, a tan jacket, low workshoes and a small white cap under which she had tucked her fine light brown hair. "I consider you a contemptible sneak, with the morals of an alley cat. You may or may not be a prostitute; I can only suspect."

"Now then!" cried Vita Palas. "Don't you go slanging me, you raddled old hussy! I know your kind, all skin and spleen, and wrinkles to wrap over all! Your own morals are sewage, you with your dancing-boys and gigolos! Don't you try slanging me anymore, or I'll snatch off your wig and really explain what I think of you! It will not be nice! It will turn your long nose blue!"

Dame Hester turned to Henry. "Expel Dauncy and this slut from the house. If they offer resistance, Myron will deal with them quite brutally, so I suspect. Am I right, Myron?"

"I suspect that they will go peacefully," said Myron. "While you are at it, discharge the two stewards as well; they are comic dancers at the Club Kit-Kat."

Dauncy signaled to Vita. "Let us leave with our dignity. This woman has obviously gone mad."

"One moment!" cried Dame Hester brassily. "I want you to take note of this." She turned to Myron. "I believe that you are trained in cosmology, and know the Gaean Reach from end to end?"

"That is for the most part true," said Myron.

"And you are capable of navigating the *Glodwyn*?"

"Certainly, so long as the autopilot works properly."

"Good," said Dame Hester crisply. "I now appoint you captain of the *Glodwyn*. You will make all necessary preparations for the voyage." She swung around once more to confront Dauncy. "Now, you ingrate and traitor, what do you think of that?"

Dauncy pulled at his mustache. "As before, I think you are a silly old woman."

"Henry! Eject these people!"

"This way, if you please," said Henry.

"What of us?" demanded the chief engineer. "That Dauncy fellow hired us from the list at the space terminal."

"You may leave your addresses and telephone directions with Henry; also your references, if you care to leave these documents overnight. I will look them over tomorrow. That is all for now."

The spacemen departed; Dame Hester and Myron were alone in the room.

"Now then, Myron," said Dame Hester, "I have a statement to make. Your function is to manage the *Glodwyn* so that I am happy, secure and comfortable. I wish to enjoy the voyage."

"I hope that this will be the case," said Myron guardedly.

"Very well. Now then, as captain, you are a symbol of authority. You are not to slouch about, or peek through doorways. Therefore, cultivate a proper bearing! Throw your shoulders back! Speak in a resonant voice! Further, you must make decisions on your own; I do not want to be pestered by problems or complaints. You are captain; be as firm as necessary. Authority is yours; use it without compromise and without apology. Is all this clear?"

"Oh yes, it is clear enough."

"Hmm," said Dame Hester. "You show no signs of elation."

Myron gave a short laugh. "There will be challenges to the job. I was thinking them over."

"Hmmf," said Dame Hester. "So long as we reach our destination in a proper fashion, and I am not rendered numb with boredom and apathy along the way, there should be no severe challenges. And, naturally, I wish to return to Sarbiter House in good time and in good health, and—so I hope—revitalized, if not rejuvenated."

"It will be an interesting voyage," said Myron.

TWO

1

The *Glodwyn* lifted from the Salou Sain spaceport, up through the clouds and was away into space. The sun Dianthe drifted astern. Dame Hester saw Vermazen become a small disk, then a luminous point. She heaved a sigh and turned away from the observation port. "It is a lonesome feeling to see the sun move away with such definite finality. It provokes emotions which I cannot put into words."

Myron responded with a rather ponderous dignity which his responsibilities and the influence of his uniform had worked upon him. "You should enjoy the comfort of your wonderful spaceyacht, which protects you from the emptiness, just as a boat floats you above the water in which you might otherwise drown."

Dame Hester seemed not to hear. "When one watches a sunset, the mood of tragedy gives way to certainty that the sun will rise in the morning. Now it seems that black space lies ahead forever and ever."

Myron forced a laugh. "That is dismal symbology. Come; here is the sofa! Relax, and I will order aperitifs from the steward."

"That, at least, is a constructive idea." Dame Hester seated herself. "How is our dining schedule arranged?"

"It is simple enough. Our clocks are set to Salou Sain time; that is the pattern we shall follow until there is reason to change. Lunch, therefore, will be served in about a hour."

Dame Hester nodded. "That will give us a break in the monotony."

Myron started to speak, but changed his mind.

Lunch was served to them in the main saloon: a relatively simple repast which Dame Hester found a trifle dull. After the meal Myron explained to Alois the chef that Dame Hester required more elaborate meals of several courses, if only to punctuate the routine which otherwise she might find a bore. "So it shall be," said Alois. "The dishes will move in classical succession. She shall know the grandeur of my art!"

"Good," said Myron. "That is one problem solved, at least."

Dame Hester had no taste for reading, and required that Myron involve himself in card games and a backgammon tournament: all played for rather high stakes. Myron would have objected had he not managed to win as often as he lost. After a time, as Myron's skills sharpened, he began to win consistently, and Dame Hester lost interest in the gaming.

The voyage proceeded. Dame Hester discovered an abundance of spare time which rasped at her volatile temperament. She made a peevish complaint to Myron: "For a fact, I had no idea that space travel was like this! There is nothing to do but eat and sleep! The routines are invariable. It is the next thing to catatonia!"

Myron, using tact and delicacy, tried to make light of the complaint. "Some people enjoy the tranquillity. It gives them time to take stock of themselves. Sometimes they learn to play a musical instrument. Now that I think of it, there is a concertina in the cabinet yonder."

Dame Hester curled her lip. "Myron, sometimes your ideas are almost imbecilic. I am not sure whether the word 'bathos' applies."

"I would think not. 'Bathos' is when someone tries to make an absurdity seem important or exalted. I suppose that the idea of you playing the concertina is a bit far-fetched."

Dame Hester was not listening to him. In a pensive voice she said, "Dauncy was an ingrate and an irredemptible monster, not to mention his deceit. Still, despite all, he was amusing. I will not say that I regret expelling him from my life; nevertheless, if he were here he would take instant steps to relieve my boredom."

"He called you a silly old woman, so I believe."

Dame Hester smiled in wistful recollection. "Yes, I remember. But it was just a fit of pique. Ah well, Dauncy aside, I think I would enjoy the company of a few lively guests. The ship, as of now, is a social vacuum. I do believe, Myron, that you might have foreseen this sort of thing."

"Don't blame me!" declared Myron. "You yourself insisted that guests would grate on your nerves! You called them opportunists! You said that, above all, you wanted rest. Now that you can rest, you want something else!"

Dame Hester spoke with dignity. " 'Rest' and numb apathy are a bit different. You put me in a false position."

"Not so! I only want to set the record straight before I am crucified and burned at the stake."

"Myron, be good enough to face facts. You have long celebrated the joys and romance of space travel. Now, I am out here in this interminable void and I ask myself: 'Where is the joy? Where is the romance?'"

Myron pointed to the observation port. "Look yonder! Observe the stars. Watch them drifting past. It is the most romantic spectacle of all!"

Dame Hester shuddered. "The stars are far away. Space is dark and silent. Out there is where all the dead souls drift and wander."

"Nonsense!" scoffed Myron. "There is nothing of the sort out there! Come! See for yourself!"

Dame Hester shook her head. "If I looked and saw something staring in at me, gibbering and grimacing, I should never stop screaming."

Myron turned a glance over his shoulder toward the window. "It is an eerie thought."

Dame Hester dropped into one of the chairs. "Fetch the Frugola; pour us each a splash or two. Then sit down; I want you to explain something to me."

Myron poured the brandy and cautiously lowered himself into a chair. "Yes? What is it that I must explain?"

"Simply this. You know our destination; am I correct?"

"Certainly. It is the world Naharius."

"You know the exact dimensional coordinates of this place."

"I do, indeed."

"Further, you can manipulate your engines to move us at great speed—far more rapidly than the speed at which we are now crossing space. Am I right?"

"Yes and no. It is a complex compromise, which is calculated by the auto-pilot. The slower we move, the more accurately we arrive at our destination. We could easily proceed a hundred times faster than now, but we could not bring the ship into ordinary space anywhere near our destination, except by luck. The errors inherent in the machinery make such speeds impractical. The auto-pilot calculates optimums, and space voyages are generally of a length which suits almost everyone."

"The system should be perfected," said Dame Hester. She drained her goblet and signaled to Myron for a refill.

"Are you sure you want more?" asked Myron. "It is time for you to dress for dinner."

Dame Hester groaned and scowled. "Sometimes, Myron, you can be most tiresome." She rose from the chair. "But yes, it is time that I dress. Tonight I shall wear my green and scarlet fandango costume, for the delectation of my soul, and we shall have a gala dinner!"

"A good idea!" said Myron, without conviction.

On the following day Dame Hester took breakfast in her cabin. Myron saw nothing of her until mid-morning, when he found her in the pilothouse deep in conversation with the chief mate.

"Aha, Myron," said Dame Hester. "Here you are at last! The chief mate and I have been looking over the charts, and we notice that there is an inhabited world not too far away and only a trifle off-course. The world is known as 'Dimmick.' The attendant star is—" she turned to the mate "—what is the star?"

The mate touched his finger to a button and the screen displayed a pattern. "Maudwell's Star, Leo JN-44. There you have it, sir! The fifth world is Dimmick!"

Dame Hester spoke brusquely, in tones calculated to forestall argument. "You are to land at the Dimmick spaceport, since I wish to stretch my legs for a bit, and perhaps we can search out a local fiesta, or pageant, where we can enjoy some gay music and general merriment. I also would like to do a bit of shopping, if there is anything quaint for sale at the market, or wherever the folk sell their crafts."

Myron asked the mate, "Have you checked the *Handbook*?"

"Not yet, sir."

Myron went to the desk, opened the red-bound volume and found the entry labeled "Dimmick." He skimmed the table of physical characteristics and read the section entitled "Miscellaneous Comments." The *Handbook to the Planets*, a compendium notorious for cautious understatement, described Dimmick as a "graceless world, shrouded by a dismal overcast which often condenses to a pall of lugubrious drizzle. The cloud-cover insulates the world and few extremes of temperature are to be found anywhere. Despite this fact and the presence of several convenient land-masses, the population is concentrated in a district surrounding the city Flajaret. Dimmick is not notable for pleasant scenery and the only occasions of touristic interest are the weekly dogfights.

"In the absence of interesting vegetation, landscapes are bleak; even the mountains seem little more than dour heaps of slag and rubble. The oceans are sodded over with foot-thick pads of algae. These mats spread to the horizon flat as billiard tables. They oxygenate the atmosphere and nurture countless swarms of insects. The antics of the red and yellow tumblebugs are said to be amusing, as are the disciplined tactics of the monitor fomories. Before venturing out upon the mat, however, the traveler should be advised that the sting of the blue whiptail may be fatal, and that the clouds of gnats, winged grubs, squeeches, and the like are unendurable in the absence of special precautions.

"Flajaret, the largest town, is a service center for personnel at the nearby mines; these mines, in fact, are the only reason why any sane Gaean would choose to live on Dimmick, since the food is bad, as is the local beer, brewed, according to a cynical rumor, from ocean algae. The most popular recreation is a program of dogfights, which arouse passionate emotions in the audiences. Not infrequently riots ensue, in which packs of roving dogs joyously participate, biting at random.

"In early times malefactors were dressed in boots, a breechclout, and a respirator, and then were discharged a metered distance out upon the algae mat. The more flagrant the crime, the farther from shore was the culprit banished, to a maximum of five miles, after which any other increment was considered supererogatory. At present, the only crimes for which such penalties are inflicted are attacks upon an IPCC agent, in which case the offender is released at the very center of the ocean mat, thereby driving home the lesson.

"Sexual customs are most peculiar and complex, and cannot be analyzed here. The visitor, however is earnestly warned never, under any circumstances, to make overtures to local women, since unpleasant consequences may be expected, the extreme penalty being marriage to the woman involved, or her mother."

To protect himself from potential reproach, Myron insisted upon reading the "Miscellaneous Comments" to Dame Hester. As he had expected, she listened with only half an ear; and when Myron asked, "You are still anxious to land?" she gave a fretful response: "Of course! Land at once!"

2

Dimmick grew large below: a globe swathed in gray mist, showing no physiographic detail. Sensors aboard the *Glodwyn* located the Flajaret spaceport and the ship settled into the bright fog, emerging at an altitude of three thousand feet. Below were tumbled mountains of black and gray stone to the side of a flat ocean, tinged here and there with streaks of pale blue.

Dame Hester, looking down through the observation port, sniffed in deprecation and glanced sharply toward Myron.

"This place seems neither exciting nor exhilarating."

Myron shrugged. "The *Handbook to the Planets* told us as much, if you recall. You might enjoy the dogfights."

Dame Hester clamped her lips together, but said no more.

The *Glodwyn* settled upon the terminal at Flajaret. As soon as entry formalities had been completed, Dame Hester and Myron went off to explore the town. An avenue led from the terminal, through the central district, past a set of concrete administration buildings, then up a long slope through tumbles of gray boulders to the gaunt structures surrounding the mines themselves. Beyond rose ridges and peaks of naked gray stone.

The town Flajaret lacked both charm and architectural interest, since all structures were built of rock-melt to uncompromising four-square dimensions. To the right of the avenue tiers of cubical gray cottages ascended the hillside; to the left were larger structures: warehouses, workshops, and a massive building with a large sign on the roof. The sign depicted, at one end, a huge ruffed mastiff standing on its hind legs, showing its fangs; and, at the opposite end another dog, snarling with equal ferocity. Between were the words: NAC-NAC SPORTING ARENA.

The avenue entered a square overlooked by the Apollon Hotel, and lined elsewhere by small shops. Dame Hester walked swiftly from shop to shop, examining the merchandise with sharp eyes and probing fingers. She saw little which appealed to her. In a clothing boutique she came upon a skirt fashioned from dogs' teeth strung on threads and woven together to create an unusual fabric. Dame Hester studied the skirt, which was quite distinctive, and which would be sure to cause a stir should she wear it to a dinner party back at Salou Sain. In the end she decided that it was rather heavy and failed to drape gracefully around her legs.

The next shop sold comestibles: small bitter kumquats; cakes of compressed honeygrubs; cartons of yeast; strings of myriapods, dragged squirming from the sea, drowned in formaldehyde, then dried and cured in the smoke of smouldering algae. Dame Hester reeled back from the combination of odors and hurried away. In the next shop her attention was caught by a display of small stone effigies, each crudely carved to represent a squat short-legged man, half-crouching, with a heavy head thrust forward. Dame Hester picked up one of these objects, fascinated by the leering features. Who, she wondered, had troubled to carve objects so repulsive, and for what purpose, except, perhaps, to sell to off-worlders? The proprietress, as squat and heavy-featured as the effigy itself, bustled forward, holding a finger high to signal Dame Hester's attention. "That is a fine piece—very rare, very valuable! I make you a good price, because I like you!"

"How can it be rare?" demanded Dame Hester. "I took it from this tray where there are thirty more just like it!"

"You do not see with the eyes of a connoisseur! That is an image of the Garre Mountain effrit, who casts thunder stones. This piece is especially lucky and will win your gambles at the dogfights! Since I am poor and ignorant, I will let you have it for the laughable price of twenty sols!"

Dame Hester stared at her in angry amazement. "It is true that I am laughing! Clearly you lack all decency to ask any price whatever for this repulsive little gewgaw! Do you take me for a fool? I am seriously insulted."

"No matter. I insult better folk than you several times a day. It is no novelty; in fact, it is a pleasure."

Dame Hester brought out a coin. "This is the value I place upon that horrid little item, and only for the pleasure it will give me when I describe your miserable shop to my friends."

"Bah!" said the woman. "Take it at no charge. You shall never gloat that you outdid me in noblesse oblige. Take it and be gone!"

"Why not? I shall do so. Please wrap it for me tastefully."

"I am too busy."

Dame Hester dropped the effigy into her handbag and marched from the shop. Myron paused long enough to place a sol into the tray. The proprietress, once more perched on her high stool, watched impassively, making no comment.

Back in the square, Dame Hester halted and made a comprehensive assessment of the surroundings. The town Flajaret, against the background of gray mountains and dreary sky, seemed a monochromatic photograph of great complexity. A half-dozen vehicles moved slowly along the avenue. A few pedestrians marched here and there around the square: short scowling men with black beards stumping along the sidewalks in company with heavy-bottomed women wearing black knee boots and broad-brimmed hats. These women walked with ponderous steps, as if conscious of an inner majesty. They looked neither right nor left. As Dame Hester turned from her inspection of the hotel, she inadvertently jostled one of the women. Dame Hester stepped back, eyebrows raised in haughty annoyance. The woman was portly, of middle age, with a broad face, close-set black eyes, and a large wen on her cheek. The two women inspected each other coldly, from head to toe, before each turned with dignity and went on as before.

Dame Hester spoke aside to Myron: "What a frump! Her hat is a farce."

The woman also muttered something to her husband as they walked away. Both paused to look back at Dame Hester, then turned and continued along the sidewalk, smiling to themselves.

The episode provoked Dame Hester to indignation. "If I were not a gentlewoman, I would give that old hen a piece of my mind! I am not accustomed to that sort of insolence."

"Why bother?" Myron advised. "It is not worth the effort."

The two continued around the square, and came upon a café at the front of the Hotel Apollon. Six small tables were ranged along a narrow terrace, each sheltered under a faded red and blue parasol, which guarded against drizzle rather than nonexistent sunlight. Two of the tables were occupied. At the far end, a pair of elderly men wearing heavy black coats huddled over mugs of a steaming brew. At another table sat a young man, tall, self-assured, with a bushy black mustache, rich black ringlets, glistening brown eyes—an off-worlder, to judge by his clothes. Myron acknowledged the man's presence with a polite nod and seated himself at the adjoining table. Dame Hester, meanwhile, went off to inspect the shops in the arcade at the front of the hotel.

A waiter came forward. He gave the table a cursory wipe with the napkin he carried slung over his arm, then looked Myron up and down. "Well then, what will you be taking?"

"I don't know until I see a menu."

"There is no menu; and at any rate it is inside and I don't care to fetch it. Just give me your order and have done with it."

"How can I order if I don't know what is available?"

"It's your choice," said the waiter. "I can't make up your mind for you."

Myron pointed to the two men at the far end of the terrace. "What are they drinking?"

"That is our lucky toddy. It is recommended if you plan to gamble on the fights."

The young man at the next table spoke up. "Give it a miss. It is boiled up from the tailbones of dead dogs."

"Thanks for the warning," said Myron. "What do you suggest?"

"It's all bad. There is nothing worth ordering. The tea is like liniment. The coffee is brewed from burned hair and dead birds; their liquors are unmentionable. The pale ale is what they serve children, and is what I am drinking. It is not good, but everything else is worse. Another thing: he has not shown you the menu, which means that he plans to charge you three sols for a flask of pale ale. The price is seventeen dinkets."

Myron turned to the glowering waiter. "Bring me two flasks of the seventeen-dinket ale."

"And what to eat?"

The off-worlder again offered advice. "Take imported biscuits and cheese, on clean plates."

Myron told the waiter: "We will try an order of biscuits and cheese, at the menu price, on clean plates, if you please."

"You must pay a premium for the clean plates. It is how we amortise the expense of dishwashing."

The waiter departed.

The off-worlder at the next table rose to his feet. "May I join you?"

"If you like," said Myron, without enthusiasm.

The man settled himself at the table and introduced himself. "Marko Fassig is what polite people call me; I am by trade a ship owner, temporarily without a ship."

"I am pleased to meet you," said Myron stiffly. "I am Captain Myron Tany, of the ship *Glodwyn*."

"That's very nice," said Marko Fassig. "Who is your lady friend? Surely not your wife?"

Myron fixed Marko Fassig with a cold stare of incredulity and distaste. "Of course not! That is an idiotic idea! She is my great-aunt, Dame Hester Lajoie, and she owns the *Glodwyn*."

Marko Fassig laughed with great good humor. "Come now! Surely you are not all that naive! Stranger things have happened."

"Not to me," said Myron fastidiously.

The waiter arrived with the ale and the biscuits and cheese. Marko Fassig looked at the plate. "Take notice! This is not a clean plate; you may not charge the premium."

"It is clean enough."

"There are crumbs here, and a smear of grease, and dirty fingerprints."

"It was a mistake. What difference does it make?" He turned the cheese and biscuits out on the table, wiped the plate with his napkin, replaced cheese and biscuits, and set the dish in front of Myron with a flourish. "There you are, clean plate and all; take it or leave it, but pay just the same."

"I will take it under protest, but I will pay no premium!"

"Bah," grumbled the waiter. "In that case, you must double my gratuity."

Dame Hester came from the arcade and seated herself at the table. She looked questioningly at Marko Fassig. "And who might this be?"

"I really can't say," Myron told her. "He's a bird of passage, of some sort; that's all I know of him." He spoke to Fassig. "You must excuse my candor, Marko, but I am not quite so naive as you think. Now, you may return to your table, since Dame Hester and I have important matters to discuss."

Dame Hester cried out: "Myron, not so fast! I don't understand you! Here is a perfectly nice young man, with an interesting air about him, and you want to send him away?" She turned to Marko Fassig, who had been listening with a smile of easy complacence.

Dame Hester said, "Tell us something about yourself, Marko. What brings you here to this desolate hellhole which Myron foisted upon me?"

"We must not blame Myron; he is surely doing his best. As for me, how shall I describe myself? I am, in essence, a wandering philosopher and a connoisseur of all that is exquisite and delectable, including beautiful mature women. My life is a series of culminations, followed by brief periods during which I ponder and formulate wonderful dreams."

"How interesting! But this place is absolutely insipid! Why come here for your pondering and your dreams?"

"There are two reasons—or chains of events, let us say. They run in parallel. One is spiritual and the other is practical. The two forces twine around each other, each exerting its influence. Am I confusing you? Myron seems a bit distrait."

"Oh, never mind Myron. He is often a bit prim. Please elucidate."

"The first element is as I have adumbrated. Perhaps it is an exercise in self-discipline, so that when I come upon a place of utter tedium, I force myself to enter a metamorphic state. I become a chrysalis, so to speak, from which I ultimately emerge, renewed and revived, so that life is all the more splendid for the contrast. It is a foolhardy style of life, but I make no excuses. I like to think of myself as an adventurer sailing a sea of romantic emotion, occasionally making landfall at a port where I find a kindred soul."

"Amazing!" declared Dame Hester. "Your philosophy piques my interest, since it is not unlike my own. But tell me of the other, practical, reason for your presence here."

"Very well. I shall withold nothing. A man named Goss Jylstra and I were owners of a small spaceship. We specialized in the fruit transport trade. For the most part we worked in harmony, but the day finally came when we could not agree upon future plans. Our ship was the *Darling Boreen*, and when we landed at Flajaret, the time had arrived when we must go our separate ways. Neither of us could buy the other out, so we agreed to place everything, lock, stock, and the *Darling Boreen*, up to a decision of chance. We had a dozen ways of putting our fortunes to the test, but in the end we visited the dogfights and gambled on the dogs. Jylstra's fice was a spavined cur named Smaug; my beast was named Tinkifer. The fight began, and from the first it was clear that Smaug's tactics were unfair. At last he jumped on Tinkifer and tore out his liver, but the gallant Tinkifer chewed at Smaug's jugular vein, so that the fight ended in a draw, with both beasts dead. Goss Jylstra and I were momentarily at a loss; then we agreed to hazard all on a single hand of three-card layabout. I laid first, a nine; Goss laid a three, to his dismay. I laid an eight, for a score of seventeen, while poor Goss had to be content with a seven, for a score of what is called 'crooked ten,' and the *Darling Boreen* was as good as mine, for how could he match now? But the sly villain moved away from the window and a blast of air blew our cards, including my third laydown, to the floor. As quick as lightning Goss played his third card, a two, and cried huzzah! ending the game, winning the *Darling Boreen* with a score of two, since my cards were on the floor. So here I sit, a wandering vagabond, a true scion of Dionysus, always ready to quaff the wine of Life, then throw the dregs into the teeth of Destiny, as is my custom."

Dame Hester asked, "And your old companion left you here at Flajaret? That seems a bit heartless."

"I am inclined to agree. Still, we parted amicably enough. He flew off into space, and I entered one of my regenerative modes. It is now at an end, so that once more I am ready to undertake new ventures. But surely, my dear lady, that is enough of me and my sorry vicissitudes! Tell me about yourself."

"Gladly!" Dame Hester raised the mug of ale to her lips and tasted. "Faugh! What is this stuff?"

"That is their pale ale," said Myron. "Apparently there is nothing better on hand. I agree that it is totally rank."

"Ha! You tasted it?"

"I took a cautious sip, which was more than enough."

"Then why did you not warn me, before I drank a great swallow?"

"My mind had wandered. I was thinking of something else."

Dame Hester told Marko Fassig: "In a way this is symptomatic of our voyage. We set out from Salou Sain in high excitement; we were embarked upon what, in a sense, would be a quest for life and youth. We were determined and serious; still, we resolved that the venture should never become grim or austere. Myron concurred with this program; he assured me that the voyage would be rife with gay episodes and marvels of exotic pageantry. What was the reality? We drifted forever through a stultifying void! The hermetics immured in their caves could not have known greater boredom! When I mentioned entertainment, Myron wanted me to look out the windows and admire the blankness of space. I refused! It was a foretaste of death! The voyage continued and the tedium was profound. I yearned for diversion and Captain Myron finally saw that apathy was destroying my health. This is the puddle he selected for my enjoyment. For entertainment he has promised me a dogfight and has served me this vile liquid to drink."

"You have my sympathy," said Marko Fassig. "But cruising space need not be dull. Aboard the *Darling Boreen* we had many jolly times, I assure you! In this respect Goss Jylstra and I were of the same mind. Between us we knew every haunt of delight and gaiety, innocent and not so innocent, in all the Corvus constellation."

Dame Hester cried piteously: "That is how I want to cruise, with a bit of fun now and then, not just blinking out through the portholes at nothing whatever. Still, I have seen all I care to see of Flajaret, and I am quite ready to depart. Myron, what of you?"

"In a certain sense Flajaret is interesting, but I am ready to leave."

Dame Hester gave her head a curt nod and turned to Marko Fassig: "What are your plans?"

Marko Fassig blew out his bushy mustache. "They are simple enough. Before long I hope to find a berth aboard some passing spaceship in need of an experienced hand."

Myron said coldly, "We cannot help you. The *Glodwyn* is more than adequately crewed at the moment."

"Nonsense!" cried Dame Hester. "Myron, you are far too hasty! Marko, you may report aboard the *Glodwyn* at once. I will have a word with Captain Myron, and something will be arranged."

"That is extremely satisfactory," said Marko Fassig. "I shall do my best for you, and perhaps I can even enliven the voyage."

"That is what I have in mind," said Dame Hester. "Get your things and report aboard *Glodwyn* as soon as possible!"

Dame Hester and Myron returned to the ship. Dame Hester made explicit suggestions to Myron so that, when Marko Fassig boarded the *Glodwyn*, Myron somewhat glumly informed him that he would be entered on the roster as "Purser." Marko Fassig declared himself well-satisfied with the arrangement.

3

The *Glodwyn* rose from Flajaret spaceport, pushed up through the overcast, and broke out into the light of Maudwell's Star. The chief mate and Myron set the autopilot on the proper course, and Maudwell's Star dwindled astern.

Myron returned to the main saloon, to find Dame Hester and Marko Fassig sitting at their ease, each with a frosty goblet of Pingaree Punch. Dame Hester was explaining the purpose of the voyage, while Marko lounged in the cushioned chair, lazily attentive. "As you will now understand, the voyage is essentially a very serious and important expedition. I hope to validate Dame Betka Ontwill's claims by personal observations, and of course I will gladly undertake a revitalizing program. Psychologically I concede to no conventional categorization. I am as daring and flexible as ever I was. I act as I see fit, and a fig for the consequences! I am sorry to say that sometimes my body complains of what I do, and I must take heed. I cannot scamper across a sandy beach to plunge into towering surf, or dart off on some madcap escapade as once I managed without a second thought. It is this sad ebbing of resilience that I am anxious to repair. And why should I not? I command zest and the spirit of adventure in its richest form. I have a single goal: to pluck all the fruit from the Tree of Life; and consume it down to the rind!" With a dramatic gesture Dame Hester drank deep from her goblet. "Now you know the force which drives this expedition on its way!"

"I salute you!" declared Marko Fassig. "You are a woman in a thousand!"

Dame Hester turned to look at Myron. "Yes? What is it now? You are standing there first on one leg, then the other. What is the problem?"

"There is no problem. I want to show Fassig where he will take his meals and then I shall explain the work he will be doing."

Dame Hester raised her eyebrows. "Truly, Myron, you are being a bit stiff-necked. I am interested in what Marko has to say. He has led a fascinating life, from which you yourself might learn."

Marko Fassig lazily rose to his feet. "I must not keep Captain Tany waiting." He bowed to Dame Hester. "I hope to continue our discussion another time."

At the evening meal Dame Hester was short with Myron. Finally she said, "I see no reason why Marko should not dine in our company. He is both amusing and sympathetic, which is a rare combination."

Myron said, "It is not proper for the crew to dine in the saloon. There are distinctions which should never be relaxed, at the risk of impairing ship's discipline."

"Bah! There is no need for such rigidity. Please ask Marko if he would care to take a liqueur with us."

Myron rose to his feet, bowed with impassive formality, and went to execute Dame Hester's orders. On the following day, Dame Hester told him: "Marko henceforth will be taking his meals in the saloon. Please inform the chief steward of the change."

As the voyage progressed, Myron became ever more disenchanted with Marko Fassig and his confident conduct. Dame Hester, if anything, seemed to encourage Marko's inappropriate behavior, and Myron soon learned that his complaints fell on deaf ears.

Partly in response to Marko's anecdotes, Dame Hester decided that a halt at some picturesque world along the way might well enliven the voyage. She suggested as much to Myron, and explained with pointed emphasis that she did not want him to take her to a place where the best entertainment was a dogfight.

Myron, using the full scope of his dignity, stated that, naturally, he would do his best to gratify her demands. However, said Myron, she should realize that they had now entered a relatively remote section of the Reach, and that the worlds of high sophistication and urbanized culture were for the most part far astern.

"So what is out there now?" demanded Dame Hester. "Jungles and swamps and jumping red-eyed savages?"

Myron laughed politely. "I'm sure that such places could be found. Out here nothing is certain."

"Hmmf. Doesn't your famous *Handbook* tell you what to expect?"

"Of course, and I will make good use of it. First, I want to find a world that is not too far off our course."

"Also, if you please, a world that is amusing, with beautiful people, appetizing cuisine, interesting entertainments, and very good shopping opportunities."

"I'll see what I can find."

Myron examined the sector charts and studied *Handbook to the Planets*, and finally decided that the world Taubry by the sun Vianjeli best approximated the requirements. He reported his findings to Dame Hester. She acceded to his choice without enthusiasm. "There is no mention of exotic ceremonies or anything which sounds particularly interesting, except that criminals are placed in cages and displayed for public edification in the central plaza."

"Perhaps you will see an interesting prisoner. The report says that the back-lander's market often offers interesting items for sale."

"What do they mean by that?" demanded Dame Hester. "Twenty-pound turnips? Trained mice?"

"I don't know."

"Very well. Let us try this world Taubry and its rather ambiguous entertainments."

Myron at once altered course toward the star Vianjeli, which in due course grew bright, and the world Taubry became large below. When Myron went to the pilothouse in order to use the macroscope, he found Marko Fassig lounging beside the equipment, lazily hobnobbing with Chief Mate Atwyn. Myron's smouldering resentment flared into anger, and he decided to abate the nuisance personified by Marko Fassig once and for all. For the moment he said, "Be good enough to attend to your duties, Fassig. The pilothouse, as you know, is off-limits to the crew."

"Certainly, sir," said Fassig, with easy good humor. He straightened, winked at Chief Mate Atwyn, and sauntered away.

The *Glodwyn* landed at Port Tanjee terminal. Myron immediately confronted Marko Fassig. "Sir, as of this moment you are discharged. I find that we have no need for a purser aboard the *Glodwyn*. Take your belongings and leave the ship at once!"

Marko Fassig pulled at his mustache, lifted his eyebrows into quizzical arches, then shrugged. "That is your option, Captain Tany, and I make no protest. Five minutes will be enough. I shall wish Dame Hester a happy voyage, and then I shall be off the ship."

An hour later Myron Tany, still wearing his captain's uniform, stood forlorn and alone outside the terminal, his great-aunt's rebukes still echoing in his ears. The suitcase at his feet contained his belongings; Dame Hester had allowed him sufficient funds to buy his passage home to Vermazen. As she concluded her remarks, she told him, "Myron, you were given your chance, but you failed miserably! You quite lost touch with reality. You are a dreamer, an allegorist, and—dare I say?—something of a moon-calf. My advice is this: return to your home; study another four years at the Institute, then go to work with your father at the Exchange. That, so I believe, is your métier, and where you will earn whatever success life has to offer you."

THREE

1

Myron noticed a uniformed official, middle-aged, extremely neat and erect, standing about fifty feet away. He seemed interested in Myron and his conduct. Odd! thought Myron. Why was the man so alert?

Myron turned away, and surveyed the landscape. A boulevard led from the terminal to the center of town, with a line of trees to either side. Myron recognized the trees from their description in the *Handbook*; these were the famous cloudtrees of Taubry: enormous masses of billowing gray foam clutched in black tendrils, towering high into the air like small thunderheads.

Myron looked over his shoulder. The official had not changed his position. His manner seemed curious rather than hostile. Still, the attention was disconcerting. Once again Myron adopted the role of an innocent tourist and pretended to study the landscape. The scenery, for a fact, was pleasant and, so Myron noted, both neat and orderly, without a weed or a scrap of litter to be seen. A few small vehicles moved slowly and carefully along the boulevard. Cloudtrees reared overhead, the foam swaying and slipping to the touch of the soft afternoon breeze. At no great distance the boulevard opened into a plaza. The buildings within Myron's range of vision were constructed to a similar architecture: complex, florid, at times almost rococo, with high-pitched roofs and many dormers. The materials were uniform: dark timber, terra cotta, tinted glass in tall narrow windows. The folk of Port Tanjee, thought Myron, had definite ideas as to how they wanted their town to look.

Myron darted a glance toward the official. He stood as before, watching with bland vigilance. Myron's patience wore thin. He swung about intending to demand an explanation, but the official bestirred himself and slowly approached, halting at a respectful distance of three yards. Myron was able to read the legend embossed on his badge. It read: PUBLIC MONITOR.

Myron spoke sharply: "Why are you watching me with such suspicion?"

"No suspicion, sir; merely ordinary interest. I take it that you are a newcomer to Port Tanjee?"

"I have only just arrived."

The monitor indicated the pamphlet which Myron had received in the terminal and which he still held in his hand. "You have studied the Advisory, sir?"

"No; not yet." Myron glanced at the pamphlet. "It seems to be a brochure of some kind."

"True. It is a valuable reference and the maps will guide you about the town. There is an interesting historical survey, and a summary of certain local regulations, with which you should become familiar. We are an orderly folk at Port Tanjee. Our off-world visitors naturally follow the same rules."

"Naturally."

"Just so. The Advisory will make you aware of our special customs, which you should keep in mind. For instance—" he pointed to the suitcase which Myron had placed on the sidewalk "—I believe that you were about to abandon that object so that it became an article of litter."

Myron asked incredulously, "Is that why you were watching me so carefully?"

"It is my duty to apprehend miscreants in the full flush of their guilt."

Myron controlled his annoyance—with an effort, since today his disposition had already been severely tried. He spoke carefully. "That is my suitcase! It contains my belongings! I need them. They are important to me."

The monitor shrugged. "The facts suggest otherwise. It is a very small case, and you have placed it where it might have escaped notice."

"The suitcase is small because I have few possessions. If I owned more things I would carry a larger case. I set it down when I came out upon the street, because I did not want to hold it suspended in the air while I looked about the surroundings. When I decide to move on, I will definitely retrieve the suitcase."

"Aha! That seems straightforward enough!" said the monitor heartily. "All is explained. Still, I recommend that you study the Advisory. It defines areas of approved and disapproved conduct, and you should definitely know the difference."

"I will read the 'Advisory' as soon as possible. Can you direct me to an inexpensive hotel, of good quality?"

The official rubbed his chin. "Your requirements contradict each other; still, I suggest the Rambler's Rest, as a reasonable compromise. I might mention that it is not considered polite to haggle."

"Oh? Suppose the landlord asks an exorbitant rate?"

"Then you merely bow and go your way. The landlord may take pity and call out a new figure, whereupon you may return or keep walking until the landlord calls out a rate which suits you."

"Very well. How do I find the Rambler's Rest?"

"Proceed up the boulevard to the plaza. Turn right, up Fimrod Lane, and you will come upon the Rambler's Rest."

"Thank you." Myron took up his suitcase with exaggerated care, and set off up the boulevard. For a moment or two his mind reverted to the *Glodwyn*, to his Aunt Hester and the obnoxious Marko Fassig. Resolutely he put the thoughts from his mind; rancor was a useless emotion; it would restrict his activity and muddle his thoughts. At some time in the future, if and when conditions allowed, he would give serious attention to the righting of wrongs, but at the moment such hopes were visionary. They would not be forgotten, he promised himself.

Myron arrived at the plaza. Looking around, he saw shops, markets, agencies, several restaurants and cafés, and to his left, across the plaza, a row of cages, evidently for the display of miscreants. Trees lined the plaza and grew behind the structures: for the most part cloudtrees supporting nimbuslike masses of gray foam.

Myron turned up Fimrod Lane and presently came upon the Rambler's Rest: a large two-storied structure under a roof of many ridges, and steep-sided gables. He entered a loggia panelled in strips of varnished wood, where he was met by a stout middle-aged woman wearing a voluminous gown of flowing green fabric. She listened impassively as Myron explained his needs; then, wasting no words, she took him to a neat room with adjoining bath on the second floor. Myron found the premises satisfactory but before he could start negotiating the price, she took three sols from him for three nights' rent, and marched silently from the room. Myron looked after her, nonplussed. He had been too slow; the time had come and gone. Myron turned away; perhaps next time he would do better. He seated himself in a chair beside the window, and took stock of his situation. His options were so limited as to merit no serious consideration. With funds at hand he could pay for his passage home—a safe, sensible, if somewhat inglorious, program. The single alternative was to find a job aboard a passing spaceship, as a steward or a cook; he lacked technical skills for anything better, notwithstanding his degree in cosmology.

Myron sighed. His expertise was profound, but focused in the wrong direction. Still it would do no harm to make inquiries at the terminal. Even if the effort proved fruitless, he could return to Salou Sain with a clear conscience.

Local time was middle afternoon. Myron decided to stroll down to the plaza, but first it might be wise to acquaint himself with the Advisory. He picked up the pamphlet, which was entitled:

– – > ADVISORY < – –

HAPPY WELCOME TO OUR VISITORS!

Herein: a friendly whisper as to our world, our rules, and our regulatory measures, including a schedule of penalties.

WE HOPE THAT THIS ADVISORY WILL FOSTER THE JOY
AND DELIGHT OF THE TRAVELER!

On the first page Myron found a preface, which read:

Welcome to our world of wonder! Taubry, so you will discover, includes regions of inspiring natural beauty. The contrasts are profound! Two of the three continents, Farst and Wints, while of great interest, are accessible only to special expeditions, by reason of natural dangers and often savage fauna. The casual visitor, nevertheless, will be thrilled and excited by the wonders of the third continent Liro, where conditions for the most part are salubrious and comfortable. The local inhabitants, despite their picturesque differences, are more often than not congenial and kind.

Port Tanjee, Melanchrino, and Semmerin are urban centers of highly sophisticated culture, ranking with facilities to be found elsewhere. The visitor should ignore thoughts of parsimony and attempt to explore each and every canton of Liro, in order to enjoy the rich diversity of custom and costume, not to mention the unfamiliar and often exotic foods, all nourishing despite appearance. But—is it not true? One eats with tongue and teeth, not eyes! Pay no heed to expense; each canton provides an ambience of felicitous interest, which will linger long in the memory.

Port Tanjee is the principal city, and offers all needful facilities, while the Museum of Non-motile Amphibian Carapaces ranks with any to be found elsewhere.

The visitor to Port Tanjee will be impressed by the order and logic of all arrangements, though he will never be stifled by regimentation. Each visitor may conduct himself with full personal franchise, since our philosophy presupposes personal will and responsibility. At Port Tanjee there are no accidents; for every occurrence a sponsor exists, and if you suffer injury or inconvenience of any kind, be assured that the perpetrator will be identified and subjected to a penitential procedure.

The word "offense" includes acts of both positive and negative volition. The same regulations apply to all—even to you, yourself, though we are loath to indicate these unpleasant things to a careful and genteel tourist.

Nevertheless, to assist the visitor, below is a general summary of the more ordinary rules of conduct. The explicit statutes are delineated in Sections II and III. Please thoroughly familiarize yourself with this Advisory. Below is a short summary of the civil proscriptions:

Distribute no litter, nor articles extraneous to the ordinary condition of the landscape. Cause no disorder; indite no signs, symbols, messages, instructions, exhortations, advice, or condemnation in a place public or private, including the walls adjacent to public or private commodes.

Cause no ugly blemishes or eyesores, anywhere. If you come upon litter, trash, blemish, or eyesore, the regulation requires that you mitigate the offensive condition.

Do not expectorate at random. Do not inappropriately void bowels or bladder; use designated receptacles. Do not perform an indiscreet flatulence except in designated areas. Make no loud, unpleasant, or unreasonable noises; play no offensive music from a mechanical device; display no prurient images.

While dealing with shopkeepers a special code of gentility is suggested. Refrain from inciting confrontations with service personnel. If the prices are beyond your means, depart. Do not berate or plead; do not scorn the merchandise as if it were mean and worthless. Do not haggle; that is not our way. To ensure the good opinion of the shopkeeper, pay his price with casual grandeur and aristocratic style. Such behavior will enhance the self-esteem of everyone concerned.

In regard to public conduct: obey the advice of the civic monitors.

If you are taken into custody, you will be judged by the nearest magistrate. He will immediately impose the penalty, which ordinarily will be fair and mild. Trivial misdeeds incur confinement in one of the cages at the eastern edge of the plaza, for one-half day, one day, or longer. More serious offenses may require a session of work therapy in the quarries. It is to be hoped that such information will be of purely abstract interest to visitors.

Our recommendations are succinct! The three affirmatives are: Be prudent! Be correct! Be munificent!

The three negatives are: Mulct no one! Pain no one! Inconvenience no one!

A few wise suggestions:

Attempt sexual interaction with circumspection. Certain conduct is considered a non-revocable offer of marriage.

Inebriation may be illegal, since only properly taxed liquors may legally be consumed! Always demand to see the tax certificate before imbibing! Or perhaps you will prefer our fruitwaters, which are tasty!

Visitors will find exhilarating entertainment at Port Tanjee! Gaze with eager enjoyment upon the artistic arrangements in the park! Participate in the nice society and graceful dancing in the houses of public entertainment. These are rated by Categories I, II and III. At Category I houses, children and sensitive girls may foregather without fear of embarrassment. At Category II houses, mature men and women may indulge in serious conversation, and often will exchange jocularities. At Category III houses, the atmosphere is sometimes a trifle loose. Working spacemen are at ease. The ale is of good quality and ladies are generally less offended by frank and cordial conversation. There is general tolerance of universalities.

Above is an indication of our philosophy of life. It celebrates quiet joy and the precepts of propriety. Anyone, including tourists and visitors, may spend money without fear or stint; and no one will utter accusations of arrogance! Spend lavishly! Enjoy Port Tanjee to the fullest! We welcome you!

The next pages set forth the legal code of Port Tanjee in detail. There was also a description of the thirteen cantons which comprised the continent Liro.

Myron put aside the Advisory and changed from his captain's uniform into the ordinary garments worn by spacemen everywhere across the Gaean Reach: dark trousers loose at the thigh, gathered at the ankle and tucked into short black boots; a long-sleeved shirt of soft dark blue material, a loose-crowned black cap.

Myron left the hotel and strolled down Fimrod Lane to the plaza, where he paused to take stock of his surroundings. The precisely spaced trees, disproportionately tall, dominated the plaza. The trees, the dark timber structures, the odd clarity of the air: they created in Myron a hallucinatory perception. He felt that he was looking at a model stage setting, or perhaps a child's miniature village. He blinked his eyes and the illusion vanished.

At a nearby café Myron ordered tea and biscuits. Relaxing in the afternoon sunlight, he dismissed his troubles and watched the folk of Port Tanjee as they moved about their affairs. They approximated the standard Gaean physical type, though Myron thought to see a tendency toward stocky torsos, round faces with prominent cheekbones, square jaws, and short snub noses, with hair generally ranging from

dark brown to near-black, with no blond hair whatever. The Port Tanjee costumes were not particularly distinctive except for the headgear.
The men wore flat quadricorn hats of stiff material, dark blue, dark
green, or black, pulled squarely down across their foreheads. The
women wore elaborate headgear which they had fabricated from
starched napkins of several colors folded and pleated together—some
marvels of intricate construction.

Myron studied passing girls with special interest, wondering as to
their amiability. They carried themselves with a lively energy, the
younger girls bouncing and half-trotting to the force of their vitality.
Some of them Myron found sufficiently attractive that he tried to remember pertinent provisions in the advisory. Most of the girls and
women, however, failed to excite his admiration, by reason of their
hair styling, which decreed large puffs or large fluff-balls over and to
the side of each ear. Myron was also put off by a general air of complacence and self-satisfaction, most noticeable among the prettiest
girls, as if each had just consumed a large bowl of strawberries and
cream to which she knew she was not entitled. When they glanced toward Myron, they noticed first his sleek blond hair, which inevitably
prompted them to assess him more closely, followed by a ineffable
purse of the lips and a slight arch of the eyebrows before looking
away, as if to communicate their suspicion of spacemen and off-
worlders in general.

Oh well, thought Myron, even if I wanted to, I'd never dare to
say "Boo," for fear of a day in the cage; or worse, finding myself married.

Myron decided to waste no more time watching the girls. The afternoon was drawing to an end. The sun had dropped behind the trees.
Myron left the café and crossed the plaza to where he could look over
the cages. As he drew near, he noticed that in the middle cage a young
man of about his own age sat disconsolately hunched on a bench. Myron approached. The prisoner turned him a surly side-glance. Myron
asked politely, "How long will you be in the cage?"

"I will be freed one hour after sunset."

"What did you do?" asked Myron. "I hope you don't mind my
asking."

"I don't mind; what's it to me, after all? I came in from Birkenhal-
ter with a load of papagonies for the market. One fell off my cart, but
I did not notice. A junior guardian summoned the inspector who allowed me seven minutes to clean up the litter. I did so, with fourteen
seconds to spare. However, four seeds had rolled under a leaf, and
these I neglected. The junior guardian had been watching and pointed

them out to the inspector, who took fifty dinkets from me, by way of penalty. I waited several minutes, then crept up on the junior guardian and gave him a whumping. I was taken before the magistrate, who put me into the cage. Now you know as much as I do."

"It is a sad tale," said Myron. "What will you do when they turn you loose?"

"I have been pondering this question myself," said the captive. "I have now come to a decision. If, when set free, I were to approach the junior guardian—you can see him lurking yonder: the fat boy in the square black hat. If, by blistering his arse with a good hazel switch, I were able to right all the ills of the universe, then I would gladly pay the price of another day in the cage. But this is not possible; evil and deceit are deeply ingrained into the fabric of being. My efforts would not efface them. For this reason I shall not trouble to beat the junior guardian. Instead, I shall walk to the Owlswyck Inn and there consume a muscadine tart, and a pint of bitter ale. Then I shall find my wagon and drive from town. If the junior guardian stands nearby, I shall stroll past, oblivious to his existence. Revenge is sweet, but trundling home under the stars of night is sweeter."

Myron ruminated a moment, looking off across the plaza, now awash with pale light reflected from the sunset sky. He said, "That is a reasonable program, and it will help me deal with my own affairs."

The captive gave a glum nod. "In the end, revenge is not worth the trouble."

"Correct," said Myron. "Unless, of course, you can get the deed done and escape without detection."

"That goes without saying."

"I take it that you recommend the Owlswyck Inn?"

"Yes; the tarts are tasty. The ale is good. The house is Category III and often quite jolly. Cross the plaza, turn into Melcher Lane, proceed sixty-two yards; there you will come upon the Owlswyck Inn."

"Thank you." Myron turned away from the cage. Clouds in the western sky glowed in shades of vermilion, magenta, and pale green: a medley of unusual colors which for Myron emphasized the peculiar ambience of Port Tanjee.

2

Myron crossed the plaza, entered Melcher Lane, and saw ahead a sign overhanging the street:

OWLSWYCK INN
A hostelry of grand tradition.
Comestibles, Noble Ale, Music and Dancing
on the occasion.
Category III. Ladies welcome.

Heavy swinging doors allowed Myron entry into a large public taproom, illuminated by fading sunset light shining through high windows. Myron found a seat at a long table at the side of the room, where, for the time at least, he sat alone. Similar tables surrounded a central area with a waxed wooden floor for the convenience of dancers. Against the opposite wall a dais supported a lectern, where someone might address the company, if he were so inclined. An odd custom, thought Myron, but then this was an odd world.

A serving boy appeared at his elbow. Myron ordered a pint of ale and asked to see a menu. The boy gave a patronizing chuckle. "Ale you shall have without delay, but for 'menu' you must read the board yonder." He indicated a blackboard hanging over the bar. "No fandangles at the Owlswyck Inn!"

Myron read the list of offerings. "What is the muscadine tart?"

"It is very good, sir: duck liver, purple grape, and parsley in a crust, with a garnish of boiled mash."

"That should do me well enough."

"Take my advice," said the boy, "start your meal with a steaming pot of our burgoo, to fill the corners of your gut. The price is seven dinkets for a pot; it is a bargain you will never forget!"

"Very well; I shall try a pot of burgoo, but first the ale."

When the boy served the ale, Myron asked the purpose of the dais and lectern. "It seems a bit out of place."

The boy was amused by Myron's lack of sophistication. "Are there no such facilities on your own world?"

"Nothing like this, in the middle of the tavern."

"Well then—it is used by the constabulary and the magistrate on duty." He directed Myron's attention to a sign on the wall over Myron's head. "Have you read the notice?"

"No. It escaped my attention."

"Then read it, since it explains how things go at Owlswyck Inn."

Myron turned and read the notice:

LOCAL ORDINANCES STRICTLY ENFORCED. OBSTREPERY FOR-
BIDDEN. WINKLERS AND SKATIFINCHES BE WARNED! ALL AT-

TEMPTS AT INSEMINATION MUST BE LICENSED. DANCERS
ARE ENJOINED TO GRACE AND DIGNITY; THESE TRAITS ARE
APPROVED, SINCE THEY CONTRIBUTE TO THE BEAUTY OF
THE DANCE.

"Hm," said Myron. "It seems that you enjoy lively times at the Owlswyck."

"In moderation, sir. The constables are quick to detect excess, and the magistrate reads from his black book without compunction."

Once again Myron resolved to conduct himself with maximum discretion. He tasted the ale, and found it strong, bitter and a trifle frowsty—still, all in all, palatable. He looked about the room. The clientele was mixed. He saw local townsmen, folk from the back-country wearing leather trousers and blue twill jackets. There were a few off-world tourists and businessmen, also a half-dozen spacemen sitting at the bar. The Port Tanjee terminal was a transit and trans-shipment node from which feeder routes radiated to worlds off the beaten track: hence the number of spacemen who came to drink ale at the Owlswyck Inn.

The boy brought a pot of burgoo, along with a dish of flatbread. Myron dipped his spoon into the pot and cautiously tasted. He winced and drank a swallow of ale. He tasted again. It seemed certain that the cook, for the enhancement of zest, had used his most original spices. Myron heaved a sigh. The best policy was to eat and ask no questions; he therefore set to work upon the burgoo, from time to time swashing ale around his mouth.

The boy served the muscadine tart, which Myron devoured without qualms, attempting no analysis of the constituents.

The tavern began to fill. Women appeared, in groups, alone, with friends or husbands: some young, some old. Myron saw nothing to interest him, and was also given pause by the possibility of inadvertent marriage.

The serving boy brought four men, newly arrived, toward the vacant places at Myron's table. Myron watched their approach with interest. They were a disparate group, though to judge by their garments, all were spacemen. The first, and the oldest, was spare, erect, somewhat taller than ordinary, with patrician features, crisp locks of gray hair, a serene, if somewhat remote, expression.

Next came a short thick man, pink-skinned, with innocent blue eyes in a round amiable face. A few lank strands of blond hair lay across his scalp. He walked with delicate precision, placing his short broad feet with care, as if to minimize the discomfort of ill-fitting boots.

The third man was slim, young, and moved with the mercurial flamboyance of a harlequin. He was inordinately handsome, with a heart-shaped face, soft black curls, long black eyelashes, a crooked mouth. He loped across the floor on long bent-kneed strides, looking from side to side with head tilted, as if watchful for the unusual or the extraordinary.

The fourth of the group, once again, was notably different from each of his fellows. He was very tall, very thin, sallow of skin, with a severe long countenance. Black hair retreated from a high forehead; below were a long nose, a prim mouth, a long chin. He wore a black suit of magisterial cut, so tight that the arms and legs were like black pipes.

The four seated themselves, nodded politely to Myron and ordered ale from the serving boy.

Myron thought them an interesting group and presently fell into conversation with the short pink man, who identified himself as "Wingo," chief steward aboard the *Glicca*, a freighter only just arrived at Port Tanjee. "I am chief steward, true enough," said Wingo, "but that is not the whole story. I am also cook, bottle-washer, janitor, vermin exterminator, surgeon, nursemaid, and general dogsbody. When we carry passengers, I become social director and psychiatrist, as well. We have had lively times aboard the *Glicca*!"

Wingo introduced his shipmates. "This is Captain Maloof. He may seem austere, with all the solemnity of a Drensky Archimandrite, but do not be deceived; when it comes to conniving the shipping agent or questing for lost treasure, or feeding bon-bons to pretty passengers, Captain Maloof is on the job."

The captain chuckled. "That is a blurred portrait. As usual, Wingo's ideas are extravagant."

Wingo gave his head a grave shake. "Not so! I have learned that truth sometimes may best be conveyed in glancing tangents. The 'what-might-be' and the 'what-should-have-been' are always more interesting than the 'what-truly-is'—and often more important."

"So it may be," said Myron. "In regard to Captain Maloof, I will reserve judgment."

"That is tactfully put," said Wingo. "But let me direct your attention to the man beside him, now quaffing ale with the insolent grace of a fallen angel. His name is Fay Schwatzendale; aboard the *Glicca* he is chief engineer, also first engineer, second engineer, oiler, wiper and general technician. He is a mathematician and performs complicated sums in his head, and furnishes the results on the instant, whether they are right or wrong."

"That is most impressive!" said Myron. He glanced across the table to where Schwatzendale sat with head tilted, smiling a slantwise smile. Myron said, "He would seem almost as versatile as you."

"Far more than I!" declared Wingo. "Schwatzendale can play the concertina and also the spoons. He can render 'The Ballad of Rosie Maloney' from beginning to end. This is only a start. Schwatzendale is a practitioner of probability. He works the laws of chance as deftly as I toss a soufflé. He thrives on five-star monte, stingaree, layabout, kachinka, and any other whimsies of fate from which he thinks he can wring a profit."

"Remarkable!" said Myron. He signaled to the serving boy and ordered a round of ale. Then he indicated the tall thin gentleman in the tight black suit at the end of the table. "What of your other shipmate: is he also a virtuoso?"

Wingo spoke in a measured voice: "That is Hilmar Krim, the supercargo, and the answer to your question is a tentative 'yes,' especially if Krim himself is to be believed. He has been with us three months, and we are only gradually sorting him out. His field is jurisprudence and his learning would seem to be profound; in fact, he is compiling material for a work to be entitled: *Comparative Gaean Jurisprudence*. Am I right, Krim?"

"Possibly," said Krim. "I was not listening. What issue were you arguing?"

"I have been telling Myron Tany that you are a savant in the field of jurisprudence."

Krim inclined his head. "I am endeavoring to combine the multiple strands of local law into a comprehensive synthesis. It is a large work."

Wingo turned his blue eyes back to Myron. "So there you have it. This is the crew of the *Glicca*. All of us have gone wrong, in one way or another. Captain Maloof is a dreamer and pursues a romantic memory as if it were real. Schwatzendale is a gambler and a master of mysterious tricks; Hilmar Krim is a savant and a pundit. All of us are a bit estranged from a life of known routines; we are picaroons rather than respectable members of society."

Krim spoke with heavy jocularity: "Please excuse me from your category, Mr. Wingo. I think of myself as a syncretic pantologist, integral with any environment. I am an element of the universal Gaean society, and not a pariah."

"It shall be as you wish," Wingo told him.

Krim nodded, well satisfied. Myron asked Wingo, "What of yourself? Are you a pundit? A gambler? A dreamer?"

Wingo wistfully shook his head. "I am, essentially, nothing: not even a pariah. I am aware of the cosmic puzzle, and I have tried to discover its outlines. To this end I have read the works of the Gaean philosophers; I have learned their words and phrases, their prefaces and envois. It was a sad revelation to learn that they, I, and the cosmos all speak different languages; no gloss exists."

"So what happens next?"

"Nothing very much. What is to be learned from chaos?" Wingo scowled thoughtfully down at his thick-fingered hands. "Once I wandered into some mountains, whose name I now forget. I came upon a rain puddle which reflected the sky and some moving clouds. I looked for a moment, then looked up at the sky, which was vast, blue, majestic. I went my way in a reverie." Wingo gave his head a rueful shake. "I recall my poor feet hurting all the way down the mountainside—as always when I try them too hard. In the end, I enjoyed the relief of bathing my feet in warm salt water and applying an ointment." After a pause he went on. "If I came upon another puddle, perhaps I might look again."

"I don't quite understand," said Myron. "You seem to be telling me that it is a mistake to search too hard for knowledge."

"I suspect that this is what I mean," said Wingo. "Even if 'Reality,' or 'Truth'—whatever it is called—were discovered, and scientifically codified, it might be something trivial and years might have been wasted in the search. I might well recommend mystics and zealots to caution, lest after decades of fasting and penitence they are allowed Truth, only to find it to be some miserable scrap of information, of no more account than mouse droppings in the sugar bowl."

Myron began to feel light-headed—whether from the ale or the effort to grasp Wingo's theories, he could not be sure.

Schwatzendale joined the conversation. "The *Glicca* is a hive of deep thinking. Krim is planning a legal system which will be standard everywhere across the Reach. He wants to charge a royalty every time a crime is committed. As for me, I live by a simple rule: if I point with excitement to the east, everyone will jump up and look to the east while I eat their lunch. Captain Maloof takes pains to appear grave, sober, and respectable—but it is all a façade. He follows a will-o'-the-wisp everywhere across the lands beneath all the stars."

Captain Maloof listened with a faint smile. He said, "My quest, even if it were real, would be little more than a nostalgia and not worth talking about." He spoke to Myron: "What of you? Do you too follow a will-o'-the-wisp?"

"Not really. I can explain myself very quickly, and you may laugh if you wish. My great-aunt Hester owns the spaceyacht *Glodwyn*. We set out on a cruise. I was nominally captain. My aunt became restless, until a man name Marko Fassig came aboard. When we arrived at Port Tanjee, I ordered Fassig off the ship, but my aunt put me off instead, and I am now at liberty, drinking ale at the Owlswyck Inn."

"You tell a melancholy tale," said Captain Maloof.

Myron reflected, then put a tentative question. "I should ask if you are short of crew in the areas of my competence. If so, I would like to apply for the job."

"You were captain of the *Glodwyn?*"

"Well, yes. That was my designation."

Maloof smilingly shook his head. "The *Glicca* is fully staffed at the moment; the entire crew is sitting here at the table."

"Ah well," said Myron, "I just thought I would ask."

"No harm done," said Captain Maloof. "I'm sorry that we cannot oblige you. We definitely have no need for two captains."

Myron gloomily drank more ale. A group of musicians had arrived at the tavern. They mounted to the bandstand at the far end of the room and brought out their instruments: a flageolet, a concertina, a baritone lute, and a trambonium. They tuned to the concertina, producing the usual squeaks, warbles, tinkles, slurs and scales; then began to play: first a tune of simple construction, but one which jerked along at a good gait. Fingers began to drum on the tables and toes tapped the floor. Soon folk went out to dance: sometimes singly, sometimes in pairs.

Night had come to Port Tanjee; the tavern was illuminated by small colored lanterns. Myron drank another mug of ale and sat back enjoying the occasion. Wingo solemnly informed him that, while he liked dancing, the impact of the floor upon his sensitive feet caused him nervous distress.

A stalwart red-haired woman, in the full bloom of her early maturity, approached Schwatzendale and suggested that he join her in the dance. Schwatzendale declined the honor with so many graceful compliments that the woman stroked his head before walking away. "Schwatzendale is wise," Wingo observed to Myron. "The marriage customs to be found from place to place are never the same. Often the stranger performs some innocent act, or suggests a casual intimacy, only to find that he has committed himself to a marriage which must be executed upon penalty of a large fine, or perhaps a good beating by the girl's relatives or a term of occupational therapy. When you are in a new place and the customs are unfamiliar, I advise you never to take liberties with a woman—or, for that matter, with a man. Schwatzendale is wily, but even he will take no chances. Listen now." Wingo addressed Schwatzendale. "Suppose a beautiful lady approached wearing a basket of fruit on her head and tried to hang a wreath of amaranthines around your neck: what would you do?"

"I would run at full speed from Owlswyck Inn and hide in the *Glicca* with the covers pulled over my head."

"That is expert advice," said Wingo.

"I will take care," said Myron. "Such hints are extremely valuable."

The orchestra had started a new tune, an energetic two-step propelled by the rhythmic pulses of the trambonium and chords in the powerful lower register of the lute. The dancers again took to the floor, executing steps of several sorts. One of the favorites started with a man and woman, arms clasping shoulders, standing poised and impassive, before setting off at a bent-kneed running glide of four steps, a halt, then a high swinging kick first to right and then to left, then the same evolution in reverse. Other folk twirled this way and that, in rollics and hornpipes. Myron thought the spectacle highly picturesque. He chanced to notice Hilmar Krim, who sat tapping his fingers and wagging his head in time with the music. Wingo said with a chuckle: "Krim has taken four ales, which is two past his usual complement, and now the music is revealing its meaning to him. He has a mind of great tenacity, and is now searching for precedents."

Krim swallowed ale from his mug, ran his fingers across the table as if playing an imaginary keyboard. The exercise proved to be unsatisfactory, and Krim rose to his feet. He drained the ale from his mug and, stepping out on the floor, attempted a jig, at first tentatively, then with increasing confidence. His face was rapt in total absorption; he jerked and shuffled, arms rigid at his sides, long legs kicking out forward and backward, while he swung and shuffled across the floor.

A plump self-assured gentleman of middle years had entered the tavern and was now performing the local dance with one of the town belles. He wore a jacket of rich dark brown velvet and glossy black shoes adorned with silver rosettes; he seemed to be a person of importance, and performed the stylish dance with conspicuous elegance. Up and down the room he swooped, performing his kicks with supercilious precision. Other dancers made way for him, and watched with respectful admiration. Up the room, kick right, kick left, with toes properly extended; back down the room, swooping and gliding, then a kick to right, a kick to left, with something of an extra flourish. Hilmar Krim, absorbed in his own boisterous dance, was smartly struck by the gentleman's foot, directly between his shoulder blades.

Krim uttered a cry of surprise and halted his jig. The dancing gentleman was loath to interrupt the rhythm of his movements, and made an easy gesture by which the contact was acknowledged but dismissed as a matter of no great importance, so that he was able to dance on to the music without losing the beat.

Krim was dissatisfied and stood in the gentleman's way, so he was compelled to stop short to avoid collision. Angry words ensued. Krim explained his theory of how the dance should properly be conducted. The gentleman returned curt comments of his own, then resumed his dance; but almost immediately, responding to a final instruction from Krim, he seized a flagon of ale and hurled the contents into Krim's face, to penalize Krim for talking too much. Krim first boxed the gentleman's ears then commenced a bewildering jig, dancing, prancing, meanwhile kicking the portly gentleman with amazing dexterity: into the rump with cavorting heels, into the belly with his toe. Round and round Krim danced, his long legs performing a fine jig into the gentleman's body, in truly artistic syncopation with the music, which had not halted. Indeed, the musicians played with enthusiasm, indicating that they would be pleased to play as long as Krim chose to continue his dance.

The performance was cut short by a pair of constables who rushed across the floor to seize Krim, and the music came to a halt.

Wingo gave his head a sad shake. "Krim's footwork was creditable, but I doubt if that fact will do his case any benefit."

"It is a pity," said Schwatzendale. "He showed some interesting moves."

Captain Maloof stated, "He was reckless, even for a legal expert."

The constables dragged Krim toward the podium. The gentleman whom Krim had belabored led the way, moving with a jaunty step. He climbed the podium and seated himself behind the lectern.

The serving boy, who had come to the table with fresh pints, spoke in awe. "Your friend is daring, but also foolhardy. Now he must demand justice from the very magistrate whom he kicked so stylishly."

"You admire his work, then?" asked Schwatzendale.

The boy shrugged. "A good performance deserves its due."

The portly gentleman took a moment to arrange himself upon the chair, then called: "Bring forward the culprit!"

The constables dragged the crestfallen Krim to an area before the lectern.

"Your name?"

"I am Hilmar Krim. My occupation is supercargo aboard the spaceship *Glicca*. I attended the Achernar Central School of Forensic Linguistics where I specialized in admiralty law. I took a second degree at the Erasmus Institute of Social Science, where I edited the *Law Review*. My professional skills are finely honed."

"Aha! And where did you learn to dance with such pertinacity?"

Krim acknowledged the quip with a rueful smile. "I mention my background only to indicate that I am versed in several phases of jurisprudence. In this present matter, certain codes of legal doctrine and a number of germane precedents are defined in Articles Ten and Twelve of the Basic Admiralty Statutes. The indices, so I recall—"

The magistrate held up his hand. "Allow me to speak, counselor, if you will! I appreciate your helpful erudition, though I suppose that you take me for a back-country loon."

"That finding is not in evidence, sir!"

"No matter. We know the scope of your guilt; we need now only reckon the proper penalty, which of course transcends a simple visit to the public cage."

Krim drew himself up to his full height. He spoke severely. "I object to that entire imputation, sir; it is irrelevant, prejudicial and nuncupatory. Further, no grounds have been laid."

The magistrate nodded and rapped his gavel. "The objection is sustained! I will ignore the remark I just made."

Hilmar Krim gave his head a curt inclination. "This being the case, I move for a dismissal of all charges."

"The motion is denied. The case is as yet undeveloped."

"There can be no doubt as to the facts," stated Krim. "The juxtaposition occurred when you interposed your person into contiguity with the area I had previously and lawfully demarcated by explicitly functioning as a dancer. You invaded this space through careless malice, and inconvenienced me by thrusting your body against my leg, to my great anguish and discomfort. A man more stringent than myself might call for punitive damages; however, your simple acknowledgment of guilt will suffice."

"The motion is out of order, having been superseded by a prior complaint, filed by myself. We need not go into details. Do you plead 'guilty' or 'not guilty'?"

"I am guiltless, by reason of reckless and malicious invasion of recreational space previously preempted by me, and also the intolerable provocation visited upon my person: said acts forming the *res gestae*."

The magistrate pounded his gavel. "Let us proceed. I will not call for testimony, since any witnesses in your behalf would be guilty of perjury and would face a harsh penalty. It is easier to assume that all witnesses will have testified for the plaintiff. The verdict is guilty as charged. Now then: in regard to the sentence, allow me a moment while I glance into my black book." He produced a volume bound in black fish-skin from a shelf, lay it flat on the lectern, swung open its covers.

Hilmar Krim spoke urgently: "Sir, justice is too fragile and fine to be crushed between the pages of a book! Justice springs from human understanding, and is laved with the milk of human sympathy. I know of several four-square precedents to guide us on this occasion."

The magistrate again held up his hand. "Your erudition is impressive, but the black book is quick. Notice: I turn the pages to 'Public Brutality.' I find the subsection: 'Assault upon an official of dignity,' and here I read the instruction: 'Specify the severity of the offense, by counting the number of blows inflicted.' Next, 'designate the style and degree of the outrage; apply an increment to express the prestige of the victim.' "

Hilmar Krim managed a tremulous smile. "Sir, special circumstances apply; I am a member of the intelligentsia!"

"Your stipulation has merit," said the magistrate. "As a concession, I will make a special evaluation. I have already taken note of your graceful agility; and your intelligence, so I believe, is many-sided. Am I right?"

"Conceivably so, but—"

"Now then: if you were to meet the quarrymaster at Dartley Hole, could you show him the most efficient manner of carrying heavy rocks from place to place?"

"I would do so gladly," croaked Krim, "but I shall not have time, since—"

"You shall have all the time needful." The magistrate consulted his black book and performed a calculation. "For offenses such as yours the exact duration of the penitential period is four months eleven days and nineteen hours. Constables, remove the prisoner and take him out to Dartley Hole. His sentence begins on the instant he passes through the gates."

Krim attempted further expostulations, and indeed was still citing precedents as he was led from the tavern. The musicians took up their instruments; the music flowed as before. The magistrate stepped down from the podium, found his partner, and resumed his dance.

Wingo said at last, "A sad culmination to Krim's entertainment. He danced with both flair and skill."

"Either too much ale or too much deep thinking warped his judgment," said Captain Maloof. "It is hard to strike a balance."

Schwatzendale lifted his mug and looked to the empty chair. "I propose a toast to Hilmar Krim. I wish him health, endurance, and pleasant company at the quarry. May the time pass with lightning speed!"

"May the rocks prove interesting!" said Wingo.

The toast was drunk, and the group fell silent.

After a period Myron addressed Captain Maloof. "Sir, it appears that the office of supercargo aboard the *Glicca* is now vacant."

Captain Maloof nodded soberly. "So it seems."

"In that case, I wish to apply for the position."

Captain Maloof gave Myron a cool inspection. "You have experience along these lines?"

"As you know, my last post was that of captain aboard the *Glodwyn*."

Maloof, somewhat nonplussed, said, "You would seem to be overqualified."

"For me, it will be the start of a new career," said Myron. "I am sure that I will be competent to the job."

"I believe you," said Captain Maloof. "You look to have both intelligence and natural ability. You are hired."

FOUR

1

The *Glicca*, an ungainly old hulk of moderate capacity, carried freight in three cargo bays, or a fluctuating number of passengers in second- and third-class accomodation, or a combination of both. The crew consisted of Captain Adair Maloof, Chief Engineer Fay Schwatzendale, Chief Steward Isel Wingo, and the new supercargo Myron Tany.

The entire crew of the *Glicca* departed Owlswyck Inn at a relatively early hour. Myron went to his lodgings at the Rambler's Rest, while the others returned to the *Glicca*.

In the morning Myron packed his belongings and descended to the office. The landlady, standing behind the counter, observed his approach without reaction.

Myron spoke with crisp authority. "I will not be needing the room any longer."

"As you like."

Myron waited, but the landlady had no further comment.

Myron spoke again, raising his voice a trifle. "You may pay me a refund of two sols."

The landlady folded her arms across her chest. "There will be no refund."

Myron studied the impassive face. He opened his mouth to speak, but the statements which entered his mind seemed inadequate. He closed his mouth. In any case, why should he wrangle with this insipid woman over a paltry two sols? As the Advisory had suggested, an attitude of aristocratic condescension, or even disdain, was more suitable. He spoke haughtily. "It is of no consequence. Do not, however, expect a gratuity." He turned on his heel and marched from the Rambler's Rest. In the largest sense, the victory was his. He had departed the premises with dignity intact, while the woman even now must be squirming with shame. Further, he had learned a valuable lesson which at the price of two sols was cheap.

Upon entering the plaza, he seated himself at a café where he made a breakfast of tea and fish cakes. Then he walked along the boulevard, under the cloudtrees, to the spaceport. The security officer gave him a polite salute. Myron responded with a crisp nod. He passed through the terminal and located the *Glicca* a hundred yards out on the field: a vessel larger than the *Glodwyn*, built for durability rather than aesthetic flair, with none of the *Glodwyn*'s self-conscious elegance. The hull, which at one time had been enameled smart blue-gray with dark red trim, now showed the lusterless gray-white of undercoat, along with daubs of orange primer, where it had been thought necessary to seal scrapes, abrasions, and meteor marks. A loading dock had been drawn up to the starboard cargo hatch, though at the moment there was no work in progress.

Myron walked out on the field and approached the *Glicca*. A gangplank led up to the entry port, now ajar. Myron climbed the steps and passed through the port into the main saloon. He found Maloof and Schwatzendale lingering over their breakfast. They greeted him with casual amiability. "Sit down," said Maloof. "Have you had breakfast?"

"I had two fish cakes in red sauce and a pot of pepper tea," said Myron. "It was, in a sense, breakfast."

Wingo, in the galley, heard the interchange and immediately brought Myron a bowl of beans with bacon, and two toasted scones. "The food one finds in remote places is often substandard," said Wingo severely. "Aboard the *Glicca* we are not epicures, but neither are we faddists; we feel no compulsion to explore every intricacy of the local cuisine."

"Wingo acts as our arbiter in these cases," Schwatzendale told Myron. "If he finds a stuff in the market which intrigues him, it is served up for our dinner. Wingo watches carefully, and if we appear to enjoy the dish he may sample it himself."

Wingo grinned broadly. "I hear few complaints," he told Myron. "If you care to step this way, I will show you your quarters. Schwatzendale and I have already taken poor Krim's belongings to the transport security locker. The cabin has been well aired and the linen is fresh. I think that you will be comfortable."

Myron took his suitcase to the cabin, then returned to the saloon.

Maloof now sat alone. He said, "Your quarters are suitable, or so I hope?"

"Yes, of course, and I am ready to go to work."

"In that case, I will explain the scope of your duties. They are more various than you might expect." Maloof looked thoughtfully toward the ceiling. He said, "You may find difficulties rationalizing Krim's methods. Despite his many fine qualities, Krim was a man of the sort known as *sui generis*."

Myron nodded. "I am not surprised."

"Often Krim was short with the passengers and generated unnecessary friction. In response to a request which he found irrational, rather than taking five minutes to gratify the passenger's needs, he would explain why the passenger should alter his philosophy. At other times he might prescribe a holistic remedy for the passenger's indigestion rather than issuing the pastille requested, and the two would debate the case for hours, until the passenger, overcome by cramps, was forced to rush off to the latrine. When I tried to intercede, Krim declared himself a man of principle, and I was made to feel a charlatan."

Myron nodded and wrote into a small notebook. "Instruction One: conciliate passengers. Dispense medicine as required."

"Correct. Now then, as to records and accounts: again I must criticize Krim. He was so preoccupied with his monumental compilation of jurisprudence, that he avoided the drudgery of keeping accounts. When he was censured, he claimed that he had memorized all pertinent figures and that they reposed accurately in his mind. One day I asked him, 'What if by some unexpected freak of fortune you are forced off the *Glicca*, as it might be if you were killed by a bandit or suffered a brain spasm?'

" 'Nonsense, sheer bullypup!' Krim declared, quite emphatically.

" 'Still,' I persisted, 'what if you were taken up by the police and dragged off to jail? Who, then, would interpret your cryptic notes?'

"Krim became rather cross. The idea, so he stated, was farfetched; no police would think to molest a man of his forensic skills. But Krim was wrong. He was taken off to jail and his vast store of mental records is lost. The episode, I believe, speaks for itself."

Myron wrote in the notebook. "Instruction Two: keep proper records. Avoid police."

"Exactly." Maloof went on to describe Myron's other duties. He must tally the loading and discharge of cargo; he would prepare bills of lading and arrange for import and export licenses when necessary. He would supervise loading, and at each port of call he would verify that the proper parcels were discharged, even if he must carry them out to the dock himself.

Myron wrote. "Instruction Three: expedite cargo on and off vessel; cargo to be recorded in detail."

Maloof went on. "The supercargo must make sure that freight charges have been paid before cargo is loaded; otherwise chances are good that we will be carrying freight without profit, since the consignee often refuses to pay the transport bill, forfeiting to us the possibly useless merchandise, which leads to many difficulties."

Myron wrote: "Instruction Four: before all else, collect fees and charges."

"As you can see," said Maloof, "the ideal supercargo is a man of iron will and grim disposition. He has a mind like a trap and tolerates no impudence from the warehousemen, no matter what their pugnacity."

"I will do my best," said Myron in a subdued voice.

"That should be sufficient," said Maloof. "We journey short-handed aboard the *Glicca*. Everyone is versatile, especially the supercargo, who at times must assist the cook, the engineer, or function as general roustabout. You are aware of all this?"

"I am now."

During the early afternoon Captain Maloof and Myron visited the terminal lobby. At one end a number of shipping agents sat in small offices. Before each office a bulletin board listed parcels of cargo which the agent wished to place for shipment.

"This is where the business becomes complex," Maloof told Myron. "If it were merely a matter of carrying cargo from A to B, then instantly picking up another cargo from B to C, then from C to D, and so on, we would all be rich and nervous hysteria would be unknown. But it is never that simple."

"What about passengers?"

Maloof pulled a dour face. "Passengers are, at best, a necessary evil. Otherwise, they are capricious. They complain. They change their minds. They quarrel. They demand extras which they hope will be provided free. They prowl the pilothouse. They sit in my chair and read my books. Wingo is much too nice to them. Schwatzendale ogles the women, and gambles with whomever he can befuddle. Freight is better. It is quiet and never demands to be entertained. Come; let us discover what is being offered today."

Maloof and Myron made a circuit of the bulletin boards. Instead of taking notes or conferring with the agents, Maloof photographed the listings. "This is the simplest method," he told Myron. "Another thing to remember: Cargo with an inconvenient destination can often be dropped off at a junction port for transshipment. Much of the cargo listed today was discharged here for just such a purpose."

"The business is more intricate than I had expected," said Myron.

"Quite so. Putting together a profitable cargo is one part logic, two parts intuition, and three parts luck, especially if we hope to pick up cargos of opportunity along the way."

The two returned to the *Glicca*. Maloof placed his photographs into the scanner of the ship's computer, where the information was assimilated and processed. Maloof told Myron, "I have directed the machine to solve what once was called the 'traveling salesman problem.' Do you know it?"

"No, I don't think so."

"The question is how a salesman should choose his route among a number of cities so as to minimize the distance to be traveled. It is a difficult problem in its simplest form, and I have made it several orders of magnitude more difficult by introducing two new variables: the third dimension and profit. Unfortunately, the machine cannot factor in cargos of opportunity picked up en route, so the solution will not be exact."

Five minutes passed. The computer produced a tinkle of three chimes. "The solution is at hand," said Maloof. "The machine is pleased with itself." He directed Myron's attention to a projection box, which displayed a multitude of white sparks and three filaments of colored light, red, blue, and green, each pursuing a zigzag trail from spark to spark.

Maloof asked, "Do you understand what you are seeing?"

"Yes. The sparks are stars; the colored lines represent possible itineraries from star to star. They all start at Port Tanjee and end at different stars."

"Correct," said Maloof, "although where the routes end is flexible and depends on cargos of opportunity." He took a printout from a slot in the computer. For several minutes he studied the data, then looked back to the projection box. "The 'blue' course will be best. Duhail, on Scropus, will be the first junction; next, to Coro-coro; then out to Cax on Blenkinsop, which is another junction." He folded the data sheet and tucked it into his pocket. "Now the real work begins, which is negotiating the contracts. It is like snatching red meat from the jaws of a wolf to wring profit from the agents. Still we can only try, and in the end they sometimes allow us a morsel or two."

Maloof and Myron returned to the terminal lobby. With the printout from the computer in hand, Maloof was able to contract for cargos along the "blue" itinerary. Myron watched the negotiations with interest. Maloof's methods were casual and almost absentminded. But it seemed to Myron that the work went with dispatch, yielding results which Maloof evidently found satisfactory. Myron finally asked for an explanation. "Why does everything go so smoothly?"

Maloof smiled. "Several reasons. I demand no outrageous concessions so that no one feels insulted. More important, these are orphan cargoes, with destinations far off the scheduled routes, where service is uncertain. The agent must wait until he finds a vagabond ship like the *Glicca*. Since he pays demurrage on the cargo, he loses money every day the cargo sits in the warehouse. In most cases, the agent is more anxious to move the cargo than I am to carry it. Today we did fairly well on our contracts, but I doubt if we are anywhere up to capacity. We'll have to see what else we can scratch up."

During the evening Myron prepared a manifest and planned efficient stowage for the new cargo. In the morning the parcels to be transported were moved from the warehouse to the loading dock, then shifted into the cargo bays of the *Glicca*, under Myron's anxious supervision. As Maloof had feared, the cargo was insufficient, and an entire bay remained empty.

During the middle afternoon Maloof and Myron returned to the terminal lobby, hoping to discover newly posted parcels of cargo, but nothing had changed and only a few offices remained open. In one of these offices, a stocky black-bearded man wearing a brown- and black-striped caftan conferred with the agent, his manner by turns wheedling and insistent. He emphasized his remarks with vehement gestures. Not to be outdone, the agent responded with gestures of his own, expressing his inability to fulfill the other's demands. His patience at last wore thin. He leaned back in his chair, shaking his head in final rejection of the demands. With almost palpable relief, he noticed Maloof and pointed; the black-bearded man wheeled about, peered toward Maloof, then instantly left the agent's office and crossed the lobby at a trot.

Maloof had noted the sequence of events and his expression became glum. He muttered to Myron, "Here comes bad news! I detect a passenger."

The man in the caftan halted. He was of moderate stature, small of hands and feet, with a modest paunch. Black ringlets covered his head; his black beard was trimmed square two inches below his chin; bulging dog-brown eyes looked from a round and earnest face. He introduced himself. "I am Deter Kalash, from Loisonville on the world Komard. My status, as you can readily detect, is good; in fact, I am perrumpter of the Clantic Sect, and I now serve as wayfinder for a contingent of ten pilgrims. We are bound for Impy's Landing on Kyril. So far our trip has not been serene. In full trust we took passage aboard the *Bazard Cosway*, assured of a journey direct to Impy's Landing. But Captain Vogler quite ruthlessly altered course and discharged us here along with our baggage. This has caused us a great inconvenience, since, for us, time is of the essence."

"Very sad!" said Maloof. "Nevertheless—"

"One moment, if you please! I am told that your itinerary takes you out through the Pergola Region toward Kyril, if not to Kyril itself! Therefore, at this time, I wish to negotiate passage to Impy's Landing for eleven persons, in the 'Choice Comfort' category, along with eleven cases containing sacred stuffs. We will naturally qualify for eleemosynary rates, with our consecrated cases transported off the billing, free and clear, as is no doubt your usual practice."

"Not always," said Maloof. "In fact, never."

Kalash's eyes grew round with surprise. "I must insist upon the usual sacerdotal concessions!"

Maloof heaved a deep sigh. "Excuse me a moment." He crossed the lobby to the office of the shipping agent. He asked a question; the agent brought out several charts, which Maloof consulted, and also studied a projection from the agent's computer. Then he returned to Kalash and Myron and indicated they be seated. When the three had settled themselves, Maloof addressed Kalash. "I assume that you carry funds to pay your transit charges?"

"Naturally," said Kalash, in a voice of offended dignity. "Do you take us for Spurionites, or the Brotherhood of the Damned?"

Maloof shrugged. "It's all the same to me, once the fares are paid." He brought out a pad of yellow paper and a stylus. "Now then: first things first. You want passage for eleven persons with baggage to Impy's Landing on Kyril."

"Exactly! We prefer the semi-deluxe 'Choice Comfort' category. The baggage, owing to its nature, should receive special handling."

"Describe this baggage, if you will."

"There is nothing to describe," said Kalash peevishly. "Each of us among his personal effects carries a quantity of sacred material."

"In a case? Is this your usual practice?"

"To some extent. Now then! As to the cuisine; we are just a bit fastidious . . ."

"No doubt. But first, a few more questions. What do these cases contain?"

Kalash frowned. "Each of us brings consecrated material to enrich the substance of Kyril."

"The cases are similar in size?"

"They are identical."

"Aha! And what is the dimension of each case?"

Kalash made an expansive gesture. "I have no notion; such details are of no interest to me. Now then, in regard to the cuisine."

Maloof refused to be diverted. "The cases are about so high?" Holding his hand two feet from the floor, Maloof looked questioningly at Kalash.

"I expect so, more or less. Somewhere in that neighborhood, I should say."

Maloof raised his hand another foot. "This high?"

Kalash laughed. "Perhaps—but remember! I am neither a mathematician nor a trained estimator."

Maloof raised his hand to a level five feet above the floor. "As high as this?"

Kalash scowled. "No, certainly not so high."

Maloof scribbled a note. "We shall tentatively say four feet, subject to correction. How wide are these cases? About so?"

Kalash eventually conceded that the dimensions of each case was about five feet long, three feet wide and four feet high.

Maloof made notes. "And there are eleven such cases?"

Kalash gave a curt nod. "Remember: all are pervaded by a strong spiritual afflatus."

Maloof made calculations. "They will occupy a quarter of a cargo bay. The gross substance will command our usual rates, inclusive of afflatus. As a special concession, the afflatus will be carried free of surcharge."

Kalash cried out in protest, but Maloof ignored him. "There is another aspect to the matter. Our itinerary does not include Kyril. We will discharge you at Coro-coro on Fluter. This is the junction node from which you can transship to Kyril."

Kalash's eyes became round and moist. "That is not a happy prospect! We are anxious to pursue our Five-year Roundel! Surely you can veer off at a slant so as to include Kyril on the route, and put us down at Impy's Landing! It would be a relatively minor deviation."

"Yes; in a sense that is true. Although the 'deviation' you mention takes us off-course at right angles, and you would pay a surcharge."

Kalash said cautiously, "This would seem a convenient choice—provided that you quote us an all-inclusive fare to match the depth of our purses."

"The purse I worry about is my own," said Maloof. "I can quote you rates, however, if that is what you wish."

"Of course!" declared Kalash eagerly. "Calculate on a blank sheet of paper with a fresh stylus. Use a light touch! Naturally, I expect the full religious discount!"

Maloof smilingly shook his head. "Your expectations are unsound. Our fares are not excessive."

Kalash uneasily pulled at his beard. "That is good to hear, certainly. And the fare?"

Maloof calculated. "Let us say, a hundred sols each for pilgrim and baggage to Coro-Coro, and an all-inclusive surcharge of five hundred sols for the detour to Kyril."

Kalash cried out in anguish, "The price is outrageous!"

"If you think so, you may exercise a third option," said Maloof.

"And what is that?"

"You may take passage aboard another ship."

"That is quite impractical! No other ship is scheduled for the Pergola Region."

"That is beyond my control."

In poignant tones Kalash pleaded: "Think beneficially of us and our pilgrimage! Like the paladins of old, we are dedicated to deeds of glory! Our way is often stark, often bitter! Still, as we traverse the wastes of Kyril, we shall acclaim the altruists who helped us along the way!"

Maloof chuckled. "We also pursue glorious goals, such as profit, survival, and the sheer joy of wringing revenue from parsimonious passengers."

"That is a crass philosophy!"

"Not so!" declared Maloof. "Rationality is never crass. It suggests that if you can afford the luxuries of an expensive religion, you can afford to pay full rate, plus all applicable surcharges on your baggage."

Kalash struggled for an adequate response. Myron watched with close attention. Each minute, or so it seemed, he learned an important new aspect of the theory and practice of interworld transport.

Kalash was not yet defeated. For another ten minutes he cajoled, blustered, cried out in despair, supplicated, used all the resources of transcendental doctrine, but at last lapsed into sullen defeat. "It seems that I must accede to your exorbitant charges. I select the first option; we will ride as far as Coro-Coro and trust to luck for the final leg of the voyage."

"As you like."

Kalash said bravely, "At this moment I will give you a draught upon the headquarters of the order, for payment in full, and I will need a receipt witnessed by your assistant."

Maloof smiled and shook his head. "That is the last despairing prayer of a religious zealot."

"I do not understand you," said Kalash stiffly.

"If the draught is worthless, what is my recourse?" asked Maloof. "Do I search the wastes of Kyril? Do I force your return to Port Tanjee? Or simply accept your apologies for the mistake?"

Kalash raised his dog-brown eyes to the ceiling. "Have you neither faith nor trust?"

"Neither."

Kalash grumbled further but Maloof remained unmoved, and in the end Kalash paid over the fares in cash.

During the evening Myron supervised the loading of the pilgrim's cases into Number Three cargo bay. The cases were of identical style and dimension, built of a dense dark brown wood, waxed and polished to a high gloss; bound with bronze straps and secured by three locks. In response to Myron's question, he was told only that the cases contained goods of extreme sanctity.

The pilgrims trooped aboard the *Glicca:* a disparate group ranging in age from Cooner, brash and plump, to the truculent old Barthold. In temperament, Zeitzer was mild while Tunch was surly, sardonic and suspicious. Between the vacuous Loris and the savant Kershaw existed an even greater gap, this time of the intellect. Kalash the perrumpter, though ordinary in most respects, was at times overzealous in his efforts to extract concessions for which he was unwilling to pay. After a single glance at the accomodations, Kalash made a strong protest to Captain Maloof, asserting that the term "choice comfort" could not reasonably be applied to the dormitories assigned to the pilgrims.

Maloof shrugged. "Since we provide only one class of accomodation, the term 'choice comfort' is as suitable as any other."

Kalash tried to expostulate further, but Captain Maloof refused to listen. "In the future, please address all complaints to the supercargo, who will adjust the deficiencies, if possible."

The pilgrims made an immediate complaint to Myron as to the amenities of the dining saloon. Instead of the long table with benches to either side, they wanted to be served at tables set with linen napery. Myron agreed at once, and prepared a menu with each item priced as it might be at a deluxe restaurant, along with a daily couvert charge of one sol per man.

Kalash studied the menu with surprise and disfavor. "There is much here I cannot understand. What is this item: 'Boiled beans after the style of Wingo' at one sol? And here: 'Salt mackerel au naturel' at one sol seventy dinkets? At this rate we can't afford to eat!"

Myron said, "You might prefer the ordinary menu, which is often quite decent, and is included in your fare."

"Yes," growled Kalash. "We will give it a try."

Wingo served them a fine dinner of goulash, dumplings, and his special salad, and Kalash was too busy eating to complain.

Maloof told Myron, "I see that you are learning the elements of the trade. You may become a successful supercargo after all, despite your innocent appearance."

2

The *Glicca* departed Port Tanjee, and set a course toward Tacton's Star and the world Scropus, where the town Duhail was the first port of call. At Duhail the *Glicca* would discharge a consignment of chemicals, drugs, and general medical supplies, destined for the Refunctionary, a penal institution housed in an ancient palace. With luck, the *Glicca* would find additional cargo of compressed pollen, or aromatic gums, or possibly a pallet or two of precious woods for onward transport.

Myron quickly adapted to the routines of his work. He found rather more difficulty dealing with Hilmar Krim's accounts and his extraordinary methods of bookkeeping. Krim had used a system of abbreviations, jotted notes in an abstruse shorthand writing, as well as a set of unintelligible hieroglyphics. Additionally, many financial details, such as port charges, wages paid to warehousemen, cash advances to members of the crew and other incidental expenses, Krim had never recorded. He preferred to keep a running total in his memory, until such time as he felt inclined to transfer the lump sum to his books. These occasions seemed dictated by caprice, and Krim seldom troubled to identify the numbers.

In the end Myron devised a method of computation which he called "creative averaging." The system was both straightforward and definite, though its basis might be considered intuitive, or even arbitrary. To use the system, Myron replaced Krim's hieroglyphics with imaginary quantities, which he adjusted until they produced an appropriate result. By this means, Myron restored the books to a state of order, though he made no guarantees of instant precision. Myron discovered that the exact numbers meant little, so long as they were written in a bold hand and produced a reasonable summation, so that, in the end, all accounts were balanced. Maloof had always reviewed the accounting, but Krim's processes exceeded his understanding. Now, with Myron's "creative" methods and simplified entries, he was well satisfied.

As the days passed, Myron became acquainted with his shipmates. Schwatzendale, so he discovered, was spontaneous and volatile, with a lilting imagination rife with surprises and wonders. In contrast, Wingo was placid, methodical, and a thinker of profound thoughts. Superficially, Schwatzendale seemed a charming rascal of slantwise habits and antic good looks. His heart-shaped face with its widow's peak and luminous eyes often prompted strangers to take him for a languid young aesthete, or even a sybarite. Such theories were wildly incorrect. Schwatzendale, in fact, was brash, restless, extravagant in his moods and attitudes. He skipped and hopped like a child, without perceptible self-consciousness. He attacked his work with disdain, as if it were too contemptible for a person of style to take seriously. In this regard, Schwatzendale was both romantic and vain; he thought of himself as a combination gambler and gentleman-adventurer. Wingo occasionally spoke of Schwatzendale's exploits in a mixture of awe, grudging admiration and disapproval.

In total contrast to Schwatzendale, Wingo was short, thick, blue-eyed, with only a few strands of blond hair across his pink scalp. Wingo was mild, amiable and sympathetic. He was an avid collector of curios, small trinkets, and interesting oddments, prizing them not for their inherent value but for their craftsmanship and cleverness of execution. Wingo was also a dedicated photographer, and was engaged in compiling a collection of what he called "mood impressions," which he hoped ultimately to publish in a portfolio entitled: *Pageant of the Gaean Race*.

Wingo was greatly interested in comparative metaphysics: the sects, superstitions, religions, and transcendental philosophies, which he inevitably encountered as the *Glicca* traveled from world to world, endlessly fascinated him. Whenever he wandered strange places, he gave careful attention to local spiritual doctrines: a practice which aroused Schwatzendale's disapproval. "You are wasting your time! They all talk the same nonsense and only want your money. Why bother? Religious cant is the greatest nonsense of all!"

"There is much in what you say," Wingo admitted. "Still, is it not possible that one of these doctrines is correct and exactly defines the Cosmic Way? If we passed it by, we might never encounter Truth again."

"In theory, yes," grumbled Schwatzendale. "In practice, your chances are next to nil."

Wingo waved a pink forefinger. "Tut! One can never be sure. Perhaps you have miscalculated the odds."

"I can't answer you properly," growled Schwatzendale. "Odds of zero in a thousand are much the same as zero in a million."

Wingo's only response was a benign shake of the head.

The pilgrims settled into routines of their own, drinking tea, criticizing the cuisine, performing rites, discussing the world Kyril, where they proposed a circumambulation, which would require about five years, and earn them the honorific title "rondler."

Once Myron had brought the accounts into order, he occasionally found himself with time on his hands. In such an event he assisted Wingo in the galley or Schwatzendale in the engine room. Myron found Schwatzendale an unending source of fascination. He was physically beautiful: a fact which Schwatzendale himself recognized but ignored. In the engine room, he worked with speed, precision, absolute certainty and his characteristic panache. Typically, he finished each job with a flourish and a glance of disdainful menace at the repaired part, as if warning it never to repeat its mistake. Myron soon came to see past the epicene beauty to an inner hardness, which was intensely masculine. Myron studied Schwatzendale's slantwise attributes with covert fascination. They manifested themselves in many tricks and habits: sardonic jokes and oblique ideas; in the tilt of his head and the angle of his elbows; in his quick loping strides. Myron sometimes fantasized that all Schwatzendale's parts were askew, so that they necessarily fitted together on the bias. All was asymmetric, quirky, "slantwise." Schwatzendale was like a knight on a chessboard who could move only by eccentric hops and bounds.

One day Myron found Schwatzendale sitting at the table in the saloon, occupied with a deck of playing cards. Myron watched for a time, admiring the deft flicker of Schwatzendale's fingers. Schwatzendale suddenly asked Myron if he knew any amusing games of chance by which they might pass the time, and perhaps wager a coin or two. For instance, was Myron acquainted with the game Hurlothrumbo?

Myron said that he knew nothing of "Hurlothrumbo," or any other game. "I have noticed that when these games are played, money changes hands. If I played and won, it would give me no pleasure; but if I lost, I would be haunted by remorse. I would also feel foolish."

Schwatzendale showed his crooked grin. "You do not understand the joy of the hunt. To gamble is to play at prehistoric savagery."

"The metaphor is apt," said Wingo. "The victor is a cannibal, feeding upon the substance of the victim."

"That is the thrust of our instincts!" Schwatzendale explained. "It is the contrast which generates so much triumph—or such tragic despair."

Wingo shook his head. "When Fay gambles, he often forgets what I shall call 'amour propre.'" He addressed Myron. "I advise against gambling in general and with Fay in particular. He will deprive you of assets so neatly that you will never notice until you grope in your pocket and find not so much as a soiled handkerchief."

"Wingo is correct!" said Schwatzendale. "Given the chance, I will win the trousers from your arse, so that you have not even a pocket for the groping!"

"Fay does not exaggerate," said Wingo somberly. "Only Moncrief the Mouse-rider has beaten him, and Fay still smarts at the recollection."

Schwatzendale clutched his head. "Why must you utter that name? I shall never rest until—"

"Until you have played him again, and lost more money, and known more shame?"

"Never, never, never!"

"Let us hope not," said Wingo virtuously.

3

Tacton's Star grew bright ahead, then passed to the side as the *Glicca* descended into the plane of the orbiting planets. Fourth in the order was Scropus: a world six thousand miles in diameter with a dense core and standard gravity.

Scropus became a sphere; the horizons expanded and the geography took on definition. A pair of large continents clasped the north and south poles, both marked by swirling clouds, indicating fearful storms. Ayra, the third continent, was shaped like a salamander and sprawled across the world in the zone immediately north of the equator, where it was secure from the storms, blasts of rain and sleet, thunder, and lightning which ravaged the polar continents. The soft sunlight diffusing the hazy atmosphere seemed to enhance the clarity and character of color. Blues, reds, and greens glowed with the purity of a child's perception. The sky was a deep cobalt; by night the moon Olanthus showed a silver-green shine. The seas were ultramarine and the surf a dazzling white effervescent froth.

The *Glicca* landed at the rambling old town Duhail, at the center of Ayra, close by the Refunctionary.

Thousands of years previously the world Scropus had been lost in the far Beyond, immune to the laws of the Gaean Reach and safe from the IPCC. At this time Scropus had been the private domain of Imbald, the so-called Sultan of Space, whose reputation had been such that, when his name was mentioned, conversation came to a frozen halt. Imbald had been a large man, seven feet tall weighing three hundred pounds. His concepts were as large as his person; his intellect was keen; his imagination ranged the sweep of human history, while his atrocities commanded a grotesque magnificence by reason of their incomprehensible scale. Near the town Duhail he ordained a palace to excel every other edifice built by the will of man. It must be supreme in architectural elegance, the splendor of its appointments, the beauty and grace of its attendants, its all-pervading luxury. The palace came into being and was named Fanchen Lalu. To celebrate its dedication, Imbald despatched a thousand small ships into every quarter of the Gaean Reach. They returned to Scropus, bringing with them the most eminent folk of the time. They included scientists, musicians, philosophers, statesmen, celebrities of every description. Some came willingly; more were kidnapped and brought willy-nilly, despite their complaints. In either case, they were conveyed to Fanchen Lalu, and housed in splendid suites, provided a retinue of servants and a wardrobe of fine garments. At Imbald's command, they participated in the rites which certified the existence and the quality of Fanchen Lalu and—by extension— the grandeur of Imbald, Sultan of Space, himself.

The formalities continued for three days, after which Imbald executed a few of the notables who had annoyed him, then sent the others home.

Less than a year later the IPCC sent out a battle fleet and destroyed Imbald's pirate flotilla. Imbald could not credit his great defeat and remained at Fanchen Lalu, where he was besieged by IPCC troopers. Imbald was trapped; there was no escape for him and his capture was imminent, along with his execution. The idea put Imbald into a great fury; he was not yet ready to die! He would have no choice in the matter. In the extremity of his despair he began to destroy Fanchen Lalu, hall after precious hall. The commander of the IPCC, Sir Ralph Vicinanza, a sensitive man, refused to tolerate the wanton destruction of so much beauty. He called Imbald to a parley, where he offered what he considered a reasonable and even generous proposal. Imbald must desist from further destruction and surrender his person to the IPCC. He would then be placed aboard a spaceship with the pilothouse sealed and the navigation system isolated from his control. The ship would be directed up and away from the Gaean Reach, on a course which would take it away into intergalactic space. Imbald would be alone aboard the ship, with provisioning to sustain him for three lifetimes. He would fly out into unknown regions and see sights never before seen by the eyes of man. He would never return.

Imbald reflected only five minutes. He made several stipulations, regarding the quality of the food and wine to be supplied, the interior decor of the spaceship, the scope of the ship's library. Then he assented to the proposal, which, so he considered, offered him a dignified retirement from his previous occupation. He confided to Sir Ralph that

he had long wished for leisure in which to write his memoirs, and finally the opportunity was at hand. Sir Ralph wished him many placid
years and sent him off into space. By such a tactic much of Fanchen
Lalu was preserved. Over the centuries the property passed from hand
to hand. A number of restorations had been attempted, with indifferent success. Fanchen Lalu now served as a penal institution, known as
the Refunctionary, along with the Institute of Advanced Penology, and
a laboratory for psychopathological research.

The current inhabitants of Scropus were for the most part descen-
dants of the sultan's henchmen, who had been allowed estates about the
countryside. They showed little of their original ferocity, living somnolent lives, disapproving of the Refunctionary, and occasionally visiting Duhail for a meeting of the Garden Club, or perhaps one of the
Outreach Society's Cultural Seminars.

The *Glicca* landed at the Duhail terminal, next to a line of tall blue
and teal-green cycads, which held feathery fronds on high.

Myron supervised the discharge of cargo. There were three large
cases destined for the Refunctionary, but when he started to unload
them he was approached by the superintendent of the facility, a mild-
seeming person of middle-age named Euel Gartover. He wore a neat
blue, white, and black uniform and spoke with such modest civility that
Myron was instantly sympathetic to his request. Gartover wanted the
Glicca to shift to the grounds of the institution, where the three cases
could be discharged directly and the need for drayage, which was slow
and uncertain, could be avoided.

Myron relayed the request to Maloof, who made no objection. After on-loading a shipment of pollen cake, destined for Cax on Blenkinsop, the *Glicca* was shifted to the grounds of the Refunctionary as an
act of good will.

Euel Gartover expressed his appreciation and took the crew on a
tour of the facility. Despite the effects of time and a dozen programs of
reconstruction, Fanchen Lalu retained much of its old magnificence.

No less interesting were the men and women who carried on their
affairs in the ancient halls. They were a various lot and, according to
Gartover, included supervisory staff, the college faculty, research scientists, and the criminals themselves.

Wingo expressed astonishment. "These folk wander about quite
freely, lacking all restraint! We are surrounded by desperate criminals!
How can you sit here with such calm?"

Gartover grinned. "Why should I not? Our inmates have better
things to do than cause disturbances."

"Most odd!" mused Wingo. "I assume that the truly vicious types are confined elsewhere."

Gartover, still smiling, shook his head. "You must remember that this, in a sense, is an experimental facility. Orthodoxy is not totally abandoned; we use methods both old and new, but always in a mode of what I shall call 'Dynamic Optimism.' 'Failure' is not in our vocabulary, and 'crime' is a non-permitted word; we use the term 'mistake,' or 'excessive conduct.' That is not to say that we are innocent mooncalves, who deny the existence of pain. We are pragmatic mechanics; our goal is to obliterate the thrill of wrongdoing by making such acts seem pointless and boring."

"You are trying to demonstrate the banality of evil," murmured Maloof. "Does it replace the code of morality?"

"Yes and no," said Gartover. "I can only ask, 'what is morality?'—a question you cannot answer."

Wingo looked dubiously toward Schwatzendale. "What would you say of a man who dangles a monstrous dead insect a foot above a sleeping man's face, illuminates it with a strong light, then stands back and yells: 'Help! Help! The world is coming to an end!'"

Gartover reflected, then said politely, "In the absence of all the facts, I could not justify a diagnosis. Still, I might guess the miscreant to be an imaginative rascal who finds himself bored."

"Yes; perhaps so."

Myron asked, "Here at the Refunctionary, are the criminals—or, I should say, 'mischief-makers'—aware of the harm they have done?"

Gartover pursed his lips and shrugged. "Possibly, but it is beside the point, since it relates to the past and our emphasis is the future. We want to inculcate pride, rather than shame."

"That is what is called 'rehabilitation,'" said Wingo.

"Exactly! In that connection we had a curious case recently. A man who had killed both his grandmothers declared himself rehabilitated, on the grounds that he could not conceivably repeat his offense in the absence of any further grandmothers. He asks for immediate release. The argument, I must say, has a certain merit, and the Board of Control is currently considering his petition."

Maloof frowned. "Are you possibly subordinating the real to the theoretical? In short, is this method practical?"

"Never fear! We are not only practical, but clever and flexible as well. At the Refunctionary we have learned to avoid static solutions to evanescent situations, which come and go like the flicker of fireflies. Each type of mischief-maker has a generic pattern of behavior, which can to some extent be classified. We never deal with our animal-torturers as we do our widow-swindlers; each must be processed in subtly different ways, to match his or her predilections. We must act tactfully; some of our murderers are damnably proud folk, and we do not want to inflict new lesions upon their self-image. This is how we think of venal acts—as psychic lesions to be healed. We avoid unnecessary stigma and to this end we have evolved a playful little ruse, and I refer to the color of the caps. Murderers wear white; forgers, swindlers, and counterfeiters wear black, and larcenists wear green. Blackmailers wear orange and also sport small pointed goatees. Don't ask me why; it is the fad. Arsonists wear purple; mutilators wear pink, while sexual activists wear brown, and so it goes. The system fosters a healthy rivalry, with each group vying for excellence. Our games are often exciting because of the cheers and enthusiasm. Everyone is spirited; no one is demoralized: that is our goal. A man may state, almost with pride: 'Yes! I was a wife-beater! Now I have put aside all remorse, and I feel the better for it!' "

Wingo was impressed. "It seems as if great things are being done."

Gartover made a rueful gesture. "I won't deny that we have our disappointments. Some of our folk are intrinsically antisocial. We try to avoid the word 'evil,' though I suppose it all comes out of the same bucket."

"And how do you deal with these folk?"

"We try our best techniques: friendly counsel, dramatic enactments demonstrating the positive values of decency, meditation, work-therapy, hypnosis."

Gartover noticed Schwatzendale's slantwise smile and sighed. "When I use the word 'hypnosis,' I arouse skepticism, without fail."

"I was born without illusions," said Schwatzendale.

Gartover smiled. " 'Skepticism' is sometimes known as 'dogmatic ignorance.' "

Schwatzendale refused to be daunted. "I have met a number of evil men. Just as water is wet and space is wide, these men were wicked through and through, in every wisp, shard, tangle, and tuft of their beings. You can hypnotize them as you like; they will remain irredemptible."

Gartover looked from face to face. "And you others? Are you equally skeptical?"

Wingo said soberly, "I have always considered hypnosis a parlor game. The savants tell us of the Cosmic Principle, which, so they declare, controls 'All.' When we have transcended to the seventh level, then we shall understand the ultimates of good and evil. There is no reference to hypnotism."

"A profound statement, certainly." Gartover addressed Myron. "And you, sir?"

Myron considered a moment, then said, "I suspect that many of your mistake-makers, once they are loose, will put hypnotism aside and return to murdering their grandmothers."

Gartover sighed and looked to Maloof. "What of you, sir?"

Maloof shrugged. "Like the others, I am dubious in regard to hypnotism, although I know little of the subject."

Gartover laughed. "We will not convince each other—not today at any rate. So now, allow me to offer you refreshment."

Gartover took his guests to a private refectory and excused himself while he went to see to the arrangements.

The four spacemen looked about themselves in admiration. The room retained much of ancient Fanchen Lalu. The walls were paneled in pale ivory wood, and displayed depictions of floral baskets fashioned from infinitesimal needles of colored glass illuminated from behind. The table was a four-foot-wide slab of dark brown wood twelve feet long, enlivened by a rich and intricate figure. Overhead hung a chandelier of unique design. Six horizontal disks of glass three feet wide were superimposed in layers, six inches apart. Each disk revolved slowly at different speeds in different directions. Each glowed with wavering flows of color. Myron tried to relate the colors to the movement of the disks, but after being deceived a dozen times, he decided that random processes were at work.

Gartover returned with a tray of small cakes and several flagons of wine. "Please excuse my delay; the kitchen crew had gone off to their elocution lessons. Yes, smile if you must, but we feel that self-expression is the final gloss on an integrated personality."

"No doubt you're right," said Maloof. "We have been admiring the paneling and the table. The material is all local?"

"Every inch! The native flora is marvelous. The wood of this table, for instance, grows in the sea. It is rooted underwater at a depth of four hundred feet. It sends a massive trunk toward the surface. In all directions filaments stream out, as much as a hundred feet, absorbing the submarine light. When the trunk reaches the surface, it spreads out to become a circular pad of tough tissue, and from the center of this pad grow a hundred flexible whips supporting the fruiting organs. It is a wonderful plant, and every part is useful. In fact—" Gartover jumped to his feet "—I think that I can offer you some appropriate souvenirs."

He went to rummage in the drawers of a cabinet and returned to the table with four squat wooden jars which he distributed to his guests.

Schwatzendale removed the cap and examined the contents of the jar. "What have we here?"

"It is pollen of the ultramarine tree, steeped in its own gum. It is known as 'Wild Blue,' and is occasionally used for ceremonial purposes. Naturally, it is non-toxic and quite harmless."

"Thank you very much," said Maloof. "These jars are beautifully crafted and make handsome souvenirs. The ultramarine, of course, is always welcome."

Wingo said thoughtfully, "There is none among our stores. I can't explain it."

The spacemen returned to the *Glicca*, where they were chided by the pilgrims for dallying overlong at Duhail. "Perhaps you do not reckon urgency, as we do," cried Deter Kalash in a passion. "Time is sifting through our fingers! We must get our sacred goods to Impy's Landing before the Concatenation!"

Myron made a soothing response. "As you see, we are departing Scropus at this very moment."

"Then we fly direct to Coro-coro?"

"Unfortunately not. Along the way are ports of call!"

Schwatzendale had joined Wingo in the galley, and sat with a rum punch as Wingo assembled the evening meal. Neither of the two had settled views in connection with the Refunctionary. Wingo's opinions were perhaps the more tolerant. "At the very least it is a noble effort, and Euel Gartover's dedication must be commended. For all we know his efforts may not be in vain."

"So we hope," growled Schwatzendale. "Otherwise, he is nurturing a nest of adders."

Wingo's honest pink face creased in doubt. "This is implicit in Euel Gartover's plan! He forgives their mistakes and heals their shame, so that, when the time comes, they march forth with heads high to do useful work in society!"

Schwatzendale's eyebrows slanted askew and his elbows jerked in shock. "Be real! Half of his mistake-makers are crazy! Did you notice all the song-stylists in the gray caps?"

"No matter. In most cases they are criminals because part of their brains had atrophied during gestation."

"Then Gartover hypnotizes them and scrambles what little is left."

Wingo pursed his lips. "There may be something in what you say. But remember—" he held high a pink forefinger "—no dogma fits every dog!" This was one of Wingo's favorite aphorisms. "The hour is late," he told Schwatzendale. "It is time to dress for dinner."

Schwatzendale went off to his cabin. The crew of the *Glicca* dined separately from the passengers, since Maloof liked his dinner served in an atmosphere of formality.

The four men took their places at the table. All wore neat garments and all had tinted their noses blue with ultramarine unguent from the squat wooden jars. Schwatzendale frowned at Wingo. "There is a place just under the tip which you neglected."

"Excuse me." Wingo turned away to repair the omission.

"That is better," said Schwatzendale.

Deter Kalash looked in at them. He asked in wonderment, "Why have you painted your noses blue?"

Schwatzendale said crossly, "Be off with you and your foolish questions; we are at our dinner."

Myron said politely, "It is a matter of formal etiquette, or so I suppose. I have never thought too much about it."

Wingo explained further: "Captain Maloof has never relented in regard to formality. Everything must be just so."

"I see," said Deter Kalash. "I am told that you visited the Refunctionary today. How did you find it?"

"All in all, quite tolerable," said Wingo. "The prisoners wear hats of different colors, and if it weren't for an absurd preoccupation with hypnotic suggestion, the theoretical basis of the institution seems sound."

"That is my own view," said Schwatzendale. Neither Myron nor Maloof had anything to add.

Kalash nodded to indicate his comprehension. "I am always happy to learn new things. Colored hats on prisoners. Staff tolerable. Theories good except for hypnotic suggestion, which is absurd. Am I right?"

"Precisely right," declared Wingo. "Informing you is a pleasure, since you are quick to learn."

4

Upon departure from Scropus, the *Glicca* set off on a slant, down and away from the center of the galaxy. The pilgrims noticed the shift and became disturbed. They reminded Maloof of their haste. "Dozens, even hundreds, of devout pilgrims await our coming!"

Maloof tried to soothe them, citing other cargo obligations. "We travel at the best practical speed. It is not just a matter of darting hither and yon; our course is the approximate solution to a very complicated mathematical proposition."

"Yes, yes, so I suppose! But, surely, other routes exist which may be even more practical. Why not fare to Coro-Coro directly? Or even better, make an instant swing out to Impy's Landing, then whirl about in a gallant roundabout sweep to Coro-Coro? That, so I believe, is the optimum solution! Your exorbitant charges surely justify such a concession."

Maloof said coldly, "If you think yourself mistreated, you may debark with your cargo at the next port of call, and pay me nothing."

"Indeed!" Deter Kalash was instantly attentive. "And what is this next port of call?"

"It is Dulcie Diver on the world Terce."

"And how are the connections for Impy's Landing?"

"Poor, or so I believe. You will find Terce a challenging world, should you choose to debark."

Kalash gave his black beard a defiant tug. "I am not a man who tergiversates! We will hold to our original commitment, despite its questionable provisions."

Fay Schwatzendale had been listening to the conversation. Now he told Kalash: "You are far too tense! Relax and enjoy the voyage! Have you nothing to do? Why not play a game with your friends?"

"We are serious folk!" snapped Kalash. "We do not waste our time with foolishness!"

A pilgrim named Dury came to lay a hand gently on Kalash's shoulder. "Think, Wayfinder! The Circle defines our creed! Destiny is a circle; each moving segment returns to its source!"

"Naturally!" snapped Kalash. "Such is the doctrine; is it germane?"

"Ever and always! Whatever is, is! Whatever is, is right! Whatever is right is good! Whatever is good has existence, and therefore 'is'; and the Circle is whole."

"So much is self-evident. Learn to avoid platitudes; we have serious issues to consider. Captain Maloof's obduracy has won the day and we must adapt to this reality."

Dury struck his fist into the palm of his hand. "If it is, then it must be; and it is supreme! We abide the way of Destiny and meanwhile, why not follow Schwatzendale's suggestion? I am bored with naming the stations of my prayer circle."

"As you like," said Kalash. "Do not include me in your frivolity; that is all I ask!"

The pilgrims at once brought out their cards and began to play double-moko for small stakes. Schwatzendale looked on from time to time, his expression benign. He seemed to take an interest in the game, clapping his hands at a dramatic "scumble," consoling the unfortunate victim and pointing out how the disaster might have been averted. Dury finally cried out: "If you are such an enthusiast, why do you not put down your money and take up a hand? Then we shall see how you fare against the experts!"

Schwatzendale smiled wistfully. "I am a tyro, and timid, but perhaps I will test the waters where you adepts swim so easily."

Schwatzendale pulled up a chair and joined the game. He played without skill and at last his stake was gone. "It is as I feared." he grumbled. "Now please excuse me. It is almost time for dinner and I must blue my nose."

Schwatzendale played the game on other occasions and each time lost his stake, so that the pilgrims were eager that he should join them. Meanwhile, the ultramarine pigment in the wooden jars became exhausted, so that the crew was compelled to dine with naked noses. Initially, they were embarrassed by the deficiency. "Odd," mused Myron. "My grandmother was always a stickler for such things, yet we never tinted our noses in her house."

"Nor was it usual in my family," rumbled Wingo.

"Gentlemen," said Maloof, "since we are dining informally aboard ship, I suggest that we dispense with the blue."

"Yes," said Schwatzendale in a subdued voice. "I can't imagine how we got started in the first place."

"I can imagine," said Maloof. "We can be grateful that Euel Gartover did not order us to shave our heads or tie ruffled white cravats to our genital organs before we sat down to dinner."

FIVE

1

Far ahead an orange spark grew ever brighter, and at last became the giant sun Bran. The *Glicca* descended upon the third planet, Terce: a world of moderate size with a single continent straggling most of the way around the world, creating innumerable bays, bights, inlets, brackish seas, and a single narrow ocean, notable for its violent storms.

The continent exhibited a bleak and sterile topography, with a paucity of rivers, several belts of timberland, and a great swamp along the west coast. Ferocious beasts, both large and small, inhabited the swamp; elsewhere the fauna was limited to a few leather-winged birds, lizards, fish, and armored insects. A sparse human population inhabited a half-dozen isolated areas; and after eight thousand years the original folk had evolved into five races, with widely disparate characteristics. The most primitive were the Uche: stone-age savages of the southern mountains, who were avid cannibals. At the center of the continent, near the Sholo spaceport, the Shuja and the Meluli lived in near-contiguity: one race living high on the plateau, the other below on the steppe. They hunted each other for pleasure and profit, flaying their victims, tanning the skin and exporting the pelts off-world. The sea folk of the islands off the east coast were the Tarc, a race with attenuated physiques; and in their black robes and high hieratic headgear they might have been priests of an esoteric mystery cult. They rode their long low sea barges from the islands to the Dulcie Diver market, where they traded with the Tzingals of the shore, each race restraining its hatred for the other.

The IPCC considered the peoples of Terce intractable and the world impossible to pacify. A hundred times they had tried to establish a local police corps, without success. Currently, the IPCC prohibited the import of energy-weapons, and warned off tourists; otherwise they left the local folk to their own devices.

Captain Maloof had visited the world on a previous occasion. Even before the *Glicca* entered its landing spiral, Maloof informed the ship's company as to the conditions they might expect to find on the world below. "Terce is not a tourist resort, nor a venue for amateur vagabonds. Terce is dangerous for natives and off-worlders alike. The spaceport at Dulcie Diver, where there is an IPCC presence and relative security, is near the market, which means that if you venture out into the market, you probably will not be murdered. But if you wander down along the docks hoping for an amorous interlude, you may be serviced but also robbed or beaten, perhaps both."

Perrumpter Kalash stated that the pilgrims would remain aboard ship. "We have no interest in the licentious habits of these strange folk. Why should we risk our lives to study their extraordinary conduct? It is a dubious pleasure; enjoy it as you like."

Wingo smilingly advised Kalash that new knowledge of any sort could only expand his understanding of the human condition. "Whenever a group of people professes a novel philosophy, I know that I will find material for my most significant photographs: what I call my 'mood impressions.' "

Kalash gave a cynical chuckle. "It is all cut from the same cloth. You are no better than the rest."

"Not so!" declared Wingo. "For me it is serious business. I have, so I believe, an exquisitely exact talent for capturing the essence of time and recording it as the image of a frozen instant."

"So you say. In any case, why bother?"

"I am compiling a portfolio of important photographs, to be entitled: *The Pageant of the Gaean Race*. I work with great care!"

Kalash was more skeptical than ever. "It is all titillation and pandering to morbid curiosity."

"Not so, not so!" cried Wingo. "My motives are purely artistic! How could they be anything else? I strongly disapprove of both cruelty and vice!"

Kalash had lost interest in the discussion. "So it may be."

Wingo, however, continued to explain his purposes. "Trillions upon trillions of Gaeans have come and gone; still, when I record my 'mood impressions,' I feel that I am encompassing the experience of the entire race!"

"Do as you like," muttered Kalash. "It is all one to me."

Wingo said politely, "I hope that I have reassured you as to my motives; I am not the slavering sensationalist that you take me for! It would be a shame to omit the extraordinary folk of Terce from my portfolio."

Kalash gave his beard a pull of impatience. "Say no more; I am convinced!" He hurried off to join his fellow pilgrims, to whom he confided his views of Wingo's eccentricities.

Maloof spoke to Wingo and reiterated his warning. "Remember that these people are not art lovers. Should they suspect impudence, they will cut off your nose."

Wingo soberly agreed to use full caution.

The *Glicca* landed at the Dulcie Diver spaceport, within sight of the Eastern Ocean. Myron supervised the discharge of cargo, while Maloof went off to solicit new business from the local shipping agents. He was tendered several parcels of cargo, and was advised that on the morrow the weekly freight barge would arrive from the offshore islands, with the prospect of more goods for export. Maloof agreed to delay departure for Sholo until the following day.

After lunch Maloof, Wingo, Schwatzendale, and Myron ventured from the terminal. At the gate a young man in the uniform of an IPCC agent accosted them. "Sirs, may I ask your destination and your purpose?"

"Our destination is the market," said Maloof. "We have no purpose other than idle curiosity, although Wingo intends to record a few discreet photographic 'mood impressions.'"

The agent surveyed Wingo with mild curiosity. As on other occasions, when Wingo went out to record his "impressions," he wore a voluminous snuff-brown cloak, a brown planter's hat, soft leather boots. The costume, so Wingo felt, captured the romantic flavor of the bohemian lifestyle, enjoyed by classical artists.

The agent said politely, "My grandmother is also a photographer; it is her favorite hobby."

"I prefer to think of myself as a creative artist," said Wingo, stiffly. "My portfolio consists of significant images which illuminate the Gaean psyche in subtle detail."

"A good idea. But a word of warning! Be careful out there in the market. If you take a picture of someone's psyche, he will demand a fee, five or ten sols, and they will make your life miserable until you pay."

"I am not a tyro," Wingo stated with dignity. "My techniques are unobtrusive and cannot be detected."

"That is good news," said the agent. "Still, relax none of your caution or they will steal the boots from your feet."

Wingo shook his head in disgust. "They would seem a folk without honor."

"That is a fair assessment. Now then, are any of you carrying power guns, flashaways or pinkers? It is imperative that we keep such gear from the local thugs, which is to say, most of the population."

"I am carrying my whangee," said Maloof, displaying his walking stick. "It is powered only by the strength of my arm."

The others declared themselves free of contraband and the agent signaled them through the gate. "One final bit of advice: do not leave the market! If you visit the rum shacks along the docks, chances are you will be doped and robbed, if not worse. Even in the market you can't relax. You may come upon a musician playing an accordion, while two pretty children dance and caper about. What charming little tykes, you think. About this time the boy turns a handspring and kicks you in the crotch with his iron-toed slipper. When you fall he sits on your head and pulls your nose, while the girl steals your purse; then they jump up and run away. Meanwhile the accordionist plays another tune, and demands a tip."

"We will watch out for accordion-players or any other such rascals," said Maloof. "I doubt if we will be caught napping."

"Good luck," said the agent.

The four passed through the gate and stepped out into the market. They halted to assess the surroundings. The confusion of sensory input could not instantly be assimilated: color, noise, and movement were like a jangle of discords; the reek from over-ripe fruit, dead fish, pots of boiling tripes, seemed to heave and squirm with a life of its own. At the back a row of scimitar trees cut across the enormous globe of the orange sun; black shadows were in violent contrast to the wan orange sunlight. A grid of aisles criss-crossed the market, serving a clutter of stalls, barrows, and booths. The merchants were members of the Tzingal race: sinewy folk, intensely active, with olive-tan skins, black hair, sparkling brown eyes in hollow-cheeked faces. They wore knee-length white kirtles, short white shirts, colored kerchiefs around their foreheads. They plied their trade with extreme zeal, striding back and forth, gesticulating, darting out into the aisle to grip the arms of passersby, performing curious little jigs; all the while advertising their goods with melodic cries and whoops of synthetic enthusiasm, each trying to drown out his rivals.

The four spacemen began to explore the market, never relaxing their vigilance against thieves and tricksters. Consequently, they encountered only a few trivial incidents which might have been considered unpleasant.

The first of these episodes later brought them a degree of wry amusement. After wandering about the market for half an hour, they climbed three steps up to a refreshment platform, in order to sample the local beer. The serving woman, while approaching their table, shuffled the menus she was carrying in a peculiar fashion before tendering one to the group.

Schwatzendale's suspicions, never dormant, went on full alert. He called out, "Hoy there, madame! Give us one menu for each of us, if you please!"

The woman spoke brusquely over her shoulder: "That is not our custom here! One menu is enough, since one person can read to the others."

As soon as the woman walked away, Schwatzendale switched the menu she had supplied for a similar menu which he took from a nearby table. When the woman returned, she listened to their orders in a manner of surly condescension, then presently served them mugs of seedy beer and a platter of fried sea-stuffs. When they had finished and signaled for the reckoning, she asked for the sum of three sols and twenty dinkets, plus the gratuity.

Schwatzendale, tilting his head slantwise, uttered a caw of fleering laughter. "You have made a serious mistake!" He pointed to the menu. "We owe for four pints of beer and a platter of fried fish. The charges total sixty dinkets. In view of your mendacity, I see no need for a gratuity. Here is your money." He put coins upon the table.

"What nonsense is this?" screamed the woman.

Schwatzendale signaled Wingo. "By all means, record this 'mood impression.'"

"A good idea," said Wingo.

The woman cried out in a passion. "The menu is explicit! We allow no cheating at this establishment!"

Schwatzendale held up the menu. "The prices are clearly noted. See for yourself."

The woman stared incredulously, then ran to the kitchen.

Maloof, gaining his feet, called, "Quick! Away from here!"

The four jumped down from the platform. The woman came running from the kitchen with a bucketful of fish guts which she threw toward them. The men, however, were well out of range and the slop struck an unsuspecting passerby, who flew into a rage. Climbing to the platform, he overturned several tables and beat the woman soundly. The occasion gave Wingo a number of interesting "impressions," and the crew moved on.

In the central aisle a second incident occurred, where a troupe of six acrobats stood waiting for employment. As the spacemen approached, they were accosted by the leader: a squat muscular man with a shaved head, massive legs, a full black mustache, and sad down-drooping eyes. Like his five agile young assistants, he wore loose scarlet breeches tied at the knees and a tight purple shirt. He called out, "Sirs! We are the Scarbush Lorrakees; for a small fee we will show you miracles of strength and grace, to the concord of vocal harmonies. Our price is moderate."

"Stop!" cried Maloof, holding up his hands. "Do not perform! We will not pay! We will not even look!"

"Quite all right," said the leader. He swung up his arm in a gesture of reckless gaiety. "Pay or no pay, we will perform anyway to show our respect." He braced himself and barked, "Yip! Yip! Huzza!" His assistants jumped upon him, climbed one on the other, to form a human tower of four tiers, supported upon the shoulders of the leader, who stood with mustaches quivering and teeth bared in exertion. A slip! A mistake! An imbalance! The tower tottered; the leader took a staggering run forward, as if to maintain equilibrium—to no avail. The tower collapsed, falling upon the spacemen, to send Myron and Wingo sprawling under a tumble of writhing bodies. Myron felt nimble fingers at work; he writhed and struggled; he heard a swishing sound and shrill yelps of pain. At last he was free and rose to his feet—but where was his cloak? It was gone! Wingo lay on his back, crying out in fury as the leader worked to pull the boots from his feet. Schwatzendale stepped forward, pointed his finger. A jet of mist sprayed into the leader's face. Hissing and gasping, he tottered away. Maloof dealt further blows with his stick. One of the acrobats staggered into a stall selling foodstuffs, to send a tray of small yellow fruits to the ground. In a fury the merchant struck the acrobat with a large salt fish. The acrobat fled with the merchant calling curses after him.

Maloof handed Myron his cloak. "I gave the thieves several raps where it hurt the most; they will attempt no more mischief today."

Wingo spoke in outrage, "The villain intended to take my boots, with no regard for my poor feet! We must report this episode to the agent!"

"A good idea," said Maloof. "I doubt if he will be surprised. Many of these folk cannot be trusted. Shall we proceed? They seem to be selling some interesting fabric at the booth yonder."

Wingo brought his outrage under control. "Very well. Now that I think of it, we need a new tablecloth or two, and those intricate patterns will work quite nicely."

The third untoward incident of the afternoon now occurred.

Several pieces of material had been draped down the front of the stand, seemingly to advertise the range of pattern and color. Wingo leaned over the table to inspect the fabric, his pouch, dangling from his shoulder on leather straps, swinging close to the front of the table. The cloths hanging down the front of the stall stealthily parted. Through the slit came a pair of scissors, then a gnarled hand, then a gaunt gray arm. The scissors cautiously closed upon the straps supporting Wingo's pouch. Maloof, standing to the side, noticed the operation. He seized the arm, heaved hard, and out from under the table tumbled an old woman with an enormous nose, straggling gray hair, gaunt arms and legs. She rolled out into the aisle, then, wheezing and groaning, tried to crawl away. Maloof whisked down his stick and struck her a smart blow on the backside, then two more for good measure. She pulled herself to her feet and faced Maloof, howling imprecations. Maloof held her away with the point of his stick; frustrated, she spat at him and cursed even more intemperately. Maloof told the others, "I find this sort of language offensive; it is time that we were returning to the ship."

"I agree," said Wingo in disgust. "I have lost interest in the fabric. In any case, it is of poor quality."

Maloof addressed the woman: "Madame, you should be ashamed of yourself! Your conduct is wicked and your language is vile. For punishment, I intend to confiscate your scissors."

"No! Never! Not my best Glitzers!"

"You should have thought of this before you tried to rob poor Wingo! Next time you will know better!" Maloof turned to his comrades. "Are we ready?"

The four returned up the aisle. The old woman hobbled in pursuit: hopping, skipping, shouting, reviling Maloof and all his works. Wingo, while pretending to adjust his cloak, created several "mood impressions," which he later discovered to be striking. Maloof finally relented and placed the scissors down on the ground. The old woman scuttled forward, snatched them up, shouted a final volley of horrifying abuse, performed an obscene gesture, then hobbled back the way she had come, waving the scissors in gleeful triumph.

"A depressing spectacle," said Wingo sadly. "The woman has quite demeaned herself."

They reached the gate without further incident. The young IPCC agent greeted them with: "How did you find the market?"

"Interesting but not to our taste," said Maloof.

"We stopped by the refreshment platform," said Schwatzendale. "The beer was flat; the fish was sour; the serving woman was surly and cheated us, as well. I cannot recommend the place."

"I will keep your opinion in mind," said the agent. "I take it you won't be back?"

"Not on this occasion," said Maloof. "We are off to Sholo in the morning."

"Hm. I will give you some unofficial advice. Dark deeds are done at Sholo! Go nowhere alone. Carry your gun at the ready. Shoot first; ask questions, not second, nor third, but much later, if at all. Still, it is easy to lose one's pelt at Sholo."

2

In the morning the *Glicca*, departing Dulcie Diver, skimmed westward: across a succession of badlands, salt deserts, mountain ranges, an arid steppe. Spires and monoliths thrust high into the slanting orange sunlight, casting stark black shadows. The steppe continued, mile after mile, finally to abut against the Panton Scarp (named for the original locator Jule Panton). The scarp reared half a mile above the steppe, with the village Sholo huddled at its base, along with the spaceport.

The scarp separated two antagonistic races: the Meluli, who inhabited the plateau at the top of the scarp, and the Shuja who ranged the steppe below. The races were culturally similar, but physically distinct, which prompted each race to abhor the other.

Maloof had visited Sholo on a previous occasion. "The Shuja and the Meluli are quite different, one from another," he told Myron. "The Shuja are pale—sallow ivory, if you like—with light brown hair. Their ears are pointed at the top; the children often have the look of little fauns, and can be charming if you don't allow them behind your back. The Meluli are thin and angular, with rapacious faces the color of clay; and they move in nervous jerks and jumps. The Shuja are more civilized, if the word in this context means anything. It is possible to visit the tavern which is adjacent to the terminal at Sholo without instant danger, provided you are suitably cautious. Both Shuja and Meluli export bales of leather tanned from human hides. They both claim that they have nothing else to export, so they must make do."

"Interesting, if macabre," said Myron. "Who furnishes the hides?"

"Anyone with a hide, whether he needs it or not. Shuja and Meluli hunt each other, and raid the Uche savages. Any corpse is useful, if it has not gone stale. Off-worlders are often converted into corpses, blond corpses being especially desirable." Maloof appraised Myron's sleek blond hair, but made no comment.

Myron asked dubiously, "Are we taking aboard a cargo of hides?"

Maloof shrugged. "Why not? The hides go to Cax on Blenkinsop; Cax is already on our itinerary. If we don't take the cargo, the next ship will."

The argument was unassailable, thought Myron. He asked, "What happens to the hides at Cax?"

"They become furniture, wall hangings, objects of virtu. Artists use the pelts in their compositions. I saw one such artwork entitled *Children at Play*. A large panel was painted to represent a garden. Pelts of at least eight children were glued flat to the panel, to show them at their games: leap-frog and ring-around-the-rosy. The faces were like flat masks, the mouths twisted into grins of delight, the eye-holes staring out at the viewer. The picture sold for a very high price. But no matter! We are spacemen, not art connoisseurs. The *Glicca* is indifferent to what it carries."

The Panton Scarp stretched across the landscape. The *Glicca* settled upon the Sholo spaceport, close under the scarp. Seen from above, Sholo was unimpressive. A crude foundry, a few bedraggled shops, a tannery and its sump, a shipping agent's office, a warehouse, and the Glad Song Tavern ranged around a central quadrangle. A clutter of huts straggled off across the steppe, each with a patch of garden planted to beanbushes, kibber, and scruff.

The *Glicca* landed. Captain Maloof assembled the ship's company in the main saloon. "I have visited this place before," he told them. "Conditions at the time were strange and dangerous, and I don't think that they have changed. If you leave the ship, guard your life, as if it were as precious to you as your pelt is to the Shuja! Go nowhere alone. If you visit the Glad Song Tavern, be careful what you drink. Avoid the shops; they sell nothing you might wish to buy. There are no prostitutes; they would be redundant, since chastity is unknown. But control your quick emotions! Should you pay your respects to a Shuja lady, she will appraise you, not as a gallant gentleman, but as a walking pelt, of greater or lesser value."

"Incredible!" declared Deter Kalash in disgust. "There is nothing here to attract us. I suggest that we leave immediately for Coro-Coro!"

"Not so fast!" said Myron. "We have cargo to discharge."

"Also," said Wingo, "these folk are truly interesting, if only because they live by what we would consider a distorted social philosophy. I would like to give them at least a cursory glance."

"Do as you like," snapped Kalash. "But remember! If you are killed and stripped of your pelt, or otherwise injured so that the cuisine suffers, we shall demand a substantial rebate from Captain Maloof."

"Well spoken!" declared Schwatzendale. "Any such rebate should be deducted from Wingo's salary!"

"Be serious if you please!" said Wingo. "These folk live by a set of mysterious rules which function as moral principles. It would be interesting if we could codify these rules, and make them more understandable to us."

"No doubt," said Maloof. "But please attempt no research! A party of ethnologists and graduate students came here about ten years ago with such ideas in mind. Their equipment was modern, their theories profound. The Uche ate some of them; the others donated their pelts to the Shuja."

Wingo shook his head despondently. "That is a sad tale. Still, it is a mistake to become exercised, or so I suppose. Sometimes I feel that virtue and vice are like bats flitting through the Gaean subconscious, and can never be defined even by consensus."

"Well put, Wingo!" said Maloof. "You have an undeniable knack for turning a phrase!"

Schwatzendale said, "If Wingo records some of his 'mood impressions,' even only at the Glad Song Tavern, he will surely capture the inner nature of these people, and some of the mystery should be illuminated."

"That is my hope!" said Wingo. "It is a challenge but I will do my best."

3

At Sholo spaceport there were no formalities. Myron saw to the discharge of cargo, while Captain Maloof and Schwatzendale visited the export agent and arranged that the merchandise on hand should be crated, invoiced, and delivered to the *Glicca* on the following day.

Schwatzendale returned to the *Glicca*, unshipped the flitter, then summoned Myron. "Do you own a gun?"

"No."

"It is time that you did."

Schwatzendale rummaged through a locker in the saloon and brought out a squat black gun, which he handed to Myron. "This is a Detractor Model Nine, the Blue Spot version, very useful. One of the passengers left it aboard. Can you use it?"

"Certainly."

"It is now yours."

"Thank you. Who am I to shoot?"

"Possibly no one. We're going up to Mel, at the top of the scarp. Bring along the gun. We will be talking to the Meluli hetman and perhaps a few others. Keep your gun in evidence at all times. Brandish it, flourish it, catch their attention! If anyone so much as sniffs, shoot him. This is the kind of conduct they respect."

Wingo had come into the saloon. "You are discussing the Shuja?"

"Both the Shuja and the Meluli. They kill easily, but they are terrified of dying themselves; it means that they must wander forever across the steppe by night, without their skins. They are gentle as songbirds when you wave a gun in their faces."

Wingo mused, "Most curious! At Sholo brutal intimidation is the first of the social graces." He noticed Myron's gun, and looked dubiously toward Schwatzendale. "What are your plans?"

"We are flying up to Mel at the top of the scarp. They may have cargo ready for shipment."

Wingo glanced at the gun in displeasure. "Myron is still inexperienced. Perhaps he should not undertake such tasks until he is a bit more seasoned."

Schwatzendale cocked his head at an angle and appraised Myron critically from head to foot. "He is probably not the innocent lamb you take him for."

Wingo said in disgust, "You have the silver tongue of an orator. I will go up with you and sit at the Ruptor with my hand on the trigger. If I fire off a burst or two and scorch their laundry, they are sure to treat you nicely."

"That is a sound idea!" said Schwatzendale. He jumped to his feet, all angles and sidewise slants. "I am ready; shall we go?"

The three climbed aboard the flitter and flew up the face of Panton Scarp, to the brink and over. The plateau stretched away, bleak and forlorn, to a far range of low hills, dim in the hazy orange light. A mile inland from the brink the village Mel occupied a strip of gravelly barrens beside a small dark pond.

The flitter flew to the village, turned, circled at an altitude of three hundred yards. Mel seemed even more cheerless than Sholo. A clutter of ramshackle huts surrounded the pond; to the side stood a line of nondescript shops, a market, and several large structures built of timber and rock-melt housing the tannery, the foundry, the warehouse, with the office of the shipping agent adjacent. There seemed to be neither tavern nor inn. Out on the plain a number of cattle grazed at the sparse brown sedge.

The flitter continued to circle the village until folk came out to stare; Schwatzendale then landed the flitter on a flat about fifty yards from the warehouse. He and Myron jumped to the ground, guns at the ready, while Wingo stood by the forward Ruptor. He had pulled a black cap low over his pink face, to make himself look grim and menacing.

Five minutes passed. Beside the tannery a man appeared. He called out, "What do you do here? This is Mel; I am the het-man!"

Schwatzendale moved two steps forward. "We are spacemen from the ship *Glicca*. What cargo, if any, is ready for export?"

The hetman called out, "Put aside your guns! I am not yet ready to lose my pelt!"

"You need not fear," said Schwatzendale. "If we were of a mind, we could destroy your entire village with three bursts of our Ruptor. Your pelts would be blown to bits and useless for export."

The Meluli hetman came slowly forward. He was middle-aged, with wings of stiff black hair projecting over his ears; his face showed a prodigious beak of a nose, hooded eyes, and skin the color of bronze, with an overtone of green shine. He wore a black leather tunic, and black breeches tucked into boots. Myron noticed that most of his attention was fixed, not upon Schwatzendale, not upon Wingo, but upon himself, with a curious brooding fascination—the next thing to an amorous fixation.

Wingo chuckled. "Do not be vain. It is your pale gold hair they covet! They think that your pelt would be a thing of beauty."

"So it may be," said Myron. "But I want to keep it for myself."

Wingo handed Myron a large white kerchief. "Tie this over your head and they will not stare so avidly."

"I feel like a naked virgin at the slave market," Myron grumbled, as he tied the scarf over his head.

Schwatzendale and the hetman had moved to within ten yards of each other. Schwatzendale asked, "What about cargo?"

The hetman turned and called over his shoulder. A man older than himself, with an even more majestic beak of a nose, came forward, showing no fear of the guns. The hetman said, "This is the export agent; you must deal with him."

The agent said, "The situation is good. There are two lots, fifty to the lot, ready for the crate. Tomorrow you may take them."

"That is satisfactory, but I am required to examine and count the lots, since the Meluli are known to be careless in their count, and the carrier is held responsible."

"As you like," said the agent. "You may count to your heart's content. The warehouse is yonder."

"Very well," said Schwatzendale. "We will visit the warehouse. The hetman must stand just yonder and wait until we return. In the event of treachery and pelt-taking, Wingo will first kill the hetman, then he will destroy Mel and all the Meluli. Why are you laughing? You sneer? You do not believe me? That is easy to fix! Wingo, be so good as to demolish that ruined hut yonder."

Wingo pushed the red button at the side of the Ruptor and a tumble-down but a hundred yards distant exploded into splinters of stone.

Both the hetman and the agent jerked back in shock. The hetman complained that the pelt of the old woman who lived in the hut had surely been damaged beyond repair. "It is a waste."

Wingo was crestfallen and said he was sorry, but Schwatzendale waved the incident aside. He spoke to the hetman: "As you can see, we are killers, plain and simple! We kill whomever annoys us, without remorse."

The hetman threw out his arms in a gesture of annoyance. " 'Remorse'? What is that? Speak so that I understand you!"

"No matter. Obey my conditions, or we will go away, and leave your pelts here to rot! Perhaps we will kill you and a few others for practice."

Conditions were finally arranged to Schwatzendale's satisfaction. The hetman stood to the side, with the Ruptor trained upon him, which caused him to fidget. None of the Meluli loitered near the warehouse where they might conveniently attack the spacemen. Myron and Schwatzendale, holding their guns at the ready, accompanied the agent to the warehouse. Here they were joined by the tanner: a small thin man of indeterminate age, milder and less coarse than either the agent or the hetman. With a tired smile, he assured Schwatzendale that the warehouse held no threat and was vacant except for himself and his apprentice. He readily acknowledged that vigilance was necessary, that mistakes in counting and declarations of quality had occurred in the past. "But not under my auspices," he stated. "It is easier to do things correctly."

"Still, I have been ordered to count," said Schwatzendale.

"And you are an expert as to the quality of these fine leathers?"

"No, not at all. But if there is trouble, we will return and cause far more trouble than the theft was worth."

"That is only sensible," said the tanner. "Come then; count the pelts. The warehouse is safe; no ambush has been organized. At least not to my knowledge." He looked inquiringly to the agent. "What plans are afoot, if any?"

"None! These men are clearly killers."

"We are pleased for your good opinion," said Schwatzendale. "I should mention that we are easily startled and kill at random. Whatever moves is killed and everyone within range of our guns will wander the night forever without their pelts."

"Enough of such grisly talk," growled the agent. "We are here to export pelts, not to soothe your apprehensions."

"We are nervous for the best of reasons," said Schwatzendale. "And for you to be more nervous than we are is optimal."

The tanner spoke impatiently, "No more blather; come count the pelts." He led the way into the warehouse, followed by the agent, then Myron and Schwatzendale.

The interior of the warehouse was cavernous and gloomy. Low orange sunlight slanted through a row of high windows, arousing a dozen tones of brown from the wooden walls, posts, planked floor, tables, and heaped pelts. Charcoal brown shadows obscured the far walls. The hides ranged in color from dark ivory through the brown of tobacco into umber. The air smelled of tanning compounds, sizing resin, camphor, and an indefinable overtone which caused Myron's stomach to twitch.

Myron examined the premises with care. At the back of the room a wizened youth, hollow-cheeked, with a predacious nose, worked at a table, scraping a pelt. The tanner spoke a few sharp words and the apprentice sidled off into the shadows.

Myron took a position by the entrance, gun at the ready. The agent went to lean against a stack of pelts, for the moment passive and indifferent. Schwatzendale, after a quick glance around the room, gave his attention to the tanner. "So what shall I count?"

"These are the hides ready for export." The tanner went to a table stacked high with pelts. "We can have them crated and ready for shipment by noon tomorrow." He began to flip over the pelts for Schwatzendale's inspection. "As you can see, these are top quality, properly tanned and well cured, with only trivial killing holes."

Myron watched in fascination. Under the tanner's hands the leather seemed supple and fine. The processing had flattened the faces so that the features were artfully subdued, the eyes staring round holes. "It is an interesting business," said the tanner. "I am beset by truly abstract speculations at times. I wonder how much personality resides in the pelts. What do they feel? What are their hopes and dreams? Often I have uncanny sensations along these lines."

"And what are your conclusions?"

"The mystery remains as profound as ever," said the tanner.

"These are interesting concepts," said Schwatzendale. "But for myself, I do not care to grope among such tenuous ideas. I deal only with what is here and now. Everything else is foam and mist."

"Yours is a simple methodology," said the tanner politely. "Perhaps, ultimately, it is the wisest way of all, since the theorist is forced to wrestle with a dozen possibilities, each making its special pleading."

Schwatzendale laughed. "I have not theorized even to this effect! I celebrate the concrete! If I locate an itch, I scratch it! If I discover a leek and mutton pie, I eat it. If I come upon a beautiful woman, I make myself agreeable."

"You will avoid a hundred unfulfilled longings," said the tanner. "You will waste no time pursuing unattainable goals. I wish that I shared your discipline! I regret to say that my aspirations take me into a land of mirages, where all excellent things are possible! Sometimes I dream of tanning a gamut of twelve faultless pelts, representing sheer perfection in each of the catalogued styles! At other times I long for what can only be called the 'ineffable.'" The tanner paused in his unfolding of the pelts. "Aha! Notice here; a true curiosity!"

Myron saw that the color of the leather was pale. The tanner explained. "It is the pelt of an off-worlder!"

"A tourist, I hope, and not a spaceman?" asked Schwatzendale.

"Yes, a tourist, with a most unusual pelt. Notice the tattooing! It is splendid, is it not? For instance, here: the whorls of red and green on the abdomen, and the fine floral pattern along the buttocks! Pelts of this quality are rare, and I shall invoice it as an expensive specialty."

"Interesting," said Schwatzendale. "You are clearly a master of your craft."

The tanner smiled wistfully. "The real artists work elsewhere. You are a sensitive man; I will show you true art." From a shelf under the table he brought out a large loose-leaf volume. "See here!" He threw back the cover, and turned to a photograph, evidently cut from a glossy periodical. The caption read:

> Rector Fabian Mais stands in the exquisite drawing room of his manor at Tassa Lola. He examines his wonderful new acquisition entitled *Sylvan Passage*, created by the artist Fedore Coluccio from exotic materials.

In the photograph an elegant gentleman stood beside a panel twelve feet wide by eight feet tall, depicting a procession of distorted human forms emerging from a forest. The group had halted where they could look forever into the drawing-room from their vacant eyeholes. First in line came a man, then a woman staring over his shoulder; and behind, half lost in the gloom, a child; and then, further back, the suggestion of other shapes.

Beside the photograph was a clipping from a journal which read:

It is a most effective use of a striking and unique medium. Rector Mais finds the work soothing and placid, conveying, so he declares, "a sense of"—and here the Rector falters, unable to find the exact word to describe his mood. "A sense of eternity," he says at last.

The tanner turned to another photograph which depicted the interior of a large and sumptuous bedroom. To either side of the bed a panel framed a pelt staring solemnly at the occupants of the room. The caption read:

Here we are vouchsafed a glimpse into the great bedroom of Babbinch House at Ballymore, and our immediate attention is drawn to what Lord Shioban smilingly calls his "memento mori."

The tanner murmured, "Is it not impressive?" He turned to another photograph. "This is from a journal called *Architect's Vantage*. It is another composite work by Fedore Coluccio. It is called *The Lovers*." Coluccio had painted a formal garden with a bench in the foreground. He had posed a pair of pelts, as if they were sitting on the bench, their arms awkwardly clasped as if in affection. As always, the eye-holes stared from the panel and seemed to say, "Look at us! Our love is forever!"

The tanner asked Schwatzendale, "What is your opinion?"

Schwatzendale said, "It is absolutely fetching, and very smart!"

Myron, standing by the doorway, tried to see the photograph. A hand touched his arm; he turned about, startled, to discover the apprentice boy, smiling shyly and making a sign to enjoin silence. He spoke in a whisper. "I will show you something even more beautiful! Come."

Myron stared at him in perplexity. "What do you mean, 'beautiful'?"

"Come! Let the others buy and sell! Step around here, into the shadows."

"I must remain here," said Myron. "I am on guard."

"Come," the boy whispered. "They are looking at picture-books; they will never notice." He tugged at Myron's arm. "Come."

Schwatzendale had been watching from the corner of his eye. He darted forward, and struck the boy with his fist, so hard that the boy fell. Something tinkled across the floor. Schwatzendale cried, "You poisonous little imp! This is your lucky day! Or you would now be dead if I were not a merciful man!" He bent and snatched up the object which had fallen. He showed it to Myron. "It is his flaying knife. Keep it for a souvenir!"

From the boy came an instant wail. "Give me my knife! It is my thing of value!"

The tanner and the agent stood, tensely watching. The tanner said, "There is nothing more to say. Tomorrow I will have two bales packed and ready for shipment. Now our business is at an end."

Schwatzendale motioned to the tanner and the agent. "You go out first."

From the boy came a yammer of pleading: "My knife, my good knife! Oh where will I get another? Give me back my property!"

Neither Myron nor Schwatzendale heeded the plea. From the shadows the boy called out in fury, "Ugly milk-fed tourists! Go back to your wallow! In two more seconds I would have had the squonk's hide, and now I have lost my knife!"

Myron and Schwatzendale returned to the flitter. As they flew back down to Sholo, Myron asked, "What is a 'squonk'?"

Schwatzendale reflected, then said at last, "I believe it to be some sort of hairless white rat."

Six

The flitter slid down to land beside the *Glicca*, where it was lifted aboard and secured into its cradle. The time was late afternoon. Wingo set out a meal for the pilgrims, who had become more querulous than ever. Barthold, a crooked hot-eyed old man who wore his gray hair in a straggle, demanded, "Why are we waiting here on this wretched outpost? Where is the need? Every instant of delay is a new barb in our flesh! We are fearfully far from our destination!"

Captain Maloof responded in a reasonable voice, "We are more or less at the mercy of the shipping agents. If their cargo is not ready, then we must allow them at least some small latitude. This is our business, after all."

Deter Kalash snapped, "Are you forgetting the responsibility you owe your passengers? Think of it! Precious hours go by while we crouch here on this arid steppe, surrounded by savages."

The bumptious young pilgrim named Cooner cried out, "Even while we wait, diddling and twiddling, the brethren are marching from Impy's Landing singing their songs of triumph!"

"And what of us?" demanded Tunch. "Where is our triumph? Only when we conquer each other at double-moko! In all truth, the situation is vexing."

"I am sorry to hear this," said Maloof. "Why not visit the tavern? It will be a change, and you will be safe so long as you do not wander off in search of women."

"Bah!" muttered Kalash. "We have no money to pay for that sort of foolishness."

"No need to pay," said Maloof. "Chastity is unknown, but unless you fornicate in a group, you may lose your pelts."

Kalash rejected the advice. "We prefer to do this sort of thing in private, since we all have our secret methods."

"In that case, I cannot advise you."

"No need! We will remain aboard the ship."

During the early evening, Wingo, Schwatzendale, and Myron set off toward the Glad Song Tavern. The orange sun Bran, its large diameter magnified even further by the thick air, trembled at the horizon, with far peaks and spires in silhouette. As they approached the tavern, Bran sank behind a pansy sky leaving the world in lavender gloom.

The three spacemen entered the tavern to find themselves in a long room with walls of white-washed concrete. Travel posters, gay with the scenery of far worlds, decorated one wall; on the wall opposite hung skulls taken from ferocious creatures of the western swamps. The landlord presided over the refreshment counter, drawing ale and beer from wooden kegs, dispensing liquors from tall black bottles. He was middle-aged, placid and portly; gray hair hung past the points of his ears. His face was typically Shuja: broad across the forehead, narrowing from cheekbones to a pointed chin. From the wall behind him, three signs addressed his patrons. The first read:

TOURISTS! WE CAN ARRANGE SAFE EXCURSIONS TO THE RE-MARKABLE GALAHANGA SWAMP, WHERE SAVAGE CREATURES CREATE A FEARSOME SPECTACLE FOR YOUR INTERESTED OB-SERVATION. SAFETY IS EMPHASIZED; THERE IS LITTLE IN-JURY, AND FATAL ACCIDENTS ARE RARE. FOR DETAILS, CONSULT THE COUNTERMAN.

Another sign read:

DRINK OUR SPECIAL BEVERAGES! THEY HAVE BEEN APPROVED BY OFF-WORLD CONNOISSEURS. THE FLAVORS ARE UNIQUE AND ENTICING. WE RECOMMEND BOTH OUR BOOMING ALE AND OUR SWEET FRUCTER BEER.

A third sign read:

WARNING TO TOURISTS: DO NOT VISIT FRIENDS IN THE VIL-LAGE BY NIGHT. RUFFIANS LURK IN THE DARK; YOU MAY BE ATTACKED AND SERIOUSLY INJURED OR EVEN KILLED. THIS WARNING HAS BEEN POSTED BY ORDER OF THE IPCC.

The three spacemen seated themselves at a table. A dozen other patrons sat about the room, hunched over fluted brass tankards. They drank in great pulsing gulps, with heads thrown back and ale trickling from the corners of their mouths. When the tankards went dry, they were set down with a clang, whereupon a serving girl came to take orders. She was not a typical tavern wench, so Myron noticed at once. She was slight, slender, somewhat younger than himself, definitely attractive, if quiet and grave. Chestnut curls fringed her forehead and hung past her ears. Her mouth drooped—in boredom? Discontent? Unhappiness? She wore a white frock, and sandals, with a white ribbon binding her hair. Myron wondered whether she might share the typical Shuja disregard for chastity. If opportunity offered, he might make a discreet investigation.

Presently the girl came to take orders from the spacemen. She looked from Myron, to Wingo, to Schwatzendale, without interest.

Wingo asked a question; the girl replied that the tavern served both bitter ale and dark sweet beer; also silverthorn wine, and imported spirits. Her voice was soft and controlled, which to Myron's ears seemed incongruous to the surroundings. Odd!

When she had gone off to the counter, he said, half to himself: "She doesn't seem the kind of girl you would expect to find here."

Schwatzendale laughed. "You will never find the girls you expect anywhere."

Myron looked after the girl. "Perhaps she is something other than local stock."

"Unlikely," said Schwatzendale. "Her ears are pointed. She is probably the landlord's daughter."

"Hmm. I wonder if—" Myron paused, half embarrassed. Then, trying to keep his voice casual, he said, "The captain mentioned that the local girls were, well, a bit easy—but this girl doesn't seem the type."

Schwatzendale made one of his wry faces, mouth slanting up one side, down the other. "No comment! In fact, no opinion. Personally, I like jolly ladies who bounce a bit. This one doesn't bounce. She's off in a dream world! Still, she's probably like all the rest."

"I'm not so sure," Myron mused. "She just doesn't have that look."

"Looks can be deceiving," said Wingo.

"Be surprised by nothing!" said Schwatzendale. "If this girl can murder a man for his pelt, she won't object to a friendly toss in the hay!"

Myron started to point out the flaws in Schwatzendale's logic but the girl was at the table with three tankards of ale. She turned to go, but Myron spoke to her. "Do you have a name?"

The girl looked at him in wonder. "Of course I have a name."

"What is it?"

"I don't like to say. One should not name names to strangers."

"Why not? I'll tell you mine. It is 'Myron.'"

The girl smiled. "Now, if I chose, I could tangle your soul in witchery."

"Why would you want to do that?"

The girl shrugged and glanced toward the counter, where the landlord drew ale for a pair of customers. She turned back to Myron. "Someday I will leave here, when I earn enough money. I would hope to have friends off-world. If I bewitched you properly, you might be such a friend."

"Hmm," said Myron. "This needs thinking about. In any case, I'd prefer not to be witched."

The girl spoke indifferently, "Forget what I said; it was sheer fancy. I know nothing about such things."

"That is a relief," said Myron. "Are you going to tell me your name?"

"No. These other two would hear." The girl took up her tray. She turned Myron an inscrutable glance, then went off to another table.

"So there you have it," said Schwatzendale, grinning. "No name, no bewitchments, no nothing."

"That was just a test run," said Myron. "I felt curiosity, nothing else."

The three drank ale and Myron tried to put the girl from his mind. To this end he thought of girls he had known at Salou Sain. He remembered Rolinda, a dark-haired imp with long eyelashes who had played glissandos along the register of Myron's emotions. Then there was Berrens: incredibly lovely, with long honey-colored hair and the bluest of blue eyes; alas! She wrote arcane poetry and wanted Myron to tattoo a large staring eye in the center of his forehead, after the style of the Sufic Transvisionaries. But Berrens refused to decorate herself in like fashion, and the romance had collapsed. There had been Angela, adorable Angela, who had led Myron a mad chase, only to marry a wealthy fishmonger, who later proved parsimonious. Every night he brought home a parcel of unsold fish for Angela to cook for their supper. The marriage had soon dissolved.

Myron became aware that Schwatzendale and Wingo were discussing the *Glicca* and the aspirations which, so Wingo asserted, motivated each member of the crew.

Schwatzendale refused to take the idea seriously. He defined "aspirations" as a mild form of dementia, to which he, at least, was immune.

"Aspirations are bleary-eyed hopes for the future, smeared over with honey and dead flies. As for me, I live on the curling crest of the moment! The past is a cemetery of regrets and second thoughts, the future is a wilderness."

"Never have I heard such nonsense," declared Wingo. "At least, not since your last harangue."

"I bring you truth," announced Schwatzendale grandly. "Time and existence both lack dimension! Life is real only during that instant known as 'Now.' Surely that is clear!"

"Oh, it is clear enough," scoffed Wingo. "You cite the most limpid banalities as if they were cosmic truths. For an unsophisticated person the effect might be startling."

Schwatzendale peered sidewise at the complacent Wingo. "You may or may not intend a compliment."

Wingo shrugged. "I feel only that it is a wasted man indeed who lives without a spiritual focus, or who fritters away his dreams. But no matter! That man cannot be you."

"And why not?"

"Need I mention the name Moncrief the Mouse-rider? You will never rest until you have beaten him, and taken his property! These are your aspirations!"

Schwatzendale threw his hands into the air. "That is no aspiration! That is simple thirst for revenge! Aspirations are quite different; they are mutable and change by the hour. Each exerts the force of a mayfly; each comes and goes and then is seen no more!"

"Irrelevant, if true," said Wingo. "Your subconscious mind guides you night and day, along the route ordained by your inner self—which is to say: your aspirations. This is true of us all."

"Enough theorizing!" cried Schwatzendale. "Be real! Prove something! Start with Captain Maloof; where are his aspirations?"

Wingo rubbed his pink chin. "In all candor, he has never discussed such subjects. Still, my intuition tells me that he is searching—for something or someone; that he lives in hope of fulfilling his quest."

"Hmmf," said Schwatzendale. "You are romanticizing in all directions at once. Where is your evidence?"

Wingo shrugged. "We have both seen him in the pilothouse, brooding out over the stars. There is mystery in his past."

Schwatzendale considered, half-convinced despite himself. "What could he be looking for?"

"He seeks something lost which must be found. That is the nature of a quest."

"Quite so," said Schwatzendale. "I could not have expressed it better. Do you also admit to aspirations? Or are they secret, like those of Captain Maloof?"

Wingo chuckled. "Nothing about me is secret, as you well know. My goals are simple. I want to live at peace with myself and in harmony with the universe. That is all."

"These are rather insipid objectives," said Schwatzendale. "Still, they are simple and probably harmless."

Wingo sighed. "Myron is not yet a cynic. He will be proud to affirm the aspirations which guide his life."

"I will answer for him," said Schwatzendale. "He has two principal aspirations. First, he wants to violate the landlord's innocent daughter. Next, he wants to return to the *Glicca* wearing his own pelt. Otherwise, Myron is a spaceman and a vagabond, without a care in the world."

"Partly true," said Myron. "But I own to a third aspiration which never leaves me. It is focussed upon a man named Marko Fassig and my great-aunt Hester who are now cruising aboard the space-yacht *Glodwyn*. Whenever my mind veers in this direction, I feel a strong yearning, which I suspect is a bona fide aspiration."

"Ah well," said Wingo. "Enough for now. Look yonder!" He pointed to a case against the back wall. A sign above read:

TABOO STONES CARVED BY THE UCHE SAVAGES OF THE SOUTH MOUNTAINS, USED AS INSTRUMENTS OF DREAD. THESE WERE TAKEN AT GREAT RISK! THE SYMBOLS CARVED INTO EACH COULD TELL A TROUBLESOME STORY. PRICES ON REQUEST.

Wingo rose to his feet; Schwatzendale jumped up and the two went to examine the dread-stones. Myron was about to follow, when he noticed that the girl was looking in his direction. He sat back in the chair and held up his hand in a signal. She crossed the room and stopped beside the table. "Yes, sir? Do you need more ale?"

"No. I wanted to speak with you."

The girl smiled doubtfully, looked over her shoulder toward the counter, then turned back to Myron and said in a rush: "I think that you have been educated at an advanced school."

"Yes," said Myron in surprise. "How do you know?"

"By looking at you and hearing your voice. What did you study?"

"The usual variety. I started in economic fluxions, then changed to theoretic aesthetics, then transferred into cosmology, and there I stayed. What about you?"

The girl was amused. "My education has come from what I have read. It is not what I would like."

"Oh? What would you like."

"I want to leave this place and never return! Perhaps I would go to a school like yours. Would that be possible?"

"No reason why not. What do you want to learn?"

"Everything there is to know."

Myron frowned, unsure of what it was proper to say. Realistically, the girl's prospects could not be considered good.

The girl seemed to divine his thoughts. "Does what I say sound reasonable?"

Myron said bravely, "It would not be easy. Still, anything is possible."

"That is what I tell myself. I don't have much money—not enough to pay for passage away from here. Can I work aboard a spaceship?"

Myron hesitated. "Sometimes a passenger ship needs a stewardess or a nurse. On a freighter such as the *Glicca* these jobs are not open. Even so, a captain will sometimes ship a pretty girl aboard to massage his back and keep his bed warm. It happens once in a while. Does the idea bother you?"

The girl thought a moment. "It would do me no permanent harm. I would not mind too much, if the captain were nice." She turned him a swift sidelong glance. "Are you the captain?"

Myron laughed. "If I were, you would be leaving aboard my ship tonight! But I am only the supercargo, at the low end of the scale."

"And you could not take me aboard?"

"Not a chance. But space-travel is not all that dear."

"I have some money—not very much. Probably not enough."

"How much do you have?"

"Thirty-six sols."

"Fifty sols would buy your passage to Port Tanjee, where you could probably find work of some kind—perhaps aboard a passenger packet, for Sarbane or Arcturus Legend or even Old Earth."

"That would be wonderful! But I don't have that much money."

"Will your father help you?"

"No." She glanced over her shoulder toward the counter. "He wants me to stay here, where I can work in the tavern. He gets angry when I talk to off-worlders. He thinks that I might be selling myself for money."

Myron looked at her askance. "Do you do that?"

"No—not that it means a great deal. Would you give me money?"

For a moment Myron could find nothing to say. Then he asked: "For what?"

"To help me find passage away from Terce—and also for me, if you like."

"It seems a good cause," said Myron. "I can invest, oh, five sols."

The girl turned him a side-glance. "I will be finished with my work in a moment or two. If you wish to give me some money very privately, you may. I have nothing to give you in return, except myself, and I will do so, if you are of a mind. Not just for the money, but because I like you and I want to share with you."

"The idea is agreeable, certainly."

"My chamber is halfway along the corridor, yonder. I will leave the door open a crack."

The girl moved away, turning him a single thoughtful glance over her shoulder. A few moments later Myron saw her lay the serving tray on the counter. She spoke briefly to the landlord, then quietly left the room.

Schwatzendale and Wingo returned to the table. Schwatzendale asked, "What was that all about? If it was seduction, forget it. She wants your pretty yellow hair. If she collected your pelt, she would come into a good deal of money."

"Nonsense," said Myron. "We were talking about education. She wants to leave Terce, and needs money. I told her I would give her five sols, and she said she would appreciate it. I can understand that it sounds a bit sordid, but it is not that way at all. She may share the local disregard for chastity, but what of that? She does not think that she is marketing herself."

"I agree," said Schwatzendale. "She wants your pelt. It is worth at least fifty sols, perhaps more."

"Incredible!" muttered Myron. "She is desperately anxious to leave this frightful world. Also, I believe that she likes me."

Schwatzendale gave a caw of sardonic laughter. "She serves you a tankard of ale and falls in love on the spot. Is that the way of it?"

"Such things happen!"

"And other things as well. They are expert with a special tool; they slide it into your neck, give it a turn and a swish, and your spinal cord is cut, so that death comes gently, and kill-marks are few."

"She intends no such grisly work; my instincts can't be that unhelpful! I'd bet money that I'm right!"

Myron intended only a rhetorical flourish. He had forgotten Schwatzendale's proclivities.

"Done!" cried Schwatzendale. "It's ten sols, even money, that she goes after your pelt, one way or another. Are you on?"

"Certainly!" declared Myron with more bravado than he felt.

Wingo protested: "That is not a kindly bet! Myron will be in danger, especially if she has confederates."

"We shall take precautions," said Schwatzendale. "I will watch through a crack in the door."

"No, no, no!" cried Myron. "I would feel quite useless."

"It is not a genteel suggestion," pronounced Wingo.

"Very well, then. I will stand by the door. If the girl chases Myron with a knife, he need only call and I will be there to protect my interests. I have no doubt but what Myron can take care of himself. Naturally, he will carry his gun."

"Of course!" said Myron. "While I am busy with the girl, I will grip the gun between my teeth."

"Not a bad idea," said Wingo. "Remember: when you are most distracted, that is when you are likely to be taken by surprise."

"Correct!" said Schwatzendale. "One time I was happily engaged with a girl, and did not notice that her mother had entered the room with a broom. When she raised it high to strike, I saw her and quickly rolled us both over. She struck the girl instead, a mighty wallop flat on the buttocks. During the outcry I took up my clothes and ran from the room. I never saw the girl again, and of course I carefully avoided the mother."

"In cases of this sort, one must always be vigilant," said Wingo.

Schwatzendale rose to his feet. "Well then, Myron, are you ready?"

Myron said grimly, "Yes, I am ready."

"Two last points. Make sure that she carries no knife, and look under the pillow. If she asks about your gun, tell her that you carry it by the captain's orders."

"Yes, yes," muttered Myron. "This is not as romantic as I had hoped. Come along then. I will go first. You come behind, and please do not call through the door to ask how things are going."

"Trust me!"

Myron turned into the dim corridor, followed by Schwatzendale. They passed the latrine and went on to where a door stood ajar, allowing a slit of light to slice across the corridor. Myron eased open the door and, step by slow step, entered the room. He halted and behind him closed the door until the edge touched the frame, stopping before the latch was engaged. He stood in a large room, more nicely furnished than he had expected. The ceiling was white plaster, with a decorative frieze around the perimeter, stained blue and ocher. Planks of polished dark wood and a grass mat covered the floor. A cabinet with six drawers stood against one wall, along with a small bookcase containing a dozen books and as many rather tattered periodicals. A round wooden table supported a lamp and a vase holding feathery fronds of several colors: mauve, black, a luminous brown. At the opposite end of the room was a bed, spread with a neat blue and white quilt. A large map of Old Earth covered the wall opposite, while over the bed a high shelf displayed a dozen small dolls, dressed in a variety of costumes.

In the air hung a muted fragrance: delicate, tart, and—so Myron thought—a trifle exotic. Aside from fragrance, dolls, and map, there was little to express the girl's personality: no photographs, oddments or souvenirs; only the girl herself. She sat on the edge of the bed. After a quick glance toward Myron, she turned away to look pensively down at her hands. She had discarded her sandals; her feet and legs were bare.

Myron watched her in fascination, ideas of every sort churning through his mind. Schwatzendale's cynicism had been disturbing; was it at all credible? Could a girl such as this, graceful, slight, with so much wistful charm, harbor the grisly intentions which Schwatzendale had imputed to her?

The girl turned her head and looked at him. She spoke in a soft voice. "Are you sorry to be here?"

"No." Myron gave a self-conscious laugh. "Perhaps I am a bit on edge."

"If you regret coming, you need not stay."

"It's nothing like that. Today, up at Mel, a boy tried to lure me into the shadows, so that he could kill me with his knife. The adventure left me in a nervous state."

The girl smiled. "This is not Mel. I am not a boy. I carry no knife."

"I can see this for myself—but the boy seemed so innocent, and my friends have pointed out that my pelt would pay for your passage to Port Tanjee."

The girl smiled rather painfully. "But in spite of your misgivings you are here."

"So I am. I wish I could know you better. Even more, I wish that we were somewhere other than here."

The girl looked down at her hands. "I do too. It is why I asked you if you wanted to come here. But I have been thinking. You need not give me any money. I don't want you to think that I sell myself—especially not for what you are able to give me. For five hundred sols—yes! For a thousand sols—gladly, with joy."

Myron laughed. "Sorry; I can barely imagine that much wealth. Still, I want to contribute to your travel fund. It won't be enough to startle you, but it will help take you to Port Tanjee." He laid five sols on the chest of drawers.

The girl rose to her feet. "Thank you." She went to the chest and dropped the money into the top drawer. She turned to face Myron, half-smiling. She held out her hands. "You must not be nervous! Look carefully, please. Do you see a knife?"

Myron looked down. The hands were empty. "No."

"That is not enough! You must make sure of me!" When Myron hesitated, she said, "Don't be shy! Am I not what you would wish me to be?"

"Perhaps you think me foolish," said Myron miserably, "but fears were put into my head by the boy with his flaying knife, and by my shipmates, and they won't go away."

"Search me, if you like," said the girl. "Explore my whole person. Search! Are you timid?"

"Yes, in a way. At Salou Sain it is not considered polite to search the other person before lovemaking." He went on, a trifle lamely. "Of course, cases are different."

The girl turned away from him, her face quite still. "Do whatever you like; only make sure that I carry neither skene, nor daggeret, nor flaying knife."

Myron stepped behind her and gingerly ran his hands over her body, sparing nowhere a knife might be concealed. At last, breathlessly, he stood back, his hands tingling. He said, "I have explored carefully, but found only a warm girl. The feel of you is superb; my teeth are grating together, I suppose from sheer lust."

The girl turned about. "So then? Why are you standing there like a thing of wax?"

"I will be candid with you," said Myron. "I am sweating with passion, but I still can't forget that this is Sholo Town."

The girl sighed, but made no comment as Myron went to the bed. He looked under the pillow, but found no knife or other weapon. The coverlet was taut and concealed not even a dangerous length of cord.

Myron stood back, feeling both foolish and frustrated. He had discovered nothing sinister: no reek of blood, nothing to suggest the cutting of throats. There was, in fact, nothing to trouble him except the girl herself. She continued to watch him, with no other expression than a half-smile, conveying, at least in part, amusement. Why was she not disgusted with him? Certainly he was being tiresome! Somewhere something was out of balance. The girl was far too tolerant! There should have been jeers at his pusillanimity and orders to clear out of her room. The girl's mood never altered; she was passive, rather than indifferent. Perhaps she was innocent and puzzled by his conduct. In this case, he would win ten sols from Schwatzendale, which, of course, was all to the good.

The girl gave a small shrug of resignation. She went to the table and sat in one of the chairs. Reaching to a shelf, she brought down a box, a bottle, and a tall fluted goblet of heavy black glass. She poured from the bottle into the goblet, raised the lid of the box, reached in and brought out a glazed wafer from among the contents. She nibbled at the wafer, sipped at the goblet. Looking sidelong toward Myron, she said, "You may join me, if you like."

Myron went to sit at the table. The girl sipped once more of the dark liquor, then said, "If you wish to drink, you must use this goblet, since I have no other."

Myron took up the goblet. The dark liquid smelled of pungent essences he could not identify. He grimaced and replaced the goblet. "I don't think that this is to my taste."

"You should not be so fearful!" The girl raised the goblet to her lips and sipped. "It is called 'Safrinet,' and tastes better than it smells. It is considered our best."

"No doubt," said Myron, "but I am not adventurous."

The girl lifted the lid to the box. "Try one of these wafers! They are baked from sweet seeds and the oil of marmarella. No? You should at least taste! The flavor is pleasant."

"Thank you, but I don't care much for sweet cakes."

The girl thoughtfully reached into the box and brought out a sweet wafer and ate it. "The refreshments have come and gone," she told Myron. "It is time to begin." She rose and stood facing him. "I am ready."

Myron slowly stood erect. Imminence hung in the air. His pulse throbbed. The girl turned her back. "Unclasp my white gown."

With clumsy fingers Myron slid aside the clasp at the nape of her neck; the white gown slid to the floor, revealing her body, naked save for a wisp of underwear at her hips. She turned and looked at him with glowing eyes. "Now I will help you from your clothes." She came a step forward, lifted her hands. "First, your tunic. You may touch me, if you like." She reached toward the clasp at the top of his tunic. By the merest flicker of a glimpse, Myron chanced to notice that the middle finger of her right hand was bent inward at an awkward angle. Before she could touch his throat, he seized her right wrist, clamping it so tightly that she cried out. Slowly, Myron turned over her hand. A sac adhered to the first joint of her middle finger. The sac was distended with liquid. From a small round gasket on the outer face of the sac a short needle protruded.

Myron looked into the girl's face. She stared back at him, eyes luminous but without expression. The girl had attached the sac to her finger when she had last reached into the box of nut-cakes. In a husky voice Myron said, "I was timid to good purpose."

The girl answered in a whisper. "It amounts to nothing. You have won. Take me and use me as you like."

A slow fury began to well up inside Myron's brain. Had he been only a trifle less vigilant or—more accurately—a trifle less lucky, he would now be dying, so that this girl might make free with his yellow-haired pelt.

The girl, watching his face, became frightened. She cried out: "You are hurting me." She jerked her arm, and tried to pull away. Myron held her tight. Squirming and twisting, she broke his hold and with palm rigid, struck at his face. Myron caught her arm, bent her elbow and diverted its impetus, guiding it upward, so that she struck her own neck. Without conscious purpose, Myron pressed and the needle entered her flesh. She felt the sting and gave a wild cry of utter desolation. Her arm relaxed; her hand went limp; Myron saw that the sac had gone flaccid.

The girl said in an incredulous voice: "You have killed me! I am dying!"

"It may be so. You should know better than I."

The girl whimpered. "I don't want to stare forever from a picture hanging on a wall!"

"That is what you wanted for me. I feel no pity; you have cost me ten sols."

"No, no, no! I took no money from you!"

"The effect is the same."

The girl's knees began to buckle. She wailed in terror: an eerie sound which thrilled along Myron's nerves.

The door swung open; Schwatzendale jerked sidewise into the room, head tilted, hand on his gun. He watched, grimly amused, as Myron carried the staggering girl to the bed, where she sprawled upon her back, staring at the ceiling.

"I came to save your life," said Schwatzendale.

"You are too late," said Myron. "I saved it myself."

The two went to look down at the girl's lax body. She spoke in a half-whisper: "I am frightened! What will happen to me?"

"I think that you are about to die," said Schwatzendale.

The girl's eyes closed. She grimaced, then her face relaxed.

"The upshot of all this is that you owe me ten sols," said Schwatzendale.

Myron nodded, slowly. "It is a debt I cannot evade." He looked to the chest of drawers, then crossed the room and opened the top drawer. From a tray he took the five sols he had given the girl, then took another ten sols from the tray, which he tendered to Schwatzendale. "This will cover the account, so I believe."

"Yes, why not? Money is money."

Myron spread a coverlet over the girl's body, then the two men left the room. They found Wingo sitting placidly at the table, occupied with his third tankard of ale. Schwatzendale asked him, "Are you ready to go?"

"Whenever you say. The ale is not particularly good."

Wingo rose to his feet and the three left the Glad Song Tavern.

On the way back to the ship Myron asked Wingo, "Did you record any of your 'mood impressions' tonight?"

"Of course! There is a distinctive character to the place. I think that I have captured at least an inkling of the atmosphere."

"What of the serving girl? Did you photograph her?"

"Yes, of course! Pretty girls add a numinous quality to any photograph. That is a truism of the trade."

Myron said no more, and the three walked the rest of the way in silence.

SEVEN

1

At dawn the *Glicca* departed from Sholo spaceport. It floated up the face of the scarp and landed beside the warehouse at Mel, to take on cargo; then it lifted again into the upper air. Myron, standing by the pilothouse window, looked down on Sholo Town, at the base of the scarp. He located the irregular roof of the Glad Song Tavern. Beneath that roof lay the body of the girl whose conduct even now seemed unreal. The episode, thought Myron, only went to reaffirm the principle that a pretty face often hides secret purposes.

Myron watched until Sholo Town dwindled and disappeared. The escarpment lay across the steppe like a welt, then became lost in orange-gray murk.

The *Glicca* slanted away into space. Terce became a coarse gray ball. The orange sun receded astern and presently disappeared into the galactic background.

The *Glicca* moved across space toward the world Fiametta, where it would put into two ports of call: first Girandole, then Sweetfleur.

The affairs of the ship resumed their routine. The pilgrims, ever more impatient, soothed themselves with endless games of double-moko, pounding the table with their fists and pulling at their beards when their scumbles went awry, and their gallant rambles-from-hell were ambushed and sent reeling. Schwatzendale watched from the side, and as before offered comments on the play, pointing out errors and praising sound strategies. Finally he allowed himself to be drawn into the game. By trifling increments he began to win—small sums, as if by blunder, or by happy surprise. Then he lost several goodly pots and appeared to become confused. He muttered and cursed his luck. The pilgrims, who were laughing and joking with each other, commiserated with Schwatzendale and once or twice took the trouble to explain the niceties of the game. They analyzed Schwatzendale's errors and pointed out where his tactics could be improved. Still, the general consensus was that Schwatzendale should master the finer points of the game before trying to match himself against the experts. But Schwatzendale was stubborn and insisted that all was well and that he would learn by doing. In this next phase, so he declared with dogged determination, he would play with proper caution so as to avoid the flagrant mistakes of past games.

"Just as you like!" said the pilgrims. "Don't say we haven't warned you! So long as you put your money on the table we will gladly sweep it away!"

Emboldened and jovial, the pilgrims were encouraged to try for large winnings. But now Schwatzendale's luck had returned, as if by magic. He struck lightning-like blows; his scumbles wrought devastation and presently he had won all the pilgrims' cash. The game came to a halt, to the pilgrims' glum dissatisfaction. For want of better occupation, they began to play a game which involved a flourish of the hand, then a display of one or more fingers, with the winner smiting the back of the loser's head with the flat of his hand. Even this game, for all its liveliness, eventually palled, and the pilgrims sat in surly groups, nursing their sore heads and criticizing Wingo's cuisine.

Meanwhile the world Fiametta grew large and bright in the light of the sun Kaneel Verd: the so-called "Green Star." Three moons circled Fiametta, creating dramatic nightscapes and inexhaustible resources for the soothsayers, mystics, priests and seers of the backlands.

The *Glicca* slid through the orbits of the three hurtling moons and drifted down toward Girandole, the first port of call. Horizons receded, revealing a landscape of rolling hills, wide valleys, rivers and marshes, a tumble of mountains and rocky crags. Much of the land was under cultivation; much more appeared to be empty range, marked both by dark forest, and by single trees standing in splendid isolation. Girandole appeared below: a town of moderate size surrounding a central marketplace. Weeping-willow trees shaded bungalows built of dark timber, each with its veranda, second-floor gallery, and high-peaked roof: all built to the terms of a picturesque architecture derived, if tradition could be believed, from the illustrations in an ancient book of fairy tales.

At Girandole the *Glicca* would discharge a cargo of agricultural chemicals, and probably pick up parcels awaiting transshipment, since Girandole functioned as a minor junction port where freight and travelers might transfer from long-range packets to sector shipping. At

Sweetfleur, halfway around the planet, cargoes of fabric, unctuous slabs of green jade, and exquisite blue-green porcelain bowls thrown and fired in the Mulravy Mountains, might be awaiting export.

The *Glicca* landed near the main cargo warehouse, among several other spaceships: a Black Stripe passenger packet, a splendid space-yacht, the *Fontenoy*, from Coiry Beach on the world Alcydon, and the *Herlemar*, another freight carrier, even more scarred and worn than the *Glicca*.

Almost immediately the crew of the *Glicca* discovered that the warehouses and workshops were quiet, by reason of a weeklong festival, during which all workers were on holiday.

Captain Maloof accepted the situation philosophically. The circumstances could not be considered unique, or even unusual; warehousemen and cargo handlers were notoriously capricious. Perhaps a skeleton workforce might be assembled on the morrow. If not, the crew of the *Glicca* would work the cargo themselves: no great hardship. In any case the delay troubled no one except the pilgrims, who instantly set up a clamor. They refused to venture off the ship, purportedly out of fear of thieves who might depredate the costly stuffs they carried in their ornate cases. The real reason was more poignant: Schwatzendale had won all their spare cash at double-moko. Sullenly they watched the four members of the crew leave the ship, then started a new game, using hairs plucked from their beards to serve as wagers.

As the four passed the spaceyacht *Fontenoy*, they were hailed by a handsome middle-aged gentleman, with a voice and manner defining him as a person of high status. He called out, "Hoy there! Hold up a moment!"

The four from the *Glicca* halted and waited while the gentleman jumped down from the *Fontenoy*'s entry port and approached. He was tall, loose-limbed, urbane; both his clothes and his carriage were casual. Locks of gray hair dangled over his forehead; eyebrows arched whimsically high, as if in amused surprise for the paradoxes of human existence.

"Joss Garwig here, master of the *Fontenoy*!" he said heartily.

Captain Maloof introduced his crew: "This is Chief Steward Wingo, then Supercargo Myron Tany, and over here, lost in one of his enigmatic daydreams, is Chief Engineer Fay Schwatzendale. I am Captain Adair Maloof."

"A pleasure to meet you!" declared Garwig. "But let me state from the start that my motives are not altogether selfless. My engine is giving me a problem which I hope your engineer can fix. My own man is baffled and the local mechanics are all on holiday. It is a most tiresome situation."

"Describe the problem," said Maloof. "We will listen, at the very least. I will make no larger commitment."

"Naturally not!" declared Garwig. "The problem is this: at the Ettenheim Spaceyards the mechanics installed a new type nine-mode malleator which was guaranteed to keep the entire anathrodetic mesh in synchrony. But this doesn't happen. When we put down to a landing the ship bounces, bumps and jerks like a crazy thing, and causes no end of anxiety. My engineer is without a clue and, for a fact, I suspect him of incompetence. Conceivably your engineer can advise us how best to abate this nuisance."

Maloof turned to Schwatzendale. "What about it, Fay?"

Schwatzendale tilted his head. "There are three possibilities. Number one: the tremble-rods are out of phase with the new unit. Number two: you have installed an undersized version of the device. Number three: the unit was improperly installed, which is most likely, since technical equipment is usually dependable."

Garwig asked dubiously, "Is this good news or bad?"

Schwatzendale hesitated the tenth part of a second, then said, "I'll have a look at it, though I guarantee nothing."

"All favors gratefully accepted!" cried Garwig heartily. "Come aboard! I'll see to some refreshments. My wife Vermyra concocts an excellent Pink-eye Punch, not to mention an almost infamous Saskadoodle!"

Garwig led the way into *Fontenoy*'s saloon, where he introduced his family. First, his wife Vermyra, a stylish, if somewhat buxom, lady with a beautiful pink and white complexion, large amiable features, and honey-gold hair teased into a cloud of frivolous ringlets. Next came the son Mirl, who was thin and diffident, with none of the affable ease of his father. Finally, in response to Garwig's call, his daughter Tibbet sauntered into the saloon, yawning, stretching, hitching the pajama trousers more snugly up around her rump, and going so far as to scratch the same rump with indolent fingers. She was three or four years younger than Myron, pretty, with a reckless mop of dark hair and a smoulder at the back of her eyes. She looked Schwatzendale over, after which she surveyed Myron. Then, with a rather ambiguous shrug, she turned away and thoughtfully studied her fingernails. In a voice of hushed urgency Vermyra recommended that Tibbet return to her cabin and dress herself properly.

Tibbet carelessly retreated from the saloon, returned a few moments later wearing what were popularly known as "picaroon pants," tight around her hips and upper thighs, flaring loosely, only to be caught in at the ankle: a style which set off her figure to advantage.

Myron decided that, all in all, she was quite attractive, if somewhat stagy. Not his type, at any rate, which was all to the good, in view of her careful disinterest.

Mirl, watching from the side, chuckled. "Don't be offended! Tibbet has just given you what we call the Wilmer treatment."

Vermyra made a fluttery protest. "Come, Mirl! Do not embarrass the gentlemen!"

"It is really no great matter," said Mirl. "We used to own two cats: Wilmer, who was large, proud and handsome; and Tink, who was skinny and furtive. They were served their meals in separate dishes. Wilmer ate with gusto and always finished first. He would glance toward Tink, strut over to Tink's dish, shoulder Tink aside and smell Tink's food. Then he would pretend to cover over the dish as if it contained you-know-what. Then Wilmer would stroll away, leaving Tink to stare down at the food which he had been enjoying but now no longer cared to eat. That is the Wilmer treatment."

"Aha!" said Schwatzendale. "You are telling us that Tibbet has smelled Myron and myself, covered us over, then strolled away."

"In effect—yes."

Myron and Schwatzendale turned to look toward Tibbet, who shrugged and smiled quietly.

Garwig chuckled. "Mirl and Tibbet are actually good friends, though sometimes you might not know it. Vermyra, what are you mixing for us?"

"Saskadoodle! Be patient; it's almost ready."

Myron transferred his attention from Tibbet to the saloon at large. The fittings, in Myron's opinion, were far too lavish and opulent for functional utility. Joss Garwig himself was clearly not an authentic spaceman but, rather, a collector of curios, works of folk art and the like, which, in great profusion, crammed cabinets and cases at the after end of the saloon. It was an eclectic, even indiscriminate collection. Articles of every description crowded each other in mindless confusion. Some of the objects, thought Myron, might well be valuable, but in the aggregate they seemed only part of a clutter. Looking more closely, Myron saw that each piece was identified by a label attesting to provenance, antiquity, and perhaps other information. At the far end of the saloon he discovered an object which halted him in his tracks. On a low stone pedestal stood a man-shaped effigy carved, or otherwise shaped, from a hard stony substance, gray-green in color, with the surface gloss of chert or nephrite, or possibly olivine. The figure stood about five feet tall, with heavy shoulders hunched forward over a thick torso. Long arms, ending in enormous hands, dangled to the knees. The massive head showed the caricature of a face, with features smeared and distorted.

Mirl's voice came from over Myron's shoulder. "It's real. The others may be worse."

"'Others'?"

Mirl pointed to the shadows at the far end of the saloon, where three other effigies, similar to the first, ranged along the wall.

Mirl asked, "What do you make of them?"

Myron reflected. At last he said, "If I owned them, I would give them on the instant to my aunt Hester."

Mirl laughed. "My father considers them marvels of human achievement. But then, that's because he is Director of Acquisitions at the Pan-Arts Museum at Duvray on Alcydon. Now you know why we cruise in such a litter." Mirl glanced here and there. "Most of it is junk." He frowned toward the effigies. "But not these fellows. The museum will think them marvelous! For a fact, they exert a brutal force."

Myron asked in awe, "Where do you find such things?"

"The same place we find everything else! In ancient shrines, junk heaps, old ruins, excavations, private collections, native sources; in short, from anyone willing to sell or to trade. Sometimes we find things that no one seems to own, or so we hope, and we take them! That is known as 'dynamic scholarship.'" Mirl grinned. "It's all in the interest of science, or art, or philosophy, which are all the same to my father. He is convinced that he can walk on water. Who am I to say he can't?"

Garwig, meanwhile, had taken Schwatzendale and Maloof back to the engine room. Twenty minutes passed, during which Vermyra served beakers of Saskadoodle: a pale green liquid, mildly effervescent, with a subtle bite which tingled pleasantly on the palate.

Maloof and Schwatzendale presently reappeared, followed by Garwig. "Success!" cried Garwig with great enthusiasm. "The unit was misaligned! Schwatzendale discovered the problem at a glance and put things right before you could say 'knife.' It was most impressive; he is a mechanical wizard!" Garwig raised his arm in a mock salute, then declared, "If I were a churl and an ingrate, I would instantly hire Schwatzendale away from the *Glicca*."

Schwatzendale gave his head a wincing jerk. "Not likely, unless you offered me the hand of your daughter in marriage, along with a large dowry; also, permission to throw those statues into the sea."

Garwig chuckled. "Tibbet, yes. Dowry, no. The statues you must learn to love. They are profound works of art."

Schwatzendale said politely, "Rather than contradict you, I shall simply stay with the *Glicca*. For a fact, I am not sure what the word 'art' means, if anything."

"The word has a hundred applications," said Wingo. He turned to Garwig: "Fay is a sensitive man! The statues project a baleful force. You would do well to pack them into iron crates and return them to the sculptor."

Garwig laughed again, somewhat less cheerfully. "The museum will accept them with gratitude, since they are truly exceptional pieces! My reputation will not be hurt; I may well be promoted or even granted a knighthood, with a raise in stipend."

"And then?"

"Then we are off again, on a new quest, and who knows what wonderful treasures we will find?"

"You lead an interesting life," said Maloof. "It takes you to places where ordinary folk never venture."

"Quite true," said Garwig. "The work has its challenges, but the compensations are priceless! At the very least, Mirl and Tibbet are receiving a splendid education!"

Tibbet uttered a half-sad, half-sardonic laugh. "I have learned how to make Saskadoodle, Pink-eye Punch, and Wild Dingo Howler, which was invented by a reckless smuggler named Terence Dowling. I have seen sun dances and moon dances, totem worship, snake races, and at least a dozen fertility rites. They would be more fun if I were allowed to participate, but whenever I show interest, someone always hustles me away."

Vermyra clicked her tongue. "My dear, if you please! Your jokes are truly not in the best taste! They may offend our guests!"

"Not likely," said Tibbet. "Mr. Schwatzendale is thinking secret thoughts. Mr. Wingo has not been listening."

Wingo, indeed, had been inspecting the effigies with critical attention. After a moment he spoke to Garwig. "There is more here than meets the eye."

"Oh? Really?"

"I think so. The craftsmanship is unusual: grotesque, savage, yet adept! I doubt if they were created to express aesthetic joy."

"Probably not. They are 'ghost-chasers,' or so I have been told."

Tibbet had become bored with the effigies. In a languid voice she said, "I make them to be simple garden ornaments—a bit too quaint for my taste."

"'Quaint'?" cried Myron, in shock. "They are absolute horrors! Who would want such squalid things in their gardens? And why?"

"Don't be dense," snapped Tibbet. "The people who owned the

gardens wanted them! That's why they put them there! For what purpose? To chase ghosts!"

"Personally, I'd prefer the ghosts," said Myron.

Garwig smiled indulgently. "You look at them with a layman's eye! The cognoscenti will see them differently!"

Captain Maloof asked Garwig, "How did you come by them?"

"A matter of luck," said Garwig complacently. "Are you aware of the Moabite Cloudlands? No? About a hundred miles east of here the land thrusts up into a region of rocky crags and high meadows. The scenery is wild: pinnacles reach up to catch the lightning; wind screams through gorges; mists swirl through the forests and blow out over the meadows. It is a dreary landscape, but at one time it was mined for jade by the Chan uplanders, or Overmen, as they called themselves—a strange reclusive folk, by all accounts. A few of these Overmen still occupy the old manor houses, living on their investments. They welcome no visitors, tourists, curio collectors, or anyone else. The locals suspect them of black magic and give them a wide berth. There you have the Moabite Cloudlands. On the plain below, just under the first jut of the Cloudlands, is an old market town, Zemerle, at one time the outlet for mountain jade. We put down at Zemerle, hoping to discover a piece or two of old jade, but we found nothing. Then one of the merchants approached us with a scheme. After a great deal of furtive hemming and hawing, he showed us a photograph, of what he called a 'ghost-chaser' from an abandoned Chan manor house. He said it was carved from prime jade, and possibly might be had, if I were willing to pay the price. I asked for particulars; he explained that when the Chan Overmen worked the jade mines, they used indentured Tril laborers from the Farsetta marshes. The Tril died by the thousands, leaving their ghosts to wander the fogs of the upland meadows. The Chan put out ghost-chasers to frighten the ghosts back into the forests. Today many of the manor houses are abandoned and moulder away at the back of dim old gardens. Ghost-chasers still stand on guard, allowing no incursion of ghosts." Garwig looked fondly over his shoulder toward the effigies. "The shopkeeper warned me that to obtain a ghost-chaser was no casual affair, but that he knew a pair of reckless young bravos who might attempt the job. The total fee would be a thousand sols.

"I cried out in shock! The price was far too high, but he would not yield by so much as a dinket. The risks, so he insisted, were real. The Overmen were savants of the transfinite mysteries, and that if I wanted a ghost-chaser on the cheap I must procure it myself.

"After some fruitless haggling, I left the shop. In the end, weighing all with all, I decided that the merchant had exaggerated the difficulties. Many of the old manors were abandoned; why should the Chan fret over the loss of a ghost-chaser or two?

"To make a long story short, I took the *Fontenoy* aloft and drifted high over the Cloudlands. For several days we scouted the terrain, peering through the mists and fog. After careful investigation, we selected an ancient manor which was definitely abandoned. At dusk we dropped down in our flitter and loaded aboard four ghost-chasers. All went well. The moons, rolling in and out of the mists, provided sufficient light; even so, the old gardens were melancholy and heavy with memories of the past. We became uneasy and were happy to return aloft to the *Fontenoy*.

"We proceeded directly to Girandole in order to repair our malleator, and that is the story in its essential form." Garwig again looked over his shoulder toward the ghost-chasers. "If the truth be told, I am tempted to return to the Cloudlands for a second consignment."

Vermyra called out sharply: "Put the idea from your mind! Tomorrow we go to Sweetfleur for the Grand Lalapalooza Fair! That is our definite plan!"

Garwig looked at his wife with smiling indulgence. "Did you say 'Lalapalooza'?"

"I did, because that is the tradition which is ever so old."

Garwig made a gracious gesture. "So it shall be! To the Grand Lalapalooza we shall go, without let, stay, hitch, qualm, or quandary!"

"I am happy to hear you say so!" Vermyra turned to Wingo. "From what we've been told, the Fair is ever so jolly, with parades, exhibits, amusement booths, pageants of folk-dancing: all highly picturesque, though it seems that some of the pantomimes can be a bit boisterous."

Garwig gave a fruity chuckle. "Or—let us say—a bit close to the knuckle. Still, all in good fun! It won't deter Mirl, Tibbet even less."

Vermyra started to protest, but Garwig held up his hand. "Now then, my dear, we can't isolate the youngsters from the real world! We must rely upon the example we set to guide them, steadfast and true, along their way! Am I correct, Captain?"

Maloof glanced toward Tibbet, who was smiling a prim smile. "Absolutely!"

Vermyra had picked up a sheet of paper. "Listen to this! Here is more about the Grand Lalapalooza. There will be acrobats, and stilt-dancing on fifteen-foot stilts, and mock stilt-battles! There is a troupe of comics under the direction of a certain Moncrief the Mage."

Schwatzendale jerked about. "Not Moncrief the Mouse-rider?"

Vermyra studied the descriptive passages. "I see no mention of mouse-riding. Still, it all sounds like great fun, and tomorrow we will be off to the Fair."

"Tomorrow we will discharge cargo and join you at Sweetfleur," said Maloof. "Now we must go." He bowed toward Vermyra and Tibbet, then turned toward the entry port.

Garwig cleared his throat portentously. "We truly appreciate your help with the malleator," he told Schwatzendale. Stepping forward, he tucked five sols into Schwatzendale's pocket. "With my thanks."

For an instant Schwatzendale stood quivering, as if at the receipt of an electrical shock. Then, slanting his eyes toward the ceiling and twisting his mouth sideways, he plucked the money from his pocket and dropped it upon the counter. Three long bent-kneed strides took him to the entry port. He jumped to the ground and was gone.

Garwig spoke in an aggrieved voice: "What an extraordinary fellow! If he had wanted more, he should have let me know! I'm not mean, but I can't read his mind."

Captain Maloof chuckled. "You don't quite understand. Fay is the scion of an extremely high-caste family; it is below his dignity to take money from a commoner or any sort of social inferior."

Garwig's jaw slackened. He looked ruefully down at the money. "Ah, then: he puts me in an awkward position. I am hardly a commoner, but I suppose—"

"No matter," said Maloof. "Fay has already forgotten the incident. I advise that when you see him again, you attempt no familiarity, nor explanations which might bore him."

"No, of course not," Garwig muttered.

The three from the *Glicca* departed the *Fontenoy*. Schwatzendale awaited them and the group continued across the field.

2

The time was early evening. Kaneel Verd had set; clouds in the western sky glowed pomegranate crimson and pale green, along with shadings of blue and lavender.

The spacemen strolled up an avenue toward the center of town, while sunset colors deepened into the violet of dusk. At the edge of town they came upon the Green Star Inn: a long low structure of dark wood at the back of an open-air pavilion. Tall black deodars, weeping willows, and indigenous kardoons surrounded the area. Flamboys fixed to high branches gave off plumes of colored light. A number of tables spaced around the edge of the pavilion were occupied by townspeople:

family groups, young lovers, a few elderly folk out for an evening's entertainment. The four spacemen stepped up into the covered area and seated themselves at a table beside the balustrade. They were approached by a round-faced serving boy wearing a fine green- and black-striped shirt, a white apron, and a tall loose-crowned white cap with the name "Flodis" embroidered along the front band. He announced the dishes available for service: a soup of tubers, leeks, and plantains; a confiture of reedfowl; fried loup-fish with sea fruit; a roast of cavies in special sauce, along with bread and side dishes. If they were inclined only to drink, he was prepared to supply deep-cellar ale, new toddy, arrack, dark or light rum, and several varieties of wine. The group opted for tankards of ale, to be followed by soup, then reedfowl with swamp rice and fried leeks.

The four drank ale, while two moons drifted across the zenith and a third moon rose in the east. Myron watched the moons in surprise; their surfaces seemed to swim with a pale green luster. An illusion? Or might the ingestion of strong ale have contributed to the effect?

Flodis served the soup in deep earthenware bowls, and Myron's attention was distracted. The soup was followed by roasted reedfowl on beds of brown rice seasoned with pods of local pepper.

The tables around the pavilion and within the covered area became occupied, by folk of many sorts and many classes. From one of the passenger packets at the terminal came a noisy group of tourists, who sat marveling at the three moons and drinking both ale and the new toddy. Nearby sat a farming family who dined on soup and bread, while covertly watching the tourists. Four young bravos of the town also seemed interested in the tourists and exchanged badinage from a table nearby. Flodis the serving boy watched them sourly. "They'll make trouble before the evening is over," he told Myron. "They hope to attract the tourist girls, and one way or another there is always a wrangle. It's up to me to sort things out, which like as not earns me a sound thumping. Am I paid a bonus for such work? As you can guess, the answer is, in every respect and in all degrees: no!" Flodis gave his head a glum shake and went off about his duties.

Next to arrive was a group of spacemen from the freighter *Herlemar*, who ranged themselves along the bar. A moment later Joss Garwig and his family appeared. Noticing the four from the *Glicca*, they approached and seated themselves at the adjacent table. Garwig eyed Schwatzendale warily, then said in his most affable voice: "So—here we are again!" He looked around the chamber. "A picturesque place, if a bit—shall we say?—raggle-taggle?"

"Perhaps so," said Maloof. "Nevertheless, the ale is quite good."

Flodis the serving boy approached, took orders and departed. Vermyra pointed and called out in happy anticipation. "I do believe that we are about to have music! Perhaps there will be dancing, as well! Tibbet, this is your enthusiasm! Aren't you excited?"

"Profoundly," said Tibbet.

From the back of the room came six small men, swarthy and sharp-featured, moving at a crouching, half-furtive run. They climbed upon the bandstand and arranged themselves in a semicircle. After them came a group of small boys: pallid, thin-featured urchins, with ragged mops of dark hair, arms and legs like sticks. They gathered at the base of the bandstand, and began to peer around the room, pointing and whispering sly comments.

Tibbet muttered, "What is going on? I understand none of this! They carry no instruments! The boys are like avid little rats!"

Joss Garwig uttered a mild reproof: "Hush, my dear! You must learn forbearance! Artistic excellence is never obvious, especially to a stranger! We must listen before we judge; these odd little men may be virtuosos of the first water. We must wait and try to understand!"

"I'm sure that you are right," said Tibbet. "I won't listen until you tell me whether or not they are talented; it will save me mental energy."

"Hush, Tibbet!" snapped Joss Garwig. "You fail to enhance your charm!"

"Everybody quiet!" cried Vermyra. "They are about to play."

The men on the bandstand brought out long pipes, and without preliminary remarks puffed out their cheeks and blew, producing a shrill squealing uproar punctuated by warbles and squeaks. The boys at the base of the bandstand put fingers to their mouths and, with eyes popping from their heads, set up a blast of ear-shattering whistles.

Joss Garwig cried in outrage, though he could not be heard: "What in the name of everything awful is going on? This is not music, not even of the avant-garde sort!"

Two of the boys took up trays and danced around the room, thrusting the trays under the faces of the inn's patrons. Their dance was a prancing hip-jiggling strut, which they accompanied with curious belching sounds to mark out the rhythm of their steps. As they moved coins were grudgingly dropped into the trays.

Myron yelled up at Flodis, who stood beside the table with a bland expression. "What is going on?"

Flodis leaned over and called into Myron's ear. "They are clowns from River-Isle. They perform free, so we allow them to stage their acts on the premises. It is a good arrangement; we pay nothing for the entertainment, which is being offered free of charge, though, as you see, they solicit gratuities with zeal. As soon as the take reaches ten sols, they will instantly stop the entertainment."

The dancing boys came to Joss Garwig. With an angry expression he made as if to elbow aside the tray, but Flodis lunged out to restrain him, and shouted into Garwig's ear: "Do not be hasty! The whole group will come to dance and entertain at your table!"

Emotions twisted Garwig's face, but at last he dropped a few coins into the tray. Then he watched, half-furious, half-amused, as the four from the *Glicca* gave over a few dinkets and the boys moved on. In due course they finished their circuit of the room and returned to the bandstand, where they turned out the trays. The noise halted abruptly, while musicians carefully counted the take. It seemed adequate; at once they slid down from the bandstand and ran at a hunching lope from the premises.

Joss Garwig called to Captain Maloof: "Never before have I so deeply appreciated the solace of quiet. The cessation of sound is a joy in itself!"

"It is a soothing anodyne," said Maloof.

"A pity that the substance cannot be bottled and sold on the market, as a general elixir," mused Wingo.

"The need has already been met," Schwatzendale told him. "It is known as tincture of blue cyanide."

Wingo smilingly demurred. "That sort of elixir is too extreme. The effect is irreversible."

"Wingo is correct," said Maloof, and, after some analysis, Schwatzendale conceded the point.

At the next table Vermyra was pulling at Joss Garwig's arm. "This place is not particularly interesting, and those young men yonder are ogling Tibbet in a most vulgar manner! I am quite ready to leave."

Joss Garwig looked from face to face around his table: from Tibbet to Vermyra to Mirl. "What of it, then? Shall we depart?"

Vermyra said, "Don't forget, we have a big day tomorrow and the hour is growing late."

Tibbet twisted her mouth into a wry pout, and appraised the young men whose attentions had annoyed her mother. They were not particularly attractive, and two of them wore rather ludicrous mustaches. She asked Flodis, "Are there to be more entertainments?"

"Not in the next few minutes. The string-twisters will be here presently, or so I believe."

"Are they noisy?" Garwig asked.

"Yes, to a certain degree."

"Then we will not wait." Garwig turned to the four from the *Glicca*. "I expect that we shall meet at Sweetfleur, but for now, good night and good luck."

Garwig and his family departed the Green Star Inn. Maloof asked his crew: "Shall we try another round of this quite passable ale?"

"I am willing," said Schwatzendale. "If the string-twisters are boring, we can always leave."

Wingo and Myron were of similar opinion; Maloof, therefore, signaled Flodis, who brought four fresh tankards.

After half an hour the string-twisters had not yet appeared, and Flodis admitted that they probably had been detained at the Lucanthus Tavern or, even more likely, had gone home to their beds.

Flodis's voice dwindled away and broke off in mid-sentence. His attention had been caught by the arrival of two elderly gentlemen wearing long black cloaks and low-crowned black hats. For a moment the two stood in the entrance, looking about the pavilion. Myron wondered at the disquiet the two had aroused in Flodis; could they be penal officers of the town come to apprehend Flodis for a misdeed? Probably not. More likely they were officials from an outlying township. Both were of middle stature, thin and erect, as if by some ascetic discipline, with pinched pale faces, round black eyes, pointed chins.

The two moved to a side table, settled themselves, and became still. Unnaturally still, thought Myron. He beckoned to Flodis, who reluctantly approached. "The two men yonder," Myron pointed. "Are they the string-twisters?"

Flodis licked his lips. He blurted, "Ignore them, at all costs! They are Chan Overmen, down from the hills! They bring bad luck to someone."

Myron looked at Maloof. "Did you hear?"

"I heard."

Myron covertly studied the Chan Overmen. Except for their peculiar stillness, there was little about them to account for Flodis's uneasiness.

Myron told Flodis: "I see only a pair of polite old gentlemen who are sitting quietly. Why are you so timid?"

Flodis gave a husky laugh. "They are shrikes of the deepest dye! They consort with ghosts and know what human men should never know. Don't so much as look at them! They will send poulders to sit on your neck of nights."

Maloof asked, "Do they often come to the Green Star Inn?"

"Not often—but even once is too many." Flodis drew a deep

breath. "Now I must go to serve them. For any trivial mistake they will look at me and take down my name."

"No need for despair," Myron told him. "They are leaving."

Flodis was not reassured. "I failed to serve them promptly! They took notice and left in a fury! I will suffer; you will see!"

"Possibly so," said Maloof. "But I suspect that they came to watch the string-twisters, and now are on their way to Lucanthus Tavern."

Flodis nodded dubiously. "You may be right. If so, I am much relieved."

Flodis went off about his duties. A moment passed. Maloof rose to his feet. "I have had enough ale, and I think that now I shall return to the ship. Also, I am curious as to how affairs are going aboard the *Fontenoy*."

"A good idea," said Wingo. "Let us all return to the ship."

The four spacemen departed the Green Star Inn and set off toward the terminal, moving like shadows under the tall trees. They arrived at the terminal and went out upon the field. One moon floated at the zenith. Another hung halfway down the sky, while the third sat with its lower limb on the western horizon. Myron still thought to discern a faint crust of green luster on the otherwise pale faces of the moons. The field stretched stark and empty to its far limits. A night-light glowed in the main saloon of the *Fontenoy*; elsewhere, darkness and silence. The four continued across the field to the *Glicca*, and retired to their cabins.

At some unknown hour of the night Myron awoke. Through the porthole he saw that the last of the moons had reached the horizon. He lay listening. A sound had awakened him, but now the night was quiet. Once more he tried to sleep.

Time passed: several minutes, perhaps longer. A soft hooting sound came to Myron's ears. His eyes snapped open. After a moment he slipped from his bunk and went to the porthole. In the starlight he recognized the shape of the *Fontenoy*. To the side, half-concealed by the hull, was another smaller shape, an unnatural presence which he could not identify. He ran from his cabin to the saloon. Maloof stood by the window, looking out over the field. He told Myron: "Something is happening at the *Fontenoy*. Get dressed; bring your gun."

Myron ran back to his cabin. As he dressed, he heard Maloof instructing Schwatzendale.

Myron returned to the saloon. Maloof asked, "You are carrying your gun?"

"Yes sir."

"Come along then."

3

Tibbet awoke, blinking and confused. The echo of a sound still rang in her ears. It had been a strange, soft call, like nothing she had heard before. She lay rigid, listening, then slid from her bunk and went to the porthole, where she stared in perplexity at the object just beside the *Fontenoy*. It seemed a large, if rather ungainly, flitter. She thrust her feet into slippers, donned a dark blue robe, went to the door. Here she hesitated, then summoning all her courage, opened the door and stepped out into the corridor. From the saloon came the stir of movement. She heard her father's voice raised in angry challenge, then silence. Step by step Tibbet moved along the corridor. At last she looked into the saloon. This was nightmare, pure and simple, and could not be believed! Two squat figures were dragging the limp body of her father toward the entry port.

Tibbet opened her mouth to scream, but produced only a gurgle. Now something seized her from behind with bone-cracking power. Wrenching her head about, she looked over her shoulder into the face of a ghost-chaser, a mere six inches from her own face. The creature's touch was marmoreal; its features were even more horrid than she remembered. She wanted to scream, but, as before, could manage no more than a sick gurgle. As she stared into the face, the loose-lipped mouth quivered. The ghost-chaser was about to suck her breath, or do something else even more horrifying. Tibbet's flesh crawled.

Without conscious plan, Tibbett wriggled free and lunged toward the entry port. She fell through the opening to the ground below, rolled over and over, and struggled to her knees. A Chan bent to seize her; she kicked at him and scurried away on hands and knees; then, picking herself up, ran off into the night.

Maloof and Myron crossed the field at a crouching lope, swinging to the side in order to gain the shadow at the stern of the *Fontenoy*. They became aware of an odd whimpering sound, which grew louder as they approached. With startling suddenness a human figure lurched from the darkness. Starlight shone into a pale contorted face under a wild tangle of dark hair. Maloof stepped forward; Tibbet saw him and gave a croak of terror. Maloof called out, "Tibbet, it is Captain Maloof and Myron! Don't be frightened!" But Tibbet had sagged to the ground in sheer despair. Maloof picked her up and stroked her hair. "Tibbet! You are safe! No one will hurt you!" Tibbet gulped and made shuddering sounds in her throat. "The ghost-chaser; it took me—"

"Tibbet, listen carefully! The others need help; we can't take care of you right now. Do you hear me?"

In a muffled voice Tibbet said, "I hear you."

"Do you see the *Glicca* yonder?"

"Yes, I see it."

"Run to the *Glicca*, go aboard and wait until we come."

Tibbet said peevishly, "I want to wait here."

There was no time to argue. Maloof said, "As you like! Don't move from this spot."

Tibbet's attention had shifted; she cried out in a poignant contralto: "Look! What are they doing to my father?" She started back toward the *Fontenoy*, but Myron stood in her way and halted her. "Stay here! You can't help us!"

Tibbet stared at him numbly. Myron ran off after Maloof, toward the shadows at the stern of the *Fontenoy*. Behind him he sensed that Tibbet was following, but he could no longer control her movements.

There was activity at the *Fontenoy*'s entry port. Joss Garwig was thrust down the gangplank. He tumbled into a limp heap. Down the gangplank behind him stumped a squat shape. It lowered its long arms, seized Garwig's leg and started to drag him toward the flitter. Next came Mirl, who was also tumbled down the steps and dragged away. Finally, Vermyra was thrust out the port, to sprawl gracelessly down the steps. Two other ghost-chasers, slow and ponderous, came next, followed by the second Chan. Once upon the ground the Chan strode out upon the field, then halted, apparently in search of Tibbet; but in the shadows at the stern of the *Fontenoy*, Maloof, Myron, and Tibbet were inconspicuous.

Maloof whispered instructions into Myron's ear. Tibbet came tentatively forward, but Maloof gestured her to stand back, behind the aft sponson. Tibbet reluctantly obeyed.

Maloof stepped out into the open. The two Chan Overmen saw him at once and dropped their hands toward the side-pockets of their cloaks.

Maloof raised his gun. "Don't move! You are close to death!"

The Chan became still. Maloof indicated the nearest of the two. "Come forward. Keep your hands high."

The Chan advanced slowly, until Maloof signaled with his gun. "That is far enough. Myron, keep this gentleman under control."

Myron left the shadows and approached, gun at the ready. He halted five yards from the Chan. "I have him in my sights."

Maloof turned his attention to the second Chan, who stood near the flitter. The Chan said, "This is a private affair. Go away, at once."

"It is not so simple," said Maloof. "We are acquainted with these folk, and you are treating them very roughly."

"They are guilty of crimes, and must pay the penalty."

" 'Crimes'?" asked Maloof incredulously. "Misdeeds, perhaps."

"Desecration of our old places is a crime, as are trespass and theft."

"Minor crimes, certainly. What penalty do you propose?"

"It is appropriate. Four statues of jade will presently stand yonder, at the end of the field. Each will hold a sign: 'I stole from the Chan Overmen. I shall steal no more.' "

Maloof spoke evenly: "That is a pretty notion, but it is quite unreasonable."

"Not so, and if you interfere further there will be six statues, rather than four. Your guns mean nothing. Go back to your ship!"

Maloof said, "There is a gunship in the sky above you. Do not move. I am about to secure your weapons."

The Chan showed him a prim smile. "And I am about to secure yours." The smile became a grimace; in each of the Chan's eyes a blue spark appeared. Blue glare flashed into Maloof's brain. His senses roiled and went vague; oblivion closed in upon him. But first! Something needed to be done. Even as he sagged to the ground he tightened his fingers against the gun: a white bolt struck into the Chan's shoulder, spinning him around. He fell prone, to lie twitching with pain.

Maloof found himself on his knees, head hanging low. He managed to look over his shoulder; the second Chan stood rigid, his eyes fixed upon Myron. Maloof croaked: "Don't look at him! Turn your head!"

Too late. The blue glare had already broken into Myron's mind, and the gun hung loosely by his side. From behind Myron came the flurry of motion; a glimpse by starlight of a pale set face as Tibbet ran to the Chan and pulled the hat-brim down over his eyes. The control was gone; Myron staggered forward and struck the Chan with the side of his gun. The Chan fell to the ground, clawing feebly at his hat. Myron bent, and from the Chan's pocket took a small power-gun. Maloof did the same for the other Chan.

The flitter from the *Glicca* landed; Schwatzendale and Wingo came forward. Maloof stood back, while Wingo dealt with the wounded Chan, bandaging the injury and staunching the flow of blood. Tearing a strip from the hem of the Chan's cloak, he contrived a sling, into which he cradled the Chan's arm.

Meanwhile Joss Garwig had pulled himself to his feet. He stood leaning against the flitter while Mirl and Tibbet ministered to Vermyra, who sat huddled upon the bottom step of the gangway, only half-conscious.

Garwig gradually grasped the full extent of what had been done to himself and his family. With glittering eyes he hobbled across the field to where Maloof stood beside the wounded Chan. Garwig managed to speak coherently to Maloof: "You have rescued us! I am grateful! Later I will thank you properly. Now I must call the IPCC; they will know how to deal with these brutes." He turned toward the *Fontenoy*.

"Just a minute!" called Maloof. "Don't be too hasty! Have you thought the matter through?"

Garwig halted and turned to scowl toward Maloof. "Why delay? These creatures were intending to kill us all!"

"That may be true—but don't forget: you committed the first offense."

"What of that? I merely rescued a few abandoned statues from the bog."

"So you say. The Chan will claim that you came furtively to the Cloudlands, that you descended by night and looted a manor house of four statues which you acknowledge to be valuable works of art. You do not come clean to the case. You risk confiscation of the *Fontenoy*, and possibly a term of penal servitude."

Garwig stood uncertainly. "Then what should I do? Much as they deserve it, I can't kill them in cold blood. To be honest, I don't know what to do."

"I will make a suggestion, which you may or may not like."

"Well, then: what is this suggestion?"

"Go aboard the *Fontenoy* with your family. The Chan will load the ghost-chasers aboard their flitter and return to the Cloudlands. No one is happy, but no one is dead."

Garwig blew out his cheeks. "The scheme is untidy but rational. I am not happy, but I will comply with these terms."

Maloof asked the Chan Overmen: "Will you accept these conditions?"

For a moment the Chan looked at him stony-faced; then one of them said, "So it will be. Our plan is now canceled."

Garwig raised his hand in a gesture of resignation. He turned away and limped toward the *Fontenoy*. After three steps he stopped short and seemed to reflect upon a sudden new concept. Slowly he turned about and thoughtfully appraised the Chan. They stared back at him without interest.

"We have put an end to our quarrel," said Garwig. "From the first it was rife with cross-purposes and false assumptions. Am I correct?"

The Chan had nothing to say. Garwig went on. "A new thought has occurred to me. You may find it interesting. I suggest a transaction of mutual benefit. I will buy from you one or two of these so-called 'ghost-chasers,' providing, of course, that the price is right." Garwig peered sidelong toward the Chan. "What do you say to the proposition?"

"No."

Garwig blinked. "Is that all?"

"The idea is without merit."

"As you like," said Garwig. He bowed stiffly, turned, and limped to the *Fontenoy*. With Mirl's assistance, he helped Vermyra up the gangway and into the *Fontenoy*. They were followed by Tibbet.

The Chan prepared to leave. While one loaded the ghost-chasers into the flitter, Maloof engaged the other in conversation. The Chan spoke tersely, but Maloof persisted with his questions until the Chan would say no more. Maloof politely stood back and watched as the flitter lifted from the field and departed into the night.

Garwig had been watching from the entry port. He called down to Maloof, "Come aboard, if you like! It has been a trying evening. All of us will profit from some small refreshment."

"That is a good idea," said Maloof. He heard no objection from his crew and the four marched up the gangway and into the saloon.

4

Mirl brewed a pot of tea which he brought into the saloon along with a platter of nut-cakes. Vermyra gratefully accepted the cup tendered to her by Tibbet. She spoke in a tremulous voice: "Never have I been so terrified! It was like the worst sort of nightmare!"

Wingo tried to soothe her. "Everything is now secure! The adventure is over and you may relax without fear."

" 'Adventure'?" snapped Garwig. "I call it a damnable outrage!"

Mirl said, "Whatever the case, we are lucky to be alive—for which we can thank Tibbet and her fast action."

Vermyra cried out: "Oh Mirl, if you please! I am trying to forget the event!"

"It does no good to bury one's head in the sand," declared Garwig. "We must face up to facts!"

Myron said, "Tibbet is a real heroine. That is an important fact!"

Tibbet flung her arms exultantly into the air. "Hurrah! At last! After all these years I have done something useful! I am an important person! Now, perhaps, Mother will allow me to go out by myself."

Vermyra patted Tibbet's hand. "Please, dear, not so excitable! All in its own good time. At the moment you are still a bit inexperienced."

Tibbet snatched away her hand. "How can I become experienced when you won't let me out of your sight?"

"Tibbet had some important experiences tonight," said Mirl. "That should bring her score up."

Vermyra was not amused. "It is nothing to joke about. Tibbet, surely it is well past your bedtime!"

Tibbet gave a shrug of despair. "It is more like the time that I would be getting up."

Vermyra started to speak, but in the end decided not to order the heroic Tibbet off to bed.

Maloof, however, had put down his cup and was making ready to leave. "Just a minute!" said Garwig. "You spoke to the Chan before they left. Was that a confidential conversation?"

Maloof smiled. "Not at all; I was curious about the ghost-chasers. I asked if they were alive or dead. 'Neither,' I was told—or, if I preferred, both. I asked for more details, and finally I learned that a suitable subject is made unconscious by a hypnotic process. Next, he is impregnated with gums and syrups, which stabilize his condition and alter his metabolism. He is then pickled for two years in a solution that provides him an impervious carapace of nephrite. He is tested, then posted to an area where his services are needed. There he remains, through fog, rain, sleet and wind, perhaps forever."

"How strange that they gave you all this information!" exclaimed Garwig.

Maloof smiled again. "They wanted their handguns back. I wanted information. That was the basis of the transaction."

"Hmmf. What else did they tell you?"

"I asked about the blue flash which caused us diminished consciousness. They explained that small lasers were surgically attached to the optic muscles, so that a laser beam could be directed down the line of sight. The beam was modulated when necessary so as to exert maximum hypnotic potency. When the beam struck the subject's retina, the signal induced hypnotic coma. It is a fractious device, which requires intensive training. Next, I asked if the ghost-chasers effectively repelled ghosts. They said that they had no evidence to the contrary, and there the matter rested. Now we shall bid you goodnight and return to the *Glicca*."

Garwig conducted the four to the entry port. "Good night, and, once again, our thanks to you all. Tomorrow we'll be off to Sweetfleur, which will please Vermyra and Tibbet, and perhaps they will forget the whole ugly affair."

"No doubt we shall meet at Sweetfleur," said Maloof. "Tomorrow morning we work cargo, so that we will arrive at Sweetfleur sometime during the afternoon. Good-bye till then!"

Before leaving the ship, Myron paused beside Tibbet. He said in a low voice, "You are not only brave; you are also extremely pretty."

Tibbet smiled. "It is nice of you to notice." She glanced over her shoulder. "My mother is watching; I can't talk to you now. Tomorrow!"

"Tomorrow, I hope!" Myron descended the gangway and followed Maloof to the *Glicca*.

EIGHT

1

Shortly after noon the *Glicca* rose into the air and flew a thousand miles south, up over the Botanic Mountains and down to the Sweetfleur space terminal. The *Fontenoy* had arrived but showed no sign of activity; the Garwigs already had gone off to explore the town.

As at Girandole, the warehousemen were celebrating their holiday; no cargo would be worked until the morrow. The pilgrims, anxious to arrive at Impy's Landing without delay, urged that the crew should perform the task, but the crew paid no heed and departed the *Glicca* immediately, leaving the pilgrims glowering after them.

With jaunty steps the crew crossed the field. In the transit lobby, they discovered a placard advertising the Grand Lalapalooza, now in progress on Lilibank Field. The placard listed a score of events and exhibitions, including novelty dancing, acrobatic spectaculars, a stilt-walkers' ballet, a beauty pageant to dazzle the senses, races and tournaments, a parade of monsters guaranteed to bring nightmares to the sleep of the most placid child. Elsewhere were displays of prizewinning fruits and vegetables which also graced the menus of nearby restaurants.

A second placard hung alongside the first, its message printed in pale green, scarlet and black:

At the Lalapalooza! An exciting surprise!
Moncrief the mage, his company and their
marvelous presentations!
Witness deeds of glory, enjoy the redoubtable games where wealth
trembles on the twitch of a finger! Play for sport; play for profit! Do not
stand in the dust while the Caravan of Dreams rolls past! Laugh and

joke with Flook, Pook, and Snook!
Enjoy the artistry of
MONCRIEF THE MAGE!

Schwatzendale read the placards with a rapt expression. This could be none other than Moncrief the Mouse-rider, who so callously had defeated him at a game of Cagliostro, mulcting him to the amount of forty-seven sols and sixty dinkets.

Schwatzendale turned away, making no comment. Wingo mused: "I am partial to fairs, and the Lalapalooza sounds as if it might be quite good! Shall we make it an occasion?"

"A sound idea," said Maloof. Neither Myron nor Schwatzendale offered objections and so it was decided.

A public conveyance took the group to Lilibank Field. They paid entrance fees at a wicket and passed through and out upon ten acres of rampant color, noise and festivity. For a time they wandered through an exhibition of prizewinning provender: fruits both familiar and exotic; nuts large and small; pepperballs, truffles, green and blue tubers, smoked fish, sun-dried tripes arranged in tasteful patterns; land leeches, bogberries, pastes and patés; small tubs of so-called devil's "butter," blocks of cheese, and other items even less familiar. Much of the same produce was offered for immediate consumption by vendors serving from cauldrons, grills, and spits. As they worked they chanted the virtues of their wares, at the same time denouncing the cuisine of competitors.

Wandering musicians added to the din. Some wore bizarre costumes; others shuffled and jigged as they croaked woebegone ballads. At intervals old women huddling behind barrows uttered sudden raucous cries, like the calls of jungle parrots, hoping to promote the sale of their goods. These, for the most part, were handicrafts from the Botanic Mountains. Wingo, who doted upon curios, acquired a dozen small treasures, and also captured a number of excellent "mood impressions."

In due course the four came to an area marked off by blue and silver pennons, where the stilt-walkers performed their stately exercises. The four watched an intricate minuet, then a tournament involving four Grand Masters on thirty-foot stilts: two in blue and silver armor, the other two in red and gold. In the end a choir of clarions sounded defeat for the red and gold, and the stilt-walkers adjourned until evening.

The four moved on to the adjacent arena, where a corps of child acrobats formed themselves into living bridges, towers, and double cantilevers. A special squad performed apparently impossible feats on sets of high springboards: bounding, flipping, twisting through high open spaces with nothing below.

After leaving the acrobats, the four came upon a large windowless structure: the Hall of the Three Aeons. Within the hall were darkness and looming masses suggesting the presence of gigantic cromlechs; through the shadows moving shapes simulated a fabulous race a million years gone. In a silence broken only by wisps of eerie sound a troupe enacted "The Rite of Dawn."

The *Glicca*'s crew left the hall in somber silence. They stood in the avenue for a few moments, dazzled by the sunlight, then crossed to a refreshment hut built of wicker and palapa thatch. They were served frozen punch in dark wooden bowls, and gradually the spell cast by "The Rite of Dawn" seeped away.

They set off along an avenue, which first passed a field devoted to the asseveration of spiritual verities, then passed another where the same beliefs were ridiculed and refuted. Special cults: meta-men, paramystics, futurians, vegetarians, yaga-yagas, each convening in a private sector, where each sect celebrated its own style of reality. There was an occasional immolation and at times a boy might be sent climbing up a swaying ladder of snakes, until, with a final startled outcry, he disappeared into the sky, leaving his parents standing below, staring up in perplexity.

The avenue continued past a children's park, then entered a central compound: a place thronged by visitors and bordered by booths, cafés, and pavilions. The four spacemen halted to take stock of the area. Through an opening in the crowd Myron glimpsed the Garwig family standing near the House of Buffoons, apparently debating whether or not to enter the premises. Tibbet stood to the side, half-turned away, taking no part in the conference. She wore a pale tan pullover, snug white pants, and a small white cap controlling most of her dark locks. Myron stared in fascination.

Tibbet felt his gaze. She turned her head, saw him, and smiled. She glanced quickly toward her mother, looked back to Myron, made a secret gesture indicating—what? Myron thought he knew.

The crowds shifted; miscellaneous shoulders and torsos closed the gap; Tibbett could no longer be seen. Myron stood staring at nothing in particular. He glimpsed the Garwigs once again, near the parade yard where the Green Pygmy Dervishes conducted their maneuvers. A moment later they had disappeared.

Wingo, meanwhile, had discovered a large sign designating a rather pretentious pavilion that consisted of a low platform surmounted, in part, by a tall pink and blue tent. A sign read:

MONCRIEF THE MAGE
PURPORTMENTS! EXTUITIONS!
GREAT AND GOOD FORTUNES.
PLAY THE GAMES!

The four approached the pavilion, where several dozen folk stood awaiting the appearance of Moncrief and the next session of his games. The time for this occasion seemed imminent. Three cylindrical blocks had been arranged near the front of the platform. They were three feet wide and two feet high, decorated with glossy white enamel and bands of pink, blue, and gold ormolu. As the spacemen watched, three girls came from the tent and climbed upon the drums, where they stood smiling cheerfully down at the spectators. They were of no great age, slender, clear-eyed, beautiful as angels. Honey-colored hair hung past their ears; they wore knee-length white frocks and white sandals without ornament. Each stood with feet slightly apart, grasping the shaft of a tall flamboy, with yellow flames dancing two feet over their heads; they might have been children playing at the rituals of an ancient mystery. Even more wonderful, the girls were exactly alike.

A pair of hard-faced women, also much alike, came to stand in the shadows at the back of the platform. They were tall, built like bulls, with massive shoulders, short necks, hair like handfuls of wet hay. An impressive pair, thought Myron, though lacking physical appeal. Their hips, thick and deep, clamped tough muscular buttocks. Their breasts were stark leathery rinds.

Yet another personage appeared from the tent: a plump man of medium stature, wearing garments of subdued elegance. Moncrief? Myron had envisioned someone more severe; Moncrief—if this were he—seemed a kindly avuncular sort, perhaps a bit absentminded. A tuft of gray hair grew up from his scalp; below was a pale forehead, a long lumpy nose, a pair of dog-brown eyes that seemed to plead for faith and trust.

Moncrief looked out over the spectators. If he recognized Schwatzendale, he gave no signal of the fact.

Schwatzendale muttered to Maloof, "He has swindled so many folk that now he can't tell one from the other."

Moncrief stepped forward. "Ladies and gentlemen, I am Marcel Moncrief; I call myself a purveyor of magic and mysteries, but most of that stems from a time twenty years gone when my eyes were keen and my nerves were strong." Moncrief chuckled. "That is the way of the world! My friends, accept this wisdom from me! Remember: I am not a stranger! I have long enjoyed my visits to Fiametta and to Sweetfleur in particular." Moncrief raised his eyes to the sky and showed a sweet smile, as if he were caught up in halcyon reminiscences. With a regretful shake of the head he brought himself back to the present. "Alas! I and others like myself are cursed with wanderer's itch; we must travel, up hill and down dale, always yearning after an unattainable dream! Hence our unworldly generosity! Who cares whether the game is won or lost? Our concern is only that folk depart with happy memories! So then—come play the game! It costs so very little, and you alone specify how much you wish to win!"

Moncrief looked around the spectators. "You are impatient; you are anxious to play the game! Very well then! Allow me to introduce my company. On the drums stand the beautiful Flook, Pook, and Snook: each a vision of delight, each as pure as the driven snow. At the back of the platform are Siglaf and Hunzel: both sturdy Klutes from the Bleary Hills of Numoy, a most extraordinary world. They are simple farm girls; each in her own way is timid and demure. Nevertheless, they are anxious to earn their dowries, so that they may return to their loved ones and the home of their dreams. Later in the day, they will take part in an exciting competition which can also enrich those who participate. In this connection, notice the tank yonder, beside the pavilion. I have spoken enough! It is time for activity, to quicken the blood and jingle the wallets! Let us play one of our jolly games, which can win you as much wealth as you care to specify! You do not believe me? Play the game and be convinced! At this moment turn your attention to these three maidens, each as fresh as the morning dew! Notice that each wears a ring. Further, each ring is distinguished by a small but excellent gem: for Flook, a ruby; for Pook, an emerald; for Snook, a fine royal blue sapphire. Examine the girls carefully! Study their peculiarities; analyze their habits! For instance, when Pook smiles, you can often see the glint of her right upper canine tooth. Flook parts her hair on the left; Pook and Snook have not yet adopted this style, and so it goes! Now then, at this time—"

"Hold hard!" A birdlike old man with lank gray hair, red-rimmed eyes, and an unkempt nose mustache thrust himself to the front, where he now cocked his head from one side to the other, staring and peering.

Moncrief said with gentle insistence: "If you have concluded your study, it is now time for us to proceed."

"Not so fast! My investigations are not complete! I want to study Flook at greater length!"

Moncrief made a gracious gesture. "By all means! I ask only that you neither loiter nor lallygag, since we do not wish to delay the game."

The old man moved close to the edge of the platform and leaned forward. "Hah! Harrumph!"

Almost at once Flook set up a complaint. "He is acting strangely! It is most unusual! He is breathing on my knee! It tickles!"

"We must be patient with our senior customers," Moncrief told her. "Perhaps his eyesight is faulty."

"Not so! His eyes are sharp! He is counting the hairs on my leg!"

Moncrief frowned down upon the old man. "What, sir, are your intentions?"

"Quiet; do not distract me or I shall lose my count!"

Moncrief pulled at his chin. Then he said, "Our rules specify that you may approach the platform no closer than three feet! You are in violation of this rule, and you must desist!"

"La la! I was not born yesterday! Show me this rule!"

"The document is lost, but the rule remains. May I ask how much you intend to wager?"

"Nothing. I am practicing."

Moncrief threw his arms in the air. "Stand back! Go away! Practice on your grandmother!"

Shaking his fist and expostulating, the old man staggered off down the avenue. Moncrief drew a deep sigh and smiled affably at the company. "I take it that everyone is ready for the game? One moment, then." He stepped behind the girls, collected their flamboys and placed them into sockets at the side of the stage. "Now then, all is in order! Girls, girls, on the alert! One, two, and hey presto; off we go!"

Flook, Pook, and Snook turned their rings so as to conceal the stones, then jumped down from the drums, to clasp hands and whirl around in a circle, tossing their heads low, then high, like a trio of young maenads. They broke apart, turned, twisted, swung around each other, mingling in a confusion of lithe young bodies, then once again broke apart, and marched to form a line at the front of the platform, where they stood grinning in triumph. Which was Flook? Which was Pook? Which was Snook?

Moncrief stepped forward. He spoke dolefully, "Today I feel the pressure of bad luck; but I am driven by Destiny and cannot turn back. So who will wager ten sols on what amounts to giveaway money? You need only point out Flook, or Pook, or Snook with accuracy; what could be easier? Come then, lay down your wager. I suggest ten sols, or more if you are so disposed."

Wingo muttered to Maloof: "At the far right stands Pook! Is this your opinion as well?"

Maloof shrugged. "I was not watching. I have no opinion."

Schwatzendale told Wingo, "If you are sure, bet!"

Wingo hesitated, but, before he could move, a gentleman stepped forward and laid five sols on the platform in front of the girl in the center. "This is Pook! Pay me my money!"

The girl in the center displayed a ruby. "I am Flook."

"Ha ha!" cried Moncrief, scooping up the five sols. "I fear, sir, that you were inattentive. To win, you must watch carefully!"

The girls climbed back upon the drums. Wingo proudly told Maloof: "I was right! The girl I named as Pook now stands on the middle drum."

"That is good work!" said Maloof. 'You have a keen eye."

"True. My training as an art photographer is responsible."

Moncrief called for another game. "Hey, presto! Down and about! Let the patterns of Destiny play themselves out!"

The girls performed their evolutions as before: twisting and winding through a confusion of arms, legs, agile torsos, finally to array themselves in a line, where they stood panting and grinning.

Moncrief called: "Now then! Which of you will place his modest ten-sol wager?"

Wingo bravely marched forward. "I hereby bet one sol upon the identity of this person!" He carefully placed the money upon the platform. Moncrief peered down at the coin. "What is this? Your allowance for the week?"

"Not at all! Under the circumstances, it is all I care to risk."

Moncrief gave a sigh of resignation. "Ah well, just as you like! Name the girl whom you have identified."

Wingo tapped one of the girls on the knee. "I declare this person to be Pook!" He took her hand and looked at the emerald of her ring. "I am correct."

"So it seems," grumbled Moncrief. He paid Wingo a sol. "You should have gambled with more audacity."

"Possibly so."

"Well, no matter; we are wasting valuable time. Girls, back up on your drums, where you perch so prettily!"

A new game proceeded. Wingo decided to enrich himself at Moncrief's expense and bet five sols. On this occasion the girl he identified as "Pook" showed a sapphire ring and declared herself to be "Snook." Wingo looked on glumly as his money was taken up.

Moncrief set a new game into motion. After the usual evolutions the girls formed a line and Moncrief called out for wagers.

Myron turned suddenly to Schwatzendale. "I have broken the code! The girl on the right is Pook!"

"Oh? How so?"

"She is grinning and I can see the glint of her right upper canine tooth!"

"Bah!" said Schwatzendale. "All are grinning and all are showing their teeth. That is not the answer!"

Myron scowled. "Well then, what of you? Can you pick out one from the other?"

Schwatzendale glanced at the girls. "I should think so."

"Then why do you not play the game?"

Schwatzendale made an airy gesture. "Perhaps I will, in due course. Look yonder, over by the Green Dervishes: surely it is Joss Garwig and his family, including Tibbett, whom you seem to fancy."

Myron shrugged. "To a certain extent."

The Garwigs turned away from the jumping dervishes and their heavy-voiced songs. They noticed the group from the *Glicca* and crossed the compound to Moncrief's pavilion. There was an interchange of greetings; then, in response to Vermyra's question, Wingo explained the nature of Moncrief's game. Vermyra was fascinated. She turned to Garwig. "The girls are exactly alike; I can't tell them apart! What of you?"

Garwig laughed confidently. "I'm sure I could find a clue if I chose to do so." He addressed Maloof: "Have you had a go yet?"

"Not I. The odds are too long."

"Sensible man! I hope that you are enjoying the fair?"

"Yes; it's clean and orderly, and the only evidence of venality seems to be Moncrief."

Garwig inclined his head, pleased that Maloof had validated his own views.

Vermyra cried out enthusiastically: "The floral displays are exquisite, and I very much enjoyed those clever little dervishes; they are truly quaint!"

Garwig said: "I was even more impressed with the stilt-dancers. I have never before seen such skill! They stride around on twelve-foot stilts, jumping, hopping, dancing, pirouetting on a single stilt! Their costumes are flamboyant: red and gold and purple, with long skirts and pantaloons draping far down their stilts, as if they were princes of Bjorkland! They danced the most complicated steps—polkas, saltarellos, and the like, with precision and utter grace. Sometimes they are led by a pair of Grand Masters on thirty-foot stilts; we watched them dancing the Formby Rounds."

"It was really a splendid sight!" declared Vermyra.

Garwig said: "All in all, the festival has maintained commendable standards."

"Except for that tawdry 'Tunnel of Love,'" said Vermyra with a sniff. "I'm sure it's not at all nice, with all sorts of tasteless things going on."

"So it could be," said Garwig with a laugh. "Maybe we should send Mirl to investigate."

"Hmmf!" sniffed Vermyra. "Mirl has too much self-respect for a visit to such a place."

"Send me instead!" said Tibbett. "I have no self-respect whatever."

"Hush!" snapped Vermyra. "You should not talk like that, even in fun! One day someone whom you revere will hear you, and you will have lost your most precious possession."

"My what?"

"By that, I mean your reputation!"

"I will give the matter some thought," said Tibbet.

2

Moncrief requested that the girls do their routine once again. A gentleman placed a small wager upon the identity of Flook. The ruby in her ring proved him correct.

Moncrief cried out in woe. "Luck is against me! I shall be a pauper if I play this game for long! Girls, let us continue! With full energy!"

Sportsman after sportsman marched up to the platform to lay down his money and identify one or another of the girls. Sometimes the contestants won; more often they were proved incorrect by the flash of Flook's ruby, or Pook's emerald, or Snook's sapphire. Some accepted defeat with resignation; others deplored their bad luck, and glowered toward Moncrief, who remained equable. At times he tried to console the victim, stating his belief that their bad luck could not last forever and that they were welcome to try the game again. One such contestant, a civic official named Eban Doskoy, had lost the game three times in a row, but each loss seemed only to intensify his will to win. Doskoy, a short sturdy man of middle years, with a square pugnacious face framed in short russet curls, could not accept defeat easily. Three times he had laid down a wager of five sols and had identified Snook, only to be confronted with Flook's ruby, then Pook's emerald, then once again the ruby. After the third loss, he slowly raised his head and fixed his steel blue eyes upon Moncrief. "There is something peculiar going on," said Doskoy. "It eludes my intellectual grasp."

Moncrief said politely, "My dear sir, all is open and aboveboard, as you can see for yourself!"

"So it appears. But—if only to speculate—suppose that you were able to augment your winnings by means of some mechanical device?"

Moncrief laughed. "I would be pleased to discover such a device—though, naturally, I would never use it to the detriment of my clients."

"Well said! Still, I have noticed that when the wager is small, you occasionally lose, but seldom otherwise."

Moncrief's smile became fixed. "Coincidence only. I am here; the girls are there; you are where you now stand. We occupy the corners of a triangle, without intervening connection. Your suspicions are illusory."

"But, what if you were able to circumvent such an arrangement by the use of a magnetic ray?"

"Then I would be a wealthy man. Since I am not wealthy, either your ray is imaginary, or I am honest. That is a syllogism, in its purest form."

"Very well," said Doskoy through a tight-lipped grimace. "Let us try another game, using proper precautions."

"As you like," said Moncrief with dignity.

Doskoy turned his back on Moncrief. He inserted money into an envelope, then wrote a name on a slip of paper, then tucked the paper into the envelope. He turned to Flook. "Your left hand, if you please."

Flook shrugged, then extended her left hand. On the inside of the ring finger, just above the band of the ring, Doskoy drew a small circle. He went to Pook and did the same, inditing a small cross, rather than a circle. On Snook's finger he drew a square crossed by a diagonal. "Now then," said Doskoy, "we shall proceed. In the envelope is my wager and the name of the girl I shall designate after you complete your cantabulations." He placed the envelope on the platform, and stood back. "You may proceed."

Moncrief spoke to Flook, Pook and Snook. "Girls, sadly enough, we have here a man who doubts our bona fides. We shall take no offense, but proceed as usual. Hey presto! Let it happen, with a will!"

Schwatzendale said to Maloof, "The gentleman is no fool. I admit that similar thoughts crossed my mind, until I saw their absurdity. Moncrief needs no tricks; he has the laws of chance at his beck and call."

Joss Garwig asked, "What of you? Are you planning to bet?"

"Conceivably! The doors of opportunity are open; I shall take my long-deferred revenge upon Moncrief the Mouse-rider."

"Then you have solved the mystery?"

"So I believe."

"What, then, is the secret?"

"Aha!" Schwatzendale showed one of his slantwise grins. "You must be observant! If I told you, Moncrief would know at once!"

The girls had formed their line. Moncrief said politely to Doskoy: "Sir, the conditions are as you have arranged them. Can you now make your identification?"

Doskoy stepped forward, tapped the knee of the girl in the center. "This is she whom I have named in the envelope."

"Well then! Let us see!" Moncrief took up the envelope, withdrew first ten sols, then the strip of paper. He read the name aloud. "He has named Flook." Moncrief looked toward the girl in the middle: "If you are Flook you wear a ruby ring and a circle. Is this the case?"

The girl said, "No! I am Pook! I wear an emerald and a cross. The gentleman has made an unfortunate mistake."

Doskoy took up the girl's hand, stared dumbfounded at the emerald and the cross. He pulled at his russet beard, then looked up at Moncrief. He muttered, "It is past my understanding. I will play no more."

Moncrief spoke in fulsome tones: "Do not reproach yourself! I, for one, find your conduct both gallant and commendable; no more need be said."

Doskoy grunted, swung away and strode off up the avenue.

Moncrief turned to the girls. "Back up on your drums, if you please! Other sportsmen have been inspired by Doskoy's example and now await their turn! Who will be next?"

Schwatzendale argued with himself. Had the time arrived at last? Or should he prolong the suspense, in order that the drama might ripen? He inclined first one way, then the other, but in the end he was influenced by a dictum of the mad poet Navarth: "When opportunity comes fleeting past, seize it by the heels before it seizes you!"

Schwatzendale sidled forward. "The time has come when I must play the game!" he told Moncrief. "I have developed a mathematical equation, which specifies that I attempt five trials, increasing my wager at each trial. That is my intent, if you are agreeable?"

Moncrief bowed with smiling affability. "My dear sir, you may test your equation as you like. How will you wager?"

Schwatzendale advanced to the platform and placed down a sum of money. "I hereby wager exactly four sols and seventy-six dinkets."

Moncrief frowned up toward the sky. "That is an odd number! I suspect that somewhere, symbolic significance might be at work."

"So it might be," said Schwatzendale. "I am ready."

"Then, hey presto! Down, around, and about; let the money flow like wine!"

The girls performed their routine permutations and lined themselves in a row.

"Now then," cried Moncrief. "Let us test your equation! Show me a girl and call out her name!"

"I wonder," mused Schwatzendale. "Which shall it be? Flook? Pook? Or Snook?" He looked over his slip of paper. "I will specify Flook. She is the girl in the middle!"

Flook showed her ruby ring. Moncrief cried out: "The equation is valid! You are right!" He paid off the wager. "And now?"

Schwatzendale consulted his notes. "The factor of ten is applied, and the wager becomes forty-seven sols and sixty dinkets."

"That is another peculiar sum," Moncrief mused. "Do you apply the factor of ten to each successive wager?"

"Correct," said Schwatzendale. "Let the game proceed!"

"As you wish." Moncrief signaled the girls. "Hoy! Hoop! Hoop! Huzza! Up, around, and over!"

The girls formed a line. Schwatzendale said, "I nominate Pook, with the emerald ring, standing at the far left!"

Pook displayed the green gem. Moncrief gave a small grunt of vexation. "Right once again! How much was the wager?"

"Forty-seven sols and sixty dinkets."

"Ah yes, just so." Moncrief sighed. "I will pay forty-eight sols, since I am not a man for paltry trifles. You may keep the change."

Schwatzendale shook his head. "I am bound by mathematical rigor! Here is forty dinkets, and now we shall play another game."

Moncrief pulled at his chin. "And you will again apply the factor of ten?"

"Of course! I now wager four hundred and seventy-six sols and no dinkets!"

Moncrief's shoulders sagged. He gave three sharp coughs and thumped his chest smartly: once, twice, three times. At the back of the platform Siglaf and Hunzel took up heavy mauls and struck a gong. "Ah, too bad!" cried Moncrief. "The afternoon session has come to an end! However, be of good cheer! For the keener sportsmen among you, we now offer a new cycle of games. I call your attention to the gaming tank beside the platform. It has now been uncovered and you will see that it contains a viscous substance resembling mud, to a depth of four feet. This tank is the special province of our brave Klutes, Siglaf and Hunzel, who will help with the new contests."

Vermyra had become bored and restive. She spoke to Garwig:

"Haven't we been here long enough? It is definitely time that we were leaving!"

Garwig sighed and made a tentative suggestion: "The new contests might be amusing."

"Pish! In the presence of mud, I expect only the gratification of morbid sexual fantasies."

"No doubt you are right," sighed Garwig.

Vermyra gave a brisk nod. "Come then. Mirl? Tibbett? We are about to go."

"Any time you are ready," said Mirl.

Vermyra looked from right to left. "Where is Tibbet? This is truly vexing! We are on the point of leaving, and she is nowhere to be seen!"

Mirl looked blankly this way and that, then said: "Oh yes, I remember now! She and Myron went off together."

Vermyra stared dumbfounded. "What! She said nothing of this to me! Where did they go?"

Mirl shrugged. "They mentioned the Tunnel of Love, but I can't say that they were serious. Still, it's a possibility! Myron said that they might take dinner out, and not to worry if they weren't back till late."

For a moment Vermyra could not speak for shock. Regaining her composure, she turned upon Garwig and gave him his instructions. He must instantly set off and track down the miscreants. Myron must be treated to a stern reprimand and Tibbet taken into parental custody.

Garwig agreed in principle, but pointed out practical difficulties. In the end, after evasiveness and logic both failed him, Garwig flatly refused to obey Vermyra's commands. She cried out, "In that case, I will find them myself, no matter what the effort!"

"You must do as you think correct," said Garwig.

Vermyra went out to stand in the avenue. She looked first right, then left. Most of the passersby seemed distinctly of the lower classes, some even a trifle vulgar. One of these, a swaggering black-bearded lout, paused as if intending to ask what she needed. Vermyra quickly rejoined Garwig.

Moncrief was speaking. "Please notice that a section of the platform borders on the tank. This is known as the playing area. At the far end a brace supports a gong. The goal of the player is to start from 'Safe Station' at the near end of the playing area and make his way to the far end, where he must strike the gong. He thereby wins his wager. But there is an obstacle! Halfway along the playing area stands one of our gallant Klutes; either Siglaf, or Hunzel. She will try to impede the contestant and protect the gong. She may not kick, strike, butt, bite, or strangle the contestant. His basic wager is ten sols. If he sounds the gong he wins a hundred sols. If he decamps from the playing area, he loses his wager.

"Now then, as to his options! He can increase his winnings to a thousand sols if he pits himself against the two Klutes, working in tandem. He can choose to shackle the ankles of his adversary, but he thereby reduces his potential winnings to fifty sols. If he elects both to shackle and blindfold her, he wins only ten sols. If he shackles both her arms and legs, and she is blindfolded, then required to spin in circles at the starting bell, his winnings are reduced to a single sol. That, in essence, is the nature of the game. Who, then, will be the first contestant?" Moncrief surveyed the spectators, but none seemed eager to play the game. Moncrief turned to Schwatzendale. "What of you? An equation might help you win the prize!"

Schwatzendale shook his head. "Not unless it is you who guards the field, instead of Siglaf or Hunzel."

Moncrief chuckled. "I am far too slow for such work, also too wise." He looked here and there. "I am disappointed! Where are the gallant sportsmen?"

From the back of the crowd came a peremptory call: "Not so fast! I am here with my secret techniques!"

A middle-aged gentleman, broad and squat, with a round pink face, pushed forward, waving his arms. He evidently had been celebrating the fair in all its aspects and was in a state of elevated spirits. Several ceremonial ribbons adorned his jacket while two plumes had been affixed to his hat, now rakishly askew. "Stand back; do nothing! Omar Dyding is coming and you will know his secret at last!" Dyding swaggered confidently forward. "I am here, and this is my wager!" He threw ten sols down upon the platform. "Bring out Snook or Pook or Flook, I will select one of the three for my adversary!"

Moncrief spoke with unctuous courtesy: "The three you mention are resting after their work. Siglaf and Hunzel have agreed to take their places. Choose one or the other!"

"I prefer the thousand-sol prize," said Dyding. "Why should I stint myself? I will subdue both at once, using my secret method."

"As you wish," said Moncrief. "We shall watch your tactics with interest."

The contestants took their places. Moncrief gave the signal. Dyding stepped forward. Siglaf and Hunzel strolled to meet him. Dyding spoke to them, but they would not listen. Siglaf seized his wrists; Hunzel grasped his ankles. They swung him once, twice, then pitched him into the tank. Moncrief terminated the contest and took the ten sols of the wager.

Dyding floundered to the side of the tank. Wingo captured several excellent "mood impressions," then helped Dyding crawl out upon the walkway, where he lay in a puddle, while Wingo, taking up a pole, retrieved his hat.

After a moment Dyding stood up and started to clean himself. Wingo obligingly turned water from a garden hose upon him. Dyding was no longer in a jovial mood. Wingo nevertheless ventured a comment: "I thought that you had a secret plan of attack. Something must have gone wrong."

"Bah!" muttered Dyding. "These girls are healthy enough, but they are overly coy. I spoke to them, outlining the program, but they refused to listen."

"What, then, was the plan?"

"It is simple and natural. If the contestant caresses his adversaries, fondles their buttocks, lays hold of their private parts, they become embarrassed and confused; thereafter he can do as he likes with them. Those, in general, are my tactics; you may try them if you like."

"Hm," said Wingo. "It is a new approach to the pugilistic art."

Moncrief, finding no more interest in the contest, had closed his operation for the night. He then had taken Captain Maloof aside and engaged him in conversation. Maloof finally agreed to transport Moncrief and his troupe to Cax on the world Blenkinsop, a port already on the ship's itinerary.

"I have eleven pilgrims aboard," Maloof told Moncrief. "They will be with us as far as Coro-Coro on Fluter; it may be a bit tight aboard until then. Still, we'll manage one way or another."

3

Fiametta's long afternoon passed. Kaneel Verd, the Green Star, settled below the horizon, leaving behind a welter of orange and coral red, along with a scatter of apple-green cirrus.

Evening came to Sweetfleur. Two of the three moons climbed the sky, casting a pale greenish light over the landscape. The Lalapalooza had closed down for the night and was quiet except for a few dim resorts where the murmur of grave voices attended the consumption of Pingaree Punch, Gaedmon's ale, and wines of the region. At the space terminal a few dim lights glowed from the *Glicca* and the *Fontenoy*, indicating wakeful presences within.

Time passed. The moons arrived at the zenith and drifted down the sky. Across the landing field two figures moved through the moonlight.

They approached the *Fontenoy* and paused in the shadow of the hull, where they drew close together. After a time they spoke, in soft sad voices. Myron said, "The time has come at last. We must say good-bye."

Tibbet made a mournful sound. She took his hand and placed it between her breasts. "That's my heart beating! A week ago you never suspected that such a heart existed! Now you have found it and now you must go."

"I have no choice. Your father and mother would bar me from the *Fontenoy*, and Captain Maloof would not ship you aboard the *Glicca*, even if your parents agreed."

"Small chance of that."

Myron said musingly, "At one time I hoped that my aunt Hester would give me her spaceyacht after taking a cruise or two. If it ever happened, I would locate the *Fontenoy* and come for you."

Tibbet laughed sadly. "Sheer fantasy! Nice, though." She looked up at the sky and for a moment watched the course of the moons. Then she said softly, "I'll never forget tonight, as long as I live. And now—" she straightened, threw her shoulders back "—I had better go in, before I start to cry."

"I'll come in with you. If there is to be thunder and lightning, I'll collect some of it."

The two approached the gangplank. Someone sat on the top step in the dark. "I've been waiting for you," said Mirl.

"We are here at last," said Tibbet. "How is the climate inside?"

"Not too bad. Worry but no hysteria." Mirl rose to his feet and slid aside the portal. Myron and Tibbet preceded him into the saloon.

Joss Garwig and Vermyra sat side by side on a couch. "So!" growled Garwig. "You finally decided to come home."

Tibbet managed to laugh. "In a word—yes. Here I am, the errant daughter, awaiting execution."

Garwig looked at Myron. "And what do you have to say for yourself?"

Myron shook his head. "Nothing—except that it was a very nice fair and we'll never forget it."

Tibbet ran to the couch, hugged and kissed her mother. "I hope you haven't worried too hard."

Vermyra sighed. "The years have gone by much too quickly, even though I tried to hold them back! You aren't my baby anymore."

"I suppose not. At least, not altogether."

Vermyra rose to her feet. She looked at Myron. "I suppose that this is the end of it, so far as you are concerned?"

Myron said somberly, "The *Fontenoy* is returning to Duvray on Alcydon. The *Glicca* is headed for Cax on Blenkinsop, then who knows where."

Vermyra gave a grim nod. "That is what I thought you would say."

Myron found that he had no proper words to express his feelings. He turned away and started for the portal. Tibbet followed him through the opening and out upon the landing at the head of the gangplank. They stood close and kissed. After a moment Myron said, "We may never see each other again. The Reach is a very large place."

"In a way, so it is. In another, it's not so large."

"It feels large when we are going off in different directions."

"You can write me care of the Pan-Arts Museum at Duvray," said Tibbet. "If I don't hear from you, I'll know that you have forgotten me."

NINE

In the morning the spaceyacht *Fontenoy* was gone from its pad. The *Glicca* worked cargo, then departed Sweetfleur on a course which would take it first to Pfitz Star and the four stations of Mariah, thence to Coro-Coro, finally onward to Cax, on Blenkinsop.

The six new passengers brought an immediate animation to the ship. The saloon resounded to laughter and jokes, as well as conversation on a more serious level. Wingo discussed aspects of his philosophy and Maloof offered an occasional wry witticism. Myron told of his tenure as captain of the spaceyacht *Glodwyn*, to such good effect that even Hunzel and Siglaf, if contemptuously, recognized his right to existence. Only Schwatzendale seemed pensive, and took himself to a corner of the saloon where he sat in sardonic silence. The three girls, as always, were happy and gay and quite at ease in the new environment. They wore modest blue frocks with white collars, white stockings, white slippers, and small white caps; they looked crisp, clean, delicious enough to eat. The pilgrims, who had not seen them before, were duly impressed. They stood in small groups, darting covert glances toward the girls and muttering bleak comments to each other.

The exception was the moist brown-eyed, plump, and pink-cheeked Cooner. While naive and more than a little prim, Cooner also was garrulous and abashed by nothing. Finding the girls sitting at the long table, Cooner ambled across the saloon and dropped his large buttocks into a chair. With fulsome bonhomie he welcomed the girls aboard the *Glicca*, and vowed that he would take it upon himself to make their voyage both joyous and memorable. The girls, after a moment of slack-jawed amazement, responded politely. Cooner hitched himself forward. In a hearty voice enlivened by chuckles and intimate asides, he identified himself as a "unique individual with a prismatic personality."

"Interesting!" said the girls. "We haven't seen that sort of thing before."

Cooner made a casual gesture. "At home I am known as a real blue-tailed goer, which means 'a person of dynamic competence.'"

"Marvelous!" said the girls.

"Just so and more. At the yearly rally I was in charge of the senior ladies' high jumps, and I instructed in classic genuflections at the Noble House."

"Heigh-ho!" said the girls. "Quite fascinating."

Cooner smiled and nodded. "Now then, would you girls like to learn some of our interesting customs? I will teach you the Ten Dithyrambs, and the 'Cleansing Ceremony,' if you do not object to an ablution in the nude. Most tastful, of course!"

From Siglaf came a gruff sound. The girls left the table and joined her across the saloon, where she spoke a few terse words. Cooner looked after them, eyebrows raised in displeasure. He started to follow, but Wingo came to join him at the table.

"I see that you have developed an admiration for the three girls," said Wingo.

"Of course!" declared Cooner loftily. "They are devout and modest. They deserve my ungrudging help!"

"I see. Which of the three do you fancy above the others? Snook? Or is it Pook? Or perhaps it is Flook?"

"I don't know," said Cooner peevishly. "All are quite gracious."

"You are bold!" said Wingo. "Have you noticed Siglaf and Hunzel? They are Klutes from the Bleary Hills, and they have been watching your every move."

Cooner said proudly, "They have a right to do so, and I grant them that privilege."

"Aha!" said Wingo. "You do not suspect the truth?"

"What do you mean?"

"You are a mouse sniffing the cheese of a very sinister trap!"

Cooner's confidence began to slip. "How so?"

"Suppose, in your innocence, you committed an infraction of the Klute intersexual code. In such a case, either Siglaf or Hunzel, or both, would claim you in marriage. Captain Maloof would be obliged to perform the ritual, and you would find a new meaning to your life."

"That is beyond imagination!" gasped Cooner.

"Just so," said Wingo. "The Klutes are estimable ladies, but perhaps you have other plans."

"Of course! I am on an important pilgrimage!"

Wingo had no more to say. Cooner sat motionless for a time; then, after a covert glance across the saloon, he went quietly off to his quarters and read eighteen pages in the book of Primal Verities.

Time passed. The ship's company gradually adopted routines which seemed congenial. Flook, Pook, and Snook ignored the gloomy disapproval of the two Klute women, and ranged the ship like a trio of active kittens. Their capacity for pranks and mischief seemed limitless. They involved Cooner in a game of blind man's buff and locked him in the aft latrine, where he stayed until his bellows finally aroused the attention of Kalash. They played a different game with Wingo, descending upon him in a sudden tumble of young femininity, to sit in his lap, kiss his nose, ruffle his sparse locks, and blow in his ears, until he promised them nut-cakes and cream gateaus. They set ambushes for Schwatzendale, fondling him, clambering upon his back, kissing him, and declaring that he was so pretty they intended to put an embroidered collar around his neck and keep him for a pet. Schwatzendale hugged them benignly and patted their bottoms, and said that the scheme would suit him well enough, provided that he were well-fed, well-groomed, and exercised every day. Ah yes! cried the girls in delight. They would all run together on the beach at Sha-la-la, and they would throw sticks for Schwatzendale to fetch.

Siglaf and Hunzel watched the antics with dour disapproval, muttering to each other from time to time. Moncrief was more tolerant. "So goes the world!" he told the Klute women. "The tide always ebbs before it flows. The water is still the same water, and it is now time for poor old Moncrief to float quietly away to his repose."

Siglaf, swinging around, stared down at Moncrief with eyes like flints. She spoke tersely. "Before you float too far, and before your repose becomes too tranquil, please pay over the monies owing to us. We have waited long enough."

Hunzel also spoke. "We know that you are happiest when you are swindling someone and taking all their money. We do not want you to enjoy this pleasure at our expense." Both spoke brusquely, without concern for decorum, and neither heeded the half-open door which gave upon the supercargo's office.

Siglaf went on to state: "At this moment we carry no funds whatever. It is an outrage!"

Moncrief smilingly held up his hand. "Ladies, ladies! Let us have no more caterwauling! Your assets are safe."

"Bah!" sneered Hunzel. "Our assets consist of numbers in a notebook which no one can read! How can you expect us to believe you?"

Siglaf spoke forcefully. "Do you want us to walk the street like paupers? Pay us the money at once!"

"All in good time," said Moncrief. "I can do nothing until I draw up the balances."

"Never mind 'balances'! Just give us money!"

"It is not all so simple," Moncrief explained. "First I must reckon your earnings. From this sum I deduct costs: charges for transit, lodging, cuisine, and the like. The balance is what remains."

Siglaf made an angry gesture. "Then strike these balances now, and pay us our due!"

"Impractical!" said Moncrief. "As you well know, for reasons of security, the records are noted in a secret cipher. They cannot be decoded without time and effort."

"Do not dissemble!" Hunzel cried out. "We know the truth! You have gambled like a crazy man! The funds have been squandered and there is nothing left. Am I not right?"

"In a technical sense only. I intend to collect fees and amortize holdings along the way. When the grand total is struck, that will be the time to consider your accounts. We cannot act in an atmosphere of hysteria; the calculations are complex."

"In that case you should be working at them now."

Moncrief spoke with dignity. "At the moment I am planning a new set of spectacles for the troupe and I cannot be distracted."

Both Klutes made sounds of bitter amusement. Hunzel asked, "What troupe? You are living in the past."

Moncrief gave an indifferent shrug. "We shall see. Now you may go away; you are disturbing my rest."

"Ha hah! That has been our intention!"

Hunzel asked, "Why should you wallow here at your ease while we mourn the loss of our funds? At Cax we shall see that you are placed in the Aquabelle Island work camp!"

Moncrief had nothing to say. The Klute women strode away.

A few minutes later Myron emerged from his office. The Klutes had retired to their quarters and the saloon was quiet. Flook, Pook, and Snook sat at the dining table, looking through Wingo's portfolio of "mood impressions." The pilgrims had gathered in the cargo bay, where they rehearsed a cycle of devotional exercises. Moncrief still sat in a corner of the saloon. At the sight of Myron he signaled, and Myron went to join him.

Moncrief indicated the door to Myron's office. "I assume that you overheard my exchange with the Klute ladies?"

"So I did. I was ready to intervene if necessary."

Moncrief chuckled. "The need was never acute. They strut; they posture; they clamor like gilgaws, but in the end they trot meekly off to their quarters."

"I am impressed by your aplomb," said Myron. "The threat of incarceration in a work camp does not seem to trouble you."

Moncrief shrugged. "I am like a well-found vessel sailing the ocean of life, careless of wind, wave or storm. For the most part, my voyages are calm."

"And what of this present voyage?"

Moncrief grimaced. "We have drifted into a belt of unwise investment. The losses included funds which Siglaf and Hunzel hoped might be their own. Now they are unhappy."

Myron said, "I heard Hunzel suggest that you had 'gambled away money like a crazy man.'"

Moncrief heaved a sigh. "One cannot reason with an angry woman. Meanwhile, having no money, I have nothing to lose. It is liberation, of a sort."

"Another small matter," said Myron. "Captain Maloof insists that fares be paid in advance. But I find no record on my books of such payment, either from you or others of your troupe."

Moncrief said languidly, "I have made special arrangements with Captain Maloof. My personal fare will be paid from monies collected on Mariah and Coro-Coro, on Fluter. The Klute women must make their own arrangements."

"What of the three girls?"

Moncrief's expression became sour. "The Klutes have custody of the girls; they must pay all fees and fares."

Myron was puzzled. "But you are master of the troupe!"

Again Moncrief sighed. "The girls are indentured to the Klutes for four hundred sols each. The Klutes control the girls' services until the indentures are paid off—but this will never happen. At Cax the Klutes will sell off the papers to a rich padroon for an enormous price. The girls will be taken to a Skyland palace; they will disappear into the seraglio, and will never be seen again."

"This is hard to believe!" said Myron in a shocked voice.

"Nevertheless, it is the way things are done on Blenkinsop. The padroons do as they please."

"It sounds to me like slavery, and slavery is illegal!"

"Indenture and slavery are sometimes alike—except that you can buy your way out of indenture."

"Hmf," said Myron. "Something should have been done long ago."

"That is easy to say! The indentures are twelve hundred sols in all. I have no such sum. Do you?"

"There is not that much money aboard the entire ship."

"Now then, a second matter: even if I had the money, the Klutes are not obliged to settle with me. Only the girls themselves may dissolve the indentures by paying off the Klutes. In effect, the Klutes can do as they like."

Myron slumped back into the chair. "I don't understand how such things can happen!"

"Simple enough. On the world Numoy, in the Enders Valley, several institutions take care of lost children. The largest is the Enders Valley Foundling Farm, under the Bleary Hills. Siglaf and Hunzel worked in the refectory, and took out papers on the girls. For two years they have worked with the troupe, but now, as soon as we put into Cax, they will sell the indentures; Siglaf and Hunzel will be wealthy and return to the Bleary Hills of Numoy."

"This is truly sickening!"

"I agree," said Moncrief.

An hour later Myron came upon Maloof, alone in the pilothouse. Myron reported what he had learned from Moncrief.

For a time Maloof sat motionless; at last he stirred. "It is an ugly situation."

Myron asked, "Is there any way we can interfere?"

"Dozens of ways. One way might even be feasible. Another might be legal."

Myron and the captain stood silently, staring out the port into space. Finally Maloof spoke. "It's still a long way to Cax. I will give the matter some thought."

2

After a time, the pilgrims once again began to play their game, using beans for counters. In the absence of financial pressure, they played in a style more dashing than they had dared when real money had been on the line. At the same time, they took occasion to analyze their play, evaluating the tactics of positional flux, totting up the weight of power-increments which previously they had considered too paltry to note. With their new insights they confidently told each other that at last they understood Schwatzendale's tricks, and spoke of the strategies by which they would rout his forces should he dare to play with them again.

After a few days of pushing beans back and forth, the pilgrims devised a new currency consisting, as before, of chips equivalent to one of the packets in their cases.

The game proceeded at the old level of excitement. The pilgrims were now convinced of their expertise, confident in their skills, and many still rankled from the defeats inflicted by Schwatzendale. Emboldened they challenged him to join the game, so that they might attempt to recover their previous losses.

Schwatzendale pretended disinclination. "I sense a trap! You have honed your skills until they fairly dazzle the eye! Your scumbles rain down like thunderbolts! You are the new demons of double-moko!"

"Bah! That is an illusion! We are the same duffers as before!"

"Is this really true?" asked Schwatzendale, as if his resolve were melting.

"Absolutely! You can depend upon it!"

"What are the stakes? I already hold all your cash."

"We are using specie even more precious than cash," declared Zeitzer. "The units are chips, identical to the last issue. Each chip represents a packet of sacred material, worth at least a sol and perhaps as much as ten sols at Impy's Landing."

Schwatzendale performed one of his most picturesque gestures. "Do you take me for a lumpkin? The chips are worthless, until I know what they signify. If I should win a few, how, when, and where would I convert them into ordinary cash?"

Zeitzer reluctantly responded. "Is it not clear? At Cape Pallorquin there will be hundreds of pilgrims who have neglected to bring proper tokens. We will supply what is needed at a benevolent price, which of course is subject to market factors. This price determines the worth of both the packet and the chip."

Schwatzendale hesitated, drawn by the lure of the game. He remembered the triumphant sallies from the corners of hell; the sidelong scumbles, like slashes of a scimitar; the moans of the stricken pilgrims. In the end, Schwatzendale agreed to sit in for a hand or two, to see how the game went.

Zeitzer, a man of conscience, held up a restraining finger. "It is only fair to warn you that we are no longer quite as inept as before. Some of us have learned the rudiments of the game. Will you still take the risk?"

"I have committed myself," said Schwatzendale. "I would feel a sorry cad if now I showed the white feather."

"Then let the game begin!"

For a time Schwatzendale played modestly, while he appraised the tactics of the others, but presently he became infected by the spirit of the game and began to play with his usual bravura. His "diabolos" crashed down like balls of iron; his "scumbles" instantly found their marks; at his cries of "Out Gehenna!" his "rambles" carried all before them. In the end the pilgrims sat stunned, with neither chips nor cash, and so the game might have come to a dismal end had it not been for an unforeseen circumstance. Moncrief had wandered past the table once or twice, watching the play with benign disinterest. When the game seemed about to collapse, he settled himself at the table, and meekly asked permission to join the game. The permission was granted and play resumed. Suddenly all went poorly for Schwatzendale. His diabolos never reached the third card, while his scumbles were brushed aside as if they had been puffs of smoke. Schwatzendale endured the reverses with stoic fortitude, and his responses inflicted little damage. He made only timid display of his dragons, while his half-hearted sallies only seemed to arouse Moncrief's amusement, so that he struck back with ever more novel combinations.

After a dreary two hours Moncrief had won all Schwatzendale's chips. He would have continued the game had not Schwatzendale called a halt.

Moncrief chided him gently: "My dear chap, why do you stop so soon? The game is at its height! Open your purse! Throw down a few sols! Then let the game proceed!"

Schwatzendale smilingly shook his head. "I have exhausted my bait."

Moncrief raised his eyebrows. " 'Bait'? Explain, if you please."

Schwatzendale hesitated, then gave his head a modest shake. "All taken with all, it might be as well to put the subject aside."

Moncrief was not to be diverted so easily. "Come, my good fellow! Speak up! Let us have neither mysteries nor evasions!"

Schwatzendale shrugged. "Just as you like. The chips, so I suspect, are worthless, since they take on real value only at Impy's Landing, which is not on our itinerary. Therefore I put the chips to practical use. I played, with care, surrendering my chips in a measured flow, so that I could observe and analyze your game in detail."

Moncrief sat back in his chair. "Ha hah! Your schemes were subtle, but—naturally I diagnosed them at once. In response, I showed you a few childish feints, and a set of outmoded positions—all of which you studied with fascinated interest."

"True," murmured Schwatzendale. "So I did."

Moncrief went on. "I wonder as to your purposes—unless you expect more gaming."

"The possibility exists," said Schwatzendale seriously, "so long as the stakes are neither chips nor religious items."

Moncrief tapped his chin with a white forefinger. "This being the case, what stakes do you propose?"

"Money is useful."

Moncrief smiled wanly. "That is a dictum worthy of good Baron Bodissey himself! At the moment, my finances are in a state of flux, for which I blame a series of unwise speculations."

"I gather, then, that you are without funds?"

"Correct. But I am not without resource, since the troupe itself must be considered an asset of value."

Schwatzendale was perplexed. "How can your troupe be used as the stake in a gambling game?"

"By an indirect means. I propose that, using the troupe as security, you advance me, let us say, a thousand sols. With this money I will enter the game, and we shall compete on equal terms."

Schwatzendale pulled at his chin. He mused. "There is stuff here which requires sober thought."

Moncrief waved away the idea. "No need! I have done all necessary thinking. The scheme is excellent!"

"So you say. What if I lose my entire stake?"

Moncrief smiled and shrugged. "Need you ask? I would immediately return the thousand sols, retain my troupe and use the winnings to advantage."

Schwatzendale twisted his mouth in a grimace of distaste. "On the other hand, suppose that I won: what then?"

"Pish!" said Moncrief grandly. "I shall not lose."

"Let us think the unthinkable," said Schwatzendale. "Assume that I have won the game and the money as well, then I gain full control of the troupe and all its adjuncts; am I correct?"

"Far-fetched, of course; but, yes, essentially correct."

"I would also control the services of Flook, Pook, and Snook. Again, am I correct?"

Moncrief laughed indulgently. "Your plans become clear. But your conclusions are incorrect!"

"Indeed?"

"Indeed. Siglaf and Hunzel are resigning from the troupe, and taking the girls with them."

Schwatzendale inquired, "How can this be?"

"There is no mystery. The Klute women control the girls by the force of legal instruments known as papers of indenture. The girls must obey until the indentures are paid off."

Schwatzendale flung himself back in his chair. "This comes as a shock!" After a moment a new thought occurred to him. "The troupe which you value so highly is an empty shell! It includes only you."

Moncrief spoke loftily. "Along with my reputation, repertory, spectacles, costumes, formulas, musical scores, a vast store of goodwill, and all my glorious experience."

Schwatzendale sadly shook his head. "That is flapdoodle. When I control the troupe, it shall be like old times! And you shall once again be Moncrief the famous Mouse-rider, and once again the troupe shall prosper! You shall ride like a man possessed, with fury and zeal. I will collect the wagers, and pay out the winnings: all to the exact dinket. There shall be no more chicanery, nor flights in the night, no longer need we disguise ourselves as old women to avoid the ruffians we have cheated!"

"Eh? Eh? What's this!" cried Moncrief. "The Mouse-riders were models of rectitude, in every respect!"

"Not always," said Schwatzendale. "I know someone who was mulcted of forty-seven sols and sixty dinkets at a game of Cagliostro! He identified the scoundrel as Moncrief the Mouserider and swore revenge!"

Moncrief dismissed the anecdote with a weary sigh. "In my time I have heard endless poor-mouthing. It is all water under the bridge and the topic is moot, since the days of mouse-riding are gone."

"They shall be revived, with all their old fanfaronade! Buffoonery is popular with the gamesters and helps to open their wallets. You still command your adroit tricks, and you are quite agile, for a person of your age."

Moncrief grimaced, and started to speak, but Schwatzendale forestalled him. "You mentioned a thousand sols: a fine sum, I agree! But we now must descend from fantasy and speak of what is real. When I look into my cash box, I find less than two hundred sols. From this I can spare, at most, a hundred sols. This must suffice."

"Surely you can't be serious!" cried Moncrief. "The figure is preposterous!"

"It is no more preposterous than your scheme! Think of it! If I win, I lose. If I lose, I lose even more. That is not sound practice."

Moncrief heaved himself to his feet. Looking down at Schwatzendale he said, "I see that the scheme is impractical. Dismiss it, if you will, from your mind." He stalked off across the saloon.

3

Aboard the *Glicca*, in accordance with standard practice, the diurnal unit was arbitrarily divided into twelve hours of day, followed by twelve hours of night. When the ship took departure from a port of call, the on-board computer adjusted shipboard time by small daily increments, either positive or negative, so that upon arrival at the next destination shipboard time was in synchrony with local time, and travelers were able to disembark without temporal jar.

The days passed in orderly sequence. About halfway into the voyage, Schwatzendale noticed a curious alteration in the mood of the pilgrims. From time to time they gathered in small groups, whispering and smirking, turning bland faces toward him as he passed. Once or twice he came upon them chortling, snapping their fingers, clapping each other on the back, though when he drew near, they became stiffly sober.

One day Cooner came ambling across the saloon and, with a grunt, settled into a chair beside Schwatzendale. He peered to right and left, as if to ensure privacy, then asked, "Do you care to learn something of interest?"

"Certainly; why not?" replied Schwatzendale.

Once again Cooner peered over his shoulder. "This is information of a quasi-confidential nature."

Schwatzendale looked at him blankly: "How is that term defined?"

Cooner chuckled. "Oh, you know! It is matter for select ears only!"

"Very well. My ears have been selected and I am listening."

Cooner bent forward and tapped Schwatzendale's knee. "Some of the pilgrims, I regret to say, have performed an act which may or may not be considered irregular."

"What sort of act?"

"They have established a clubhouse in the corner of the aft cargo bay. They amuse themselves with a new game, which they find quite novel."

Schwatzendale was puzzled. "That is somewhat irregular, but I doubt if anyone will object, unless they molest the cargo."

"No; nothing like that. Everyone has been careful."

"Then why tell me?"

"For a simple reason. They think that you might care to join the game."

Schwatzendale grinned. "I took all their assets! What are they using for stakes?"

"It is the same as before. They have issued new chips, secured by the contents of other cases."

"Amazing! I thought that the old chips controlled all the cases."

"Not quite; we are too wise for that! Only about one third of the goods were put at hazard. This new issue represents three other cases."

"What do you carry in the cases that is so valuable?"

Cooner pursed his lips. "We are members of the Clantic Sect, well and truly, but we are also prone to hunger, thirst, pain, fatigue, and ordinary misery. Most of all, we hope to return home after our pilgrimage. To pay for these indulgences, we must undertake practical enterprises."

"All very well," said Schwatzendale. "But what do you carry in the cases?"

Cooner gave his hands a flutter of genteel distaste. "I must explain. When pilgrims arrive at Impy's Landing, some come lacking articles of critical importance. We carry supplies of these stuffs, properly formulated and sanctified, which we sell at ten sols or more per unit. The process is a trifle crass, but, since we lack funds, we rely upon sharing the wealth of more fortunate brethren."

"You are certain that you can sell these items?"

"Absolutely! They are much in demand! Once we arrive at Impy's Landing, we shall enjoy an amplitude of funds."

"Then why do you want me to play your game?"

Cooner grinned rather foolishly. "Is it not clear? Think back to the last game! You came at us like a storming tyrant, to take all our chips. We hope to win them back."

"You have come to the wrong man! The chips were of no use to me, so I let Moncrief win them all."

Cooner gave a poignant cry. "You own no chips whatever?"

Schwatzendale gave his hand a brave flourish. "I can win them back anytime I like. The old mountebank has lost his cunning. Come; show me the game."

Cooner seemed suddenly hesitant. "We shall go sedately, like gentlemen. There is no need for a headlong rush. In fact, they may not be ready for you."

"No matter! I am ready for them!" Schwatzendale jumped to his feet. "I will first look the game over; be kind enough to lead the way."

Cooner stood irresolute. "You will need money."

"We will stop by my cabin. Come along with you, or I shall find my own way."

Cooner set off slowly, at a pompous strut.

Schwatzendale finally cried out: "Is this the slow-march at the high abbot's funeral? You walk like a constipated owl! Come, come! Show a bit more brio!"

Cooner halted and looked over his shoulder. "Are you tired? Perhaps we should rest."

"I am not tired."

"A bit of a delay is sometimes nice."

"Why a delay? We have only just started!"

"They may not be finished practicing, if you must know."

"What are they practicing?"

"Oh—" Cooner made a vague gesture "—this and that. One thing or another."

"I will watch the practice; I might learn something of interest."

Cooner rolled his dog-brown eyes in distress. "I wonder if it is politic?"

"Aha! You have aroused my interest! Let us look in on this famous practice, and let us go softly."

In a corner of the aft cargo bay, the pilgrims had shifted bales and crates to open up a space large enough for their table. Schwatzendale halted in the corridor, well back in the shadows and, despite Cooner's uneasiness, watched the game from concealment.

Six men sat at the table. Schwatzendale recognized Zeitzer, Quantic, Dury, Tunch, Kimmel, and Lolling; they were playing with stiff cards two by three inches in dimension, similar to the chips used at the previous gaming. They were building houses, leaning the chips one against the other, delicately placing floors on the construction, then starting new tiers. They worked with a nervous tension, darting vigilant glances at their opponents, pausing only long enough to send one of their chips skimming across the table at a house which had been built to a respectable height. If the builder were deft, he caught the chip and added it to his own stack; if he were unlucky, the chip would strike his building and send it toppling into ruins. When this occurred, all the other players lunged forward to seize the fallen chips, while the builder sought to protect his belongings.

Schwatzendale asked Cooner: "What is the object of the game?"

"Each player tried to build a house six tiers high. If he succeeds, he wins all the chips which have gone into the other houses. Now, it is time that we show ourselves to the players."

"Not yet! I want to see how the game goes."

Cooner grumbled under his breath. With a mulish set to his face he started forward. Schwatzendale seized his collar and jerked him so that his head snapped back. "Stand quiet! Or I shall cut off your nose by the roots!"

Cooner sullenly stood back. "There is no need for rude behavior!"

Schwatzendale continued to watch the game. Quantic, using intense vigilance, built a house five tiers high and was starting on his sixth tier when the thin and rapacious Tunch hurled two chips in quick succession. Quantic was able to fend off the first chip, but the next struck his house full at the second tier, and the house collapsed, to Quantic's outrage. The ruins were instantly attacked by Dury, Kimmel, Tunch, and Zeitzer. Quantic, despite his best efforts, lost half of his chips. In a fury he rose and shook his fist at Tunch, who responded with a fleering laugh of contempt. Meanwhile, Zeitzer took advantage of the diversion to salvage four more of Quantic's remaining chips.

Before Quantic could react, Lolling held up his two hands, bringing order to the group. He started to speak, but the peculiar timbre of Lolling's voice, together with the acoustics of the chamber, muffled his words. He seemed to be instructing the group, who listened with earnest attention, nodding from time to time. He held up a white forefinger and spoke. The others nodded. Lolling held up two fingers, and again the others nodded. Lolling held up three fingers; the others broke into grins and chuckles. Lolling spoke another minute then looked from face to face to gauge his effect. Satisfied, he sat back in his chair.

Cooner now took the bit between his teeth and moved forward. He cleared his throat loudly, so that the gamesters all turned to look; Schwatzendale, willy-nilly, followed Cooner into the room.

Cooner called out, "I am here with the gentleman Fay Schwatzendale, whom you all know and admire! I mentioned that a game was in progress and he expressed interest. Perhaps, if you politely offered him a place at the table, he might be induced to join the game."

"Of course," cried Lolling. "We all respect Schwatzendale's skill! He is a sportsman and one of our kind. Welcome, Fay Schwatzendale! Do you care to join our game?"

"Just for a moment or two," said Schwatzendale. "I cannot hope to hold my own against six keen experts; still, I shall give the game a sporting try! What are the rules?"

Lolling explained. "First, you must know that this is a children's game, active, happy, and full of fun!"

"Good! I approve! What next?"

"We buy our chips. I act as banker."

"Very well, and then?"

"Then we all set to work building houses, after the pattern you see in front of Zeitzer. Our goal is to build six tiers high, which signalizes victory!"

"That sounds simple enough. Is that all I need to know?"

"In the main, yes. There are a few little tricks by which we hope to gain advantage, but the rules are strict!"

"Explain these rules, if you please."

"You may not touch another player's house with your hands or feet, nor propel more than a single chip at the same time. We refer to these propelled chips as 'missiles.' Should the house fall, any chip lying loose on the table may be 'salvaged'—that is the word we use. Reserve chips stacked at the edge of the table are out of bounds and safe from salvage."

"Simple enough. What if, let us say, three players set up a cabal against another? What are the rules in this regard?"

"There are none, since such cabals are barred from play. It is every man for himself!"

Schwatzendale bought chips and the game commenced. He played with extreme caution, building a single tier, meanwhile hurling missiles at the structures of fellow gamesters, especially the houses of Zeitzer, Tunch, and Kimmel, which were rising apace. A missile flung by Dury destroyed Lolling's house. Schwatzendale was quick to salvage a round dozen chips. One of his own chips brought down the four tiers which Tunch had erected, and again Schwatzendale alertly salvaged more than a dozen chips. Playing in this conservative style, he began to amass chips, while never himself building up from the first tier. His tactics began to irk the others, and they started to utter sneering remarks: "Well well, Schwatzendale; what a fine doghouse you have built!" And: "Come alive, Schwatzendale! This is not a game for dandified pretty boys! Play like a man!"

Tunch and Quantic, hoping to embarrass Schwatzendale, began to build tier upon tier at a reckless pace, with the result that Schwatzendale's missiles, skimming with force and accuracy, brought disaster to both. Neither accepted the event with aplomb. Quantic waved his fists in the air and uttered sibilant curses, while Tunch's face became rigid with fury. Meanwhile Schwatzendale adroitly salvaged thirty chips. By this time Kimmel, Dury, and Tunch had lost so many chips that they were forced to apply to Lolling for reinforcements. Zeitzer remonstrated with Schwatzendale. "You don't understand the spirit of the game! We build recklessly, like gallant champions bent on glory!"

Schwatzendale said meekly, "I am still learning the rudiments of the game; you must not expect me to match your flair."

Lolling said peevishly, "Whatever the case, you have already accumulated far more chips than you were issued."

"That is known as 'beginner's luck,'" said Schwatzendale.

"Ha hm," said Lolling. He glanced around the table, catching eyes, then held up a single white forefinger. "Let us proceed," he said.

The game now seemed to change. The pilgrims played with caution, building rarely, guarding their modest two- or three-tier structures with both hands at the ready. Schwatzendale noticed the alteration in mood, and began to pile chip upon chip at top speed. Up went his tiers: two, three, four, five. Lolling rapped on the table and showed a single finger. Instantly each pilgrim sent missiles hurtling toward Schwatzendale's house. They came in a salvo; he could not ward them off and his house collapsed into a ruin. Schwatzendale clasped the heap of chips with one arm and with the other struck at the onslaught of salvaging hands, to such good effect that he lost only a dozen chips. He turned to Lolling. "I understood that the rules barred both collusion and cabals."

"So they do," said Lolling severely. "Everyone must obey this rule!"

"Then why did everyone act in close cooperation to destroy my house?"

"It must have been a freak coincidence, if indeed the case were real."

"Then why did you hold up a finger? Was it a signal?"

"Of course not!" Lolling indignantly blew out his cheeks. "I reached up to scratch my nose! I suspect that you were misled by the gesture." He looked around the table. "Schwatzendale is, in a sense, our guest; we must be sure that he is satisfied with the play; is that understood?"

From around the table came gruff sounds of assent.

"Very well then! Let us play the game!"

The house-building, the skirling of missiles, and the groans of rage went on as before. Schwatzendale tried a new tactic, concentrating upon slow steady construction and deft interception of enemy missiles, and once again raised an edifice of five tiers. Watching in all directions at once, with nerves keyed to maximum alertness, he could build with one hand while capturing missiles with the other. Schwatzendale began to feel that he might win the game. At this point Lolling glanced around the table, as if assessing the levels of construction. Absent-mindedly he scratched his chest with two fingers.

Schwatzendale tensed, but no one seemed to notice. Across the table Cooner leaned against the cargo, idly toying with a length of dangling string. All was placid. Schwatzendale returned to work on his sixth tier. Behind him sounded a tremendous jangling crash, which set Schwatzendale's nerves to vibrating like bulrushes in a wind. He jerked around to find that a bale of metal goods had fallen from on high to the deck. Schwatzendale whirled back to the table: too late! His house was a tumble of ruins. Only by dint of furious action was he able to rescue a dozen or so chips. Schwatzendale ruefully gauged his depleted reserve stockpile. There were enough chips for him to attempt one more house. He glanced around the table. The other players smiled and shook their heads in condolence.

Schwatzendale made sure that no other bales were ready to fall, then doggedly returned to construction. The pilgrims seemed absorbed in their own building. Cooner was engaged in another mindless game at the other side of the table, kicking at some loose dunnage.

Schwatzendale worked with both diligence and caution, capturing the occasional missiles hurled in his direction. No question but what he had the knack for this sort of game, he told himself, provided only that he used the proper vigilance. His tiers once more rose high: three, four, five. He laid the first chips in his sixth tier; once again he was close to victory. Lolling leaned forward in grave concern, and in order to support himself, lay three fingers flat upon the table. Schwatzendale went instantly on the alert, but no one else seemed to have noticed and their play went as usual. Tunch caught a missile thrown by Kimmel, while Dury, to better effect, sent a chip skirling on a fierce swoop to destroy Zeitzer's house. In the space beyond the table Cooner was bobbing foolishly up and down. Schwatzendale paid no heed. Beneath him something was amiss. His chair tilted over backward, sending him sprawling to the deck. Instantly he sprang erect and threw himself at the table, thereby saving eleven chips from the ruins of his house.

"Ah! Very sad!" Tunch commiserated. "A sad blow!" said Kimmel.

Schwatzendale adjusted his chair and reseated himself. Lolling cautioned him. "That was a serious mistake! You should sit squarely and solidly in your chair, and refrain from tilting back."

"Quite right," said Schwatzendale. "It does not pay to be careless!"

"You have lost most of your chips. Do you wish to buy a fresh supply?"

"Of course! I am just now learning how to play the game, though I must visit my cabin for more money."

Lolling said courteously, "You are a keen sportsman! We await your return with anticipation."

Schwatzendale left the chamber and was gone for several minutes. As before, when returning, he halted in the shadows of the corridor and observed events at the gaming table. As before, he discovered Lolling instructing the other players, holding up first one finger, then two, then three. Lolling then made a comment which aroused laughter in the other pilgrims, even the dour Tunch. At this juncture, Schwatzendale reentered the chamber. He was greeted with friendly banter and smiles. Kimmel called, "Perhaps you will enjoy better luck and not fall off your chair!"

Dury spoke a few words of reassurance, "We all go through ups and downs, but we find our true joy in the sport itself!"

Schwatzendale nodded without comment. He bought chips from Lolling, then returned to his chair. Quantic called out facetiously: "So now, Schwatzendale, it's back to the drawing board, eh?"

"I'm afraid so," said Schwatzendale. "My old tactics were not productive, but I am not discouraged! I plan ever more important construction. My houses shall rise high! Tier after tier; high as the sky, while all look on with wonder!" As Schwatzendale spoke, he raised his left hand and swept it back and forth in a series of ascending swerves, attracting the fascinated attention of the other gamesters. Meanwhile, with his right hand he squeezed a dispenser, to lay a line of clear gel along the edge of the table just behind his wall of chips. "But do not expect me to build as recklessly as before; I cannot trust you others to sympathize with my goals, so I must fend for myself. That, after all, is the philosophy of the game!"

"Just so!" "Absolutely right!" "Most wise!" were the responsive remarks.

Schwatzendale looked to Lolling. "I take it that in my absence the rules have not been altered or amended?"

"Certainly not! The rules are immutable!"

"In that case, let us play the game!"

Each builder bent forward at once, and with guarded looks to left and right began their constructions. Schwatzendale built with the same methodical manner as before, but now each chip was unobtrusively touched to the adhesive gel at points of contact with the other chips, so that, when put in place, it instantly became part of a rigid unit. He worked without apparent haste, but, relieved of the need to fend off missiles, he was able to build at speed. Up went his tiers: two, three, four. Lolling began to show interest. After a look around the table to catch his comrades' attention, he unobtrusively laid a single finger upon his chest. At once a salvo of six missiles hurtled down upon Schwatzendale's house. Two struck his house, causing no damage; Schwatzendale captured the other four and added them to his stockpile, while the pilgrims looked on in surprise.

Play continued. Lolling showed two fingers. Down from the ceiling came a flapping hairy insect a foot in diameter; it struck Schwatzendale on the chest. As he recoiled in horror he thought he heard Cooner's chortle. At the same time a torrent of missiles struck down at Schwatzendale's house, which only vibrated to the strikes.

The insect was a contrivance of wire, paper, and hair, with a grotesque head molded from dough. The string which had guided it lay across the table and disappeared into the shadows. Cooner stood by innocently. Schwatzendale tossed the contrivance to the floor and added the spent missiles to his reserves. He called out to Cooner: "Why did you throw that insect at me? You might have cost me a large number of chips!"

Cooner showed no remorse. "The thing was just a toy. It escaped from my control. Need you be so surly? It was only in fun!"

Lolling said, "Do not victimize poor Cooner; he was only playing with his toy! After all, you suffered no damage."

Tunch muttered, "It is a mystery! Schwatzendale's house is like a fortress of alloy steel! It is beyond my comprehension!"

"The house is only a house, as you can see," said Schwatzendale. "Do not maunder over trifles! Let the game proceed!"

Schwatzendale began to fit chips to his sixth tier.

Lolling gave a groan of anguish, and placed three fingers upon the table. Schwatzendale instantly cried out to Cooner, who stood by the wall, "Take your hand off that switch! Do not turn off the lights, or I will lock you into the latrine for a week; the charge shall be 'interfering with ship's electrical gear'!"

Cooner reluctantly turned away from the switch. Schwatzendale completed the sixth tier of his house. "The game is done!" he cried. "I claim victory!"

The other players slumped back in dismay. Schwatzendale swept their houses into a pile of something over two hundred chips, which he stacked in front of him. A problem remained: how to dismantle his own house without exciting suspicion? He looked around the table. "I take it that we are keen for a new game? I am at the top of my form, and ready for anything!"

"Not I!" growled Tunch. "You have impoverished us all with your weird antics."

Lolling had trouble finding his voice, but at last managed to say, "I too am done for the day." He rose to his feet and stalked from the chamber.

"I will remain for a bit," said Schwatzendale. "I want to count my chips. Perhaps I will practice my techniques, in case we play another game."

"Practice all you like," snapped Tunch. "I doubt if it will do you any good, since I for one will play no more games with you." He walked stiffly away.

"Nor I," said Kimmel. "There is something about you and your play which afflicts me with a sick dismay." He too left the chamber, followed by the others.

Schwatzendale dismantled his house, scraped adhesive from chips and table, gathered up his booty, and went his way.

TEN

1

In *Handbook to the Planets*, Myron learned that Mariah was the sixth world in orbit around the white star Pfitz. At this point a footnote explained that the locator, Abel Merklint, had named the star Laura Ardelia Pfitz, to memorialize a childhood sweetheart, but time and usage had abbreviated the name.

Myron learned further that Mariah, though slightly larger than Earth, exerted somewhat less gravitational force by reason of a lower overall density.

Abel Merklint, like many others of his calling, was both a man of letters and a romantic philosopher. He described Mariah as a protean world, endowed with innumerable beauties, and at the same time haunted by much that was dark and terrible. In the General Remarks, at the bottom of his original report, Merklint had noted:

Mariah shows a hundred guises, a thousand faces, and ten thousand moods. Four continents are spaced at regular intervals around the equator. Viewed from space they seem like four dainty demoiselles dancing in a circle, but on closer approach the impression vanishes and the continents reveal their special identities.

Alpha is bleak and rough, with four mountain ranges, a variety of deserts, both high and low, and the whole fringed by a cheerless seaboard of crags, cliffs, and narrow beaches of groaning shingle.

The second continent, Beta, has been subjected to a great deal of tectonic stress, and displays a wonderful variety of geological formations. The blasted hills of Beta provide great mineral wealth. In the pegmatite sills I have seen perfect tourmalines a foot long; the metamorphosed amphibole produces a blue jade with the unctuous texture of frozen butter.

On the edge of the Great Shinar Forest, and perhaps one or two areas, there is a suggestion of ruins and artifacts of enormous age, as if half a million years ago the place was home to a race of beings now vanished. The evidence is ambiguous and surely will arouse controversy.

Gamma is the largest continent, and is abundantly watered by frequent rains. At the center of Gamma is a vast swamp inhabited by a fecund mix of flora and fauna, all violently disagreeable. Nine slow rivers drain the swamp, then make their way to the sea across savannahs populated by grazing quadrupeds and a complement of predators who react to the human presence with only a mild curiosity. When approached they move away with quiet dignity, as if to say, "I don't know who or what you are, and I prefer not to find out."

The fourth continent, Delta, is like a pretty girl in the company of three bearded ruffians. Everywhere on Delta are delightful landscapes of halcyon beauty, where everything harsh or cruel is forbidden. On the shore of Songerl Bay I shall build a rambling home of rustic timber, with a porch overlooking the beach. In the morning barefoot maidens shall serve my breakfast. Later, they will bring flasks of rum punch to where I sit on the porch, watching the sunset fade and the stars come out. By day Songerl Bay is placid and blue, but I shall neither swim nor wade in the surf, since the water festers with all manner of noxious life; still, it is here where I wish to live out my days. Will it happen so? Who knows? For a man with a locator's soul, nothing is ever certain.

Myron consulted the map. There were four spaceports, one for each continent: Station A, near the town Ascensor, on the continent Alpha; Station B on Beta, with Cambria Town on the west and the Great Shinar Forest to the east; Station C on Gamma, at the brink of the Great Gorge at Felker's Landing; Station D, near Sonc Town, beside Songerl Bay, on the west coast of Delta.

The *Glicca* carried cargo for each of the stations, and so would visit each of the continents. Cargo accessibility dictated that the first port of call should be Station D beside Songerl Bay, near the site of Abel Merklint's rustic homeplace.

The *Glicca* landed at noon. The cargo was discharged expeditiously, and cargo awaiting transshipment was loaded into the appropriate bay. There would be a delay of a day or two pending the arrival of goods from outlying depots. For tramp freighters plying space without schedule, such delays occurred more often than not. Only the pilgrims complained, especially since, lacking funds, they were unable to visit the village adjacent to the spaceport. To placate them, Wingo promised an amplitude of fresh fruit for an after-supper treat. They were further gratified when Schwatzendale tendered Kalash the Perrumpter an envelope containing eleven sols for distribution among the pilgrims, thus allowing them to visit the village market.

Siglaf and Hunzel came into the saloon. They looked left and right; then, discovering Moncrief sipping tea and reading a journal, strode across the saloon to confront him. Moncrief sighed, put down the journal, and looked up. "Ladies! Are you out for a stroll along the beach? Take heed; do not swim in the sea without a green bathing cap; otherwise you might be devoured by a monitor-trapenoid. Even the green cap may not protect you."

"We will neither stroll nor swim," stated Siglaf. "Other matters concern us."

Hunzel spoke curtly. "You have had time to reflect. When will you pay what you owe us?"

Moncrief replaced the journal into a rack. "I have not been idle. To the contrary! I have made collections, and I am now ready to settle our accounts."

Taken aback, both Siglaf and Hunzel surveyed him in silent wonder. "If true, that is good news," said Siglaf at last.

"Yes, yes; good news for us all," said Moncrief. "Still, we cannot ignore the formalities."

"What formalities?" demanded Siglaf. "Mind you: we will not be satisfied with verbiage!"

Moncrief gave his hand a tolerant wave. "Correct business practice must be observed. First, have you prepared a receipt? I thought not. Very well then! At this moment write the following document, in a clear hand: 'Received in toto and in full from Marcel Moncrief, this day, settlement for all debts or obligations, tacit or otherwise, incurred during that period from the first instant of recorded or unrecorded time, whichever came first, to that moment when the last glimmer of energy fades from the universe, whether the principals to this instrument be living or dead at the time.' Then date and sign the document."

Siglaf bawled in outrage, "Bah! Bosh! Sheer bullypup! Are you truly serious?"

Hunzel spoke idly. "Just give us our money, and let there be an end to the blather."

Moncrief said politely, "Of course, but first I must have proper invoices, with all credits and debits itemized. No doubt you have prepared such a statement?"

Hunzel threw a paper down upon the table. "This is all we need. It is a tally of our joint unpaid salaries: Siglaf, myself, the three girls. Please pay this sum."

Moncrief took up the paper, scanned it judiciously then looked up in mild astonishment. "Is this a joke? Where are your deductions for ongoing expenses? I refer to transport, sustenance, and miscellaneous outlays."

"I believe that you refer to what are known as 'perquisites of the trade,'" said Hunzel. "We are not required to deal with them."

Moncrief tossed the paper aside. "Your figures are incomplete. Luckily, my own records are here at hand. The correct system is simple. You are credited with your salary, from which you must pay your personal expenses, such as transportation, lodging, and victualing." He brought out his account book and also a packet of the chips he had won from Schwatzendale. After consulting his accounts, he wrote a number upon the discarded document. "This is the sum owing to you at the moment. You must still settle your transit charges from Sweetfleur to Cax with either the supercargo or Captain Maloof."

Siglaf and Hunzel read the number in quivering outrage. "Preposterous!" cried Hunzel. "We refuse to be victimized!"

"Nevertheless, this is the amount I am prepared to pay. You may inspect my figures if you like."

"By all means; pay us in part! Anything is better than nothing! At Cax we will complain to the Red Coats, and they will soon set matters right!"

Moncrief gave a good-natured shrug. "You still must give me a receipt for any sum I pay over to you." He began to count chips. The Klutes watched with suspicion. Siglaf demanded, "What are those bits of trash?"

Moncrief responded with dignity, "These are securities issued by the pilgrims. Each item is worth ten sols, a value secured by the precious articles they carry in their cases. I consider it quasi-legal tender, and I shall use it as such to pay off your accounts."

From Siglaf and Hunzel came bellows of furious laughter.

"Never!" cried Siglaf. "Do you take us for fools?"

Hunzel demanded, "Pay us in real money and pay us now! Otherwise we shall turn you over to the Red Coats! They will drag you howling and squealing to the Aquabelle Island workhouse!"

"I shall file countercharges," said Moncrief. "It is you who will be dragged off in disgrace."

"Never! Our charges shall carry the day, since you owe us money! This fact will be construed as your motive, and the cat will be out of the bag."

"Absurdity and nonsense," declared Moncrief. "Right shall prevail!"

Hunzel gave a fleering laugh. "Remember only that the Aquabelle work camp is stark, and that the food—what there is of it—is sour and bitter."

The Klutes departed the *Glicca*, and went out to saunter along the beach. Moncrief remained in his chair, reviewing the events of the day. They brought him no cheer. Uncertainties lurked wherever he looked. And meanwhile, the worst enemy of all, the great colossus Time, loomed ever taller over his mental landscape. The years were advancing; there was no turning them back.

Moncrief winced and sat up in the chair. This sort of rumination must be avoided. True: he was no longer a nimble young bravo but his mental capacity had declined no whit! He was as clever, subtle and audacious as ever—but, if truth must be told, he had gone soft and lazy! Still, and on the other hand, could he not trace his tendency toward ease and self-indulgence to the advent of years? Was he supposed to be an acrobat and turn cartwheels for the rest of his days? Surely not. What then? The answer was plain. He must revitalize his temperament, now that youthful organs no longer pumped quick reactions and surges of stimulation into his blood.

"Rumplety-bang and a yo-heave-ho! Kick down the valve and away we go!" sang Moncrief under his breath. No more of this maundering. Despite all, he was Moncrief the Mage, the same Marcel Moncrief who had elevated mouse-riding to the status of a fine art! There had been many triumphs, a few tantalizing failures, and even now in his present troupe there was the potentiality for new glories, if he could only keep it together! At the moment he must rouse himself and take control of his small predicaments, as well as others not so small.

First, the repair of his finances! Almost his only tangible assets were the chips he had won from Schwatzendale. What, if anything, was their value? Moncrief rose to his feet and strolled back to the cargo hold where the pilgrims' cases were stowed. Here, to his annoyance, he found a grizzled old pilgrim named Barthold, who stood guard over the cases during the absence of the other pilgrims now wandering the village market. Barthold was squat, with a crooked leg, coarse gray hair, bleary blue eyes, and a pugnacious chin. He sat on a keg, his staff and a jug of juniper ready to hand. Behind him the cargo hatch stood ajar, admitting Pfitz-light and draughts of cool air fresh with the tang of the sea.

Moncrief asked, "Why are you not ashore, sporting about with your fellows?"

Barthold lurched to his feet; he waved his staff toward the cases.

"These are valuable objects, and someone must stand guard. To this end the brethren have invested their trust in me."

"For the best of reasons, no doubt," said Moncrief. He advanced into the hold and examined the cases more closely. They were constructed from heavy dark wood, bound by bronze straps of ornate design. Each case was secured by a ponderous bronze lock. Moncrief attempted an ingenuous question: "Which of the cases are open for inspection?"

"None whatever! All are sealed with sacred seals. No one may transgress and perhaps commit a mischief. I will tolerate no exceptions to the rule."

Moncrief spoke with pompous authority. "Stand aside, if you please! I wish to examine the cases, which is my right, since I own most of the contents, as you must be aware."

"Ha ha! Goose-wipe and poodle-juice! You may own the objects but you don't own the cases, nor the bronze, nor the sacred seal, nor have you earned my trust!" He flourished his staff. "I stand resolute in my duty!"

Moncrief warned him: "If Captain Maloof passes by and you strike him with your staff, you will find yourself in serious trouble!"

Barthold's response was a snort of disdain and a twitch of his staff. Moncrief departed the hold and returned to the saloon. Schwatzendale stepped from the galley, where he had been testing Wingo's special Sea Island Punch, a compound of fresh coconut milk*, lime juice, rum and a dash of apricot brandy. At Moncrief's signal, Schwatzendale crossed the saloon and joined him. "You look morose. What has happened now?"

"If you must know, I fear poverty, not to mention its ancillary effects."

"No less do I. It is how I justify taking money from the pilgrims, though as well, a fine exhilaration is to be had from the deed."

Moncrief made a gloomy sound. "Profit is probably an illusion."

"Oh? How so?"

"We gambled with these cunning pilgrims in sterling good faith. We put down our sound currency; they used bits of hardboard which they valued at ten sols. All very well, but where can these chips be redeemed? Only on the world Kyril, at Impy's Landing. But the *Glicca*

---

* The coconut palm, native to Old Earth, had been transferred across the Gaean Reach wherever climate and salt water permitted, and now seemed native to the entire universe.

will fare nowhere near Kyril—which leaves us with stacks of worthless chips!"

Schwatzendale threw his arms into the air, elbows at sharp angles: a gesture denoting rueful amusement mingled with outrage. "We have been swindled by rascally pilgrims!"

Moncrief nodded somberly. "That is my reading of the case, which has prompted me to a stint of serious thinking. As we have already noted, the *Glicca* will not put into Kyril. The pilgrims and their cases will be discharged at Coro-Coro, where they must transship to Impy's Landing, while we continue to Blenkinsop—foolishly clutching our worthless chips."

"Correct: a fiasco!"

"But hold! A spark of hope remains. The chips are secured by items in the cases. These items are purportedly valuable, but the reason for this value has never been defined for us. Perhaps they are ancient relics studded with precious gems! Or Khorasan miniatures! Or pink turbans embroidered in black! It is this information which is lacking to us."

Schwatzendale clapped his hands together. "We should redeem our chips at once, the sooner the better! Of course we can expect a great howling from the pilgrims, but what of that?"

Moncrief stated, "What is right is right. At least, that shall be our contention. It is a maxim which the pilgrims will find hard to dispute."

Schwatzendale jumped to his feet. "I suggest that we act at once. The pilgrims are at the market, probably haggling with the town prostitutes, trying to strike bargains."

Moncrief also rose to his feet. "First we must deal with a preliminary detail. The cases are guarded by an old bowser named Barthold, who is truculent to a fault. If we can distract him from his duties, can you open one of the cases?"

"Certainly! No problem exists."

"In that case, let us set the process in motion."

Moncrief found Flook, Pook, and Snook in the galley, where they were testing Wingo's Sea Island Punch. Moncrief summoned them into the saloon, and settled them around a low table. He spoke in a grave voice. "I have many things to discuss with you, but each topic must wait its turn. At the moment we will deal with a matter of urgent importance."

"Aha!" cried Snook. "Then you too believe that Siglaf should cultivate a more charming manner?"

"I do indeed, but it is not what concerns us now." He went on to instruct the girls in the work which lay ahead. The program was not to their liking.

"It is far too tiresome," Flook told him. "Not at all in our style!"

"It is even a bit grotesque," said Pook. "What will you demand of us next?"

Snook gave a little shudder. "As to that, I would not care to speculate."

Flook said reasonably, "Another day will do as well."

"I have the answer!" cried Pook. "Why not turn the job over to Siglaf and Hunzel? They have nothing better to do."

Moncrief spoke sternly. "Come now! I will hear no more grumbling!"

Pook wailed piteously. "Ah! Have mercy! We are not apt for such mischief—especially in connection with someone so scurrilous!"

"I have heard enough!" declared Moncrief. "You must obey at this instant, or you will be looking in vain for the little treats you enjoy so much!"

"Nonsense," declared Snook. "We know how to get anything we want from you."

Moncrief chuckled. "Regardless! Today you must do my bidding and there will be a box of bon-bons for each."

"Ah, well! In that case!"

The girls ran to the stern cargo hold, where they fell to teasing Barthold. They sat on his lap, pulled his nose, blew into his ears. Pook raised his shirt while Snook tickled his back with a wisp of straw.

"You are a sturdy fellow!" they told him. "We seldom see a man so brave and fierce! You frighten us!"

"Ha, what a joke!" Barthold refreshed himself with a pull from his jug. "Still, no question but what I am strong and ready! Very ready indeed!" He seized Pook, drew her down on his lap and began to caress her. "You girls are choice morsels indeed! Ha! What is this?"

"Oh—you know. We're all the same."

"May I touch them both?"

"Of course! Are we not your innocent little friends? Even so, now we are all excited."

Barthold gave his head a sad shake. "A pity that only one can be first."

"True—but which of us?"

"I shall determine by my secret method. Stand up in a row; I will pat your lovely little bottoms and so come to a decision."

"But not in this dismal place. Let us go down the ramp into the open." The girls ran down the ramp and Barthold followed.

"Now then: line up, according to the plan," said Barthold.

"Ha ha! You must catch us first!" The girls scampered off down the beach. Barthold called for them to slow their pace and set out in pursuit, hobbling and lurching and waving his jug of juniper.

Moncrief summoned Schwatzendale. "Bring some tools and we shall learn the worth of a pilgrim's chit." The two went to the cargo bay, closed and locked the doors against the return of Barthold. Then Schwatzendale took up his tools and set to work on the most convenient of the cases. After a quick examination of lock, seals and bronze straps, he carefully pried open the back of a case, leaving the seals intact. The contents were neatly packed in cardboard boxes: many small sacks of dry soil of no obvious value.

Moncrief and Schwatzendale exchanged glances and both shrugged in dour exasperation. Wordlessly Schwatzendale repaired the box. After reopening the cargo door, the two departed the bay.

2

Near the site of Abel Mirklint's original homeplace the Sonc Saloon overlooked Songerl Bay. It was a crotchety old structure of weathered timber, with a wide verandah and a roof broken by a dozen fanciful dormers. An annex to the side functioned as a dining room, with tables ranged around a dance floor.

Schwatzendale and Moncrief, on their way to the inn, came upon Flook, Pook, and Snook playing in the surf, running in and out of the foaming water. Pausing, they told an excited tale of how they had eluded old Barthold and left him thrashing about in a thicket; now they were proposing to divest themselves of their clothes and frolic in the surf. Moncrief clapped his hand to his forehead. When he could speak he pointed to a black tube lifting six feet from the sea a hundred yards offshore. "Do you see that tube? It supports the eye of a monstrous creature known as a 'monitor-trapenoid.' As soon as you entered the water three or four tentacles would reach out to seize your ankles and drag you to its jaws. If the monitor were absent, there are knife-fish out there with dorsal ridges hard and sharp as butcher knives. They would instantly slash you into gobbets and carry the pieces down to the bottom to feed their babies. There are also nefring with needle-noses; and gakkos with heads like little sponges. If the sponges touch you, a green fester appears, which kills you if it is not cut away. Songerl Bay is not a favored venue for aquatic sports."

The three girls cried out in alarm and jumped away from the water. Pook spoke in a hushed voice. "We were minutes short of death!"

"To think of it!" cried Flook. "We were on the point of learning what Cooner calls the 'forbidden mysteries.'"

"Everyone would have grieved most bitterly!" said Snook in tones of awe. "Undoubtedly there would have been a memorial raised at this very spot!"

Pook lamented, "Our afternoon is spoiled! What shall we do now?"

Moncrief spoke with authority: "First of all, a serious talk is in order. We must make plans for the future."

"That is unnecessary," said Pook, rather grandly. "According to Siglaf, our future has already been planned to best advantage."

"Indeed!" said Moncrief. "Did either of these wise Klute ladies describe your future in detail?"

"Yes, of course," said Flook offhandedly. "At Cax we are to become princesses, which is not at all the ordinary thing. It is a matter of knowing the right people."

Snook explained. "At Cax social position means everything, and we will be running with the right set."

Pook said, "Siglaf and Hunzel have told us what to expect, and it seems very pleasant. We will ride in golden cars and eat all manner of nice things. We shall be the envy of everyone!"

Moncrief sighed and shook his head. "Ah, my little pets! So debonair and yet so innocent! The truth is very much different. Come; let us sit over yonder and I will explain what you need to know."

Schwatzendale continued down the beach to the Sonc Saloon. He found his shipmates sitting on the verandah, drinking rum punch and enjoying the view across Songerl Bay. The group included a pair of pilgrims: Cooner and Linus Kershaw, a gray-haired gentleman of erudition. Both had refrained from gambling and so retained most of their private funds. Wingo, upon learning that Kershaw held degrees both in doxology and in ontological science, engaged the savant in conversation. They touched upon several topics, including the doctrine of the Clantic Rasborians. Wingo expressed his confusion and asked for a definition in clear language: a requirement which brought a smile to Kershaw's face.

"It is a large subject and the matter, by its own nature, is abstruse. Still, I can offer you what I call a 'bare-bones' survey, if that will suffice."

Cooner cleared his throat and spoke in his most cultured voice. "If I may say so, I have pondered the subject at length; in fact, I have compiled a codification of the Thirteen Punctilios—"

"Thank you," said Kershaw. "At this time we need venture no farther than the 'Prima Facie,' since we do not wish to encumber Wingo's mind with more than the most basic adumbrations."

Cooner gave a rather lofty shrug. "It won't amount to much unless we go into the Inverse Corollaries."

"Something is better than nothing," said Wingo. "That is a dictum of great antiquity, which still seems valid today."

"Just so," said Kershaw. "I will do the best I can."

Cooner said bravely, "If and when Kershaw chances to overlook some small element of doctrine, I can no doubt supply the missing detail. Or, if you like, I can undertake a running commentary."

Kershaw turned him a glance of mild inquiry. Cooner went abruptly silent. After a moment he rose from his seat and stepped down to the beach, where he occupied himself throwing stones into the surf.

"Our creed is not immediately accessible to the casual amateur," said Kershaw. "Still, in a sense, it is simplicity itself. The basic doctrine tells us that each individual, willy-nilly, generates his own universe, of which he, or she, is the Supreme Being. We do not, as you will notice, use the word 'God,' since the individual's power is neither transducive nor pervasive, and each person will have a different concept as to the nature of his divine program. Perhaps he will merely manipulate the tenor, or—let us say—the disposition of a standard universe. In effect, each individual inhabits the sort of universe he deserves, as if it were sweated out through his pores. For this reason, if the environment lacks charm, he is often reluctant to admit his responsibility, and claims control over only a limited personal ambience."

Wingo pursed his lips. "These persons might be motivated by modesty, or even humility, which, in view of their creed, seems only appropriate."

"An interesting point," said Kershaw politely. "Still, under the Clantic doctrine, each individual lives by the terms of his own capabilities. The implications are often disturbing."

"I can appreciate this," said Wingo. "I might add that the difficulties of cross-codification would seem an endless task."

"Exactly! It is tantamount to finding the solution to a very large number of simultaneous equations involving an indefinite number of unknowns, without recourse to matrices. At the Institute, for a fact, I thought to develop an equation which would resolve all such disharmonies. My tactic was to cancel out what I call 'aberrations' and 'wolf-terms,' on both sides of the equation."

"And the upshot?"

"I achieved success, along with a modicum of perplexity. In the ultimate resolution I was yielded a highly significant equation: nullity equals nullity."

"Most odd!" muttered Wingo. "The matter at this point would seem to enter the realm of mysticism. It is as if you were traveling a road by moonlight and came upon a tall faceless figure holding up his hand to bar your further progress."

Kershaw nodded somberly. "On that day all that I needed to know was quietly made clear. Since then I have given up research, though I ponder the many ways of life as I wander."

The two men sat silent, watching the surge and retreat of the surf. Cooner was now shying stones at the eye-tube of the monitor-trapenoid, which had eased considerably closer to the shore. One of the waiters called to Cooner and pointed to the tall eye-tube, now swaying sinuously back and forth. Cooner, startled, drew back from the line of the surf and desisted from throwing stones. The eye-tube gave a series of irritated jerks and once again moved offshore. Cooner seated himself upon a log and watched the white star Pfitz settle into a bank of cumulus at the horizon.

Kershaw remarked, "Perhaps I am mistaken, but Cooner seems a bit forlorn. I wonder what has caused him such distress."

Wingo chuckled. "I think that I can guess the circumstances. He feels that Moncrief, by one means or another, has mulcted him of five sols."

"Most odd! Cooner is extremely careful with his money!"

"No doubt. He thought he had caught Moncrief out in a blunder, and he could not resist winning an easy ten sols."

Kershaw nodded. "Ah yes. In many respects Cooner's nature is innocent and trusting. How was his trust betrayed?"

"By his own avarice, I fear. Moncrief was playing with a loop of string, creating cat's-cradles and the like and defying Cooner to predict the outcome of each, the wager being ten dinkets, which Cooner consistently won. Thus, he was emboldened when Moncrief handed him a sharp knife and, holding the loop stretched between his hands, defied Cooner to cut the string, so as to break the loop into a simple length of line. Cooner was assured that he could easily do so, and when Moncrief offered to bet him ten sols to five, he readily placed down his money and cut one of the taut strands Moncrief held between his hands. Moncrief called out: 'Alakazam! Let the string be whole!' When Cooner took the string, the loop was unbroken. Moncrief thereupon took up the five sols. Cooner stamped his feet and tore his hair, to no avail. He still carries the loop of string which he examines from time to time, hoping to find where he made the cut."

Kershaw gave his head a wry shake. "Cooner should not brood upon this event, since it might compromise his grasp upon the universe for which he is responsible."

Wingo glanced up the beach toward Cooner, who sat as before, moodily tossing pebbles into the surf and watching the decline of the star Pfitz.

"Ah well," said Kershaw. "Cooner might not find my advice useful."

The two men drained their goblets and signaled for refills. After a moment Wingo said, "While you were reminiscing, I remembered one or two of my own experiences. You may be interested in their substance."

"Speak on," said Kershaw with a fatalistic wave of the hand. "Every event of existence, like every grain of sand, is a marvel in itself."

"That is my own opinion," said Wingo. "Like yourself, I have long hoped to synthesize the vagaries of the cosmos into a harmonious unity. I have traveled a long road, and from time to time I have resolved some of the more flagrant paradoxes—but I am not yet at peace. A pair of quandaries still hang in my mind."

Kershaw gave a sardonic chuckle. "Only two? Your thinking must be profound! Describe these quandaries."

Wingo gathered his thoughts. "Both are basic, though quite different. I encountered the first at a colloquium I attended when I was young. During the event, two respected pundits found themselves at odds. The dispute was fundamental in nature. One declared that a primal divinity had created the universe; the other insisted that the cosmos itself was the seminal agency, and had generated a special ad hoc divinity to function as a self-replicating model of itself. For a time the arguments were sharp, since if one doctrine were correct, the other was doomed to oblivion. At the time I could not decide where truth lay, nor can I do so now."

"It is an uncomfortable condition," said Kershaw. "A serene philosophy rests upon a foundation of indisputable truth."

Myron, who had been following the conversation, ventured a comment. "I am told that Unspiek Baron Bodissey was once called upon to define Truth. His views are not exactly relevant, but, as always, they are illuminating."

"Don't stop now," said Schwatzendale, who also had been listening. "On with the anecdote!"

"It goes like this. One dark midnight a student entered the Baron's chamber and awoke the Baron from his sleep. The student cried out, 'Sir, I am distraught with anxiety! Tell me once and for all: what is Truth?'

"The Baron groaned and cursed and finally raised his head. He roared, 'Why do you bother me with such trivia?'

"The student gave a faltering response. 'Because I am ignorant and you are wise!'

"'Very well, then! I can reveal to you that Truth is a rope with one end!'

"The student persisted. 'All very well, sir! But what of the far end which is never found?'

"'Idiot!' stormed the Baron. 'That is the end to which I refer!' And the Baron once more composed himself to sleep."

"Most amusing," said Kershaw. "It is as responsive to Wingo's dilemma as any statement I could make." He turned back to Wingo. "And what of the second problem?"

"It is a paradox which disturbs me greatly," said Wingo. "It does not seem amenable to pure reason."

"At the very least you pose us an interesting challenge," said Kershaw. "Continue, if you please."

"Once again I must revert to my early days, when I was a student at the Organon. My mathematics professor was unconventional; further, he was contemptuous of cant. He explained that ordinary mathematics was a fraud and a deception, lacking correspondence with reality. The fault lay in the use of the symbol 'zero' as an integer to designate 'nothing.' This, so the professor claimed, was a travesty, since no such entity as 'nothing' existed. He pointed out that the absence of 'something' was in no wise equivalent to 'nothing'; to calculate using 'zero' as an integer was a logical farce and conventional mathematics was a tool useful only to idiots. I feel that the arguments are valid, but when I use a multiplication table based upon true and proper mathematics, nothing comes out right, and I am at a loss to explain it."

Kershaw gave his head a dubious shake. "Even if the usual multiplication table is wrong, no one will want to change now. Best let sleeping dogs lie."

"That is also my opinion," said Myron. "Use the old system, even if it is wrong. Otherwise, whenever you pay out money, you'll find yourself arguing over the change."

Wingo gave a despondent grunt and drank from his goblet. "Somewhere a fallacy exists."

The sun Pfitz sank behind the roil of cumulus and passed below the horizon. The sky glowed scarlet and pink, then faded through magenta and plum, as evening came to Songerl Bay. Small fires along the beach flickered where local folk boiled pots reeking of a hundred nose-twitching ingredients.

At Sonc Saloon, dim lights behind colored shades began to glow in the annex, illuminating a row of paintings in sepia, black, and umber, which hung on the walls. A platform at the far end of the annex supported a battered old marimba, apparently home-built, using hardwood blocks strung out along a bamboo frame. At the side of the room Myron saw Moncrief, deep in conversation with a burly red-faced man wearing a white apron and a tall white hat. Both were waving their arms high and low, and tapping the palms of one hand with the fingers of another, as if stipulating the terms of a transaction.

The tables along the verandah and in the annex became filled, and the kitchen staff began serving the evening repast: bowls of fish stew, bread, cheese, and cold meat with pickles. In the sand of the beach a pair of waiters dug a shallow trench eight feet long, in which they started a fire of gnarled black logs. A long grill resting on six splayed legs was placed over the trench; when the fire had dwindled to coals a long object wrapped in banana leaves was placed upon the grill and left to roast.

Meanwhile, dramatic events were taking place in the annex: notably, a quarrel between the burly landlord Isel Trapp and one of his minions, a weedy youth named Fritzen. Trapp's fury was extraordinary. He shouted imprecations of an original nature; he performed wild gesticulations, so that Fritzen often was forced to sway backward to avoid the sweep of the great arms. At one point, Trapp dashed his tall white hat to the floor and stomped on it. Fritzen stood with shoulders hunched, head drooping. When he dared mutter a protest, Trapp only roared the louder, so that in the end Fritzen threw up his arms in defeat. Turning, he sought here and there for a place of refuge and finally stalked across the floor to the side of the platform.

From behind the marimba he brought out a weary old bass drum that he carried to the front of the platform, then seated himself in the shadows behind the marimba. The drum, a veteran of many musical episodes, had most likely originated on Old Earth, to judge by the scene painted on its front face. Depicted was the image of a vagabond cat wearing a broad-brimmed black sombrero with little bells around the edge; he lounged upon a marble bench playing a guitar, his upturned face expressing the rapture of his song. He played in the light of a yellow crescent moon. Three coconut trees leaned across the background, suggesting tropical romance.

Isel Trapp, meanwhile, had picked up his hat, slapped it against his leg in order to restore its shape, then fitted it to his head with an air of satisfaction for a deed well done. Then he returned to the kitchen. As soon as he had gone Fritzen sullenly began playing with the marimba mallets, striking discordant notes at random. As if at a signal, into the room by way of the back entrance slipped a curious creature: a man of so many mutational characteristics as to seem almost a member of an alien race. He was short, with skin the color of slate. At the top of a large pop-eyed head grew a shock of gray-yellow bristles, stiff as quills. Long thin legs supported a plump torso of no great dimension. He wore a ragged brown tunic and dull green trousers tight as a second skin. He hopped up to the platform and settled cross-legged behind the drum. Fritzen continued to toy with the marimba. He put down the mallets, adjusted the soundbars, took up the mallets again, and struck a long arpeggio, from low to high. This was enough; Fritzen was bored. He put down the mallets, sat back down on the edge of the platform. The dwarfish drummer began to stroke the drum with long thin fingers and rap with his knuckles, producing a soft propulsive rhythm. Isel Trapp emerged from the kitchen, and bawled something which Fritzen pretended not to hear. Trapp took an ominous step forward. Fritzen languidly rose to his feet. He waved Trapp back toward the kitchen, picked up the mallets, and attacked the marimba. For a time he struck aimlessly at the blocks, producing random clinks and plangent thumps; gradually he took charge of the mallets, and wistful melodies began to issue from the instrument.

Fritzen at last brought the music to a halt by means of a clever eight-bar coda. He grinned wolfishly down at the drummer, who returned a blank pop-eyed stare.

Only for a moment; Fritzen remembered his dignity and erased the smile before Trapp, glancing benignly from the kitchen, could notice.

Now, for want of better occupation, Fritzen scowled down at the marimba and began to adjust the blocks, all the while muttering, or, possibly, cursing under his breath. At last he was satisfied, and ran the mallets up and down the blocks, creating a fine flourish of sound. He set forth into a brave new tune at a loping tempo, issuing musical commands, then halting, while the drummer inserted ingenious whirligigs of thumping and bumping into the breaks.

So it went for twenty minutes, the marimba producing a soft blurred sound, dull notes without overmuch brilliance; with the drum, muffled and soft, creating unobtrusive thrust. One melody followed another: tunes wistful, pensive, tragic. There were no lively tunes: no jigs, merrihews, or whirlaways; no stomping, leg-kicking essays into the upper areas of musical verve.

Curious! thought Myron. He stopped one of the waiters. "Those are unusual musicians! Are they part of the regular staff?"

The waiter looked critically toward the platform. "Not the drummer; he's a Klugash, from Gamma; he came around begging and Trapp thought that, being a savage, he might be able to work the drums. As for the marimba, Trapp's grandmother sent away for instructions, then built the thing out of bits and pieces. But it only mouldered out in the shed until Trapp decided that his kitchen staff was overpaid and under-worked. He took the scullions, pot-boys, and skulkies aside; he told them that too long they had been dogging their work. From now on they must go out and play the marimba. They told him that they had no ear for music, but Trapp said he knew a trick worth two of that. He took his grandmother's book of music and tore it apart, so that each lad received a section. Fritzen was allotted a collection of laments, tristes, mournful ballads, and the like." The waiter chuckled. "Fritzen runs in bad luck. Tonight, while scouring his leeks, he paused to blow his nose, and Trapp caught him out with a great roar, and Fritzen was sent off to the marimba." The waiter, catching sight of Trapp, hurried off about his duties.

Ten minutes passed, then Myron became witness to another odd event. Three young women slipped into the annex through the back door. Keeping to the shadows, they approached the platform. Colored lights, flickering and dim, made their faces indistinct; Myron could see only that they were slight and slender, with dusky-brown skins and dark hair which fringed their foreheads and hung past their ears. From the waist up they were naked, save for small cups over their breasts; be-low the waist they wore skirts of fiber strings which rippled sinuously as they walked, to reveal their legs. They carried small guitars; unob-trusively, they stepped close to the side of the platform and began to pick out chords to the music in progress.

The tune ended. Fritzen looked down at the three girls without enthusiasm.

The girls struck an introductory sequence and began to sing softly, perhaps in an exotic dialect, so that their words were incomprehensi-ble. But it made little difference; the spirit illuminating the music was clear. Fritzen listened, shrugged, and began to play a muted obbligato. The voices were sweet and quiet; the girls sang songs of longing and homesickness for places unknown. They sang of fading memories and anguish too heavy to be borne.

Another surprise! In the shadows beside the platform appeared a shape wearing the costume of a wayfaring musician: a loose black cloak of flamboyant cut, and a broad-brimmed slouch hat, tilted down over the face, already half-concealed by a pair of drooping black musta-chios. He carried a concertina; seating himself on the platform beside

the three girls he began to work the bellows of his instrument, finding
his way by sighs and whispers into the music.

So the tune ended. The concertina player slid free of his cloak to
reveal a jacket of black velvet decorated with two panels of red and
blue embroidery and silver buttons. He pulled the brim of his hat even
lower, so that it almost met his swooping mustache. He drew four long
chords from his instrument; the girls chanted a ballad so softly that the
words were lost, though their tragic import was clear.

The music stopped and for a time nothing could be heard but the
rush of the surf up and down the beach. Then once more, to the tinkle
of guitar chords, the girls began to sing another slow sad song, yearning for something gone and irretrievably lost. The music slowed; the
marimba became quiet; the voices sighed away, as if receding along the
wind, and then became still. The music was finished.

Fritzen stepped down from the platform and went to sit in the
shadows. The drummer jumped to the floor and trotted to the back
door and disappeared. The musician in the black velvet jacket put
down his instrument. He spoke a few words to Fritzen, then, from a
table to the back he took a wide bowl, into which he dropped a handful
of coins.

Aha! thought Myron; priming the pump, was he? Moncrief, had he
been on hand, would have used the same trick without compunction.
Into Myron's mind came a sudden queer speculation. He studied the
vagabond musician carefully. Could his surmise be accurate? Of
course! There could be no doubt. The concertina-player, with the raffish hat and the jaunty mustachios, was none other than Moncrief the
Mouse-rider!

A second startling thought entered Myron's mind: What of the
three dark-haired maidens? He turned to look, only to see them slipping out the back way. But no mistake! They could only be Flook,
Pook, and Snook in disguise! And what a disguise! It was enough to
make a man's head reel.

Moncrief carried his bowl from table to table, rattling the coins, at
the same time conversing with the tourists from Sonc Town hotels,
who found him picturesque. After an adequate gratuity had been
placed in the bowl, he continued to the next table, and the next.

Finally, the versatile mountebank arrived at Myron's table. In a
plaintive voice he spoke: "Sir, I am a musician born to the trade, and in-
ured to hardship and fearful toil! Tonight I have given the best of my
bent, so that all ears might be ravished with charm. It is a noble deed,
and I will not refuse compensation. So now you may give from a full

heart! Give without stint! Give of your many sols, with both hands and a soul full of gratitude."

Myron tossed a sol into the bowl and Moncrief continued on his rounds.

Flook, Pook, and Snook entered the verandah. The wigs were gone; the skin tone had been rinsed away; they wore skirts and pullovers of white and blue. The alteration was total. They came to the table occupied by the group from the *Glicca*; Wingo and Schwatzendale gallantly found them chairs. Moncrief presently appeared, now wearing his usual garments.

Waiters from the inn brought a long table out to the beach and placed it near the fire. They surrounded the table with chairs, spread a cloth, set out bowls of green sauce, hunches of bread, platters of raw vegetables, plates, and table utensils. Moncrief stepped down from the veranda, along with Flook, Pook, and Snook. They took seats at the table, and in due course were joined by others from along the veranda, until the table was filled.

The waiters brought a plank to the grill and placed upon it the long parcel which had been cooking for over an hour. They carried the plank to the table, stripped away the leaves to reveal an enormous armored sea-worm a foot in diameter, eight feet long, fringed with twin rows of small jointed arms. The waiters cut away the forward proboscis and the frontal processes, as well as the terminal organs, from which exuded a yellow froth. They detached the jointed arms, then cut the carcass into vertical slices an inch thick, which were served to the diners with tongs. Within each slice was a layer of blood-red cells, like pomegranate seeds; the diners scraped these into bowls of sauce, then cut the slices and ate the pungent white flesh as they might devour slices from a watermelon, using the red kernels in the green sauce for a relish.

At midnight the group from the *Glicca* took lights and flares, both to illuminate the beach and to warn away the night-visioned flying creatures which often attacked men. Thus protected, the group returned to the spaceport and to the security of the *Glicca*.

In the morning a few more parcels of outbound cargo were loaded. The freight agent reported that there would be no more for a week. Captain Maloof immediately shifted the *Glicca* to Station C on Gamma, near the town Felker's Landing.

ELEVEN

Felker's Landing was situated at the brink of the Great Gorge of Gamma. The spaceport, at the eastern edge of town, also overlooked the gorge, at this point about five hundred feet wide and two hundred feet deep.

A mesh of fragile walkways—the so-called "sprangs"—suspended from trusses extending over the Gorge, provided access to the kiki-nuts which grew on stalks rising from the swamp below.

Felker's Landing had been founded in ancient times by a folk quite different from the current inhabitants. These were the Peregrine Fellows of the Phillippic Society, who had come to Mariah in order to create a community based upon rationality and harmony with nature. They intended to make logic and efficiency instinctive habits, as automatic as breathing. All structures would be built in the round, to avoid cracks and angles where dirt might collect. Every aspect of life was analyzed and simplified, so as to yield maximum effect for minimal exertion.

As the centuries and millennia passed, the customs of Felker's Landing altered until only the most tenuous continuity remained. The current conventions were even more rigorous than before; now, however, they were comprehensible only to the initiated. Distinctions of dress and color guided many phases of interpersonal relations, allowing a person to specify, in broad terms, the role he wished to play in the events of the day. A person disinclined for social contact might choose to wear a black headband, thereby shrouding himself in a mantle of invisibility. No one might notice him, and so he became unseen. At puberty men wore blue-fringed headbands and girls red-fringed headbands; thereafter, they were oblivious to each other save as sexless blurs. Marriages were arranged and at the conclusion of the ceremony the bride and groom removed the colored fringes from each other's forehead, the presumption being that now, for the first time, they saw each other's faces, and perhaps in many cases it was so. The act had strong erotic symbolism, being tantamount to breaking the maidenhead. The excitement affected everyone present. At the raising of the fringes, bride and groom were required to feign gladsome surprise, then dance a traditional dance symbolic of initiation into the erotic mysteries. Everyone enjoyed the occasion, approving a proper performance of the dance, criticizing incorrect postures, reminiscing as to other dancings.

The river Amer flowed down the center of Felker's main boulevard, on its way to pour over the brink of the Great Gorge. The north bank was considered female, the south bank male. When men wished to visit the north bank they must clip small scarlet cockades to the bridge of their noses. The women similarly must fix tufts of blue hair to their cheeks when they visited the south bank, usually when they wished to patronize one of the three taverns: the Prospero, the Black Tamber, or the Fazirab.

The Great Gorge, with its web of sprangs, dominated the life of the town. A dense growth of enormous black ferns choked the swamp. The fronds rose a hundred feet, with the central stalk pushing thirty feet higher, terminating in a spherical case, six to eight feet in diameter. Pods sprouted from the surface like warts, each containing a cluster of the kiki-nuts, which had engaged epicurean appetites everywhere across the Reach.

Kiki-nuts, together with the tourist trade, nourished the economy of Felker's Landing. The ferns could not be climbed from below to harvest the pods, by reason of poisonous insects inhabiting the fronds. Laminated poles penetrated the swamp at intervals; they were joined to narrow walkways, "sprangs," then connected to each other and to landings along the edge of the gorge, creating an intricate network. The sprangs were narrow and light, often no more than a foot or two wide, and supported mainly by catenary cables hanging from the trusses above. The men and women who ran along the sprangs, carrying baskets, were the "sprang-hoppers." Over the centuries certain spranghoppers had become legends, through feats of agility, remarkable leaps; also for gallantry in connection with the dramatic duels which had occurred out along the sprangs, the loser toppling into the soft blue-green core of the ferns, to be swarmed over by foot-long insects.

The sprang-hoppers harvested the nut pods and carried them to the sheds. The pods were husked, the kiki-nuts extracted, cleaned, graded, and packed in casks for shipment to the civilized worlds.

The *Glicca* would remain in port for two, possibly three days, and the crew was given liberty to pursue its own inclinations.

When time allowed, Wingo sometimes set up a little market, where he would sell toys, pots, pans, cutlery, colored pencils, and the like. The enterprise earned him no great profit, but he enjoyed dealing with the local folk, and his camera was always ready to capture a quaint "mood impression." On these occasions, the better to project the romantic ambience of ancient artistic tradition, Wingo liked to wear his wide-brimmed brown hat, the brim set at a rakish angle; and his sweeping brown cloak and expensive boots, custom-made to protect his sensitive feet.

During the afternoon following the *Glicca*'s arrival at Felker's Landing, the crew tested the ales offered for sale by the Prospero Inn, and also the Black Tamber, and were favorably impressed. On the following day Wingo set up his booth near the entrance to the space terminal. Almost at once a small crowd of potential customers gathered to inspect his merchandise, so that Wingo was encouraged to hope for a profitable day. However, on this occasion Wingo's hopes were not to be realized. Neither his artistic garments nor his stern demeanor dissuaded the Felks from acts of mischief. After approaching the booth and examining the stock, they moved away and slipped the black bands of invisibility over their foreheads. Now, assured that their misdeeds would go unnoticed, they returned to the booth and began to steal Wingo's merchandise.

Wingo wrathfully cried out: "Come now! This must stop! I cannot allow such thievery!"

The protests went unheeded. Wingo quickly took several "mood impressions" for his records, then began to squirt the perpetrators with bad-smelling tick repellent. The act aroused so much outrage that Wingo was forced to desist.

"Very well," Wingo told the angry thieves. "Since you cannot behave like ladies and gentlemen, I regret that I must close the market. I am amazed to find petty dishonesty so rampant at Felker's Landing!"

Wingo carried his stock back to the *Glicca*, then went off into the town. He sauntered along the edge of the Great Gorge, pausing now and then to photograph the sprangs and the agile sprang-hoppers. Across the river he noticed the Prospero Inn, a hostelry of three stories shaded under the black and green palps of six tall dendrons. Wingo crossed the Amer by one of the six bridges and investigated the premises of the Prospero, but found no sign of his shipmates. Returning to the boulevard, he set off toward the Black Tamber. Along the way he passed a side street with tall three-story houses to either side. One of these houses had been converted into a shop. A sign hung over the street:

MUSEUM OF THE NATURAL MAN
On display and for sale:
Objects of virtu. Curios. Artifacts illustrative
of lore and ritual.
Professor Gill, Curator, is a savant of trans-galactic reputation. He is currently showing a collection of objects odd, arcane, and often imbued with mystery. Serious collectors are welcome. Faddists, dabblers, and casual tourists, please pass on. We have no time to waste.

Wingo entered the shop. At the back sat a small man with a pinched pale face, a few untidy locks of gray hair, eyebrows raised in chronic annoyance. He wore a threadbare black coat, tight trousers of snuff-brown velvet, and pointed black shoes of a style long outmoded. A large leather-bound book lay open on the table before him; as he read, he tapped quick flurries upon the keys of a coding machine. Wingo waited a polite moment, then began to look about the shop. A row of tables supported trays heaped with miscellaneous oddments; shelves along the walls displayed a similar clutter.

With ponderous deliberation Professor Gill put aside the ledger and gave his attention to Wingo. He said crisply, "I specialize in materials to interest only the serious student. Tourist shops are along the main street. Let me advise you: wear a green and white mercantilist's ribbon before you attempt to deal with the local shopkeepers; otherwise they will cheat you without remorse."

"That is good advice!" said Wingo gratefully. "Where can I obtain such a ribbon?"

"As it happens, I have a stock of such ribbons on hand. All are of high quality, but I suppose I can spare one of lesser value."

"It will serve me well enough," said Wingo. "What is the price?"

"Ninety-two sols," said Professor Gill quickly.

Wingo blinked. "I will give the matter thought."

"As you like."

Before Gill could return to his book, Wingo asked, "You are a native of the town?"

Professor Gill shot Wingo a scornful glance. "In no manner, shape, form, or degree! Surely this is obvious?"

Wingo hurriedly apologized. "Of course; it is quite clear! I spoke without thinking!"

Professor Gill was not to be mollified so easily. "I am a pure cosmopolitan! I hold degrees from six universities and my publications are seminal. As soon as my treatise is documented, I shall be gone from here in the blink of an eye! Meanwhile"—he made a curt gesture— "you are at liberty to examine the items on display."

Wingo asked ingenuously, "These are artifacts of the early spranghoppers, or so I assume?"

Professor Gill spoke with studied patience. "Some of the material is Felker. Rather more is Klugash."

Wingo started to speak, but Gill held up his hand. "I lack the time to chat with you about the Klugash."

Wingo spoke with dignity. "I only wished to mention that I saw one of this sort a day or two ago, at Songerl Bay. It was small, freakish, with a little round belly and long thin legs. It seemed inoffensive enough."

Professor Gill chuckled sourly. "I know of at least three research teams which thought to study the Klugash. They entered the Shinar forest and never returned. Still, the Klugash occasionally show themselves at the Cambrian digs, to beg, or steal, or trade." Gill suddenly lost patience with the conversation. He pointed with jerking motions here and there about the room. "The items are open for your inspection! Perhaps you will find something to interest you."

Wingo looked into a nearby tray. He noticed a pair of earshells, carved from oily black seed-pods. The carving was carelessly executed and Wingo thought to recognize the Felker technique. He put the items aside. In a glass box he found a set of insects preserved in transparent gum, apparently intended for use as ladies' ornaments. The set included a large green scorpion; a necklace terminating in three tigerbeetles; a small black-and-gold butterfly; and a hundred iridescent flies floating inside a crystal sphere. He pushed aside a tattered rag doll and came upon a small mechanism of no obvious purpose. He turned it this way and that, trying to coax the parts into motion, without success. Professor Gill watched him with a small smile, and finally said, "That is a Felker device, used to trim the hair from their noses. It has failed because of corrosion. Perhaps you might see fit to repair it."

"Possibly so," said Wingo. He replaced the object in the tray and took up a small sketchbook. Ornate block letters on the front cover read:

THE MOST IMPORTANT THOUGHTS OF DONDIL RESKE, AGE 13.

Inside Wingo found first several sections of crabbed script, most of which had been scribbled over in red wax-pencil, making the script even less legible. Some of the pages had been torn away, leaving a collection of drawings. The first, executed entirely in tones of brown and

gray, showed a two-story house of complicated architecture, surrounded by stark black dendrons. An arrow pointed to an upstairs window, with an attached legend: "My room!" On the next page Wingo
found a drawing of a different sort: a portrait labeled: "Everly Prase,
age 11," depicting the wan face of a young girl, almost lost in a tumble
of curls. Wingo smiled benignly and turned the page. Here he found
another sketch, more complicated, also somewhat more tentative, as if
Dondil had been less sure of his material. He had drawn a nightmarish
creature, half gargoyle, half pterodactyl, with thirty-foot wings of
brown membrane folded back beside the thorax. To the side stood a
tall thin man, narrow at hip and shoulder, with a rapacious face. He
wore a cylindrical helmet two feet high, ending in a point. Dondil had
labeled the sketch: SKY-MAN OF THE GASPARD CRAGS WITH MOUNT.

To Wingo's disappointment, only blank pages remained in the
book. He showed the sketch of the "Sky-man" to Professor Gill.
"What do you make of this?"

Gill gave the sketch a perfunctory glance. "The book is about four
thousand years old. You have here a schoolboy's impression of a Gaspard Arct. The draftsmanship is quite good. They have changed little
in four thousand years."

Wingo looked up in surprise. "This man and this beast: surely they
are imaginary?"

"The Arcts are an ancient race. They still inhabit a dozen crags in
the Gaspard fastnesses of Gamma. They are notorious for their feuds
and vendettas. They also raid the lowland cattle ranches, where they
are greatly feared. Like the Klugash, they are a peculiar race and a
rather sinister people."

"So it would seem," said Wingo absentmindedly. He considered the
sketchbook. Gill's price might be high, or it might be low. There was
one way to find out. He asked, "What is your price on the sketchbook?"

"A hundred sols," said Gill without hesitation. "It is an object of
rare charm."

"Ha hm," said Wingo. He laid the sketchbook aside. Everly Prase's
wan little face would haunt him for weeks.

Wingo looked into another tray and at random picked up a fragment of broken stone. After a glance he started to drop it back into the
tray, then looked again with greater attention. The fragment, carved
from black diorite, represented the broken forequarters and head of a
large beast. Wingo noted that the carving was of excellent quality, and
even in its broken condition, it pulsed with vital energy.

Wingo held up the piece for Professor Gill's inspection. "What
sort of thing is this?"

Professor Gill spared the object a casual glance. "It is a Klugash fetish. If you owned all thirty-seven pieces to the set, you would control a great deal of Klugash magic. The set would also be valuable and you might become rich, or—more likely—dead."

Wingo appraised the item dubiously. "Do you stock other such carvings, perhaps for your own collection?"

"Ha ha! I never see any to collect! If I did, I would hesitate for a variety of reasons, including fear."

Wingo said wistfully, "I am drawn to such little trinkets, especially when they are parts of a set."

"That is known as 'collector's pruritis,'" observed Professor Gill.

Wingo muttered, half to himself, "I wonder if a complete set might be obtained from the Klugash themselves?"

Professor Gill chuckled. "The chances are remote."

Wingo sighed. "What is your price on this fragment?"

Gill chuckled again. "You want the piece with great fervor! I could ask an exorbitant price and you would pay!"

"Try me," said Wingo grimly.

"Do you take me for a man without honor?" cried Gill. "The thing is broken and useless. Take it, free of charge; it is yours."

Wingo grunted, and laid two sols upon the counter. "This is the price I was prepared to pay. Add it to the fund which will whisk you away from Mariah."

"On that basis, I agree to the transaction."

The two bowed to each other. Wingo took up the fragment and left the shop.

TWELVE

1

Late in the afternoon, while Pfitz still hung high in the dark sky, the *Glicca* rose from the Felker spaceport and drifted eastward: over plain, ocean, and into the mountainous heart of Beta. With the coming of dusk the *Glicca* settled upon the Cambria spaceport. The terminal office was already closed for the night, as were the warehouses and docks. At the far end of the field the dark face of the Great Shinar Forest rose like a wall. In the opposite direction, a spatter of light indicated the extent of Cambria Town. Beyond, the Mystic Hills loomed across the twilight sky.

Over the course of time the area had been racked by tectonic violence. Under the Mystic Hills drifting continental plates had collided, curling up and over, to produce cataclysmic landslides; sometimes the plates ground at each other, face to face, until one was subdued and thrust down into the underlying magma, meanwhile squirting bursts of flaming gas and incandescent lava upward through parallel fissures, along what in effect were fractionating processes, forming ledges of precious metals.

During the five thousand years after the arrival of Abel Mirklint, Cambria underwent many phases of history. Settlements waxed and waned, in proportion to the activity along the Great Mother Reef, where the mines yielded rare-earth elements too difficult and too expensive to be synthesized.

Halfway through the history of Cambria, a new factor of sensational import burst upon the Gaean Reach. Its source was a row of fourteen statues seven feet tall, discovered only a few yards into the shade of the Great Shinar Forest. At first the statues had been assumed to be the work of the Klugash, and so had been neglected. Then, by chance, a team of biochemists had examined the statues and, for various reasons, declared them to be the relics of an alien race. The news, while not inherently unreasonable, excited an instant storm of controversy. A hundred study teams and research groups descended upon Cambria. The area was subjected to an inch-by-inch scrutiny, while the statues were analyzed from every direction.

The end result was ambiguity, with no one wiser than before. Since the stuff of the statues refused to incandesce, it gave off no spectroscopic signature, nor did it emit radiation of any detectable frequency by which its half-life could be measured. The material was impervious to all known reagents. In the end the stuff was announced to be a subnuclear gum, and the problem was declared solved. The age of the statues remained in doubt, as did the methods by which they had been sculpted, transported, and emplaced.

Such was the nature of the first mystery: a puzzle for physical scientists. The second mystery occupied xenologists and social symbologists. Who or what were the statues intended to represent? Ostensibly they depicted fourteen large Klugash squatting upon their haunches, in positions suggesting either introspection, or, conceivably, submissiveness. Were the statues attempts by an alien race to memorialize the Klugash? Were the Klugash themselves the alien race? Helmets like squat cones shadowed the faces, where the features were only playfully suggested, and not always in an andromorphic mode.

The controversy persisted; scholars developed fresh speculations; the site became first an institution, then, with the advent of tourists, a small multifunctional community.

The statues were disposed in a line at the very edge of the Great Shinar Forest; tourists and personnel alike were warned as to the unpredictable Klugash temperament. Often, when dusk fell over the Mystic Hills, a solitary Klugash might sidle from the forest, clamber upon a pedestal, then swing up to straddle the marmoreal shoulders and sit for an hour, resting his head on the helmet below. Why? To cogitate? To recharge his psychic batteries? The Klugash never explained and no one dared to ask.

In the morning the *Glicca* discharged cargo, then became dormant, waiting until parcels of outbound cargo could be crated and invoiced.

Wingo took advantage of the free time to further his private concerns. Without confiding in anyone, he sauntered off toward the Parade of Statues, the brown cloak flapping and a backpack slung about his shoulders. At the edge of the field Wingo halted and appraised the forest that reared above him: dismal, dark, menacing. Ribbed trunks of several muted colors rose thirty feet, to bifurcate into secondary stalks, which rose to other bifurcations, sprouting fleshy gray-green palps along the way. From the forest depths came no sound. Wingo peered into the gloom, but, as he had expected, saw nothing. In a brisk businesslike manner he set up a small collapsible table on which he placed several objects: first, a flat box divided into forty compartments, into one of which he placed the fragmentary carving he had obtained from Professor Gill. He tilted back the lid to the box and propped against it a card on which he had printed a message:

> I WISH TO TRADE FOR A FULL SET OF CARVINGS LIKE THE FRAGMENT IN THE BOX, BUT IN GOOD CONDITION.
> I PLACE MY TRADE GOODS AT THE SIDE. IF INSUFFICIENT, PLEASE ADVISE AS TO WHAT IS WANTED.

On the other side of the table he placed a set of four knives with edges of the substance irrevox, two chisels, scissors, a pair of tweezers, a small flask of lavender oil, a flashlight, and a small mirror.

Wingo surveyed the table with satisfaction, then moved fifty yards or so up the field toward the *Glicca*, where he halted and discreetly readied his camera.

Wingo waited. Time passed. Pfitz moved up the ink-dark sky. Nothing happened. Wingo brought out a tin whistle and blew a round of trills, warbles, and runs. He waited, then essayed a jig, but desisted since he had forgotten much of the tune, and the music was not going well.

More time passed, then at last Wingo thought to detect movement among the shadows of the forest. He called out, "I am here to trade! I want good carvings of animals! Bring me the set of thirty-seven such carvings, and take the cutting knives, with which you may carve many more such objects, since the edges never grow dull. I want only carvings of excellent quality!"

Wingo moved off another few yards and leaned back against a stump. More time passed. The table remained as before, seeming timid and ineffectual against the massive indifference of the forest. Wingo uttered a sad sigh. He had, after all, expected nothing better; still, perhaps it was too soon to be discouraged. He restrained himself from peering too intently into the woods, though from the corners of his eyes he thought to notice small shadows flitting back and forth.

Pfitz reached its zenith. Wingo strolled casually to the table and saw at once that his fragment of a statue was gone. Interesting! How and when had it been removed? He had noticed no such activity!

Wingo stretched, and without haste returned to the *Glicca* where he remained the rest of the afternoon.

Pfitz settled behind the Mystic Hills. Dimness slowly blurred the landscape. Wingo restlessly prowled about the saloon, peering out the portholes from time to time. It was a world of bleak melancholy. He had felt an oppression from the moment they had put down at Songerl Spaceport. He had seen no laughing at Felker's Landing, while the atmosphere at Cambria Town was even more oppressive. Most peculiar. He had waited long enough. Taking up a lantern and a pole, he went out once more and walked slowly down to the lower end of the field. Wingo approached the table and—his heart gave a leap; the trade goods were gone! Wingo hurried forward, peered down into the box. To his surprise and delight each of thirty-seven compartments contained a small stone carving.

Marvelous! thought Wingo. Here, so casually bestowed, was treasure beyond his most fervent hopes! What of the purported magic? He looked down at the carved creatures, but felt no quiver of arcane force. No matter! It was enough to own these objects of wonder and beauty.

A low voice spoke. "Why do you smirk, pink man? Have you cheated us so rarely?"

"No! Never!" cried Wingo. "Absolutely not! I smile because the carvings give me pleasure! That is not wrongful smiling!"

"Perhaps not. Still, a fitting sobriety is preferred. What else have you brought for us?"

"I brought what I could. Here is a lantern and a pole; also two flashlights, a roll of strapping tape, a jar of my private foot ointment, and a dozen custard tarts." Wingo set out his gifts, and waited. The silence was portentous.

Then: "I suppose it will do. Now be off with you, else there might be fifteen statues in a row, the last notable for its foolish smirk."

Wingo hesitated, then daring greatly, asked, "You have been generous; can you tell me why?"

The voice was silent. Perhaps it had gone. Wingo listened intently. He heard only what sounded like a soft in-drawing of breath. Wingo's heart started thudding. He mumbled something incoherent, then at best speed closed the box, folded the table, took up his gear, and departed.

Back aboard the *Glicca* and alone in his cabin, he examined the statues one by one. They were even more strange and fearsome than he had expected. He found that he was reluctant to touch them, and could not handle them without using a towel to muffle his fingers.

Wingo stood up and pondered the carvings. His euphoria was gone, leaving him deflated. Slowly he repacked the box, clamped down the lid, then stowed the box into the deepest darkest corner of his closet. At the first opportunity, he told himself, he would sell box and contents to an institution, or any one else who wanted them.

2

Rorbeck Square, at the center of Cambria Town, was surrounded on three sides by multistoried buildings: some extremely old, others modern, but built to the precepts of the same basic rectilinear architecture. On the fourth side, the square adjoined a public park with a playground for children, a bandstand, and a mineralogical museum. Moncrief, in order to take advantage of the *Glicca*'s three-day layover, arranged a pavilion for his troupe at the northern entrance to the park. A sign read:

> SCIENTISTS! ENGINEERS! TECHNICIANS! DO YOU TRUST YOUR JUDGMENT? YES? THEN USE THIS TALENT TO WIN A GRAND FORTUNE! THE GAMES ARE FASCINATING! YOU WILL BE TESTING YOUR WITS AGAINST FLOOK, POOK, AND SNOOK. COME FORWARD, PLACE DOWN YOUR WAGERS, AND TAKE YOUR CHOICE.

The three girls mounted their ormolu drums, holding their flambeaux at dramatic angles. At the back of the platform stood Siglaf and Hunzel, resolved to protect their interests. As always, they wore leather breeches and leather tunics, with iron bands clamping their oat-colored hair.

Moncrief came forward, jaunty and gay, as if laden with glad tidings. He identified himself, then presented each of the three girls, describing their virtues, whims, and special qualities. Next, he introduced Siglaf and Hunzel, whom he described as "staunch and virginal avatars of the classic Gothic war goddesses." "Now then!" cried Moncrief. "To the game! All you men of pride and honor, come forward! Never will such an opportunity appear again!" Moncrief took the flambeaux from the three girls. "Observe these dainty morsels: Flook, Pook, and Snook: each a creature of ardent mischief, daring you to seek her out! Away now, with a hi-ho douterango!"

The girls performed their evolutions and stood in a line, grinning at the spectators.

"Now then!" cried Moncrief. "Which is Flook? Or Pook? Or Snook? Make a choice and place your wager. For folk of keen intellect a problem like this will seem a bagatelle!"

"Quite so," said a small fat man with a mincing voice. "I wager five sols, and I make out this young creature to be Snook."

"Hurrah!" called Moncrief, with patently false enthusiasm. "Your eyes are keen! Well, then, to another game, and this time luck may be on my side."

The contestant spoke primly. "For a scientist, luck is never a factor! It is a matter of using the proper mental procedures at the optimal instant."

Moncrief made no comment, and set another game into motion. The scientist won this game as well, and also a third, causing Moncrief considerable disquietude. He went to the side of the platform to refresh himself with a glass of water. Here he chanced to overhear a snatch of conversation between a pair of scientists. "Have you noticed? Herman is testing his new temperature sensor! It seems to be a jim-dandy!"

"Oh indeed! It reads differences of a thousandth degree at thirty feet!"

The two men walked away. Moncrief turned to look at Herman, the plump constestant, and saw that he carried a small instrument. Herman called impatiently, "I am ready to continue the game! Let us hop to it, since I wish to play as often as possible."

"A moment while we make adjustments," said Moncrief. He signaled the girls to the backstage dressing room, where he turned a heat lamp for ten seconds on Flook; for twenty seconds on Snook, while Pook wiped herself down with a towel dipped in cold water.

Moncrief went to the front of the platform. "We are ready to continue!" he told Herman. "What is your wager?"

"I am now confident, and my wager shall be sixty-five sols! Where are the girls?"

Flook, Pook, and Snook came from backstage to stand in a line. "For this game we will omit the acrobatics, since it tires the girls. So then: which is Flook? Or Pook? Or Snook?"

The scientist examined his instrument, at first casually, then in confusion. At last he pointed a wavering finger. "Yonder stands Pook, or so it may be."

"Wrong!" declared Moncrief, tucking the sixty-five sol wager into his wallet. "You have chosen the equally desirable Flook!"

The scientist moved away, grumbling and shaking his head. Moncrief looked after him with satisfaction. He announced: "A new game is in prospect. Are we ready?" He looked right and left, then called out: "Aha! The joyful lust for competition runs deep among the bravos of Cambria! Sir, welcome to the game!"

The gentleman who had stepped forward, unlike Herman the thermodynamicist, was tall, thin, waxen pale, bald as an egg, with a long thin nose. He wore the red and yellow cap of the Hyperlogique Society, and Moncrief thought that here, perhaps, was another scientist, though he carried neither dials nor instruments. The gentleman stepped close to the platform, surveyed the girls, then placed down ten sols. "Here is my wager! Let the game proceed!"

When the girls stood in a line, the gentleman without hesitation pointed his finger. "This is obviously Pook."

"Just so!" grumbled Moncrief. "You scientists are all alike. What is it this time? Telemetry? Logarithms? I cannot cope with such technology! You must abstain from these devices if you wish to join the sport."

"Never mind your foolishness!" stormed the gentleman. "It is my right to play and here is my wager, this time a rousing hundred sols!"

Moncrief shook his head decisively. "I have heard enough! We allow no agitators to spoil our fun." Moncrief gave a discreet signal and Siglaf moved forward. "Our rules prohibit scientific instruments; they corrupt the spirit of the game."

"One moment!" cried the gentleman. "If I explain my methods, may I continue to play the game?"

Moncrief's indignation vanished. "Of course! We insist upon fair play for all."

"That is good news!" declared the gentleman. "I applaud your gallantry!"

Moncrief smilingly bowed his head, in appreciation of the gentleman's naivete. "Your high standards have carried the day! Since you insist upon frankness, you may now reveal how you won the previous game."

"Simplicity itself! I used my nose. Flook has recently ingested a rum-flavored toffee; Snook has enjoyed a taste or two of garlic, and Pook even now is sucking on a mint pastille. It is child's play. Now then, I have wagered a hundred sols. Shall we proceed?"

"Without delay!" cried Moncrief. "It is on to our new program! You have become the lucky first challenger!"

"By no means! I wish to lay my wager on the last game!"

"Tomorrow perhaps, but today your wager has already been registered to the new game!"

All arguments went unheeded, and eventually the gentleman was induced to walk out upon a teetering plank balanced across a vat of mud. Hunzel stepped up on the far end of the plank. She stretched her arms to either side, hunched her shoulders, clenching and unclenching her fists, meanwhile showing the gentleman a wolfish grin.

Moncrief explained the rules. "This is a game of both bravura and finesse, but, in the end, creative strategy will win the day! Each contestant hopes to cause his adversary to 'run through the air,' as we put it, which means trying to reach the rim of the vat before falling into the mud. The contestants earn points through classical grace, but politeness is always commended."

Myron watched the spectacle from the side. A tall thin man standing nearby caught his attention. His legs were long and thin; his face narrow, with glittering black eyes. An odd specimen, as tough and spare as a predatory bird, thought Myron. He wore the costume of a back-country rancher, with a cap pulled down over short black curls. He noticed Myron and gave him a quick appraisal. "You are a stranger here?"

Myron acknowledged the fact. "I am supercargo aboard the *Glicca*."

The man showed even greater interest. "You might be able to help me. My ranch is out on the Lilank Prairie, across the forest. I have wrecked my flitter on the Balch Rocks, and barely escaped with my life, but this is to the side. More to the point, I need another flitter. Do you carry a spare aboard your ship? I will pay well."

"Sorry! We carry only our old utility."

The rancher nodded, as if he had expected no better. "If you hear of anything, leave a message for Cloyd Tutter at the hotel."

"I'll be happy to do so," said Myron, and turned his attention back to the platform.

The gentleman was crawling slowly from the vat, still wearing his red and yellow cap. Moncrief asked him if he would care to play another game, but the gentleman responded in the negative. Hunzel stood to the side, leering down at the onlookers. Moncrief cried out: "Are there no more challengers? Hunzel is proud; see how she struts! She needs a good splash in the mud. Where are the brave scientists to take up the call? What? Are there none whatever? Evidently not. Therefore, we shall transfer to our next demonstration. I refer, of course, to the fabulous Mouse-riders, in triple stampede. The invitation applies to all! Please step around to the side."

Tutter told Myron, "I expected nothing like this. Those girls create an epic just standing still."

Myron said, "Yes, possibly so."

"And what is their function aboard ship? Are they dancers? Bait? Jolly companions?"

"One thing is definite," said Myron, "they are good eaters. Wingo the cook has spoiled them rotten."

In frowning speculation Tutter pulled at his long chin. "What is their destination?"

"We are taking them as far as Cax, on Blenkinsop."

"I have a better idea," said Tutter. "Moncrief can leave the girls with me. I'll keep them strong and fit!"

"You could make Moncrief an offer," Myron suggested. "He might listen, or he might refer you to Hunzel or Siglaf."

Tutter scanned the platform. "Who might they be?"

Myron pointed. "Yonder stand two female juggernauts in iron pants; they are Siglaf and Hunzel. They claim control of the three girls, rightly or wrongly, I can't say; but you could challenge them to a competition."

Tutter looked at Myron in surprise, then darted a glance toward Siglaf and Hunzel. "A competition? You mean, on the plank across the vat? I think not. My other business is more urgent. I need transport to the Lilank Prairie. At home I have three wrecked flitters and a barnful of parts. I can put together something that flies, even if it flies funny. When you leave here, where do you go?"

"We have a few crates for Pharisee City, but we won't be leaving for another three days."

Tutter nodded without enthusiasm. "If I can't do better, I will take passage with you to Pharisee City, where I can find transport home. What will be your charges?"

"About three sols, or so I should think."

On the platform Moncrief was addressing the crowd. "Already I seem to hear the thunder of the Mouse-riders! Adventure survives in this remarkable universe! If you doubt me, consult Flook, Pook, or Snook! So now, around to the back of the tent."

"Excuse me!" Tutter told Myron. "I must see for myself what is going on!" He set off at a lope toward the back of Moncrief's tent.

Captain Maloof arrived on the scene. He looked after Tutter. "Who or what is that?"

"He is a rancher who has wrecked his flitter and can't find a replacement. Now he wants to go home."

"Hm," said Maloof. "Where is 'home'?"

"Out on the Lilank Prairie, east of the forest."

"How much cargo do we carry for Pharisee City?"

"Not much. A few sacks of mail and four or five crates of general cargo."

Maloof nodded. "During the layover we can deliver to Pharisee City by flitter and depart this dreary place two days the sooner. We can also carry Tutter as a passenger. Charge him three sols and ask him to be on hand early tomorrow morning."

Myron followed instructions, loading cargo and mail for Pharisee City aboard the flitter. He telephoned Cloyd Tutter at the Grand Luxe Hotel. Tutter readily agreed to be on hand at the time specified.

In the pilothouse Myron studied a map of Mariah. He located Cambria beside the Mystic Hills, with the Great Shinar Forest shrouding the land to the east until it met the rise of the Gaspard Wastelands. Beyond, the Lilank Prairie extended all the way to the waters of the Aeolian Ocean. Eastward, another four hundred miles, the ocean broke upon the dreary shores of Alpha, with Pharisee City huddled behind the hook of Cape Fray.

Myron called Captain Maloof's attention to the map. "Remember Wingo's photographs of the Arct and his dragon-bat?"

"Yes; what of it?"

Myron pointed to the Gaspard Peaks. "This is where they lived four thousand years ago. If you notice, our course takes us over the Balch Rocks, north of the peaks. We might see Arct settlements—if they still exist. Tutter should have the facts."

Maloof bent over the map. "And where is Tutter's ranch?"

"Somewhere about here, I should think." Myron tapped the map. "We could deliver him directly to his home."

"I'm agreeable," said Maloof.

In the morning Cloyd Tutter arrived early at the space terminal. He was met at the *Glicca* by Captain Maloof and Myron; the three went to the flitter. Tutter started to climb aboard, but Captain Maloof detained him. "Excuse me! I must make sure that you are carrying no weapons. It is a graceless bit of routine but it must be done, for obvious reasons."

Tutter's eyebrows arched high. "Weapons? What I carry or do not carry is no concern of yours."

Captain Maloof turned to Myron. "Return to Cloyd Tutter the money he has paid us; he must find another way home."

Tutter stood still, staring at Maloof with glittering black eyes. Then, wordlessly, he reached into his coat and brought out a small dart-pistol and in the same movement jerked a dagger from the sheath which lay flat beside his haunch. He handed the weapons to Maloof, and turned to the flitter.

"Wait," said Maloof. "There is a final formality." He ran his hands deftly over Tutter's body; then, after murmuring an apology, examined Tutter's helmet. Tutter stood stock-still, outraged, but obliged to endure the indignities.

Maloof completed the search and stood back. "I am sorry for the inconvenience, but it can't be helped. I would rather annoy an innocent man than be killed by an armed bandit."

Tutter, with lips compressed, climbed aboard the flitter, followed by Myron and Maloof. The flitter rose from the terminal and set off to the east.

Tutter sat rigidly, staring down at the dark Great Shinar Forest, still rankling from the affront to his self-esteem. Myron allowed him to simmer for a few minutes, then handed him a map. "If you will indicate the location of your ranch, we will drop you off at your front door."

Tutter grudgingly decided that nothing could be gained by sulking. In a flat voice he said, "That would be convenient." He studied the map, then drew a small cross. "This is where I live: about the center of the Lilank Prairie."

Myron indicated a shaded area. "And these are the Gaspard Wastelands?"

"That is correct."

"They are not far from your home. I suppose you know them well?"

"Well enough."

"Listen to this." Myron read from the *Handbook*: " 'Lilank Prairie is the habitat of an astonishing variety of savage beasts. Some of these are of great size and truly amazing ferocity; others survive through strength, or agility, or even a measure of quasi-intelligence.' " Myron paused in his reading and asked Tutter, "How do you cope with these creatures?"

"Ha ha! By fear, stealth, and a hundred miles of electric fence. When my business takes me out on the open prairie, I stay aloft, out of their reach. Sometimes it is a near thing. When I lost my flitter in the Balch Rocks, I ran two hundred miles overland, mostly during the early morning when the beasts are torpid. When I reached my fence, I found a junction-box and called home; one of my women came out in a ground-wagon to pick me up. I had some vivid experiences along the way."

Myron returned to the *Handbook*. "It mentions a people called 'Arcts,' who live in the high Gaspard Peaks." Myron read: " 'They are rumored to ride from peak to peak on creatures called "dragon-bats," which measure as much as forty feet from wingtip to wingtip. The Arct themselves are said to be tall and spare, with ruthless faces. According to legend, they are warlike brigands who ride their dragon-bats when they conduct their bloody forays. This has not been confirmed; more likely, they use some sort of lightweight flitters built to resemble a monster. They reputedly wear complicated helmets which are both handsome and grotesque. The Arct helmet, along with his women, represent his wealth. His favored weapon is a twenty-foot harpoon, since power-guns are proscribed.

" 'A related folk, the Yeltings, live in the stony fastness at the base of the Gaspards, notably among the Balch Rocks. Yelting women are the prey of Arct warriors. The dragon-bats swoop down; the women flee in panic, but they are often seized and carried aloft to the Arct eyries. When they no longer produce children, they work the crops in the high yards.' "

Myron gave his head a shake of distaste. "Is any of this real?"

"All of it."

"You have seen them yourself?"

Tutter gave a short laugh. "Every time I fly over the peaks."

"They don't trouble you?"

Tutter laughed. "They can't catch me, but not for want of trying! Last month they put out a helmet on a grave pole, then waited in ambush. They are not too clever; while they were disposing themselves and quarreling, I dropped down in my flitter, took up the helmet and was gone, before they were ready for me. But one of them threw a harpoon, which struck my craft. I fell to the rocks, bounced a hundred yards, from hummock to hummock, and finally slid into the Wermom River. This was not at all good. I jumped to a sandbank and crawled off through the reeds, still carrying the helmet. The Arcts came down and I heard their outcries, but their bats grew tired and they failed to find me; otherwise, at this very moment I would be dangling in a wicker cage high over Slevin Gulch. Instead, I ran overland to my ranch, where I added the helmet to my collection." Tutter chortled with glee. "This was very good indeed!"

Myron, tired of boasting and vainglory, made a cool observation: "In the process you lost your flitter, which must disturb you."

"Bah!" said Tutter with something of a sneer. "Such a helmet as I won is a great prize, worth ten flitters; and in any case I shall have another flitter shortly."

"And what then? Will you go after their bait again?"

Tutter smiled. "They are a crafty lot, in some ways! In others, they are innocent as twittering birds. A fascinating folk, but not at all likeable, and their concept of humor is bizarre. If you want to see them for yourself, veer a bit south! The Gaspard Peaks will be showing in a few minutes."

Myron studied Tutter for a moment. Tutter turned an irritable scowl upon him. "Why do you stare so boldly?"

Myron collected his wits. "No offense intended! I have noticed that you yourself resemble an Arct."

"Bah!" sneered Tutter. "Where would you have seen an Arct?"

"No mystery! I saw a photograph of an Arct and his mount, copied from an old book."

Tutter gave a dour grunt. "You are half right. I was born in the shadow of the Balch Rocks; my father was Arct; my mother was a red-silk Yelting! I killed an Arct when I was still a boy. The dragon-bat toppled over and landed on its back, where it lay flapping and squealing, and pounding its tail. I rolled boulders down and trapped its tail; then I chopped away the neck and the thing lay quivering. Four days later it died. The priests wanted to sacrifice me, but I broke out of the cage. I pushed old Fugasis into the fire and ran off through the rocks, and out upon the prairie. In the end I arrived at the old Panselin Homeplace. I became a ranchboy, and after the last of the Panselin were gone, I laid claim to the ranch, and that is where I live today."

The Gaspard Wastelands appeared below. The flitter crossed a confusion of toppled blocks and boulders, then flew above a panorama of crags and cliffs. It would seem an environment too stark for human habitation. Still, from time to time a village appeared: sometimes spilling like natural detritus from a cleft; sometimes perched high on a ledge. At rare intervals dark objects glided across the gulf between crags. Tutter identified these as dragon-bats with their riders, and watched them with fascination. After one of the episodes, he told Myron and Maloof with great satisfaction, "It is as I promised! You have seen what few Gaeans have seen, or even suspect: a truly gallant conqueror of the high spaces, with his awful mount! The Arcts are lords of the firmament!"

"Most inspiring!" Maloof said. "But you are a remarkable person in your own right, needless to say."

"Ha ho," said Tutter indifferently. "So it may be. I take myself as I am."

The flitter moved onward, through an airy clarity of Pfitzlight and shadow. The high Gaspard Peaks dwindled astern; the land fell away to the prairie, in a succession of bluffs, terraces, and further bluffs, until at last it merged with a rolling expanse growing with coarse grasses, and an occasional lonely sentinel tree. At far distances between, out-crops of rotting black rock shouldered up from the soil.

Tutter presently announced that the lands below were part of his ranch. A few minutes later the flitter alighted beside an old stone and timber farmhouse, surrounded by a dozen majestic yews.

Tutter jumped from the flitter, followed more sedately by Myron and Maloof. The three stood surveying the old house. "This is quite a surprise," said Maloof. "I expected something more modest."

Tutter chuckled. "It suits me well enough. I have all the room I need, and there is no noise except the wind."

Myron asked, "Do you live alone?"

"So I do, for the most part. The farm compound lies over yonder, behind the Irfle Woods. There I keep twenty-eight Yelting women, who work the farm and patrol the fences. Once a week a young woman comes in to cut my hair and do whatever else is needful; otherwise I am alone and free to take care of my business."

"What is this business?" Maloof asked.

"Trifles of this and that. In the main I sell farm stuff to villagers along the eastern shore. But come! Step inside for a moment! I can show you objects even more surprising than the house itself!"

Myron and Maloof looked at each other. They shrugged, then followed Tutter through the front door into a large room paneled with planks of varnished rock-cedar. A pair of heavy rugs, striped black, white, and gray, lay on the floor; furniture, consisting of a long table, a few chairs, a couch, and a pair of small tabourets, were all built of black wenge and placed to the dictates of household etiquette. On the walls hung Panselin family portraits, painted upon thin slabs of wenge.

Maloof went to study the long pale faces, which stared at him from brooding black eyes. "The portraits are interesting," Maloof told Tutter. "Are these your 'surprises'?"

"No; I had something else in mind, as you will see."

"We have far to go," said Maloof. "It is time that we were on our way."

Tutter cried out heartily. "Must you go so soon? I have more to show you."

"If you have something, a surprise, or whatever, please show us now. We really must leave."

"Yes," said Tutter, after reflection. "I think that the word 'surprise' holds force. In any case, I must serve refreshments! It would be shame-ful to do otherwise."

Tutter left the room at a lope, to return a moment later with a tray which he placed upon the table. "It is our traditional fare. These are seedcakes; and here, in the pot of the Panselin, is a special tea. It is considered very good." He poured, tendered a mug to Myron and another to Maloof. "I am anxious to learn your opinion."

Maloof took up his mug and smelled the steam. His eyebrows jerked high; he replaced the mug on the tray.

Tutter watched carefully. "What do you think?"

"It is too strong for me. If anyone—even you—could drink it, I would consider it a 'surprise' indeed."

"Try just a sip!" Tutter urged. "You too, Myron! You might well find it pleasing!"

"I am afraid it will make me sick," said Maloof.

"Just a sip?" suggested Tutter.

"No, thank you."

Myron also put down his mug. "My opinion is the same."

Maloof turned toward the door. "And now—"

Tutter held up his hand. "You may recall that I spoke of the Arct helmets?"

"You mentioned that they were valuable."

"So I did, and so they are!" Tutter went to the cabinet and threw wide the doors. "See for yourselves!"

Six tall helmets faced out upon the room, staring from shadowed holes to right and left of the nasals. "My treasures stand revealed!" cried Tutter. "So much beauty is surely a 'surprise,' is it not? But there is more!" Tutter stepped forward, lifted one of the helmets from the shelf. "Look! Notice the sweep of the curves! The helmet is a symbol of Destiny! But one moment." He placed the helmet on the table and turned back to the shelves. "Symmetry is indispensable." He reached, then paused to look over his shoulder. "Beauty comes in many guises! It is everywhere! Some identify beauty with life! Others claim that the waning of life, like the fading of a sunset, is the culmination of all experience. A paradox? If so, I have not been able to resolve it."

Tutter shook his head as if baffled. He turned back to the shelves, stretched his arm, groped in the shadows and brought out a silver-blue gun. He swung about, his face a gaunt grinning mask. "All questions, both of life and death, are now moot, since I must have the flitter."

Maloof had been waiting, gun in hand. He shot before Tutter could level his weapon, and watched as Tutter slumped to the floor.

Myron came to look down at the body. "It is hard to mourn Tutter."

Maloof turned away. "Come; it is time to go. Let Tutter solve his mysteries in peace."

"Wait!" cried Myron. "There are still the helmets to consider!"

"What about them?"

"We just can't walk away and leave them! They would be loot for the first gang to look through the window!"

"You may well be right."

The two carried the helmets out to the flitter, then climbed aboard and flew off into the east through the failing light of afternoon. In due course they arrived at the dismal shore of the Aeolian Ocean. They set off across the water and four hundred miles later, they put down behind the squat stone ramparts of Pharisee City. They discharged their cargo, then went to the refectory and made a meal of fried fish and oatcakes. Returning to the flitter, they departed Pharisee City and flew back the way they had come: over the water and across the Lilank Prairie, chasing twilight into the west.

The two rode in silence, each preoccupied with his own thoughts. The prairie fell behind; the flitter drifted out across the vast black face of the Great Shinar Forest. Myron looked down from the window, wondering whether he might see the glimmer of a light, but saw only deep darkness. He drew back. "I would not care to make a forced landing down there, especially now."

"Nor I," said Maloof. "I want only to arrive at Cambria, board the *Glicca*, and put this dismal world astern!"

"I agree."

For a time they did not speak. Then Maloof looked toward the sky, where the stars were shining. "Up there is our next port of call: Coro-Coro on Fluter. It is serene and restful. The scenery is splendid. It is the ideal place for a layover, which will be useful to all of us."

"You'll hear a few complaints."

"At Coro-Coro the first phase of our voyage is over. The next phase takes us to Cax on Blenkinsop. The padroons are not always reasonable; if we hope to have our way with them, we shall need all our craft. But I am sanguine; I suspect that we will succeed and set off along the next phase of our voyage. And there ahead I see the lights of Cambria!"

3

Before leaving Mariah, the *Glicca* made a final stop at Felker's Landing, in order to load another consignment of kiki-nuts. At the first opportunity, Wingo donned his brown cloak and wide-brimmed hat and, taking up a parcel, set off toward town. He passed the Prospero Inn, turned into a side-street, approached the Museum of the Natural Man, and entered. He found Professor Gill standing at a counter, polishing a stone amulet.

Professor Gill acknowledged Wingo's presence with a curt nod and continued his work. Wingo bowed politely and placed his parcel on the counter. After a moment Professor Gill glanced sidewise at the parcel, then a second time, then finally could no longer contain his curiosity. He put down his work. "What do you have there?"

Wingo responded rather ponderously: "I believe this piece to be genuine, but I would be interested to hear your opinion."

Professor Gill made a sound of annoyance: "Sassah! Is it not always the way? Every time a tourist finds a bit of petrified turnip, he comes running to me with his prize and demands a notarized affadavit! I must start charging a fee. Well then, let's have a look."

"A glance should be enough," said Wingo soothingly. He opened the parcel. "I remember you expressed interest in such articles, so before I take it to auction—"

"Hold!" cried Professor Gill in a choking voice. "My dear sir; am I seeing correctly?"

"Of course; why should you not?"

"Because I never thought to see such a piece! What is its source?"

"It comes, so I am told, from the collection of an outlaw Arct, who no longer flies."

"It is a superb example! May I touch it?"

"Of course! In fact I wonder if we might agree on a trade."

"Absolutely! What are your desires? You need but name them."

Wingo said hesitantly, "As a matter of fact, one of your properties caught my eye: the sketchbook of a boy named Dondil Reske."

"I know it well, a charming little piece! It is yours! What more do you need?"

"That will be enough."

Professor Gill ran to fetch the sketchbook.

The two connoisseurs congratulated each other, then Wingo returned to the *Glicca*. Professor Gill closed and locked the door. He placed the helmet on a counter. To the right and left he arranged a golden candelabrum and reverently put flame to the orange candles. From the depths of a cabinet he brought a squat bottle and a goblet. He unsealed the bottle and poured a thick amber liquid into the goblet; then he pulled up a chair, settled himself to the joy of his acquisition. The universe had been opened to him; he was free to leave this frowsty little town of mad sprang-hoppers and, in dignity and pride, return to the cloisters of academia, where his wry anecdotes of life on Mariah would grace many an intimate little dinner party.

Bliss!

EPILOGUE

The *Glicca* drifted through space, unsubstantial as a puff of magic smoke. Far astern Pfitz was a dying white spark, which presently faded. Ahead, golden Frametta could not yet be seen. In the pilothouse of the *Glicca*, Captain Maloof turned from the observation window and stepped aft into the main saloon. He waited until the cheerful voices quieted, then spoke.

"Before long we will be arriving at the Coro-coro spaceport on Fluter, and you should know something of local conditions, which at times are ambiguous if not extraordinary. In general, Fluter is a tranquil world, with beautiful landscapes in every direction, and a near-total lack of natural hazards. Coro-coro is the only settlement of consequence and functions as node for the tourist trade, which is of great importance.

"Aside from the tourist facilities, there is nothing much to the town. A boulevard runs from the spaceport out to the O-Shar-Shan Hotel, with more hotels along the way; also agencies, shops, and taverns. Residences are scattered in the gardens to either side of the boulevard. These are the homes of the folk native to Coro-coro, who are different from the Flauts who live in the back-country villages. They are, in fact, a hybrid race, mixed from renegade Flauts and those few off-worlders who have been allowed permanent residence on Fluter. They regard themselves as highly sophisticated aristocrats, with wealth derived from the tourist trade.

"Coro-coro functions as an enclave, to some degree exempt from the ordinary population controls. In theory, tourists are allowed entry permits of thirty days, then are required to leave the planet. In practice the entry permit can be extended.

"If a tourist is adventurous, he can rent a vehicle and go out to explore the back-country. He will find magnificent scenery, otherwise mostly solitude. Perhaps he will come upon a village consisting of a dozen or two picturesque old cottages, a tavern, a market, and a few shops surrounding a village green. Usually there is an inn where lodging can be had. The management will be polite but not cordial. If you should visit a village, remain unobtrusive, express no opinions; drink with temperance. No one worries for the drunken tourist who has been tossed into the sump. Do not haggle or complain; ignore the girls. The village may seem a placid place where nothing ever happens, but it is almost certainly the scene of a thousand grisly events.

"The first settlers arrived from the congested world Ergard. At their first conclave, they vowed that pressure of population should never again become distressful. The number they fixed upon was ninety-nine thousand, and by great effort across the ages the limit has been maintained, and the population of Fluter is now at equilibrium. The bitter events of the past still rankle and gnaw at the Flaut soul, so that they display a peculiar personality: a kind of sullen grandiosity. Today they are a dour suspicious folk, by reason of their grim history, which I will not touch upon now.

"I think I have covered everything important. Are there any questions?"

Kalash, perrumpter of the pilgrims, raised his hand. "What of our cases? They contain valuable materials; will you relinquish them to us?"

"Certainly, as soon as you pay off the freight charges."

"Ah, bah!" cried Kalash. "Can you not take the long view? If you recall, we gambled with Schwatzendale; now we lack funds."

"That was your mistake, not mine."

Kalash grimaced. "We are quite at a loss! Ours is a pilgrimage of immense importance, but Schwatzendale avoids all talk of restitution. Our needs are urgent! Think, if you will! We must pay our fares to Kyril, then return fares home to Komard—not to mention the expenses during our march around Kyril. How can we obtain this necessary money?"

"Simple enough. Work for it."

Kalash made a face. "That is easier said than done."

"Not altogether. There is a labor shortage along the Strip. You should have no trouble."

"And the cases?"

"They shall be ready to hand. I will leave them in the transit warehouse. To redeem them, pay off storage and freight charges, and they are yours. Have you any further questions?"

"I think not," grumbled Kalash. "I had hoped for an easy generosity on your part, but I must make do with what I find."

"Anything else?" asked Maloof.

Cooner stepped forward, frowning thoughtfully, to indicate that he might have a question, possibly of a recondite nature. Maloof looked past him and addressed the group.

"I have an announcement to make. The crew of this ship needs both bodily rest and nervous regeneration. The *Glicca* itself is in need of maintenance. Therefore we shall sojourn upon Fluter for—perhaps a week or two. The pilgrims will debark and prepare to transship to Kyril. We shall miss their wise counsel and their happy songs, but after Coro-Coro we must fare onward to Cax.

"Thereafter, who knows? I can make no prediction. We are like the romantic vagabonds of old, each searching for Lurulu."

Cooner called out, "That is a place past my experience! What or where, pray, is 'Lurulu'?"

"It is a special word, from the language of myths and legends, and is as much of a mystery now as when I first yearned for something lost and unknown. But one day I shall glance over my shoulder and there it will be, wondering why I had not come sooner. As for now, it is on to Coro-Coro. Here I feel an imminence; here something important will happen; of this I feel certain. What? I do not know; it is a mystery."

Cooner's puzzlement had not yet been assuaged. "And Lurulu is part of this mystery?"

Maloof gave a noncommittal shrug. "Perhaps. I may not be happy with what I find, if and when I find it."

"And what is it you seek?"

Maloof smiled. "I can tell you this much. If I am lucky—or perhaps if I am unlucky—I will find it on Fluter."

"Interesting!" declared Cooner. He turned to Moncrief. "And you, sir! Are you also in pursuit of Lurulu?"

"I am sidling in its direction," Moncrief admitted. "I see a glimmer every time I take some of Schwatzendale's money. In the main, I hope that the Mouse-riders will resurge in all their glory! That would be Lurulu of the purest water!"

Cooner looked to Wingo. "And you, Brother Wingo? Where do you seek Lurulu?"

"I cannot put it aptly into words," said Wingo. "It is what I hope to capture in my *Pageant of the Gaean Race*. There is also an elemental equation which describes Truth, but in this regard I am reluctant to say more."

Myron called out, "I am not so diffident! The object of my quest is named Dame Hester Lajoie, and when I catch her, I hope that a jail is near, since gallantry would not allow me to do what I would like."

Cooner turned back to Captain Maloof. "Would you, sir, care to tell us a bit more of your own quest?"

Captain Maloof smiled sadly. "I will say only that I am anxious to arrive on Fluter. Out among the back-islands mysteries still abide. In any case, good luck to us all."

Cooner started to ask a cogent new question, but Captain Maloof turned back into the pilothouse. He went to look from the observation window. Frametta still could not be seen. He muttered to himself: "How will it be, if it happens at all? I must take care not to commit myself absolutely." He stared out the window to where Frametta would shortly come into view. "Whatever the case, life goes on, and I must prepare for Cax, where something ugly is certain."

For several moments more he stood gazing out the window. At last, far across the void, he thought to see the small gleam that would be the star Frametta.

LURULU

To Norma

ONE

A précis of the first book, *Ports of Call*

As a boy Myron Tany had immersed himself in the lore of space exploration. In his imagination he wandered the far places of the Gaean Reach, thrilling to the exploits of star-dusters and locators; of pirates and slavers; of the IPCC and its brave agents.

By contrast, his home at the bucolic village Lilling, on the pleasant world Vermazen, seemed to encompass everything easy, tranquil, and soporific. Despite Myron's daydreams, his parents persisted in stressing the practicalities. "Most important is your education, if you are to become a financial analyst like your father," Myron was told. "After you finish your course at the Institute, that will be the time to flutter your wings for a bit before taking a post at the Exchange."

Myron, mild and dutiful by temperament, pushed the intoxicating images to the back of his mind, and enrolled at the College of Definable Excellences at the Varley Institute, across the continent at Salou Sain. His parents, who well understood his casual disposition, sent him off with a set of stern injunctions: he must concentrate with full diligence upon his studies; scholastic achievement was highly important when a person prepared for a career.

Myron agreed to do his best, but found himself waylaid by indecision when it came time to propose a schedule of studies. Despite his best intentions, he could not put aside images of majestic space-packets sliding through the void; of cities redolent with strange smells; of taverns open to the warm winds where barefoot maidens served jugs of Mango Slurry and Blue Ruin.

In the end Myron fixed upon a set of courses which, in his opinion, represented a compromise. The list included statistical mathematics, economic patterns of the Gaean Reach, general cosmology, the elementary theory of space propulsion, Gaean anthropology. The program, so he assured his parents, was known as 'Economic Fluxions', and provided a solid foundation upon which a good general education might be based. Myron's parents were not convinced. They knew that Myron's decorous manner, though at times a trifle absent-minded, concealed a streak of irrational intransigence against which no argument could prevail. They would say no more; Myron must discover his mistakes for himself.

Myron could not dismiss the foreboding which his father's glum predictions had induced. As a consequence he attacked his work vigorously. In due course he was matriculated with high honors, and a position at the Exchange was open to him. But now an unforeseen factor disturbed the flow of Myron's life. The disruptive influence was Myron's great-aunt Dame Hester Lajoie, who had inherited great wealth from her first husband. Dame Hester maintained her splendid residence, Sarbiter House, on Dingle Terrace, at the southern edge of Salou Sain. During Myron's last term at Varley Institute, Dame Hester noticed that Myron was no longer a slender stripling with a vague and—as she put it—moony expression, but had become a distinctly good-looking young man, still slender, but of good physical proportions, with sleek blond hair and sea-blue eyes. Dame Hester enjoyed the presence of handsome young men: they acted, so she imagined, as a foil, or perhaps better to say, a setting for the precious gem which was herself. For whatever reason, during Myron's last term, he resided at Sarbiter House with his great-aunt: an education in itself.

Dame Hester fitted no familiar patterns of Gaean womanhood. She was tall and gaunt, though she insisted upon the word 'slim'. She walked with long strides, head thrust forward like a rapacious animal on the prowl. Her wild mass of mahogany-red hair framed a pale, hollow-cheeked face. Her black eyes were surrounded by small creases and folds of skin, like a parrot's eyes, and her long high-bridged nose terminated in a notable hook. It was a striking face, the mouth jerking and grimacing, parrot-eyes snapping, her expression shifting to the flux of emotions. Her tempestuous moods, quirks and fancies were notorious. One day at a garden party, a gentleman artlessly urged Dame Hester to write her memoirs. The fervor of her response caused him shock and dismay. "Ludicrous! Graceless! Stupid! A beastly idea! How can I write memoirs now when I have scarcely started to live?"

For a fact Dame Hester was not always discreet. She conceived herself a creature of voluptuous charm for whom time had no meaning. Undeniably she made a gorgeous spectacle as she whirled about the haut monde, clad in remarkable garments of magenta, lime green, vermilion and black.

Dame Hester had recently won a judgment of slander against Gower Hatchkey, a wealthy member of the Gadroon Society. In satisfaction of the judgment she had accepted the space-yacht *Glodwyn*.

Initially Dame Hester thought of the *Glodwyn* only as proof that whoever chose to call her 'a bald old harridan in a red fright-wig' must pay well for the privilege. She showed no interest in the vessel, to Myron's astonishment. She told him tartly: "Truly, I have no inclination to go hurtling through space in an oversize coffin. That is sheer lunacy and a mortification of both body and spirit. I shall probably put the vessel up for sale."

Myron groaned and clutched at his sleek blond hair.

Dame Hester watched him closely. "I see that you are perplexed; you think me timid and orthodox! That is incorrect! I pay no heed to convention, and why is this? Because my youthful spirit defies the years! So you dismiss me as an eccentric madcap? What then? It is the price I pay for retaining the verve of youth, and it is the secret of my vivid beauty!"

"Ah yes, of course," said Myron. He added thoughtfully: "Still, it is sad waste of a beautiful ship."

The remark irritated Dame Hester. "Myron, be practical! Why should I gad about empty space, or trudge through dirty back alleys in search of strange smells? Preposterous!"

Myron numbly went off to read *Transcendent Lives: The Locators and Their Model 11-B Scudders*.

During a rare moment of repose, Dame Hester chanced upon an article written by a certain 'Serena', telling of her experiences on the world Kodaira, where she had undertaken an amazingly effective rejuvenation program. Dame Hester was inspired by the article. After making inquiries, she altered her views regarding space travel and resolved to visit Kodaira aboard the *Glodwyn*.

With Dame Hester, to think was to act. She summoned Myron and ordered him to learn the exact location of Kodaira. She appointed her dear and intimate friend Dauncy Covarth Captain of the *Glodwyn*, but he disgraced himself and Myron was tendered the position.

The *Glodwyn* departed the Salou Sain spaceport, and Myron set a course for Naharius, the real name of Kodaira. For a time the voyage proceeded smoothly. Dame Hester luxuriated in the tranquility, the absence of stress, the total lack of demands upon her time. She slept late, dawdled over her meals and read several books. "The voyage," she told Myron, "is a rejuvenation in itself."

As time passed, Dame Hester's enthusiasm began to wane. She became ever more restless, and finally she summoned Myron.

"Yes, Aunt Hester?"

"How far have we come to date?"

"About halfway, I should guess."

"So little? I feel as if we have been traveling forever!"

"Naharius is a long way out, for a fact," Myron admitted. "Still, there is much to enjoy along the way: untroubled rest, calm and deep meditation, the sheer joy of easing effortlessly past the stars."

"Bah!" snapped Dame Hester.

Myron pointed to the observation port. "Observe the stars drifting past. It is the most romantic spectacle of all!"

"My wish would be to stop by a pleasant way station where the folk still abide by their ancient customs, where we could breathe new air, and enjoy the glamour of strange landscapes and quaint villages."

"All very well," said Myron. "No doubt these picturesque places exist, but if we deviate from our planned course we may not so easily return anywhere near our destination, which is Naharius."

Dame Hester seemed not to hear. "I have read of native markets where unique goods can be had: fetishes and masks, emblems of fertility, exotic fabrics. There are true bargains to be found, if one is prepared to haggle a bit."

"Yes, yes, of course! Nevertheless, such worlds are not to be found everywhere."

Dame Hester lurched up from her position on the sofa. "Please! Myron! I have stated my needs! Be good enough to implement them."

Myron spoke with harried patience. "My dear Aunt Hester, if I could produce a world of such gorgeous romance for your pleasure, I would do so on the instant. But I would be performing a miracle!"

Dame Hester spoke icily: "In that case, perform the miracle. Are you finally aware of my mood?"

"Yes," said Myron. "It is clear."

"Good." Dame Hester resumed her supine posture on the sofa.

Myron bowed and went off to consult his references.

Presently he returned to the saloon. "I have studied *Handbook to the Planets* at length," he told Dame Hester. "The most accessible world is Dimmick, in orbit around the white dwarf Maudwell's Star. It would seem queer and odd enough to gratify even the most avid taste.

"The references are somewhat ambiguous, but none seriously emphasize the world's allure. Let me read from the *Handbook*: 'Dimmick is not a world of halcyon charm, although the topography often displays a rugged grandeur. The surface is for the most part covered under harsh mountains and glaciers. A number of small circular plains, depressed below the surface, are in fact meteor craters. In these parts, the air temperature is modified by ground heat to the threshhold of livability. The town Flajaret and the spaceport are located in one of the craters.

" 'Dimmick and its people, to say the least, are unusual, though sensitive visitors may not be captivated. The efflux of hot springs creates tunnels through the glaciers, providing shelter for a debased caste of dog-breeders known as 'spockows'. The upper castes keep dogs in their homes, and dress them in fancy suits. There is an undercurrent of hostility between the castes, since one eats the creatures, while the other pampers the animals and feeds them tidbits from their tables.

" 'The principal sport is dog-fighting, which is important since it sets the tone for the society. Gambling is obsessive. Even small children crawl to the arena, to bet coins upon their favorite beast. Another vehicle for gambling is the penal system. Near Flajaret is a large lake crusted over with mats of algae. On this surface the penal exercises are conducted, to the great interest of the public at large.

" 'Dimmick is not known for its gracious cuisine, since few if any natural foods are consumed. Ordinary victual consists of synthetic gruel, enlivened by artificial flavoring, then fried, baked, boiled, or shirred, to much the same effect.' "

Myron paused. "Shall I go on? The *Handbook* provides several recipes for boiled dog, which may interest you."

"Thank you, no."

Myron looked sidewise at Dame Hester, trying to gauge her mood. Often she could be perverse simply to inject drama into a situation. He risked an opinion: "I suggest that we bypass Dimmick. We are approaching Port Tanjee on Taubry, which surely will be more entertaining."

Dame Hester spoke decisively: "We shall land at Flajaret and briefly explore this benighted world. Then we shall also halt at Port Tanjee. In this way we will be able to compare the good with the bad."

Myron performed a crisp bow. "As you like."

At Flajaret Dame Hester met an off-worlder named Marko Fassig, an engaging young scapegrace with burly shoulders, a bushy mustache, and soft brown eyes. His witticisms and general gallantry impressed Dame Hester to such an extent that she hired him as purser aboard the *Glodwyn*, despite Myron's strenuous objections.

When the *Glodwyn* landed at Port Tanjee, Myron discharged Fassig from his post, and ordered him off the ship within the hour. But half an hour later it was Myron himself who, in a morose mood, departed the ship carrying his suitcase, with Dame Hester's final remarks still ringing in his ears.

Myron wandered into town and took lodging for the night at the Rambler's Rest rooming house. During the evening he visited the Owlswyck Inn, where he encountered the crew of the freighter *Glicca*, consisting of Captain Adair Maloof, Chief Steward Isel Wingo, Chief Engineer Fay Schwatzendale, and Hilmar Krim, the Supercargo.

Each man contrasted markedly with his fellows, but Krim most of all. He was tall and gaunt, with a high forehead, a curious little mat of black hair, a long chin and hooded black eyes. Krim was given to dogmatic opinions, which his fellows never troubled to contradict. Myron learned that Krim was a dedicated student of jurisprudence, and in fact was composing a three-volume analysis of Gaean law.

On this particular evening, Krim was in good spirits and drank several tankards of Old Gaboon. When the dancing started, he jumped out upon the floor and began to dance an energetic loose-legged strut. A portly well-dressed gentleman, with a fine ginger-colored mustache, also came out upon the floor to perform what was known as 'The Chicken-thief's Trot'—a long loping prance, with body leaning far backwards and legs kicking out high to the front. The two came into contact. During the altercation which followed, Krim committed several offenses against the local law and, when the constable on duty sought to restrain him, aggravated his offenses by kicking the ginger-mustached man in the shins. This gentleman chanced to be the district Magistrate.

The Magistrate hobbled to a chair on the dais and seated himself, while the sergeant of the guard stepped forward and cited the entire list of Krim's infractions. Krim foolishly tried to argue jurisprudence using the terms 'fat lummox' and 'dunderhead': a new transgression of the local antidefamation code. He was arraigned on the spot. The Magistrate put on his judicial hat and took Krim's case under consideration. He now seemed cool and impartial, as befitted his position, and pronounced Krim's sentence in an even voice: "Sir, you have made several interesting legal points, but they fly a bit wide of the mark. My duty is both to better your legal understanding and to shield the innocent folk of this city against acts of mindless violence. Therefore, I sentence you to four months, eleven days and nineteen hours of educational exercises in the rock quarry."

Krim tried to utter further legalities, and to introduce apposite

precedents into the case, but was marched from the inn and hustled off
to the quarry.

After a decorous interval, Myron applied to Captain Maloof for
Krim's position aboard the *Glicca*. Captain Maloof ruminated for a moment. He said: "The job is not simple, and demands all the resources of
a competent man."

"I believe that I am that man," declared Myron boldly.

"We shall see," said Captain Maloof. "First, let me ask: are you familiar with the ten primary digits of the numerical scheme?"

"Yes sir. So I am!"

"And you understand their usual employment?"

"Yes, sir."

"You are able to read written documents, and translate them into
the spoken tongue?"

"Yes, sir."

"If hired, would you object to balancing your accounts, more or
less accurately?"

"No sir; not at all."

Captain Maloof gave a sigh of relief. "Your qualifications seem to
be superb. You are hired."

"Thank you, sir."

"Not at all," said Captain Maloof. "While I do not want to bring
poor Krim any unnecessary tribulation, it will be something of a relief
to have him shifting large rocks, rather than integers in the ledgers.
Your main challenge, or so I believe, will be adapting to Krim's intuitive methods of accounting. You may report aboard the *Glicca* tomorrow morning."

In the morning Myron departed the Rambler's Rest, and took his
breakfast at an open-air café to the side of the plaza. Then he walked
under the cloud-trees to the spaceport, passed through the terminal,
and found the *Glicca* a hundred yards out on the field. It was an ungainly old hulk, carrying freight in three cargo bays, and a fluctuating
number of passengers. The hull, which at one time had been enamelled
blue-gray with dark red trim, now showed a lusterless gray-white undercoat, along with daubs of orange primer where it had been thought
necessary to seal off scrapes, abrasions and meteor marks. Myron approached, climbed the short gangway and passed through the open
port into the main saloon. He found Captain Maloof and Schwatzendale lingering over their breakfast.

"Sit down," said Captain Maloof. "Have you had breakfast?"

"I had two fishcakes in a red sauce, and a pot of pepper tea," said
Myron. "It was, in a sense, breakfast."

Wingo, in the galley, had heard the interchange and immediately brought Myron a bowl of beans with bacon and two toasted scones. "The food one finds in remote places is often sub-standard," said Wingo severely. "Aboard the *Glicca* we are not epicures, but we are never faddists, and we feel no compulsion to explore every intricacy of the local cuisine."

"Wingo acts as our arbiter in these cases," Schwatzendale told Myron. "If he finds a stuff in the market which intrigues him, it is served up for our dinner. He watches us carefully, and if we appear to enjoy the dish he may even sample it himself."

Wingo grinned broadly. "I hear few complaints," he told Myron. "If you care to step this way, I will show you your quarters. Schwatzendale and I have already taken poor Krim's belongings to the transit office. The cabin has been well aired, and the linen is fresh. I think that you will be comfortable."

Myron took his suitcase to the cabin, then returned to the saloon. Maloof now sat alone.

"Your quarters are suitable, or so I hope?"

"Yes, of course, and I am ready to go to work."

"In that case, I will explain the scope of your duties. They are more various than you might expect." Maloof looked thoughtfully toward the ceiling. "You may find difficulties taking up where Krim left off. Despite his many fine qualities, Krim was a man of the sort known as *sui generis*."

Myron nodded. "I am not surprised."

"Krim was often a bit short with the passengers, and generated quite unnecessary friction. In response to a request which he found irrational, rather than taking five minutes to gratify the passenger's needs, he would explain why the passenger should alter his philosophy. At other times, he might prescribe a holistic remedy for the passenger's indigestion, rather than simply issuing the pastille requested, and the two would debate the case for hours—until the passenger, overcome by cramps, was forced to rush off to the latrine. When I tried to intercede, Krim declared himself a man of principle, and I was made to feel a charlatan."

Myron nodded and spoke as he wrote into a small notebook: "Instruction one: conciliate passengers. Dispense medicine as required."

"Correct. Now then, as to records and accounts, again I must criticize Krim. He was so preoccupied with his monumental compilation of jurisprudence that he avoided the drudgery of keeping accounts. When he was censured, he claimed that he had memorized all pertinent figures, and that they reposed accurately in his mind. One day I asked him: 'What if by some unexpected freak of fortune you are forced off the *Glicca*, as it might be if you were killed by a bandit, or suffered a brain-spasm?' 'Nonsense, sheer bullypup!' he told me, quite emphatically. Still, I persisted: 'What if you are taken up by the police and dragged off to jail? Who, then, will interpret your cryptic notes?' At this, Krim became cross. 'The idea,' he stated, 'is far-fetched. No police would think to molest a man of my forensic skills.' But Krim was wrong; he was taken off to jail, and his vast store of mental records is lost. The episode, I believe, speaks for itself."

Myron wrote in the notebook: "Instruction two: keep proper records. Avoid police."

"Exactly." Maloof went on to describe Myron's other duties. He would prepare bills of lading, and arrange for import and export licenses when necessary. He would supervise loading, and at each port of call he must verify that the proper parcels were discharged, even if he must carry them out to the dock himself.

Myron wrote: "Instruction three: expedite cargo on and off vessel. Cargo to be recorded in detail."

Maloof continued: "The Supercargo must make sure that freight charges have been paid, before cargo is loaded. Otherwise, chances are good that we will be carrying cargo free of charge, since the consignee will often refuse to pay freight charges—leaving us in possession of the freight, which is often worthless, leading to many difficulties."

Myron wrote: "Instruction four: before all else, collect fees and charges."

"As you can see," said Maloof, "the ideal Supercargo is a man of iron will and a grim disposition. He has a mind like a trap and tolerates no impudence from the warehousemen, no matter how pugnacious they seem."

"I will do my best," said Myron in a subdued voice.

"That should be sufficient," said Maloof. "We travel short-handed aboard the *Glicca*. Everyone is versatile, especially the Supercargo. You are aware of all this?"

"I am now."

Later in the day, eleven pilgrims presented themselves to Captain Maloof, requesting passage to Impy's Landing on the world Kyril, where they would undertake a five-year march around the planet. Captain Maloof explained that the *Glicca* could convey them to Coro-coro on Fluter, but thereafter they must trans-ship to Kyril. After argument, the pilgrims reluctantly agreed to Captain Maloof's stipulations.

There was further contention in regard to the fares. Kalash, the Perrumpter of the group, insisted upon a religious discount. Captain

Maloof responded with a sad shake of his head. "If your panel of deities wished you a quick and comfortable transfer to Kyril, it would have been arranged by divine fiat."

Kalash made a final attempt to explain the seeming paradox: "The gods move in mysterious ways."

Maloof nodded sagely. "Agreed! Still, either you or the gods must pay the proper fare."

The Perrumpter had nothing more to say. The pilgrims trooped aboard the ship, and were shown to their quarters by Wingo and Myron.

At sunset the *Glicca* set off on a route which would take it from world to world, through regions obscure and remote, visited only by tramp freighters like the *Glicca*. The pilgrims quickly settled into routines; drinking tea, criticizing the cuisine, performing rites, gambling, and discussing the world Kyril, where they proposed a circumambulation.

Myron adapted quickly to his work, but found some difficulty dealing with Hilmar Krim's extraordinary methods of accounting. Krim had used an abstruse shorthand writing and a system of abbreviations and crabbed hieroglyphics which baffled Myron's understanding. Additionally, Krim had never recorded financial details such as port charges, wages of warehousemen, cash advances to members of the crew, or incidental expenses, preferring to keep a running total in his memory until such a time as he felt inclined to transfer the lump sum to his books. These occasions seemed dictated by caprice, and Krim seldom troubled to identify the numbers.

In the end, Myron devised a method of computation which he called 'creative averaging'. The system was both straightforward and definite, though its basis might be considered intuitive, or even arbitrary. To use the system, Myron replaced Krim's hieroglyphics with more or less imaginary quantities, which he adjusted until they produced a reasonable summation. By this means Myron restored the books to a state of order—though he made no guarantees of precision. Maloof looked over the books, and was well satisfied with Myron's results.

As the days passed, Myron became acquainted with his shipmates. Schwatzendale, so he discovered, was spontaneous and volatile, with a lilting imagination rife with surprises and wonders. In contrast, Wingo was placid, methodical, and a thinker of profound thoughts. Superficially, Schwatzendale seemed a charming rascal of antic habits and slantwise good looks. His heart-shaped face, with its widow's peak and luminous eyes, often prompted strangers to take him for a languid young aesthete, or even a sybarite. Such theories were wildly incorrect. Schwatzendale, in fact, was brash, restless, and extravagant in his moods and attitudes. He skipped and hopped like a child, without perceptible self-consciousness. He attacked his work with disdain, as if it were too contemptible for a person of style and taste to take seriously. In this regard, Schwatzendale was both romantic and vain; he thought of himself as a combination gambler and gentleman-adventurer.

Wingo occasionally spoke of Schwatzendale's exploits in a mixture of awe, grudging admiration, and disapproval. In total contrast to Schwatzendale, Wingo was short, thick, and blue-eyed, with only a few strands of blond hair across his pink scalp. Wingo was mild, amiable, and sympathethic, an avid collector of curios, small trinkets, and interesting oddments, which he prized not for their inherent value, but for the cleverness of their execution. He was also a dedicated photographer, and was engaged in compiling what he called 'mood-impressions', which he hoped ultimately to publish in a portfolio entitled *Pageant of the Gaean Race*.

Wingo was greatly interested in comparative metaphysics. He paid more than casual attention to the sects, superstitions, religions, and transcendental philosophies which he encountered as the *Glicca* travelled from world to world and, whenever he wandered strange places, gave careful attention to local spiritual doctrines—a practice which incurred Schwatzendale's disapproval.

"You are wasting your time! There are a hundred thousand of these creeds; they all talk the same nonsense, and all want your money. Why bother? Religious cant is the greatest nonsense of all!"

"There is much in what you say," Wingo admitted. "Still, is it not possible, that by some odd chance one of these hundred thousand doctrines is correct and precisely defines the Cosmic Way? If we passed it by, we might never encounter Truth again!"

"In theory, yes," grumbled Schwatzendale. "But in practice, your chances are next to nil."

Wingo waved a pink forefinger. "Tut! One can never be sure. Perhaps you have miscalculated the odds."

"I can't answer you properly," growled Schwatzendale. "Odds of zero in a thousand are much the same as zero in a million."

Wingo responded with a wistful smile. "I will check out your formulation. Conceivably you are mistaken."

Schwatzendale agreed that this was possible, and there the matter rested.

For Myron, Schwatzendale was a constant source of wonder and amusement. He was physically beautiful, a fact which Schwatzendale recognized but ignored. In the engine-room, he worked with speed, precision, absolute certainty, and his characteristic panache. Typically he finished each job with a flourish, and a glance of disdainful menace at the repaired part, as if warning it never to repeat its mistake. Myron soon came to see past Schwatzendale's epicene beauty to an inner hardness, which was intensely masculine. He studied Schwatzendale's attributes with covert fascination. They manifested themselves in many tricks and habits, sardonic jokes, and oblique ideas, in the tilt of his head and the angle of his elbows; in his quick, loping strides. Myron sometimes fantasized that Schwatzendale's parts were all askew, so that they necessarily fitted together on the bias and all was asymmetric, quirky, 'slantwise'. Schwatzendale was like a knight on the chessboard, which could move only by eccentric hops and bounds.

The *Glicca* cruised from world to world, controlled by bills of lading and cargo destinations. At Girandole on the world Fiametta, the *Glicca* landed beside the *Fontenoy*—a large space-yacht almost as grand as the *Glodwyn*. The master of the *Fontenoy* was Joss Garwig, Director of Acquisitions for the Pan-Arts Museum at Duvray on the world Alcydon. Garwig was accompanied by his wife Vermyra, his son Mirl, and daughter Tibbet.

At Sweetfleur, the crew of the *Glicca* joined Garwig and his family for the 'Lalapalooza', a carnival of many dimensions. They watched while Moncrief the Mouse-rider and his troupe bamboozled the public with zeal and finesse. Schwatzendale took particular interest, as this was the selfsame Moncrief who had at one time taken almost fifty sols from him at a game of Cagliostro. Schwatzendale had never ceased to yearn for revenge.

Myron and Tibbet slipped away to visit 'The Tunnel of Love', and were not seen again until late in the evening. Their parting was sad-sweet, for the Gaean Reach was long and wide, and they could not guess when they would meet again. "You can write to me care of the Pan-Arts Museum at Duvray," said Tibbet. "If I don't hear from you, I'll know that you have forgotten me."

At the end of the day's business Moncrief took Captain Maloof aside, and arranged transport for himself and his troupe to Cax on the world Blenkinsop. On the following morning the newcomers boarded the *Glicca:* a party of six, including Flook, Pook, and Snook, three enchanting young maidens of lively disposition; the Klutes, Siglaf and Hunzel, a pair of truculent warrior-women from the Bleary Hills of Numoy; and Moncrief himself—all in all, a picturesque company.

The *Glicca* continued along its route. Leaving behind the four dreary spaceports of Mariah, the *Glicca* began the long run to Fluter, and fabled Coro-coro.

TWO

1

Excerpt from *Handbook to the Planets*:
Fluter, World of Glamour

There is nothing to be gained by describing the climate of Fluter: it is perfect, and as such it is taken for granted, as are most of the other aspects of this magnificent world. The landscapes are as sunny and verdant as a view across lost Arcady.

The people of Fluter share the attributes of their wonderful world. They seem to dance through life to the measures of music they alone can hear: women of many talents, noble philosophers, solitary vagabonds wandering the lonely places. In general they are friendly and gay, and anxious to appear beautiful in the eyes of the off-worlders, whom they revere perhaps unreasonably. In the main they are addicted to the joys of feasting, music, star-naming, sailing the wild seas, and love-making in a style known as 'ingesting the perfumed flowers'.

The intelligent reader will quickly observe that the article quoted above (from the periodical *Touristic Topics*) is a masterpiece of hyperbole; doubtless the writer was never any closer to Fluter than his local amusement park. Only the most naive of readers, upon exposure to the article, will set off pell-mell for Fluter hoping to find 'ineffable glamour and daily episodes of erotic hi-jinks'.

The following facts should be noted. The scenery of Fluter is very pleasant. The best hotel in Coro-coro is the O-Shar-Shan, but there is no running hot water. The girls are neither seductive, nor particularly amiable. Arrivals at the spaceport are allowed visitor's permits of thirty days' duration.

2

The *Glicca* drifted through space, unsubstantial as a puff of magic smoke. Far astern, Pfitz was a dying white spark, which presently faded. Ahead, golden Frametta could not yet be seen.

In the pilot-house of the *Glicca*, Captain Maloof turned from the observation window and stepped aft into the main saloon. He waited until the cheerful voices quieted, then spoke.

"Before long we will be arriving at the Coro-coro spaceport on Fluter, and you should know something of local conditions, which at times are ambiguous, if not extraordinary.

"In general, Fluter is a tranquil world with beautiful landscapes in every direction, and a near-total lack of natural hazards. On Fluter time seems to move at a languid pace, possibly because there are twenty-eight hours to the Fluter day.

"Coro-coro is the only settlement of consequence. Aside from the tourist facilities, there is nothing much to the town. A boulevard runs from the spaceport to the O-Shar-Shan Hotel, with more hotels along the way; also agencies, shops, and taverns. Residences are scattered in the gardens to either side of the boulevard. These are the homes of the folk native to Coro-coro, who are different from the Flauts who live in the back-country villages. The folk of the town regard themselves as sophisticated aristocrats, with wealth derived from the tourist trade—which on Fluter is highly developed, and very lucrative.

"Permanent residence is forbidden to off-worlders. Tourists are allowed entry permits of thirty days; then they are required to leave the planet, although in practice, the entry permit can be extended.

"If you should visit a village, remain unobtrusive; express no opinions, and drink with temperance. No one worries for the drunken tourist who has been tossed into the sump! Do not haggle or complain, and above all else, ignore the girls. The Flauts observe an exact sexual morality, and if you wonder why suddenly you have been emasculated, it is probably because you have committed an immoral act, such as looking under a girl's skirt. The village may seem a placid place where nothing ever happens, but it is almost certainly the scene of a thousand grisly events.

"The first settlers arrived from the congested world Ergard. At their first conclave, they vowed that pressure of population should never again become distressful. The number they fixed upon was ninety-nine thousand, and by great effort across the ages the limit has been maintained. The population of Fluter is now at equilibrium, but bitter events of the past still rankle and gnaw at the Flaut soul. They display a peculiar personality, a kind of sullen grandiosity. Today, the Flauts are a dour, suspicious folk, by reason of their grim history, which I will not touch further upon now.

"I think I have covered everything important. Are there any questions?"

Kalash, Perrumpter of the pilgrims, raised his hand. "What of our cases? They contain valuable materials. Will you relinquish them to us?"

"Certainly, as soon as you pay off the freight charges."

"Ah, bah!" cried Kalash. "Can you not take the long view? If you recall, we gambled with Schwatzendale; now we lack funds."

"That was your mistake, not mine."

Kalash grimaced. "We are quite at a loss. Ours is a pilgrimage of immense importance, but Schwatzendale avoids all talk of restitution! Our needs are urgent; think, if you will—we must pay our fares to Kyril, return fares home to Komard—not to mention our expenses during the march around Kyril. How can we obtain this necessary money?"

"Simply enough: through the process of work."

Kalash made a face. "That is easier said than done."

"Not altogether, as there is a labor shortage at Coro-coro. You should have no trouble."

"And the cases?"

"I will leave them in the transit warehouse. To redeem them, pay off storage and freight charges, and they are yours. Have you any further questions?"

"Bah," grumbled Kalash. "What good are questions when the answers are all non-sequiturs?"

Maloof nodded in agreement. "There is something in what you say."

Kalash was not yet done. "We had hoped for an easy generosity on your part, but reasoning with you is like gnawing on a stone."

Maloof turned away from Kalash. "Any other questions?"

Cooner stepped forward, frowning thoughtfully, to indicate that he might have a question, possibly of a recondite nature. Maloof looked past him and addressed the group.

"I have an announcement to make. The crew of this ship needs both bodily rest and nervous regeneration, and the *Glicca* itself is in need of maintenance. Therefore we shall sojourn upon Fluter for perhaps a week or two. The pilgrims will debark and prepare to trans-ship to Kyril. We shall miss their wise counsel and happy songs, but after Coro-coro we must fare onward to Cax. Thereafter, who knows? I can make no prediction; we are like the romantic vagabonds of old, each searching for lurulu."

Cooner called out: "The place is unknown to me! What or where, pray, is 'lurulu'?"

"'Lurulu' is a special word from the language of myth. It is as much of a mystery to me now as when I first yearned for something which seemed forever lost. But one day I shall glance over my shoulder, and there it will be, wondering why I had not come sooner. For now, it is on to Coro-coro. Here I feel an imminence; something important will happen, of this I feel certain. What? I do not know; it is a mystery."

Cooner's puzzlement had not yet been assuaged. "And 'lurulu' is part of this mystery?"

Maloof gave a non-committal shrug. "Perhaps. I may not be happy with what I find, if and when I find it."

"But what is it you seek?"

Maloof smiled. "I can tell you this much: if I am lucky—or perhaps unlucky—I will find it on Fluter."

"Interesting," declared Cooner. He turned to Moncrief. "And you, sir—are you also in pursuit of 'lurulu'?"

"I am sidling in its direction," Moncrief admitted. "I see a glimmer every time I take some of Schwatzendale's money. In the main, I hope that the Mouse-riders will resurge in all their glory! That would be lurulu of the purest water!"

Cooner looked to Wingo. "How about you, Brother Wingo? Where do you seek lurulu?"

"I cannot put it aptly into words," said Wingo. "It is what I hope to capture in my *Pageant of the Gaean Race*. There is also an elemental equation which describes Truth; but in this regard I am reluctant to say more."

Myron called out: "I am not so diffident; the object of my quest is named Dame Hester Lajoie, and when I catch her I hope that a jail is near, since gallantry would not allow me to do what I would like."

Cooner turned to Captain Maloof. "Do you, sir, care to tell us a bit more of your own quest?"

Captain Maloof smiled sadly. "I will say only that I am anxious to arrive on Fluter. Out among the back-lands mysteries still abide. In any case: good luck to us all."

Cooner started to ask a cogent new question, but Captain Maloof turned back into the pilot-house, and went to look again from the observation window. The star Frametta still could not be seen. He muttered to himself, "How will it be, if it happens at all? I must take care not to commit myself absolutely." He stared out the window. "Whatever happens, life will go on."

For several moments he stood gazing out the window. At last, far across the void, he thought to see the small gleam which would be the star Frametta.

THREE

1

The geography of Fluter as seen from space was extraordinary, and perhaps unique—certainly within the bounds of the Gaean Reach. In cooling from its primal melt the world had shrunk, squeezing up the crust into nine enormous anticlines, running north and south across all of one hemisphere, leaving the opposite hemisphere a flat peneplain. In the course of time, the sea rose, and the rock-folds became nine narrow continents running north and south, with shallow seas between. The opposite hemisphere was drowned beneath the waters of a vast, featureless ocean. The climate was benign; life came to Fluter, and clothed the land in verdure of innumerable varieties.

In time, a band of Gaean pioneers arrived from the crowded world Ergard, to settle all nine continents. Five years later, at the First Conclave, they bound themselves to a set of strict covenants by which to control their population, so that never should Fluter become the congested jungle of concrete towers, underground warrens, smells, stinks, and pollution, crowded streets, and cramped space which they had left behind. Time might pass—a hundred years, a thousand years—but never, so they swore, would they allow their wonderful new world to be so desecrated. The Flauts, as they called themselves, surveyed the nine continents and divided the arable land into sections, with each section rated for a population which might never be exceeded. A thousand years later, the population of Fluter occupied one hundred and forty-seven villages scattered at random across all nine continents, along with a special node surrounding the Coro-coro spaceport on Continent Five. A population of ninety-nine thousand Flauts had long since been reached.

The native flora co-existed amiably with dozens of exotic imports, from Old Earth and elsewhere. The ubiquitous coconut palm* leaned across a thousand beaches; exotic hardwoods, softwoods, flowering shrubs, and vines grew in the Fluter forests and along the mountain slopes. The fauna consisted of a few lizards and insects on land and a variety of marine life, which made the waters fascinating but dangerous.

At Coro-coro was the famous O-Shar-Shan Hotel, as well as a dozen other tourist hotels more or less fashionable. Although the calculations were complicated, Coro-coro was subject to the same population controls as the rest of Fluter, and would never grow larger than an oversized village.

2

The *Glicca* landed at the Coro-coro spaceport and was boarded by a team of local officials. Their routines were unusually careful; a pair of medics tested ship, crew, and passengers for noxious diseases, while another technician filtered samples of air in search of undesirable viruses, pollen, spores, or proteins. Finding nothing of interest, the team departed the ship.

Meanwhile, an immigration officer noted name, age, world of origin, reason for visit, and criminal record, if any, for each member of the ship's complement, issuing entry permits as he did so.

He then addressed the company. "Please listen with care! I am Civil Agent Uther Taun. I represent the administration of Coro-coro, and effectually of all Fluter.

"Civil Agents are charged with many responsibilities, but most importantly, we guard the beauty of our beloved world. Severe penalties are visited upon anyone so depraved as to distribute litter, or cause any other defilement.

"I need not enlarge upon these laws, except to state that they are enforced with diligence by a corps of special Civil Agents, and equally vigilant Land Agents, and—if appropriate—penalties of all three orders are inflicted. Neither the Land Agents nor the Civil Agents accept excuses. Wastes must be deposited in certified receptacles!

"Random micturition or defecation at large is never encouraged, for reasons which need not be particularized. Nevertheless, rather than

---

* The coconut palm, native to Old Earth, had been transferred across the Gaean Reach to wherever climate and saltwater provided a habitat, and now seemed native to the entire universe.

frowning and wincing, you should think yourselves privileged to enjoy the delights of Fluter!

"I remind you that vistor's permits are valid for thirty days but may be renewed upon timely application. I will also mention that for persons desiring temporary employment, a labor exchange is situated nearby, along Pomare Boulevard.

"A final word. If, during your excursions, you should come upon a village, you would be prudent to turn away and go elsewhere. But should you ignore my advice and enter the village, be absolutely discreet—the typical Flaut may not impress you as a graceful host; to the contrary, he may appear both unfeeling and surly. If you visit a village tavern, use total decorum; if you encounter a female, abstain from familiarity, since the Flauts have no qualms about thrashing an obnoxious tourist.

"In the end, if you are careful, and pay with a willing hand, you will encounter no trouble on Fluter.

"Now then: are there questions?"

The ineffable Cooner stepped forward, his plump face alight with eager innocence. He raised his hand on high, fingers fluttering. The Civil Agent looked down at him. "You have a question?"

"Yes, sir! Why are there both Civil Agents and Land Agents?"

The Agent frowned coldly. "The differences are real, but sometimes unclear to the public. In general, the Civil Agents patrol Corocoro, while the Land Agents keep a vigilant surveillance over the conduct of campers and excursionists."

"And which is the more severe?"

"Neither is severe. Both enforce the law of the land to the exact jot and tittle."

"Ha!" cried Cooner, with unbecoming joviality. "And what, may I ask, is the nature of the three orders of punishment? What, exactly, do they designate?"

The Agent, not happy with Cooner's flippant demeanor, answered tersely. "These matters are considered indelicate; ladies and gentlemen prefer to ignore them."

"Aha," chuckled Cooner, "but you misread your audience—aboard the *Glicca* we are all philosophers, not a lady or a gentleman in the group! You may speak on, with an easy mind."

The Agent's voice became even more terse than before. "Just as you like. Listen, then. Punishment of the first order is public chastisement. Punishment of the second order includes disgrace, confiscation of all property, and expulsion from Fluter dressed only in a bramble!

Punishment of the third order involves death, by subaqueation in Sharler's Pond."

"Hm," said Cooner, more soberly than before. "I see that you take your litigation seriously. Perhaps it is wise to stay within the law."

"That is ever the case," said the official.

"How might I detect a Civil Agent, or a Land Agent, when one is in the vicinity? How are they different?"

"The questions are nuncupatory. The most prudent conduct is to assume that you are being watched by one or the other at all times.

"To answer your question more circumspectly: the Civil Agent is never conspicuous, even though he wears a neat uniform. He is polite even when he is taking you into custody. Tradition ordains that he wear a short, square beard; he is mature but never infirm, and is notable for his punctilio. The Land Agent wears a green sash and carries a ceremonial whangee; Otherwise he is much like a Civil Agent.

"Now: to other business." From his pouch Uther Taun brought pamphlets entitled: *Legal Code, Ordinary Regulations, Duties of the Visitor*, and *Advice From a Civil Agent*.

"Everyone must study this compendium with care!" declared the Agent. "There can then be no excuses for misconduct."

Cooner muttered: "Never fear, we shall creep about our affairs on tiptoe."

The Agent pretended not to hear. He distributed the pamphlets, then departed the ship.

3

Perrumpter Kalash made a final attempt to soften the resolve of Captain Maloof. He approached, face wreathed in a tremulous smile. "Sir, in talking with my colleagues, I find that we are united in admiration for the clarity of your wisdom!"

"Thank you," said Maloof. "That is good to hear."

"But we also feel that certain of your views are so abstract as to insulate you from the woes of humanity. It is our sincere hope that you have reconsidered our unhappy situation, that perhaps you have reached a better understanding and now feel a surge of sympathy for our plight. Am I right?"

"You could not be more wrong. My recommendation is as before."

Kalash threw up his arms in defeat and turned away. The pilgrims gathered to confer, and decided to ask Schwatzendale to return his winnings. Wingo overheard their muttered plans and assured them that Schwatzendale "would rather drain blood from his leg than relinquish money, once it had come into his possession."

Schwatzendale himself joined the conversation. He asked Perrumpter Kalash: "Would you have returned my losses, had you depredated my wealth? Remember, if you will, that I too have feelings!"

The pilgrims murmured resentfully, then left the ship and straggled off toward the labor exchange.

Captain Maloof and Myron went off to the warehouse to arrange for the discharge of cargo. Moncrief, along with Flook, Pook, and Snook, set off toward the center of town, with Hunzel and Siglaf hunching behind.

Wingo and Schwatzendale changed into shoreside clothes before leaving the ship. Wingo donned dust-brown breeches, a gray-pink shirt with a black string cravat, a loose brown cloak, and his brown planter's hat with the sweeping brim—a costume harking back to those gallant artists who swaggered with such élan across the early romantic eras. His sensitive feet were at ease in the fine boots of soft leather by which he set great store. Schwatzendale wore black breeches, a shirt patterned in a black and green diaper, and a soft black cap, pulled askew over his black locks.

They set off along the Pomare Boulevard, walking under a rustling canopy of overhanging foliage and sweet-smelling flowers. The trees were of many varieties: some indigenous, others brought from far worlds. Certain of the trees towered grandly on high, while others crouched, contorted with heavy limbs, spreading fans of foliage over the roadway. Silurian elms displayed fronds of pale blue and sea-green; dendrons released lobes of gas-filled membrane, which floated off down the boulevard. Quake-trees shuddered in the breeze, dropping pods loaded with spores. Nectarcups hanging on corkscrew tendrils bobbed and bounced, spilling perfume into the air.

Schwatzendale trotted along in jaunty high spirits. He danced first ahead of Wingo's staunch and steady gait, then off to the side, to pluck a flower, which a moment later he flung over his shoulder, in flamboyant disregard for the law. Wingo watched benignly and paused to pick up Schwatzendale's litter, which he tucked into his pocket.

The two passed the Labor Exchange: a long, open-sided shed overhung by talisman trees. Behind the counter, a single clerk attended to the needs of a stout woman wearing black boots and wide orange pantaloons. The pilgrims stood in a glum huddle reading notices on a bulletin board, striking from time to time at flying insects.

Wingo and Schwatzendale continued along the way. Wingo was inclined to commiserate with the pilgrims, citing the inconveniences of their present plight. Schwatzendale was more detached. "They were not compelled to march off on this fateful expedition! Had they stayed at home, they might have slept in their own beds, or performed religious rites whenever the notion took them, each to his heart's content."

"They are driven by something called 'afflatus'," Wingo told him. "It is an all-consuming force, which cannot be explained."

Schwatzendale nodded his comprehension. They proceeded, passing the premises of the Tarquin Transit Agency, which offered rental vehicles of all kinds. Three- and four-wheeled vehicles were known locally as 'skitters', some fanciful and ostentatious, others built for speed, low in front with two tall spindly wheels behind. There were flitters so fragile and light that it seemed as if the wind might carry them away. At the back of the lot, several lordly way-cars were ranked, awaiting the pleasure of those who wished to roam the wilderness in comfort, if not luxury. The firm also announced itself as agent for the rental of houseboats moored in every river and waterway of Fluter.

Taking in the sights along the way, Schwatzendale and Wingo went on, dodging the occasional skitter which trundled along the boulevard. They noticed several bungalows, almost hidden in the foliage, then came upon a rambling structure built of old boards and panels of compressed grass, under a high-peaked roof of palm thatch. A sagging porch ran along the front, with three wooden steps connecting the porch to the ground. Above the porch hung a sign: PINGIS TAVERN.

Wingo and Schwatzendale stopped short. They appraised the raffish structure with practiced eyes, then with one accord turned aside, mounted the steps and entered the tavern.

They were met by a familiar odor: the scent of old wood permeated by generations of spilled beer, along with the must of dry palm. At this time of day, business was slow; the interior was dim and quiet. At the back of the tavern, a pair of stout ladies gossiped earnestly over small beers. A gentleman of evident respectability leaned against the bar, clasping a goblet of pale liquor in his right hand. He wore a smart blue tunic, breeches of black whipcord, and black ankle-boots of good quality. His face was long and sober, under a neatly ordered ruff of crisp brown hair. A short, square beard emphasized the sobriety of his features. He nodded politely as Wingo and Schwatzendale seated themselves at a scarred wooden table.

On the wall behind the bar, a board listed a dozen special drinks in an illegible scrawl. The brown-bearded gentleman watched tolerantly as Wingo and Schwatzendale studied the board, then volunteered advice: "Balrob, our host, is a man of good reputation, and I can vouch for his bitter ale."

Balrob bowed in gratification. "Thank you, Sir Agent! Your commendation carries weight."

The gentleman straightened to an erect posture. "Allow me to introduce myself; I am Efram Shant, Land Agent, at your service."

Wingo and Schwatzendale mentioned their own names, and the Land Agent continued his remarks.

"If you are partial to toddies, the Tingletown, the Importunata, and the Old Reliable are all well regarded. Balrob, however, feels that his first speciality is Pooncho Punch, and I am inclined to agree."

"Hm," mused Wingo. "I am not familiar with this drink."

Schwatzendale gave his head a doubtful shake. "I have tested many formulations, but never Pooncho Punch."

"I am not surprised," said Balrob. "There are four versions of Pooncho; all have been developed locally, using local ingredients only. The recipe is, of course, a guarded family secret."

Agent Shant said: "My own preference is Pooncho Number Three. It is bracing and flavorful, yet never sits heavy on the tongue."

Wingo looked at Schwatzendale. "Shall we attempt this storied tipple?"

"The opportunity should not be wasted!" declared Schwatzendale without hesitation.

"My feelings exactly," said Wingo. He signalled to Balrob. "Two orders of the Number Three Pooncho, if you please."

"With pleasure, sir."

The 'Pooncho' was served in distinctive earthenware mugs, glazed dark green. Agent Shant watched as the two raised the mugs and tested the contents.

"Well, then? What is your verdict?"

Wingo coughed and cleared his throat. "This is a drink of several dimensions. It should not be judged in haste."

Schwatzendale said: "I find the drink stimulating, well balanced, and rife with a distinctive panache."

Wingo sipped again from the mug. "Most refreshing! Might there be a Number Four Pooncho?"

Agent Shant pulled soberly at his beard. "I have no personal experience with the drink. However, I understand that it is sometimes known as the 'Pingis Rejuvenator' and is occasionally administered to the dead, or unconscious."

"Indeed!" marvelled Wingo. "To what effect?"

"I have not witnessed the cure myself. Still, I have had a broad experience of life, and I have seen some startling events, so that I no longer make absolute assertions."

"You would seem a man to be trusted," said Schwatzendale. "I would value your advice on another topic altogether."

"Speak! I shall answer to my best ability."

"We are new arrivals upon this remarkable world. How best might we entertain ourselves, at modest expense, and within the limits of the law?"

"Hm." Agent Shant again pulled at his beard. "That is like asking how to dive into water, without getting wet. But let me reflect. If you are keen botanists, you will enjoy examining the flowers in the public parks, or you may go on nature walks about the countryside. At slightly larger expense, you may hire a way-car, which affords you more latitude. Or you might rent a houseboat and cruise our incomparable waterways." The Land Agent squared his shoulders, drained his goblet, and glanced around the room. "I must be off about my business."

Schwatzendale, never diffident, asked: "With full respect, I wonder what might be your business?"

The Land Agent turned Schwatzendale a brief, rather severe look. "I am a member of the Land Committee. I supervise thirty Land Agents, and as many sub-Agents, often known as the 'Land Rovers', all of whom seek illicit rubbish and bring culprits to justice. It is a taxing job, and not without danger."

Wingo asked innocently: "Do you yourself search out litter?"

Agent Shant stood erect, with shoulders thrown back. "I never shrink from my duty, at all times and in all places. I must set an example for my men!"

Agent Shant glanced idly down at the floor, then frowned and stared more fixedly. Wingo, sensing a change in the Agent's demeanor, followed his gaze to the floor, where, to his alarm, he found that one of the dead flowers he had picked up from the road had fallen from his pocket and now lay blatantly in full view.

Wingo hastily reached down and retrieved the illicit object. The Land Agent gave a grim shrug, then turned away and departed.

Wingo and Schwatzendale discussed the episode in low tones for a moment, then decided to attempt another Number Three Pooncho Punch. They gave the order, and were served.

4

Aboard the *Glicca* Myron saw to the discharge of cargo, then retired to his office to deal with paperwork. After a time Captain Maloof appeared in the doorway.

Myron looked up. "Something, sir?"

Maloof waved his hand. "Nothing of consequence. Proceed with your work."

"I am almost finished. It won't be more than a minute."

Maloof came into the office, seated himself, and watched while Myron made a few final entries.

Myron closed his ledger and looked toward Maloof, wondering what was in the wind.

Maloof asked: "Is there outbound cargo to interest us?"

Myron nodded. "A good bit—all transshipment. About half a bay for Blenkinsop."

"I see." Maloof showed no great interest; Myron thought that he seemed preoccupied.

Presently Maloof said: "A few days ago I mentioned that I might have some private business here at Coro-coro."

"So you did," said Myron. "As I recall, you used the word 'lurulu' in this connection."

Maloof nodded. "I am inclined to think that I spoke carelessly. My quest is more prosaic; I want to resolve a mystery, which has been troubling me a long time."

"What sort of mystery?"

Maloof hesitated. "I'll explain, if you have the patience to listen."

"I'll listen, of course. In fact, I'll be happy to help you in any way that I can."

"That is a kind offer, which I am tempted to accept. But first, I should mention the very real possibility of danger."

Myron shrugged. "There will be two of us, and if nothing else, I can guard your back."

"Perhaps it won't come to that," said Maloof, without conviction. "In any case, I am pleased for the help, especially since your temperament seems suitable for this sort of undertaking. Wingo and Schwatzendale are excellent fellows, no doubt, but for this particular work neither would be at his best. Wingo is too artless, and Schwatzendale too flamboyant. What is needed is someone quiet, subtle, and unobtrusive, or who will adapt himself to such a role; in short, a person like yourself, with a cap pulled down to hide your blond hair—which is rather conspicuous."

Myron decided to take the remark as a compliment. It could be worse, he reflected.

For a time Maloof sat deep in thought. At last he stirred. "I will explain the background to the case; it is not simple, but I will try to be succinct. I must start many years ago—at Traven on the world Morlock, in Argo Navis.

"I was born into the patrician caste and spent a privileged childhood, which now seems unthinkably far away. My father was a banker, and wealthy. I remember him as a tall, erect gentleman, fastidious, humorless, and definite in his views. My mother was altogether different: she was pretty, frivolous, impulsive, and always ready to try a new fad. We lived in a grand house overlooking Faurency Weald, the countryside spread out before us all the way to Leyland Forest.

"My father and I were never on the best of terms—my fault more than his, so I understand now. When I was eighteen, I left home to become an IPCC cadet, which further estranged both my father and mother, who wanted me to become a banker.

"In those days I was wild and reckless and thought very well of myself. Six years of IPCC training ground away the worst of my rough edges and brought discipline into my life. In the end, I was commissioned a junior officer, Level Eight, and I thought that my parents might even be pleased with me.

"I was allowed a short leave of absence, which I spent at Traven. My father had become more opinionated than ever, or so it seemed; now I understand that I had never appreciated his regard for me, and that my leaving home had left him forlorn and lonely. My mother, on the other hand, seemed more frivolous and foolish than before. She fluttered and flitted about in girlish frocks, more fluffy-minded than ever. I felt concern for both of them and was sorry to return to duty.

"I was sent out on a tour of service which took me here and there across the Reach. After a promotion to Level Six, I was posted to Olfane on Sigil 92; then I was promoted Lieutenant Grade Five and posted to the town Wanne on the hard little world Dusa—at the very brink of Beyond.

"Wanne was reputedly the meanest posting on this side of the Reach, but I survived, and learned what there was to be learned. Finally, I was promoted again, to a grade just short of Captain. But by this time I was ready for something new; there was talk of transfer to a new posting, but an event occurred which changed the course of my life.

"From the town Serafim, out in the Beyond, came a dilapidated old Model 9-B Locator with a crew of four ruffians. They attacked the *Creach*, a freighter which happened to be in port, killed the master and crew, then took the ship aloft and away—presumably back into the Beyond, where our authority was nil and the law barred our presence.

"At the time there were only three agents posted to the Wanne office. We were all outraged by the contemptuous act of the pirates; it was an insult to our dignity and demanded a reaction, legal or not.

"The commanding officer was Captain Wistelrod. He promoted me to full Captain, then put me on indefinite leave and decommissioned me, so that I was temporarily a civilian and could go where I saw fit—without arousing an uproar from do-gooders and pussy-footers. I took the Model 9-B up from the Wanne spaceport and flew across the edge into the Beyond, and made for the town Serafim, where we thought the pirates would take their prize.

"When I arrived at Serafim, I put down at night, in the wilderness which surrounded the town, and ran through the moonlight to the spaceport. Sure enough, there was the *Creach*!

"To make a long story short, I killed the pirates and took the *Creach* back into Gaean space. Along the way back to Wanne, a constructive idea came to me. The previous owner of the vessel was dead. De facto title had passed to the pirates, once they had gone Beyond. By salvaging the ship from the pirates, title had devolved upon me; and since I was now a civilian, I need not surrender the ship to the IPCC. I fell in love with the ship, which was sound, secure, and competent. I renamed it the '*Glicca*'.

"At Wanne I reported briefly to Captain Wistelrod and told him of my decision, which was to remain on indefinite leave. He was sorry to lose me but wished me well. I assembled a crew and at once began to transport cargo.

"Three years passed before I put into Traven. My father had been killed in a boating accident at the lake. After a few days of mourning, my foolish mother had gone off with a man whom my aunt and cousin described as an out-and-out adventurer, who had beguiled her with romantic nonsense. Their present whereabouts was uncertain.

"The big house on Telmany Heights had been sold and was now inhabited by strangers. It was a depressing situation, with a single spark of comfort: my father, knowing my mother's impulsive disposition, had placed his assets into a trust fund from which my mother should be paid an adequate but not lavish annuity; a wise precaution, which could only frustrate her new consort.

"My father had drowned when his small sailboat capsized on a calm day. I had come to revere if not love my father; I was troubled by the circumstances of his death.

"I spoke with my aunt and my cousin; they knew very little of the man involved with my mother. She had brought him to their house only once, for a visit of half an hour. He had given his name as 'Loy

Tremaine', and seemed considerably younger than my mother; she clearly doted upon him, and acted like a moonstruck girl. Tremaine made no effort to hide his boredom.

"Neither my aunt nor my cousin found him agreeable, though they admitted that he was personable, even magnetically so. His hair was short, thick, and black and clasped his head like a casque. His eyes were black and intense, close together beside a high-bridged nose. It was a face which, in the opinion of both my aunt and my cousin, indicated a self-centered willfulness, or even cruelty. Both noticed a small tattoo on his neck, just under the turn of his jaw, a cross inside two concentric circles, in a distinctive black-purple ink.

"Tremaine had spoken little, responding to questions in monosyllables. Only when asked as to his world of origin did he respond at length, and then in an excited and exalted manner, walking back and forth, flourishing his hands for emphasis. But he gave little real information. 'It is a far world,' he said. 'Its name would mean nothing to you; in fact, it is known only to discriminating and wealthy tourists, who are allowed to make limited stays—despite their reluctance to leave! But we cannot relax, and money means nothing to us. The world must be protected; it is entrancing for its serenity, and we cannot allow it to be defiled by vulgar hordes.'

"My mother proudly amplified the statement. 'Loy claims that it is the most beautiful world in all the Reach—so beautiful that it compels the return of anyone who has lived there. I am anxious to know this wonderful place!'

"At that time, according to my aunt, Tremaine rose to his feet and said: 'It is time that we were leaving,' and a moment later they were gone.

"I made inquiries at the bank. I learned that a few months before, my mother had come to the bank in the company of a surly gentleman. She had stated her intention to travel and had requested that the trust be broken so that she might realize the full value of the fund at once. The bank officials had decisively denied the request, eliciting sharp comments from the gentleman. This troubled them not at all; they tendered my mother a set of dated coupons, which she might cash at any local bank at the beginning of each year. After a set of formalities to prove her identity, the coupons would be referred to the bank at Traven, and the value of the coupon returned to my mother. She complained that the process seemed cumbersome and was told that it was the only means to ensure that her money was paid to her, and not some clever swindler, and that she should not complain.

"I asked if they as yet had paid off any of the coupons, but none had been presented for payment. The bank had no clue as to my mother's whereabouts.

"At the spaceport, I tried to discover when Loy Tremaine had arrived on Morlock, when he and my mother had departed, and what had been their destination? I learned nothing.

"There was urgent cargo aboard the *Glicca*; I could delay no longer and departed Morlock.

"Sometime later the *Glicca* put into Lorca on the world Sansevere. I went to the Aetna University and sought out Doctor Tessing, a savant in the field of social anthropology. I described Tremaine to the best of my ability, and mentioned that he was native to what he felt was the most beautiful world of the Gaean Reach—which no one could leave without yearning to return.

"I asked if he could identify this world, and Doctor Tessing said that the chances were good. He worked the controls of his information processor, studied the output, and told me: 'The problem is relatively simple. Both man and world have well-defined characteristics, and together they indicate that the man is a Flaut, native to the world Fluter—which is famed for the charm of its landscapes.' He told me also that Flauts are obsessional in regard to their world and under ordinary circumstances would not be likely to leave.

"I asked: 'What do you make of the tattoo on his neck?'

"'It is either a status symbol, or it identifies his place of origin.'

"There was nothing more he could tell me. I expressed my thanks and returned to the *Glicca*.

"I now had a good idea where my mother could be found, and reasoned that her money would keep her safe. Tremaine could not get at her capital, but her annuity nevertheless was a substantial sum and was, in effect, her insurance policy.

"For a time the transport business kept us across the Reach and far away from Fluter. We drifted here and there, but one day settled upon the Coro-coro spaceport.

"We had three days to spend at Coro-coro. I spent the first day with the senior official in the Office of Entry Formalities. Together we searched the files, but there was no record of either the man who called himself 'Tremaine' or my mother. The official was not altogether surprised; he told me—rather reluctantly—that certain rogues and blackguards avoided the immigration laws by arranging to be set down in the wilderness, then walking into town. This was a serious offense, he told me, and if apprehended the perpetrators were liable to penalties of the third order since they were violating the basic canon of Flaut law—namely, the statutes controlling the population. Without valid entry permits, they were in constant danger of being taken up by a Civil Agent, and this would be the case if they tried to book into a hotel.

"I asked: 'What if they use forged documents?'

"'Possible,' he admitted, 'but such documents must be renewed monthly, which would soon arouse attention. After two or three such renewals the permit would be voided, and the guilty person would suffer appropriate penalties.'"

Myron grimaced. "It all seems rather extreme."

"Not when you know Flaut history. During their 'Terrible Times', they learned to accept death as the all-purpose punishment for any mistake whatsoever. It was easy, and there was no quibbling.

"On the second day, I went to the IPCC office. The commanding officer was Captain Harms, a crusty old veteran who had been sent out to rusticate at Coro-coro—a post considered a safe and comfortable sinecure, where the agent in charge could do no great damage. His assistant was an innocuous young lieutenant who had learned to exert no twitch of initiative, for fear of Captain Harms's displeasure.

"I found Captain Harms sitting at his desk. He was, in fact, a man of formidable aspect, with the broad chest and thin legs of a pouter pigeon. His face had been weathered pinkish-brown, against which jutting white eyebrows, ferocious blue eyes, an ungovernable tuft of white hair, and a bristling white mustache made a fine contrast.

"I introduced myself and explained my problem. As I expected, he produced a dozen reasons why the IPCC could not stir its majestic bulk to interfere in the local jurisdiction.

"I told him that Tremaine almost certainly had killed my father and that the safety of my mother was at risk. Harms declared that these factors were extraneous to the case, and that I should report my suspicions to the Civil Agents. I explained that, by so doing, I would be exposing my mother to a penalty of the third order. He shrugged, implying that she should have foreseen the eventuality before she indulged in a criminal act.

"I mentioned Tremaine's tattoo. Harms said that it identified his native village, but beyond that he could not help, as he had no list or compendium of the Flaut tattoos. For such information I might apply to the Office of Civil Dispositions, or the Bureau of Vital Statistics, or the Population Registry. I bade Captain Harms farewell and left the agency.

"On the third day I followed Captain Harms's suggestion and presented myself to the Office of Civil Dispositions. After two hours they referred me to the Population Registry, where, after another two hours, I was told that the information could most easily be had at the Bureau of Vital Statistics. After another wait, I learned that the clerk who might have this information had gone off to a houseboat for a two-week vacation, and nothing could be done until her return. They suggested that I make inquiries at the Bureau for Archaeological Research.

"But by this time I was certain that they were playing a game with me. I returned to the *Glicca* in a very bad mood. On the next day we departed Fluter.

"The *Glicca* has returned to Fluter. I now plan to resume where I left off."

Maloof surveyed Myron. "There you have it. Now that you understand the program, do you still care to participate?"

"Certainly, but how do you plan to proceed?"

Maloof shrugged. "I wish I had a clever strategy, but I expect that I will do as before—which means trudging around and asking questions until someone decides to answer. The clerk at Vital Statistics may now, at least, be back from her houseboat vacation."

"We have one advantage," said Myron. "Tremaine will not know that we are looking for him."

"True."

"And if we find him—what then?"

"Much depends upon circumstances."

Myron rose to his feet. "I'm ready when you are."

Maloof also stood erect. "Wear a dark jacket. We are anthropologists from Aetna University on Sansevere. And don't forget your hat."

FOUR

1

Excerpt from *Handbook to the Planets:*
Fluter: The Terrible Times

Visitors to this most beautiful of worlds are ordinarily ignorant of a dark episode in Fluter's past. When they learn the facts, more often than not the information is received with polite incredulity, or more intelligently, as just another scar on the body of Gaean history. Nevertheless, here is an outline of what happened across the pleasant landscapes of Fluter during those dark events.

The original settlers came in reaction to the insufferable overcrowding of their native world-city, Coreon on Ergard. They made population control the first and most stringent law of the land. As the centuries passed the strictures gradually relaxed, and memories of Coreon became dim. The spectre of overcrowding once again cast a dreary shadow over the land, and fervor for reviving the old statutes increased—rather hysterically, so it seems now. At the first Conclave for Population Readjustment, the old laws were emphatically renewed. Zealots ruled the day; proposals for gradual retrenchment were shouted down in favor of immediacy.

Each village was assigned an index indicating how far its population must be reduced to stay within the norms; killing became an ordinary affair. First to go were the aged and the infirm, along with the feeble-minded or anyone considered deficient in some regard. Family feuded with family; the elderly and even the middle-aged walked abroad at their peril. Ambush became a fine art, but the elderly suffered most until they organized themselves into fearsome gangs: the 'Silver Ghosts', who skulked through shadows seeking children and wailing babies, whose brains they dashed out against a rock. When at last the roster of the village declined below the index, and the need for slaughter was gone, furtive killing persisted, from habit and engendered hatred.

Eventually equilibrium returned. Population control was every-where rigidly enforced through regulation of procreation, fertility, elim-ination of abnormal children, and abortion, producing more or less the same conditions we find in the Flaut villages today.

The question is often asked: where was the IPCC during these times? It has been asserted that the IPCC was indifferent, but such was not the case. In sheer point of fact, the IPCC could function effectively only if it occupied each of the Flaut villages and Coro-coro. A force of at least fifty thousand field agents would have been needed for the opera-tion, resulting in a program so complex as to be unacceptable. When the Flauts became surfeited with killing, they would stop of their own ac-cord; and so it happened.

2

The IPCC at Coro-coro kept a low profile, and in the main there was little need for a strong presence, the influence of the Civil Agents gen-erally sufficient to maintain order and discipline among the folk of Fluter.

On several occasions the Civil Agents demanded that the IPCC re-move its office from Coro-coro; the IPCC eventually responded by constructing a new headquarters of obvious permanence, situated near the O-Shar-Shan circus.

Maloof and Myron set off along the tree-shaded Pomare Boule-vard, under dangling white blossoms from which drifted a barely per-ceptible perfume. They might have jumped aboard one of the picturesque open-sided omnibuses which plied the boulevard—long, high-wheeled charabancs carrying tourists and Flauts alike between the spaceport and the O-Shar-Shan circus—but instead chose to walk.

They passed the Labor Exchange, where business was conducted under a long, open-sided shed thatched with tawny palm fronds. Lined up at the counter were the pilgrims, now receiving referrals to poten-tial employers. None showed enthusiasm toward the prospect of em-ployment. Cooner, dissatisfied with his referral, stood leaning over the counter angrily waving his referral in the air, half-prancing with indig-nation. The clerk gave him a glance of mild wonder before turning back to his work.

At the Tarquin Transit Agency, Maloof and Myron stopped to in-spect the vehicles in the yard, intrigued—like Wingo and Schwatzen-dale before them—by the idiosyncratic constructions. Bamboo and membrane flitters, resembling disheveled winged insects, appeared to be of local manufacture except for the imported power units; each was unique, built to the dictates of possibly amateur designers. Like the flitters, the skitters were of ad hoc construction, with struts, frames, and braces installed where the builder thought they would do the most good. Controls were different from one to the next, as if a standard system were an affront to the skill and brio of the driver. The three-wheelers, appealing to persons of feckless disposition, were in a separate area; in some of these the driver rode high behind the two after-wheels, with the third wheel on a boom thrust forward like an instrument of attack. Vanities were raised aloft, on struts clamped to the forward boom: a peacock's fan; a winged cherub blowing a clarion; a grotesque head, with features articulated to contort in hideous grimaces as the vehicle moved along.

Similar vehicles coursed up and down the boulevard, high wheels whirring and thumping, the driver sitting proudly aloft, regarding other drivers with disdain as if questioning their competence.

Maloof and Myron walked on, almost brushed by the white dangling blossoms which trailed over the boulevard. They came to the Pingis Tavern and stopped short to appraise the rustic structure. Maloof mused: "It is early, of course, but I wonder if Wingo and Schwatzendale might have paused here to test the local ale."

"The idea would certainly occur to them," said Myron.

Without further words the two climbed the steps to the porch and entered the tavern. Halting, they surveyed the dim interior. Behind the bar was a bartender of middle age; in a corner two old women sat engrossed in a game of some sort.

Maloof asked the bartender: "Have our friends looked in this morning? One is plump, round-faced, with a rather pink complexion, and going bald. He would be wearing a pale brown cloak. The other is dark-haired and nervous, wearing a shirt of striking green-and-black diaper pattern, so that he seems a harlequin."

The bartender placed both hands on the bar and frowned toward the old women; then his face cleared into remembrance. "Two gentlemen stepped in this morning. One was sturdy, with a kind pink face. The other was all elbows and knees, with eyes that looked in two directions at once." He shook his head, caught up by some marvelous recollection.

"Now I recall everything. They drank three tankards each of Number Three Pooncho Punch, then, despite my earnest advice, called for a fourth tankard, which they also consumed. They are now resting in the back room. I could have given them a gill each of the Number Four Pooncho, but I thought better of it, as the Four Pooncho sometimes has startling effects. While you wait, will you each take a Pooncho, to foster your own vigor?"

"At this moment, no," said Maloof. "Perhaps the next time we pass. You say that our friends are resting in comfort?"

"Just so. They are as limp as dead eels."

Thus reassured, Maloof and Myron left the tavern.

Not far ahead, the boulevard entered the O-Shar-Shan circus, across from the wonderful O-Shar-Shan terrace, where tourists wearing their most splendid regalia sat under gay parasols, drinking fizzes, punches, and toddies from tall bamboo mugs. They were on hand early, to see and be seen; in modes of feigned languor and sophisticated indifference they covertly studied the folk at nearby tables, speculating as to their places of origin, social status, and moral standards.

From time to time, charabancs stopped before the terrace. Passengers disembarked, others were loaded aboard, and the charabanc set off on a new sortie into the wilderness. Around the circus, skitters of a dozen sorts rolled on high, spindly wheels, some decorated with arrays of banderoles, others with bouquets of artificial flowers. The drivers in the main were sportive types, sitting high and erect in the approved posture; they tended to be critical of other drivers and easily became outraged by faulty or intemperate techniques. Calling out advice, whirring and veering in and out of the traffic patterns, they waved their arms to indicate the nature of the other's mistake—which usually evoked responsive comments and significant gestures, while the skitters careened from lane to lane.

A few yards short of the circus a walkway led off under tall yew trees to an impressive stone structure. A vertical arrangement of bronze characters beside the door read: IPCC. At the approach of Maloof and Myron, the door slid aside, and after they had entered, slid softly shut.

The two stood in a large, high-ceilinged chamber, which, like the exterior, conveyed a sense of uncompromising certitude. The floor was paved with pale gray tile, and the walls were washed severely white, unadorned except for the IPCC starburst emblem high on the back wall.

Behind a desk sat a man who might have been purposely selected for the office itself. He was in his early maturity, with dark golden hair and intelligent blue eyes. A plaque on his desk identified him as 'Captain Skahy Serle'. He rose to his feet and waited as Maloof and Myron approached, then indicated chairs. "Good morning, gentlemen; be seated, if you will."

When Maloof and Myron had seated themselves, Serle resumed his own place behind the desk. "Now then, introduce yourselves, and tell me how I can be of service."

"Very well. I am Adair Maloof, master of the ship *Glicca*, now at the spaceport; this is Myron Tany, my first assistant. To begin with, we need information; after that, much depends upon what you can tell us."

"Please continue."

"We are trying to locate a certain Loy Tremaine, who may now be on Fluter. Do you care to hear the background details? They are a trifle sordid."

Serle smiled. "I am not easily disturbed! I have nothing better to do than make out the monthly reports, which I can easily assign to Jervis, my subaltern."

Maloof collected his thoughts. "About a year ago I took the *Glicca* to Traven, on the world Morlock, for two reasons. The *Glicca* needed modifications and an overhaul, and I wanted to visit my father and mother, who resided there.

"My father had substantial wealth, and I expected to find my parents in comfortable retirement in their home on Telmany Heights—but instead, I discovered that my father had died, under suspicious circumstances, and that my mother had left Morlock in the company of a man much younger than she, for destinations unknown.

"Ill health had overtaken my father, and he had lost most of his initiative, demanding no more from life than quiet and the solace of his books. My mother, on the other hand, had thrown herself into a whirl of social activities, giddy and a bit senile, desperately seeking to recapture the fervor of youth. Despite my father's complaints, she opened the house to eccentric semi-scandalous masques, and wild midnight revels.

"My father was forced to take refuge in his country home on Lake Cristel, and this allowed my mother more scope than ever. He finally became disgusted with her extravagances and put the whole of his wealth into a trust fund, from which she would be paid a moderate annuity. When notified of the changes, my mother was outraged, but was careful to keep quiet her altered circumstances, since the news would surely excite the furtive amusement of her cronies. By one means or another she managed to sustain the illusion of grandiose wealth.

"My mother became fascinated by a swashbuckling young rogue named Loy Tremaine. His appearance was striking—his hair was lustrous black, his features aquiline. His eyes burned with a black intensity, and his manners were flamboyant. The old ladies could not take their eyes from him; they were universally smitten with this picaresque rogue and hung on his every word, each trying to outdo the others in girlish verve, preening and simpering when he spoke to them, though he gave my mother—known to control a notable family fortune—the most earnest attention.

"On one occasion, Tremaine drank much wine and became vainglorious. He told of escapades and dangerous ventures Beyond—all no doubt fictitious, but which held the old ladies spellbound. He mentioned his home world, which he declared to be the most beautiful planet of the Reach! He spoke with a curious passion, more than a simple yearning for home; one day, so he declared, he would return—as soon as a small misunderstanding with the civil authorities could be adjusted.

"My mother was much affected. She said that she also longed to wander among the exotic worlds, but her husband considered such off-world travel dangerous, and a waste of money. She complained that it was his penury which prevented her from enjoying the full amplitude of the family fortune, which was her due. Tremaine listened sympathetically, making no comment; still, two days later, my father drowned when his boat mysteriously capsized—on a calm day—in Lake Cristel.

"My mother appeared at the funeral in company with Loy Tremaine. A few days later he apparently induced her to go off with him, for romantic adventures among the fabulous far worlds of the Reach; at least this was the thrust of a hurried note my mother left for a friend. They departed incognito and left no hints as to their destination.

"Tremaine's background was never clear. But he had a curious tattoo on his neck, a slantwise cross inside two concentric circles. The location and style of this mark, I understand, are typically Flaut."

Maloof paused, and after a moment continued, with delicate precision. "That, by and large, is the situation. Tremaine would seem to be a native of Fluter. He may be here—now—with my mother. It is only fitting that I make inquiries, and if the IPCC can be of assistance, so much the better."

"What do you have in mind for Tremaine?"

"There is much about Tremaine which we do not know," replied Maloof carefully. "A great deal will depend upon the way he conducts himself."

Serle sat for a moment in thought. "My instructions are not to interfere with the activities of the Agents, unless they put too many tourists—or Flauts, for that matter—to punishments of the third order. At this moment, if I were to act as they think proper, I would refer you to the local office of the Civil Agents." He leaned back in his chair. "But I will naturally do what I can for you, given the strictures under which I work.

"The tattoo on Tremaine's neck indicates his place of origin. He is not from Coro-coro—if so, the tattoo would be a sunburst. Still, it should be easy to identify. I will put Jervis on the job." He pressed a button on his desk.

A door in the back wall opened, and a young man in the blue and black IPCC uniform appeared. He was slender, dark-haired, and carried himself with almost military punctilio. "Sir, you have need of me?"

"So I do. This is Captain Maloof and his shipmate Myron Tany. Gentlemen, this is my assistant Ian Jervis."

Maloof and Myron acknowledged the introductions. Serle turned to Jervis. "Do you know where to find the artist Florio?"

"Yes, his shop is across the boulevard."

Serle drew on a card, then tucked the card into an envelope, which he handed to Jervis. "I have drawn the pattern of a tattoo on the card. Please ask Florio to identify the tattoo." Jervis took the envelope and departed.

A few minutes passed; then Jervis returned in company with a thin, white-haired man. Jervis said apologetically: "I showed the card to Master Florio, and he insisted on speaking to you in person."

"Just so," said Florio. "I must confer with you privately. Certain of my affairs may not be circulated in the public forum."

"As you wish." Serle led Florio into a side room and closed the door. Jervis bowed politely and returned to his own office.

Maloof and Myron waited in silence; the implications of Florio's conduct were too recondite to prompt speculation.

After a prolonged interval, Florio and Serle returned to the chamber. Florio gave Maloof and Myron nods of impersonal courtesy and departed the office, while Serle resumed his seat.

For a moment, Serle sat considering the two off-worlders, his face a study. Finally he roused himself and straightened in his chair. "You will wonder at Florio's insistence upon privacy. Needless to say, any information or hints of enlightenment you hear now must never be revealed, especially to the Civil Agents—toward whom Florio feels total contempt.

"To begin with, Florio identified Tremaine's tattoo as the emblem of the village Krenke, which indicates that Krenke was his place of origin. In itself this is not significant. More important is that two months ago a man answering Tremaine's description came to Florio's studio; for a large cash payment, Florio altered the man's Krenke tattoo to a Coro-coro sunburst, and also applied a sunburst tattoo to the neck of an old woman who was Tremaine's companion. Here is evidence that Tremaine and your mother have established themselves somewhere on Fluter; precisely where, it is impossible to surmise."

Maloof reflected. "If Krenke were his native village, this is where he might feel most secure from the Civil Agents."

Serle shrugged. "Possibly so. For a fact he would be conspicuous in Coro-coro."

Maloof considered further. "Where is Krenke? What kind of a village is it?"

Again Serle summoned Jervis, and instructed him to discover what there was to be learned about Krenke. After a period, Jervis returned to report that Krenke was a village of moderate size, adequately prosperous, where the Three Feathers Inn provided decent lodging for tourists.

Serle provided Maloof a map indicating the location of Krenke. "It is remote, but not too remote. If you leave now, you should arrive by this evening."

3

Maloof and Myron returned to the *Glicca* to find themselves alone aboard, with the rest of the ship's company occupied elsewhere. Maloof left a note on the galley table. "That should soothe their anxieties, if any exist."

To Myron's comment that he would have been comforted by the support of Wingo and Schwatzendale, Maloof replied, "We can deal adequately with the situation, and we are far less conspicuous alone." Myron accepted Maloof's program without protest, but checked that his hand-weapons were in good working order.

The two unshipped the flitter and stowed a few items of equipment aboard. Once aloft, they set off over the arcadian landscapes of Fluter, toward the village Krenke. As the sun traversed the sky, the continents and seas passed below.

With the sun close to the horizon, Krenke appeared below, dozing in the golden light of late afternoon. Maloof put the flitter into a slow circle over the village. A road from the east crossed a tranquil river by an iron bridge, to become the high street of the village. After passing the Three Feathers Inn, the road proceeded a hundred yards to give upon a public square, then angled away and was lost under the foliage of tall trees. Across the bridge from the inn was an area of open land, occupied by a variety of vehicles: farm equipment, drays, power-carts, a few skitters badly in need of maintenance, and a pair of antique flitters, fragile as moth-wings. Maloof found an empty bay at the back of the area and landed the flitter just as the last sliver of sun dropped below the horizon, leaving behind a tumble of clouds glowing vermilion, amber, and gold.

Dusk was gathering as Maloof and Myron made their way to the bridge and crossed the river. Ahead loomed the Three Feathers Inn, a massive structure of timber and stone with a high-peaked roof. Over the entrance hung a sign depicting three iron feathers splayed out into a fan, constrained within a heavy iron frame in the traditional style. Maloof and Myron pushed open the heavy door and entered the common room of the inn.

They found themselves in a large chamber, almost majestic in its scale. Timber posts supported gnarled cross-room baulks, on which rested ceiling joists, and the age-darkened planks of the ceiling proper. A line of tables ranged the wall to the left; a long bar flanked the wall to the right. The tables were occupied by diners: men, women, and a few children dressed in their best. They were served by a gaunt, middle-aged woman with lank arms and legs, who loped with long bent-kneed strides back and forth between tables and kitchen. She wore a loose gown striped brown and green, so long that it almost swept the floor. Her hair was piled into a pyramid, with a blue flower thrust in demurely at the apex. The diners constantly importuned her as she strode back and forth: "Dinka! More sauce is needed!" "Dinka! Bring more batrachies, with fresh vinegar!" "Dinka! The bread is musty; we need more savoury paste."

A doorway into the kitchen allowed occasional glimpses of a short, squat woman with a perspiring red face, who glared out toward the tables in what seemed a state of chronic fury.

Along the bar a dozen men in working-class garments, or the somewhat more pretentious costumes of tradesmen, sat hunched over tall wooden tankards of beer talking in gruff mutters. Behind the bar a moon-faced bartender danced nimbly back and forth, his great paunch pressed against the counter, refilling tankards, wiping up spills, and chaffing the drinkers, who stared at him blankly.

Maloof and Myron seated themselves at the end of the bar and waited.

Jodel, the bartender, noticing the newcomers, sidled down the length of the bar. He spoke: "Gentlemen, what is your pleasure?"

"We have just arrived from Coro-coro," said Maloof. "We want lodging for the night, supper, and breakfast in the morning."

"No problem whatever!" declared Jodel. "Here is the registry; you need only sign, and formalities are over."

"So it might be, providing that we can afford your rates."

Jodel made an indulgent gesture. "Fear nothing; our rates are considered moderate."

"And the specific numbers?"

Jodel shrugged. "If you like. Let us say four sols for the room and fifty dinkets for each meal, to a total of six sols."

"The charges are tolerable," said Maloof, "provided that you add on no unexpected extras, let us say, for clean linen or hot water."

"Our rates are all-inclusive," said Jodel. "However, we prefer that the score be paid in advance, for practical reasons. Certain of our clientele will rise early, take a special deluxe breakfast, then decamp before settling the account."

"That is not our habit," said Maloof. "Still, one must be on guard against scoundrels. In Coro-coro we encountered a certain 'Loy Tremaine' who thought to swindle us. By an odd coincidence, he stated that he made his home in Krenke."

Jodel gave his head a dubious shake. "Somewhere there is a mistake. Tremaines have never resided in Krenke. You misheard the name of his village."

"Probably so," said Maloof.

"More likely, he was an impostor," mused Jodel. "Only last month, a huckster of wild currants arrived in Krenke. While folk were inspecting his merchandise, he laid hold of a girl and took her behind his dray, where he lifted her skirt a full five inches! Her cries brought help on the run. The hawker was dragged away to the rollers, where he danced among the coils for two days. He was also fined the contents of his dray. It was a woebegone wretch who finally took his empty dray back to Lilancx!

"But now you will wish to visit your accommodations. You may take your supper when you come down." He placed his hands on the bar and, leaning forward, searched the chamber. Dissatisfied, he threw back his head and shouted: "Buntje! Buntje! Come at the double! Where are you, Buntje?" He listened, then called again, in a louder voice: "Buntje! Do you not hear me? Come at once! Buntje! I am calling you!"

Into the room burst a girl of about fourteen, running at speed, arms pumping and skirt flapping, so that a lascivious eye might have glimpsed at least an inch of ankle. Maloof and Myron modestly averted their eyes. She wore a tight pink blouse over a near-flat chest, and a voluminous black skirt, which barely cleared the floor. Like Dinka, she had gathered her hair up into a tall pyramid, with a flower precariously thrust into the apex. Halting in front of Jodel, she panted: "Roar no further; I am here!"

"You were slow. Can you move no faster? What kept you so long?"

The girl cried out in a passion: "Must I explain every detail of my personal conduct? If I am forced to particularize, I will state that I was occupied in the retreat! When you called I could not jump up and run through the chamber, without creating a scandal; is this what you wish?"

"Bah," muttered Jodel. "You should accomplish these acts in your spare time. While you were luxuriating, these gentlemen have been awaiting your help. Now then: escort them to their quarters at once. Make sure that all is in order."

Buntje surveyed Maloof and Myron with mouth primly down-turned. "I take them to be off-worlders, and the young one has a queer look."

"No matter," said Jodel. "It is all one. Take them to Chamber Six, and see to their needs."

Buntje grimaced and composed herself. She asked Maloof, "Where is your luggage?"

"We have only these small travel bags, and we will carry them ourselves."

Buntje's face became a frozen mask. "As you like! However, please know that I am not the thief you take me for. Your precious belongings are safe from me."

Maloof stuttered an apology, which Buntje ignored. "Come; I will take you to your chamber."

"Hold hard!" cried Jodel, slapping the bar. "I want to see six sols shining in a row, before events move another inch."

Maloof paid over the required sum. Buntje led them to a narrow staircase. Maloof and Myron politely waited for Buntje to precede them, but she indignantly jerked aside. "Do you take me for a raw innocent? I know your off-world tricks! The ruse has failed; you may go first."

"As you wish," sighed Maloof. The two climbed the stairs, with Buntje several steps behind. At the landing she slipped past, giving Myron a wide berth. She opened the door with the numeral '6', and, after looking warily at Maloof and Myron, glanced into the room, then stepped quickly back out.

"You may enter; the room is in order."

"Just a moment," said Maloof. "You were supposed to check the room carefully. Are the beds fresh?"

"And what about towels and soap?" Myron asked. "You should at least look into the bathroom."

"Everything is as it should be. If you find any rodents, chase them into the hall."

Buntje retreated and clattered down the stairs. Maloof and Myron inspected the room, and found no cause for complaint. The furniture was massive, durable, and obviously of great age. A door led into a rather quaint bathroom.

For a moment the two stood by the window, looking out over the village. A few wavering street-lights came on, casting islands of wan illumination. In the public square a number of young men were preparing for a social event of a sort not immediately clear. The two turned from the window and went down to the common room. They seated themselves at a vacant table, and waited for attention.

Dinka loped past, back and forth, and eventually halted. When Maloof requested a menu, she seemed puzzled; when he explained, she said with the ghost of a prim smile: "Sir, we have no such documents on hand."

"Then what is available for our supper?"

"That depends upon the decision of Wilkin."

"Indeed." Looking toward the kitchen, Maloof and Myron saw the squat, red-faced cook glaring at them through the doorway, brandishing a wooden spoon.

Dinka said: "She is in a bit of a tantrum. Buntje has reported that the young one tried to lure her into the bathroom, planning a lewd antic, which she took heroic measures to avoid."

"Absurd!" declared Maloof. "Ask Wilkin to step out here, and we will explain the situation in detail. We cannot let such slander go unchallenged."

Dinka shook her head. "I will talk to Wilkin and put matters right. Buntje is subject to adolescent fits; this is known, and perhaps Wilkin will see reason. If not, I can bring you some dried fish, and some dried bread with suet."

Dinka went off to the kitchen, closing the door behind her. After a time she emerged carrying a tureen of pungent soup, which she placed before Maloof and Myron. She glanced toward the kitchen and said: "Wilkin has herself in control now. It seems that tonight there is a romp; Buntje has never before dared to attend, for fear that she might fall sprawling, with legs in the air. In any case, your supper is secure."

Following the soup, Dinka brought a platter of fish stewed with ramp and small tubers, which might have been acorns, and finally dumplings in fruit sauce.

The supper was over. The two sat over mugs of herbal tea. The night was still young, and it was too early to retire to their room. For a time they watched the coming and going of patrons at the bar, but there was no entertainment here. All conducted themselves with somber restraint, and spoke in mutters to each other. Jodel darted back and forth, his great paunch pressed against the counter, his moon-face fixed in the semblance of smiling cordiality. No one took notice of the off-worlders.

After a time, Maloof and Myron rose from the table and went to the door. They pushed through and passed out into the evening.

4

For a moment they stood in front of the inn, the sign swinging gently over their heads to vagrant puffs of wind. Dusk had not yet left the sky; up and down the high street the roofs of cottages were black outlines against the gray murk.

The two set off up the high street, keeping to the shadows. Where the street entered the square, they halted to watch what seemed to be the early stages of a social event involving the adolescent population of Krenke. On one side of the square a group of boys had gathered, in the main striplings of about sixteen to perhaps eighteen. Opposite was a group of girls of similar age, perhaps a year or so younger. They chattered, laughed, made extravagant gestures, and ran a few steps back and forth, creating a spectacle of gay spontaneity, meanwhile turning covert glances toward the boys, who for the most part were quiet, gazing shamelessly toward the girls.

Maloof and Myron, beguiled by the situation, seated themselves on a bench under a tall plumeria tree and waited to discover how the event would develop. As they watched, teams of young men using ground-marking equipment laid down sets of parallel lines to create a system of lanes about five feet wide running from side to side across the square.

When the work was finished, the boys and girls at once spread out, each selecting a lane, sometimes backing away and going to another lane when they did not particularly approve of the person at the other end, running quickly back and forth. At the far end of the square a group of young men, apparently musicians, climbed onto a low platform and busied themselves setting up their instruments. They wore special costumes of odd style and color: tight open-midriff shirts of fluorescent blue; expansive breeches, vermilion, lime green, and black, ballooning out over the hips and tied at the knees, and long pointed white shoes. Now they all donned grotesque vulpine masks and were suddenly transformed into a cabal of minor devils.

Tension increased; the air seemed to tingle. The boys and girls began to jig and caper, tentatively at first but with ever more abandon. They jabbed the air with their fingers, jerked their thumbs to the side. On the far platform the tympanist arranged a battery of chimes over the great bass drum, tested a hollow wood-block with a bamboo whisk, then stood at the ready and waited while profound silence came to the square. He raised his arm dramatically high, then struck down at his cylindrical gong. The other musicians were off and away, producing a sudden din of wails, quavers, and random arpeggios, paced by a fateful booming of the great drum.

The effect took Maloof and Myron by surprise; for some reason they had expected music more structured and melodic than what they now heard. They listened carefully.

"I have the answer," said Myron. "We do not understand this music because it is too subtle for us."

Maloof agreed. "No doubt you are right."

The boys and girls at the open ends of lanes were reacting to the music with enthusiasm, and stood jerking to the beat of the big drum, the most exuberant squirming and twisting, kicking forward, knees bent, then thrusting out with pointed toes. Myron noted that the girls had tied their skirts more or less tightly to their shoes, so as not to flaunt too much ankle, though the most audacious allowed a few provocative inches to flash in and out of sight.

The drum became more urgent; the kicking and prancing grew vehement, and the energies reached a critical level. At each end of a lane a boy and a girl broke free, and advanced to meet, kicking and jigging, hands thrusting at hips. They arrived at the center and jerked to a halt, shoulders squirming, hips twisting; then, wheeling and bending so that they bumped buttocks, each returned jigging and jerking in triumph along the way they had come.

The music continued as before, the great drum maintaining its thundering beat. Another pair broke free and repeated the routine, followed by two others.

Myron suddenly leaned forward and pointed. "Look yonder—the fourth girl along the line!"

"It is Buntje, cavorting with the best of them!"

"There she goes!" cried Myron, as Buntje set off along the lane, performing with no less energy than the others.

The lanes were suddenly active, the participants each demonstrating his or her particular style: some ponderous and meaningful, others lightsome and frivolous, like careening insects. At times a boy or a girl would start out in a lane, jigging and twitching in notable display, only to find that no one was advancing from the opposite end of the lane. It was a humiliating experience. The person so slighted might halt, then return crestfallen to the starting point, or if sufficiently angry might proceed to the middle and there perform a grotesque travesty of the usual postures, hoping to shame the offender.

After a time the function came to an end. There was a cre-scendo of chimes, a wild glissando from the belp-horn, a final fateful thump of the drum, then silence. The musicians removed their masks, packed their instruments, jumped down from the platform, and disappeared into the night. The boys and girls, now ignoring each other, formed chattering little groups discussing the evening's events. Some were elated and celebrated their successes. Others were more subdued, and wondered about themselves.

"So there you have it," said Maloof. "That is how life goes at Krenke. We witnessed a hundred small triumphs and gratified hopes, and as many small tragedies."

Myron nodded soberly. "I wonder what happens next," he said. "They can't be ready to go home."

Myron's speculations were soon put to rest. The boys moved to the high street, where they dispersed to their various destinations. From the shadows beside the square, men and women materialized as if by magic, and one by one the girls were whisked unceremoniously out to the high street and away to home.

A few minutes later the square was deserted and dark, except for a light in one of the offices across the square.

"Someone is working late," said Myron. He rose to his feet and studied the office more closely; beside the door he saw a rack which of-fered journals for sale.

"It might be the local news agency," he told Maloof, "assuming that such an enterprise exists at Krenke."

The two men crossed the square. As they approached the office, they noticed a sign above the door. Gold script on a black background read:

THE KRENKE OBSERVER
ULWYN FARRO, PURVEYOR

Maloof tapped at the door. A calm voice said: "Come!"
The two entered a small, neat office, furnished sparsely. One wall

was completely covered by hundreds of photographs, depicting men, women, and children of all ages and conditions, for the most part staring blankly into the camera. The other walls were washed starkly white, and lacked all decoration.

Behind a desk sat a pale young man of unimpressive physique. A few strands of ash-blond hair fringed his forehead; his long, thin face was unremarkable, except for luminous gray eyes. He said: "I am Ulwyn Farro, as you may have guessed. Do you have business with me?"

"Nothing of consequence," said Maloof. "We happened to notice your sign and looked in out of sheer curiosity."

Farro surveyed his two visitors with curiosity of his own. "I assume that you are the off-worlders who arrived this afternoon and are lodging at the Three Feathers."

"Quite correct," said Maloof.

Myron added with a sardonic grin: "Rumor travels fast across Krenke."

Farro gave an indifferent shrug. "One way or another, I am grateful—it brings me most of my material. Do you care to sit?"

"Thank you." The two settled themselves upon straight-backed chairs. "I am Adair Maloof, master of the spaceship *Glicca*. This is my first officer, Myron Tany."

Farro acknowledged the introductions with a nod. "What brings you to this rather remote village? Are you tourists, or do you have other business in mind?"

Maloof said: "If you are hoping to develop an interesting article for the *Observer*, put the idea aside. We are ordinary tourists, wandering the far places of Fluter as the mood takes us."

"As you say." Farro leaned back in his chair and subjected his visitors to a moment of contemplation. "If I were to risk an offhand comment, I might say that neither of you fits the mold of the ordinary tourist. Still, what other conceivable purpose could bring you to a somnolent backwater such as Krenke? You are truly something of a puzzle. My speculations, I hasten to say, are no more than whimsical fancy, in no way relevant to the *Observer*."

Maloof reflected before responding. He said, rather ponderously: "You seem a sensitive man, with an agile mind. Let me float another 'whimsical fancy', to the effect that we are, for a fact, pursuing a topic regarding which we need information, but only if the topic were totally isolated from any form of publicity."

Farro leaned forward. "Let us bring the matter into closer focus. I gather that you want me to supply information, and thereafter keep the discussion hermetically secret. Is this correct?"

"Precisely so. If the reason for our presence became known, our function would be compromised."

"Very well," said Farro. "I agree to your conditions, unless your revelations are so dire and disastrous that I am forced to make them known."

Maloof smiled grimly. "You shall hear neither of disasters nor cataclysms. Shall I proceed?"

"Yes," said Farro. "Proceed."

"A year ago at Traven, on the world Morlock, I encountered a young man who called himself 'Loy Tremaine'. He occupied himself charming old women and defrauding them of their wealth. He had a magnetic presence and carried himself with incredible arrogance. On his neck he wore a tattoo, which we have identified as the Krenke insignia. During this time at Traven, he stated that he desperately wished to return to Fluter but must make an adjustment with the Civil Agents. In the end he committed a murder and induced a wealthy widow to leave Morlock so that the two could pursue wonderful adventures among the far worlds, but he had Fluter in mind.

"Two days ago the *Glicca* landed at the Coro-coro spaceport. We discovered that Tremaine was resident on Fluter. We could not find him in Coro-coro and theorized that he might have taken refuge in Krenke, which is why we are here."

Farro shook his head. "Something is wrong. There have never been 'Tremaines' at Krenke; perhaps you misread the tattoo."

"Definitely not. It was seen and certified by an expert, who had altered it to a Coro-coro sunburst."

"In that case, there is no doubt about it—your man is using a false name. What did he look like?"

Maloof gave a short harsh laugh. "Once seen, he can never be mistaken. He is tall and strong. He moves with dramatic pride—like a cavalier of old dancing the shebardigan. Dark curls fall over his forehead; his eyes burn with black intensity, close beside a lordly nose. He likes to act the rakehelly damn-your-eyes bravo, and uses flamboyant gestures."

"Hold," cried Farro, his voice husky with excitement. "I know this man. His name is Orlo Cavke! I can assure you that he is not at Krenke."

"Why is that?"

"He would not dare show his face where it might be recognized! He committed abominable crimes here but escaped punishment.

"His deeds were sickening. He took three girls, one after the other, and led them by night up the Mellamy Steeps. It was a terrible time at Krenke, with every man looking askance at every other. Orlo Cavke violated the girls in every conceivable manner, and perhaps in other ways not immediately conceivable. He vented a mad rage upon these poor children, punishing them for the beauty which they had withheld from him. He was captured and dragged back to the village in chains, but he escaped, and it was learned that he had left Fluter. I am shocked to learn of his return!"

Maloof muttered: "This casts a new light upon Loy Tremaine." He grunted. "I suppose that now we must call him 'Orlo Cavke'."

Farro regarded them thoughtfully. "What will you do now?"

"We have no choice," said Maloof. "We will look for him elsewhere. If he is on Fluter, we shall find him."

"Then what will you do?"

"I don't know. Much will depend upon circumstances."

Farro said earnestly: "If you find him, I hope that you will return him to Krenke. He has dealt us a foul wound that only he can make better."

Maloof shook his head sadly. "We can promise nothing. He has my mother in his custody, and we must be guided by what we find." He stopped to consider. "Can you provide us a picture of Orlo Cavke?"

Farro hesitated, then reached into a drawer and brought out a pair of photographs, which he pushed across the desk to Maloof.

"Thank you."

Maloof studied the two poses a moment, then passed them to Myron.

In the first photo Myron saw a tall, dark-haired man of striking appearance, standing manacled before a stone wall. Cavke glared at the camera, projecting a near-tangible fury. In the second, Cavke had swung aside, showing a profile which might have been that of an ancient demonic hero. His posture conveyed only defiance and contempt.

Farro asked: "When will you be leaving Krenke?"

"In the morning; there is nothing to keep us in Krenke any longer."

Maloof and Myron rose to their feet and gave Farro their thanks. They departed into the night leaving Farro at his desk, staring disconsolately after them.

Arriving at the Three Feathers Inn, the two entered the common room. A pair of beer-drinkers sat in colloquy with Jodel. Along the line of empty tables, Dinka stood looking out the window, engrossed in private reverie. The door into the kitchen was closed, concealing the irascible Wilkin, if indeed she were still striding about among her pots and pans, gesticulating with her spoon.

The two gave Dinka a polite good night as they passed, but she barely noticed. They climbed the stairs to their room, made preparations for the night, sought their beds, and were soon asleep.

5

In the morning, a dismal overcast had drifted down from the hills to the north, and from the window the village seemed more dank, cheerless, and worn by the passage of time than ever.

The two men dressed in silence, depressed by what they had learned, and descended the stairs to the common room. Dinka met them and took them to what she called "the breakfast saloon"—a long, dim chamber smelling of mold and wet stone. A small window in the back wall admitted a watery gray light, barely sufficient to illuminate their table.

"Wilkin is in a good mood," Dinka told them. "She has allowed you her best porridge, and also dishes of fruit."

The two were served crusty bread and marmalade, thick porridge flavored with fragments of salt fish, and dishes of boiled figs in a syrup of spiced honey. They gnawed at the bread and drank as much herbal tea as they could tolerate, then returned to the common room.

At the bar three men of middle years sat hunched over tankards of beer.

Jodel called out a jovial greeting and said: "The time is early; are you leaving so soon?"

Maloof paused. "Our visit to Krenke has been pleasant, but it is time we were returning to Coro-coro."

"Just so," said Jodel. "You must do as you think best. But perhaps you will delay your departure a few moments; these gentlemen wish to make your acquaintance."

"Indeed!" said Maloof. He muttered to Myron: "It seems that Farro found the news too dire and terrible to be kept secret."

"I am not surprised," said Myron. "In truth, he had no choice."

Jodel, looking from one to the other, said anxiously: "There is no need for diffidence. These are gentlemen of reputation; I vouch for them myself."

The Krenks stepped down from their stools and turned to face the off-worlders. They were much alike: dour, hard-featured men with sturdy torsos, heavy shoulders, and dark hair pulled back and tied with leather thongs. They wore long black coats flaring at the hip, black pantaloons tied at the knee, black stockings, and long pointed shoes.

Jodel spoke with careful deference. "Allow me to make introductions." He tapped each Krenk on the shoulder in turn. "This is Derl Mone. This is Avern Glister. This is Madrig Cargus." With a sheepish grin he looked sidewise at Maloof. "I fear that I have forgotten your names."

"No matter. I am Adair Maloof; this is Myron Tany. We both serve aboard the *Glicca*, now at the Coro-coro spaceport. What do you wish of us?"

Derl Mone spoke, his voice rasping with the effort to maintain civility. "You have taken an unusual interest in a certain Orlo Cavke. As you may have discovered, he is a criminal who escaped our justice. We are anxious to repair our mistake."

"I understand your concern," said Maloof. "Last night we learned more about Orlo Cavke—Loy Tremaine, as we knew him—than we had ever suspected."

As before, Mone controlled his voice with an effort. "Why do you seek Cavke?"

"He killed my father, and now controls my mother, living on her income."

Mone made an ambiguous sound, then asked: "What do you intend to do now?"

"At the moment, we have no idea of his whereabouts. Still, we will find him, probably by tracing my mother's annuity. If she were not receiving this money, he would have abandoned her. The foolish old lady certainly cannot be an exciting companion."

Mone made a grim sound. "Orlo's inclinations take him differently—toward innocent pretty little creatures, hardly more than children. First he took Lally Glister and led her to a forest den, where he did incredible things to her. When she died, he buried her under the mold. After a time, he stole my girl Murs, and followed the same procedure. By this time the village was wild with horror, and no one raged more wildly than Orlo Cavke! After a time, he lay in wait for Salu Cargus, and what he did to her is beyond belief. But he had become careless. The farmboy Tinnoc, who worked a plot close by Orlo's planting, noticed Orlo's absences when he should have been tending his crops. There was no sign of tillage, and the weeds were rampant. Tinnoc told us of his suspicions, and we put a tracer button in Orlo's shoe and tracked him to his den.

"We unearthed the things from under the mold which once had been our daughters, and looked to Orlo for explanation. He merely smiled and shrugged.

"We dragged him back to the village and loaded him with chains. While we pondered the best way to deal with him, he squirmed free and fled into the forest; we fell to the ground and chewed stones. Five days of mourning were decreed: one day for the lost girls, three days for the loss of Orlo, and a final day to curse the great and only god for his apathy, whom we now reject as a turncoat. You will understand why we have questioned you in such detail."

Maloof assented. "You have our total sympathy."

Cargus broke his silence. "That is not enough—you claim that you will capture Orlo Cavke, and so it may be; when you have him in your custody, you must return him to Krenke, where we will provide him a suitable home-coming."

Maloof shook his head apologetically. "We cannot make such a commitment, which might be impossible for us to implement. I can only say that if we capture him and it is practical, we will turn him over to you. Any other promise I could make would be meaningless."

The three Krenks turned back to the bar. They drained the beer from their tankards, then turned toward the door and departed the inn.

Maloof and Myron paused long enough to give Jodel a polite farewell, then also departed the inn. For a moment they stood before the Three Feathers. They looked a last time up the high street, then marched over the iron bridge and crossed the parking yard to their flitter.

The flitter rose through the low overcast and broke out into sunlight. With the autopilot set, Maloof and Myron flew back over the landscapes of Fluter toward Coro-coro.

FIVE

1

The flitter arrived at the Coro-coro spaceport during the soft Fluter dusk. Aboard the *Glicca*, Wingo and Schwatzendale sat at the galley table making a meal of bread, sardines, and onions. Maloof and Myron joined the repast and told of their visit to Krenke.

Wingo and Schwatzendale were suitably impressed. "Strange," mused Wingo, "one would think that, after so many years, they might have evolved a cuisine more subtle than what you have described."

Schwatzendale pointed out that Wingo's theories were ad hoc and relativistic, since Wingo had no information as to the gastronomical standards of two thousand years previously. "For all we know, they subsisted on grass."

Wingo ignored the remark. "Conceivably each village of Fluter has developed a unique cuisine." He pondered a moment. "Hmm. A student of anthropology might find here scope for an interesting monograph." He brought a pot of tea and a plate of fruit tarts to the table; then he and Schwatzendale recounted their own exploits of the day. They had passed the afternoon on the O-Shar-Shan terrace, where Wingo had captured a number of vivid mood-impressions for his monumental *Pageant of the Gaean Race*.

"The terrace is a vast reservoir of material," said Wingo. "I give special attention to the ladies! Each has gone to great lengths to make herself supreme. Gentlemen are also on hand, naturally, but in general they lack a certain éclat.

"The terrace has become an avenue of almost transcendental mystique. Tourists are permeated by this extraordinary afflatus, and come to think of themselves as a privileged elite—free to indulge in whatever extravagance occurs to them." Wingo gave a rueful laugh. "It is ironic that when I encountered a truly startling circumstance, I failed to record the event, and I will regret the lapse forever." Wingo paused for reflection.

Maloof became impatient. "Please be more explicit! We sit here on tenterhooks, while you reminisce."

"Sorry," said Wingo. "I shall be more direct. When we arrived at the terrace, Schwatzendale went off on affairs of his own, while I found a table beside an ornamental planting and for a time was busy capturing mood-impressions. Then I put my equipment aside and sat at my ease drinking rum punch.

"Suddenly, at a nearby table, half hidden by the planting, I noticed what I had unaccountably missed before: a pair of young ladies, both exceedingly beautiful. Most notable was their resemblance to each other, so that I felt that they must be twins. They wore their honey-yellow curls in the same style; their features were identical, and they wore identical white blouses decorated with blue and red embroidery. The planting concealed their nether garments, but I was sure that they were the same.

"There was, however, a difference between the two. One was happy; her face glowed with excitement, humor, and ardent vitality, while the other sat steeped in despair and defeat, with mouth drooping and eyes downcast.

"I sat staring in wonder: what had caused such a disparity of emotion?"

Schwatzendale leaned forward. "I have the answer. They noticed you staring at them; one was amused; the other was angry, and about to shake her fist!"

"Nonsense!" scoffed Wingo. "The facts are quite different; neither so much as glanced in my direction."

"Belatedly I thought to capture the two faces for the *Pageant*," continued Wingo. "I reached for my gear, which I had tucked under the table. The other table was just across the planter, and I knew that I must be unobtrusive. I pretended ennui, and finally was ready to record the remarkable scene. But when I turned to look, the table was vacant; while I had been occupied, the girls had departed.

"I jumped to my feet and searched along the passages, up and down the aisles among the surge of tourists, and at last I saw them! They were walking away from me, so I saw only their backs. One was of ordinary height and walked with an easy athletic grace, while the other was half her height, and scuttled along on grotesquely deformed legs.

"I finally remembered my camera, but when I made ready, they were gone, and I saw no more of them."

"Hmm," said Maloof. "There is a lesson to be learned here, but I find it hard to quantify. Where was Schwatzendale during this episode?"

Wingo gave his head a dubious shake. "For a time, at least, he sat at a table on the level above me, in company with a woman of a most unusual type. She was tall, thin, and sinuous, with long white arms and long pale fingers. Her hair was white, and surrounded her head like a nimbus of dandelion fluff. Her face was long and gaunt, with eyebrows and mouth marked with black—like the face of a pierrette. She wore a number of white ribbons dangling from epaulets—when she moved the ribbons shifted, allowing glimpses of the anatomy below—and carried a fan of lavish white plumes. When she spoke, she flourished the fan to hide their faces, evidently to ensure privacy. I asked Schwatzendale what went on behind the fan, but he refused to describe the conversation."

"Surely no surprise," said Myron. "Schwatzendale is a man of honor; he does not care to betray the secrets of a lady."

Schwatzendale gave his head a puzzled shake. "There were no secrets. The lady revealed herself to be an addict of long walks in the countryside; she wanted to know if I cared to join her on a ramble across the Maudlen Moors. I explained that I lacked a proper costume for the sport and therefore must decline. And that was the way of it."

"All is explained," said Wingo. "Still, why did the conversation take place behind her fan?"

"For no particular reason," said Schwatzendale. "It was as good a place as any."

Wingo accepted the explanation, and the conversation came to a close.

2

The following morning Maloof and Myron breakfasted in the galley, then rode the omnibus along Pomare Boulevard to the IPCC office. They found Serle at his desk, occupied with the paperwork which, because of Civil Agent sensitivity, comprised most of his official duties. He greeted the two spacemen politely and indicated chairs.

Leaning back, Serle surveyed the two with dispassionate curiosity. "You seem to have avoided serious damage. How did you fare?"

"Well enough, all taken with all," replied Maloof. "We watched the young folk of the town engage in what seemed to be an energetic courtship rite in the public square. We dined at the Three Feathers Inn and took our breakfast in a special breakfast saloon. A serving girl named Buntje accused Myron of peering at her ankles and reported his conduct to the cook.

"More importantly, we learned that Loy Tremaine is in fact a man named Orlo Cavke, who killed three children. The folk of Krenke captured him, but he broke free and fled to Coro-coro, then escaped off-world. The Krenks were surprised to learn that he had returned to Fluter. They want him badly."

"Amazing!" said Serle. "I marvel at his audacity."

"So long as he avoids the Civil Agents he is in no great danger—until we find him."

"So it would seem," Serle agreed.

"The presence of Lady Maloof reduces his options," continued Serle. "It would not be practical for him to take a house in Coro-coro; too much paperwork is involved, and the lady would surely want to make sorties to the O-Shar-Shan and other places of high fashion. After a month, the Agents would wonder about her entry papers, whereupon both she and Cavke would be in serious trouble. Cavke could set up a romantic camp in the wilderness, but Lady Maloof might not enjoy cold water, bad food, insects, or crouching over a hole in the ground when the need becomes urgent."

"This option may be dismissed," said Maloof.

"Another possibility exists, which is more probable. I refer to the use of a houseboat. They come in all sizes, configurations, and degrees of luxury, and can be taken to where scenery is most appealing and anchored without restriction. Supplies can be obtained at waterside villages; from Cavke's point of view, a houseboat would seem the optimum solution to his problems."

"Perhaps so," mused Myron. "What then? Fluter is a world with a hundred rivers, and probably hundreds of houseboats. Once Cavke is anchored on some lonely river he is lost to us."

"Not necessarily," said Serle. "There is a way to check out every houseboat on Fluter, without leaving Coro-coro."

"That sounds useful. How is it done?"

"In a most logical fashion," said Serle. "Suppose that you owned a fleet of rental houseboats. What would be your greatest fear?"

Myron reflected, then said: "I would be afraid that a drunken tourist would run my best boat onto a reef, then leave my boat to rot. By the time I learned what had happened, the tourist would be back on his home-world."

Serle nodded. "Exactly. To guard against this event, the renter installs a tracer button aboard each of his houseboats. On a map in his office, the position of each houseboat is plotted. You need only learn which vessel Orlo Cavke has rented, obtain the coordinates, and proceed to this position. Board the houseboat and apprehend Cavke, and the job is done."

"Simple enough," said Maloof, "especially if Cavke makes no objection."

"That is the only dubious link in the chain," Serle agreed. "I am sorry to say that I am restricted by IPCC protocol with the Agency; otherwise Jervis and I, wearing field uniforms, could board the houseboat and put Cavke under arrest—which would finalize the matter very neatly."

"No matter," said Maloof. "One way or another, we will get the job done, even if we have to set fire to the houseboat and make the capture as Cavke jumps overboard."

3

The *Tourist Guide to Fluter* listed two concerns from which houseboats might be rented or leased.

The Tarquin Transit Agency maintained premises on Pomare Boulevard, next to the Pingis Tavern. Maloof and Myron sought out the yardmaster, a debonair young man with a fine set of silky yellow side-whiskers. When Maloof put his initial questions, the yardmaster looked at him a trifle askance. "Are the Civil Agents concerned in this matter?"

"Absolutely not—it is the IPCC which has become interested in Loy Tremaine, and the rather haughty old lady with whom he is travelling. There is no wish to involve the Civil Agents."

"Ah, well!" said the yardmaster. "That puts a new face on the matter. For your information, then, Tarquin Transit has never, within the span of my employment, rented to a couple such as that which you have described. For the most part we serve groups of three or four tourists, often with children." He consulted his listings but was only confirmed in his statements.

Maloof and Myron went on to the Zangwill Agency, situated on a side street behind the O-Shar-Shan Hotel. The proprietor, Urban Zangwill, unlike the Tarquin yardmaster, showed no inclination whatever to cooperate, and responded to Maloof's initial inquiry with disdain. "I have an enviable reputation for discretion. Am I likely to risk this priceless asset at the behest of a pair of off-worlders?"

As Serle had predicted, Zangwill became cooperative as soon as the IPCC was mentioned. Grudgingly, he looked into his ledger and presently announced that the *Maijaro*—a luxury vessel of excellent characteristics—had been let on a long-term basis to a distinguished gentleman named Loy Tremaine, and his ailing mother, who displayed a testy temperament.

Zangwill brought out plans which depicted a fine vessel, forty-eight feet long, with a fifteen-foot beam. The plans showed a forward pilot station, a large main saloon, a galley with a pantry, two staterooms each with a bath, and forward and aft decks six feet wide.

"Where is the *Maijaro* anchored?" Maloof asked.

Zangwill took them into his inner office. A table supported a large-scale map of Fluter embossed on a surface of matte black glass, with pale tinted continents in relief, the waterways spangled here and there by white sparks.

In a voice without accent, as if detaching himself from all association with Maloof and Myron, Zangwill said: "The sparks represent Agency houseboats. There are fifty-one vessels, of four classes."

"And which is the *Maijaro*?"

Still impassive, Zangwill looked into a ledger, then touched buttons on a panel beside the map. One of the white sparks became a bright green glitter.

"That is the *Maijaro*. It is anchored on the Suametta River, to the west of the second continent."

Maloof studied the map with care, and noted the geographical coordinates which defined the exact position of the *Maijaro*.

Zangwill spoke, still in the same uninterested voice: "This is an especially fine anchorage. The scenery is excellent, there is adequate privacy, and supplies are available at a village a few miles upstream."

"The information is important," said Maloof. "You should know that Tremaine is a criminal. I tell you this so that you will feel no compulsion to warn him of our interest—by any means whatever. If you do so, you become an accessory to his crimes, which are serious. You will incur the same penalties that will be visited upon Tremaine. The IPCC penitential colonies are cold, wet, miserable, and long-term. The food is bad. Your fellow prisoners are vicious. Are these facts well understood?"

Zangwill grimaced. "You have made them clear. The Zangwill Agency operates in total accord with the law."

"Good," said Maloof. "We are reassured."

4

Maloof and Myron returned to the IPCC office. Serle looked up from his work in surprise. "You are back earlier than I had expected. Is this a positive sign?"

Maloof assented. "Our affairs seem to be moving forward." He described the events of the morning.

"Zangwill was cooperative, but he would seem a man of flexible principles. For this reason, I warned him that he would incur severe punishment if he should communicate with Orlo Cavke—Loy Tremaine, as he knows him."

"Good," said Serle. He pondered. "But not good enough." He spoke into his telephone.

The screen brightened to reveal a somber, black-browed face.

"Urban Zangwill here."

"I am Commander Skahy Serle, at the IPCC office."

Zangwill studied Serle's image. "I have not had the pleasure of meeting you before. How may I be of service?"

Serle smiled. "I am about to inform you of something which you may find unusual, but I am sure that in your lifetime you have adapted to many odd circumstances."

Zangwill responded cautiously: "I suppose that this is true."

"Then you will have no difficulty with the following fact. This morning, as you sat relaxing in your office, you drifted into what is called a fugue, a kind of day-dream. At this time you may have a vague recollection that two IPCC operatives spoke to you, in relation to a certain houseboat. Am I right?"

Zangwill's eyes narrowed in puzzlement. "I do not quite understand the thrust of your remarks."

"It is no mystery. During your day-dream, you fabricated a hallucinatory event. I now assure you that no such operatives appeared at your yard, and that for the sake of your mental health you should totally dismiss such peculiar dream-figments from your mind. Even as we speak, I am sure that these notions have disappeared—especially if someone should ask a foolish question. Am I clear on this?"

Zangwill's heavy mouth twitched. "In short, if someone asks about your operatives, I am to forget that they ever existed."

"How can you forget a fact which has never existed?"

Zangwill licked his lips. "I see that it would not be possible."

"Correct." Serle examined Zangwill's face with attention. "In general, how is your memory?"

Zangwill took time to consider. "I believe that it is good."

"Excellent. Therefore, if you do not recall a visit by anyone this morning, such event never occurred."

"That would be my conclusion; yes, indeed!"

"And you do not recall any such event?"

Zangwill grimaced. "No; I fear not."

"If anyone shows an interest in this hypothetical occasion, communicate with me immediately, and I will put matters right. I may say that your cooperation has established you in the good graces of the IPCC."

Zangwill showed a wry smile. "That is good news."

The screen went blank. Serle, frowning at some unwelcome thought, asked Maloof: "I assume that you learned the exact location of the *Maijaro*?"

Maloof responded without emphasis. "I took the coordinates from Zangwill's map." He recited numbers.

Serle brought out a map of the second continent and spread it upon his desk. Maloof repeated the numbers; Serle traced the coordinates and marked the intersection. "The *Maijaro* is here, where the river passes close under the Sumberlin Ridge." He studied the map.

"Upstream about eight miles is a small village. Its name is 'Pengelly'; it seems of no great importance." He reached into a drawer, brought out a reference book, found relevant information, and read: "Pengelly: a village of considerable antiquity on the Suametta River, with a population of about four hundred, occupied principally with fishing and agriculture. Pengelly figures to a small extent in historical lore, and at one time was the lair of the bandit Rasselbane. The single structure of importance is the 'Iron Crow Inn'." Serle put the book aside. "And there you have it. The *Maijaro* lies at anchor on the Suametta, with your mother and Cavke drowsing away the hours. Cavke will not surrender gracefully. Apart from setting the houseboat on fire, how will you proceed?"

"There is no lack of options," said Maloof. "We may dress as fisherman and try to sell Cavke some fish, or we may present ourselves as river police, looking for a stolen houseboat. During the night we could transfer the anchor line to a tree on the shore; the current would swing the houseboat up on the beach, and when Cavke waded ashore we could apprehend him. In any case, we will bring my mother back to Coro-coro, and return her to Morlock." Maloof rose to his feet. "We will keep in touch with you."

Serle also rose. "If you leave now, you will arrive at the Suametta by late afternoon. I suggest that you put down somewhere for the night and reconnoiter in the morning."

"No doubt that is what we shall do."

Returning to the *Glicca*, Maloof and Myron found no one aboard. They left a note on the galley table, then set off once again in the flitter across the pleasant landscapes of Fluter, holding to a north-westerly course.

Early in the afternoon they passed over a long line of cliffs and set out over the blue ocean beyond, reaching the white beach which fringed the second continent as the sun approached the noon meridian. They flew on, over forests, rolling hills, mountains, cultivated lands, and tracts of wilderness.

Late in the day the River Suametta appeared ahead. In the failing light of afternoon, the village Pengelly could be seen on the opposite shore, half-hidden under tall trees.

Several miles downstream, a houseboat was visible lying quietly at anchor.

The Iron Crow Inn was immediately noticeable: a massive two-story structure built of antique timber and stone under a crotchety slate roof, with ghost-chasers protecting the ridges. The single street of the village led away under the trees, past weathered stone houses. Tendrils of somnolent smoke rose from chimneys; Pengelly had succumbed to the torpor of age.

Maloof and Myron surveyed the village from above, then dropped to a landing upon a strip of wasteland beside the inn. Alighting, they stood watching and listening, but heard neither voices nor running footsteps; their arrival apparently had gone unnoticed.

They set off along a path which led to the front of the building. The sign over the door depicted a black iron crow four feet tall, in an attitude of intrepid defiance. The frame hung by iron chains from an overhead gallows. Under the sign, a pair of heavy doors opened into the inn.

Maloof and Myron pushed through the doors, and entered a large, high-ceilinged common room. Windows in the left wall overlooked the Suametta, admitting a tide of dim light. A glossy wooden bar occupied the front half of the right-hand wall, with a dining area to the rear. Alone in the room, at a table to the back, sat two children busily writing in exercise books. The boy was about eleven, the girl somewhat younger.

Entering the chamber, Maloof and Myron came forward, then stopped short, staring in fascination at the wall behind the bar. An artist of long ago had painted a remarkable mural four feet high and extending the length of the bar. In meticulous detail, and with absolute pre-

ciosity the artist had simulated a long mirror reflecting the images of
the patrons, who sat studying their simulated reflections in the mirror.
A representative group of villagers were present on that long-past occasion: young, old, men and women, a few laughing, others grave,
wearing clothes of archaic style, all concerned with the exigencies of
their now forgotten lives. The bar was untenanted, except perhaps for
the ghosts of those who sat reflected in the mirror.

The children had become aware of the newcomers. Both were
clean, alert, and self-assured. The boy jumped to his feet, ran to a door
in the back wall, called through a message, then trotted back to his
place at the table. In the doorway a grizzled old man showed himself.
He was small, bony, and dour, wearing a white apron. Muttering an
objurgation, he sidled down behind the bar to where Maloof and Myron waited. Halting, he subjected them to a brief inspection, then
spoke.

"Gentlemen, what are your needs?"

"They are quite ordinary," said Maloof. "We want lodging for the
night, supper, and breakfast in the morning."

The bartender reflected at length, nodding in slow cogitation, until Maloof became impatient. "Surely this is the Iron Crow Inn? Am I
addressing the proper official? If not, please direct us to someone in
authority."

The bartender surveyed Maloof with disapproval. He responded
carefully, using precise diction, so as not to confuse Maloof. "Be
calm—you have certainly arrived at the historic Iron Crow Inn. I am
Ugo Teybald, the proprietor. I am obliged to notify you that our clientele is select, and we cannot indulge the habits of off-worlders, except
at premium rates."

Maloof smiled grimly. "Your preconceptions are wrong. We are savants touring Fluter like vagabonds, and we are accustomed to the hospitality of Fluter inns. Nothing surprises us, and we will make do with
your standard accommodation. Put away all thought of premium rates,
since we have agreed to report all instances of over-charging to the
District Control."

"Bah," muttered Teybald. "Our rates are graven in stone. If the
goddess Hyrcania came up from her cave and wanted lodging, she
would find that our rates were immutable."

"Very well, then; we shall be content with the best you can offer, at
the immutable rate."

Teybald deliberated, then said gruffly: "The season is slack; we can
allow you a first-class chamber, which includes fine furniture and a
splendid view of the river. An adjacent lavatory is offered as an extra."

"Oh? How much extra? And what will be the immutable total?"

The two eventually agreed upon an all-inclusive price for room, lavatory, supper, breakfast, service, and view for a rate which Maloof found acceptable.

Teybald looked here and there. "And where is your luggage?"

"Still aboard the flitter."

Teybald slapped his hand upon the bar and cried out: "Berard! Sonssi! Be quick—these rich off-worlders want service! Smartly now, if you hope for a noble gratuity!"

Almost before he had finished speaking, the children had dashed from the inn, and around the building to the flitter. Myron hurried after them and reached the flitter in time to extricate the luggage before Berard and Sonssi swarmed aboard to do the work themselves. Myron passed out the luggage; the children seized the cases and carried them triumphantly back to the inn, up the stairs, and into the room which had been assigned to the spacemen.

Maloof and Myron followed more sedately, and were ushered by the children into a large room smelling of wax and old wood. The room lacked ornament, but was furnished with massive pieces clearly of great age. Maloof went to look from the window, which, as advertised, commanded a view of the river. A path led from the inn down to a dock, where several boats bobbed at their moorings.

Maloof signalled Sonssi, who sprang forward, quivering with eagerness. Maloof said: "I notice boats at the dock yonder. Are they to be used by guests of the inn?"

"Indeed they are, sir, and they provide truly fine sport or—if you prefer—calm and gentle rest. You are assured of a pleasant evening on the water."

"Not tonight," said Maloof. "Perhaps tomorrow morning."

"Still, you should reserve now. In the morning the fishermen come early and take out the best boats until nothing remains but the scow."

Berard stepped forward. "May I ask what sort of boat you require?"

Maloof considered. "Something not too large, but it should move well through the water, and be very quiet."

"Perhaps you should come down to the dock while the light still holds, and make your own selection."

"A good idea," said Maloof. "We will come down in five minutes."

"We will be ready."

Berard and Sonssi marched to the door, where they turned to stand in postures of formal decorum. Maloof and Myron paid them no heed, and began to arrange their belongings.

Berard spoke. "Sirs, we have done our best to serve you. If we have failed, then we deserve no gratuity."

"Aha!" said Maloof. "All is now clear." He gave five dinkets to each, which the children accepted, politely but without enthusiasm, then departed.

Ten minutes later Maloof and Myron walked down to the dock, with Berard and Sonssi running ahead. Four boats were moored to the dock. In the end they selected the *Lulio*, an unpretentious work-boat about twenty feet long, with a small cuddy.

Sonssi endorsed the choice. "All are good boats; they float without hesitation, and the engine propels them in a direction of your choice. The *Lulio* has a small cabin which will deflect the rain, should this occur."

Berard demonstrated the controls and certified that the boat was capable of at least adequate speed. Sonssi told them confidently: "Naturally, you will need a skillful pilot, and here I am superior to Berard—who is somewhat reckless, and likes to try sidewise swashes. He is also absent-minded and is apt to run you aground. If you trust Berard, you are likely to come back bedraggled and wet. As for me, I know all the secret places of the river and the fine streams."

Berard said scornfully: "Pay no heed to Sonssi; she is a bit of a braggart. I am by far the superior pilot! I take it for granted that you will hire me in this capacity."

Maloof explained that no pilot whatever would be needed, while the two listened glumly. The four returned up the path. Berard and Sonssi raced ahead, and stationed themselves by the door to the inn.

Maloof looked from one to the other. "So what is it now?"

"Nothing of consequence, sir," said Berard. "We were waiting in case other services might be needed."

Sonssi added: "Also, if you planned gratuities, we wanted to be ready at hand, to cause you the least inconvenience."

Maloof gave a rueful laugh and distributed five-dinket coins to each; then he and Myron entered the inn.

They went to sit at the bar, where four villagers were already present, drinking beer from tall tankards. They darted sidelong glances toward Maloof and Myron, then turned back to their beer, to mutter in undertones.

Teybald approached, now wearing a white smock and a small white cap. "What, sirs, is your pleasure?"

"You may serve us a bitter ale, if it is readily available," said Maloof.

Without comment Teybald produced two tankards of foaming ale.

"Further," said Maloof, "we want to cruise the river for a few hours tomorrow. For preference we will use the *Lulio*. I expect that this is a service that you offer to guests at the inn without charge?"

"Wrong! We rent the *Lulio* out at a rate of seven sols per day."

Maloof raised his eyebrows in shock. "That is a large sum! We can swim the river free of charge."

"True, and you will lose your private parts to the glass-fish within the minute. Swimming is a poor economy."

In the end Maloof secured the *Lulio* for five sols, payment to be made in advance. Maloof agreed to the provision, and paid on the spot.

The two were presently called to supper, which consisted of a dish of sharp greens, fried fish with sour fritters, goulash with seasoned barley, a compote of fresh fruit, and a pot of tea. Berard and Sonssi, wearing white aprons, served them deftly and again received gratuities.

After supper Maloof and Myron resisted a second visit to the bar, and went upstairs to their beds. The evening was quiet; there were no sounds from the village. After half an hour of desultory conversation, they slept.

6

Maloof and Myron arose early and descended to the common room, where they were served a substantial breakfast of porridge, griddle-cakes with marmalade, and fried sausages.

In the pre-dawn stillness, they walked down to the dock. The day was clear and crisp, without so much as a breeze to ruffle the face of the river. The two boarded the *Lulio*, loosed the mooring, and set off downstream with the first glimmer of dawn light reflecting on the water. Under different conditions, the two men would have enjoyed the peace of the river and the idyllic scenery along the shores.

The *Lulio* moved quietly at ten miles per hour, according to the meter on the console. Maloof kept the boat close to the right-hand shore, where they should be less conspicuous to anyone watching from the *Maijaro*, although it seemed unlikely that either Cavke or Lady Maloof would be vigilant at this early hour.

Half an hour passed, and the two began to search the water ahead for a glimpse of the *Maijaro*, but there was no sign of the houseboat. Another ten minutes went by while Maloof and Myron became increasingly tense; at last the *Maijaro* came into view, anchored beside a small island, the bow pointing downstream.

Maloof idled the engine. The *Lulio* drifted toward the *Maijaro*, close under the trees which shaded the water, and at last drew along-side. They watched and listened, but detected neither sound nor move-ment from within.

With the utmost delicacy, Myron transferred himself to the front deck, where he made the painter fast to a stanchion. Maloof joined him, and they let the boat swing past, to lie downstream, where it could not bump into the houseboat.

For a moment they stood listening, wary that someone within had noticed movement of the houseboat when they climbed aboard. But all remained silent.

Maloof tested the door into the front cabin, and eased it ajar. Across the cabin a doorway opened into the main saloon. From where they stood, only a section of the far wall was visible, but clearly through the open doorway came the chink of porcelain, and a faint sip-ping sound. Maloof shifted cautiously forward, and brought most of the saloon into view.

In a high-backed wicker chair sat Lady Maloof. At her side, an oc-tagonal tabouret of split bamboo supported a tray with a pot of tea, a plate of small pastries, and a saucer of what might have been honey. In her bony hand she held a fluted yellow teacup.

She wore a voluminous peignoir of pale blue silk, decorated with a fantastic array of flamboyant birds sitting on perches. Their dangling tails spread into extravagant fans, creating patterns of vivid color: tangerine-red, phosphorescent green, acrid blue. The garment was wildly unsuitable to the circumstances, and would seem to represent Lady Maloof's brave but futile attempts to deny the remorseless pas-sage of time. Apparently she had undergone surgical techniques to the same ends, and the results were not at all happy; the skin adjacent to her eyelids had been gathered, causing her eyes to tilt upward as if in querulous inquiry. The wattles under her chin were gone, leaving a long, pointed chin. Myron saw Maloof wince and shake his head.

The two searched the saloon. Lady Maloof was alone, thinking her dismal thoughts.

Holding his hand-gun at the ready, Maloof stole step by step into the saloon. Myron silently followed. Lady Maloof became fretful and raised her head, as if to call out. Maloof and Myron froze in their tracks, but she changed her mind, and drank more tea.

Maloof eased silently forward, slow step by slow step. Lady Mal-oof sat nodding over her tea until, warned by some small sound, she looked over her shoulder. At the sight of the intruders, her eyes went wide and her mouth sagged open; she started to scream.

Maloof was upon her, clamping her mouth before she could utter more than a terrified squeak. Her eyes bulged as she stared at her still-strange assailant. As for Maloof, this haggard old woman was only barely recognizable as his mother; Orlo Cavke had lavished little loving care upon the source of his income.

At last Lady Maloof's shoulders sagged, as Maloof's identity penetrated her consciousness. She clawed his hand away from her mouth. "You are Adair," she croaked. "Adair!"

"Yes, I am Adair. I am taking you back to Traven."

Lady Maloof's eyes filled with tears, which trickled down her addled old cheeks.

Maloof said: "Your friend Cavke"—he corrected himself—"Loy Tremaine; where is he now?"

Lady Maloof looked toward the hall which led to the after-cabins. Maloof followed her gaze, to find Cavke standing in the doorway, naked to the waist and barefoot.

"Here I am," said Cavke. He peered at Maloof, then at Myron. "What do you want of me?"

"I have come for my mother. I am taking her home to Traven."

Cavke took note of the hand-gun which Maloof held at the ready. "Not a good idea," said Cavke easily, apparently relaxed in the doorway.

With two sudden long strides, Cavke stood behind Lady Maloof. He seized her scrawny neck; with the other hand he swept up a knife from the galley counter and thrust the point against Lady Maloof's corded gray neck.

"You are a fine and noble son, but why should I be inconvenienced on that account? She will not go with you, or anyone else!"

Maloof studied the dark aquiline face. Remembering the Krenke photographs, Maloof saw that Cavke had become indefinably coarse. The lips had thickened; there was a puffiness under the eyes, and a slack rotundity at the abdomen marked the beginnings of a paunch. His black trousers were almost indecently tight around the hips, flaring at the knees. His naked chest was hairless, and glistened as if oiled. A gold ring hung from his left ear; the sunburst tattoo was visible under his jaw.

Cavke asked suddenly: "How did you know where to find your mother?"

"It was simple enough. You gave out the information yourself."

"Oh? How so?"

"At my aunt's house on Traven you said that you intended to return to the most beautiful world in the Reach. I took you at your word. At Coro-coro the IPCC agent suggested that you would rent a houseboat. Zangwill Transit told us where to find the *Maijaro*, and here we are."

Cavke grinned wolfishly. "I see."

"I suggest that you leave the houseboat and return to Coro-coro. But do not try to interfere with my plans."

"A good idea, if a trifle droll," said Cavke. "I have an even better idea. In a month or so I will drop this old woman off at the O-Shar-Shan, and you can do what you like with her."

"No!" squeaked Lady Maloof. "He wants to cash my annuity. To this I say no! Not another dinket for this brute!"

Maloof said to Cavke: "That seems definite enough."

Lady Maloof continued: "I cannot tell you how he has abused me. His insults have been beyond belief!"

Cavke gave her a half-amused jostle. "Quiet, you old mudlark—have you no dignity? These men are not interested in your complaints."

Lady Maloof only raised her voice. "His insults were cruel! He called me a bony old sandpiper with the molt! He said that I smelled like pickled herring, and that I must bathe—and he suggested that I use the river, since the glass-fish would give me one look, then rush off to find something edible!"

"Not at all nice," said Maloof.

"Just a bit of jocularity," said Cavke, grinning.

"He has slandered me in a hundred ways," wailed Lady Maloof. "I want to go home!"

"Not so fast," said Cavke. "Find me some clean clothes." He started for the hallway, dragging Lady Maloof along in front of him.

Myron instantly bounded across the room, and stationed himself in the opening, holding his gun at the ready. He grinned at Cavke. "You have a gun in your room. You don't need it at the moment."

Cavke saw that if he moved toward the hall, he would be putting himself between Myron and Maloof, which would not be to his advantage, since he could not watch both at once. With a sulky expression, he backed into a corner, dragging Lady Maloof stumbling and hopping. He spoke in a sibilant voice: "This stalemate must be resolved. If you behave reasonably, in three weeks, or a month, you may take custody of this woman and go your way, and I shall not interfere—unless you attempt some act of mindless vengeance upon me. Otherwise this lady shall be dead."

From somewhere came a soft thud. Myron looked toward Maloof, and the act nearly cost him his life. Cavke hurled his knife at Myron's neck. Maloof shouted; Myron saw the flicker of steel and slumped over backward, almost to the floor. Cavke then spun; in a single unbroken motion he snatched up a cleaver, which he slung with great force at Myron's head.

The cleaver spun through the air and struck Myron's shoulder, handle-first. Myron's arm went numb instantly; his gun clattered to the floor. Cavke took advantage of the occasion. Lunging forward, he scooped up the gun and lurched for the hallway, dragging Lady Maloof behind him. He gained the opening and turned back triumphantly.

"Now I will shoot you both dead. If you retreat to your boat, I will shoot you from the deck! You gambled with your lives, and you have lost at the great game; prepare to meet the judgment of your—"

Behind Cavke a heavy form appeared. A hand reached over his shoulder, twisted, and wrenched. Cavke screamed; his weapons fell to the deck. Lady Maloof fell in a whimpering heap of scarlet birds and sprawling limbs.

Cavke screamed again, as his arm was wrenched into an unnatural position; he was thrust stumbling into the saloon.

Three men entered from the rear cabin. Myron and Maloof recognized Derl Mone, Avern Glister, and Madrig Cargus, who had come up from behind Cavke, in the rear passage.

Mone and Glister advanced upon Cavke; they shackled his arms behind his back, then tied a lead-rope around his neck. Cavke stood limp, his features sagging, stricken by the disaster which had so suddenly overtaken him.

The men from Krenke, standing back, surveyed Cavke with cold satisfaction.

Mone spoke: "Orlo! Do you know me? I am Derl Mone. My daughter was Murs Mone. Do you remember her?"

Glister spoke: "Orlo, do you remember me? I am Avern Glister. My daughter was Lally Glister. She had brown hair and a tip-tilted nose."

Cargus spoke. "Orlo—do you know me? I am Madrig Cargus. My daughter was Salu; surely you remember Salu."

Cavke grinned a ghastly grin. "I know you all well, and the three girls also. The brain is a wonderful instrument, that it remembers so well." Then he added, in a voice suddenly husky: "How did you find me, so far from Krenke?"

Mone showed a small cold grin: "You have these off-worlders to thank. They flew their flitter out to Krenke and asked questions about you. We put a tracer button on their flitter and followed wherever they led. As we expected, they brought us to you."

"Be assured that you will not escape us again," said Glister. "We shall watch you with care, as if you were our ailing child!"

"Your return to Krenke will be a great sensation," said Cargus.

"The homecoming celebration will be remembered down the ages. The entire village will be in a froth of excitement!"

"Just so," said Mone. "We plan a festival of seven days, at which you shall be the dance-master. But we must not keep all of your old acquaintances waiting! Now, it is back to Krenke, in grand style!"

"You will want to make an impressive entry," said Cargus. "I will get you a shirt, a coat, and shoes."

Maloof asked Mone: "Will you be able to rise from the roof, with so much of a load?"

"Feel no concern; we came in our working flitter. It will carry double the weight, and fly like a bird."

7

The Flauts with their wretched prisoner were gone. Lady Maloof changed her costume and packed a few of her belongings into a travelling bag; then the three boarded the *Lulio* and returned upstream to dock at Pengelly.

Lady Maloof was placed aboard the flitter; there were final gratuities for Berard and Sonssi, and then the flitter rose above the village and set off back toward Coro-coro.

Maloof told Lady Maloof, "There is a final critical moment when we transfer you from the flitter to the *Glicca*. We must be as inconspicuous as possible, so as not to attract the notice of the Civil Agents."

Lady Maloof made a querulous sound. "Surely they will recognize me for what I am, and not molest me in any way."

Maloof chuckled sadly. "Unlikely. In any case, we will take as few risks as possible."

"I cannot concern myself with such affairs," said Lady Maloof. "I am anxious only for a bath, fresh garments, and a proper meal."

Maloof served her bread, cheese, and a cold meat pie, at which she nibbled with condescension, with an occasional sniff. Lady Maloof thereupon arranged herself on a bench and fell asleep.

The flitter arrived at Coro-coro during the middle evening. Maloof made sure that no Civil Agents were in evidence, then took Lady Maloof trotting and hopping at best speed to the gangway and up into the saloon.

Lady Maloof at once began to complain. "Really, Adair, have you lost all respect for propriety? You jerk me about as if I were a wayward animal. This sort of thing must not be repeated, and I shall be firm on this."

"You were not moving fast enough," said Maloof. "I wanted to evade attention."

Lady Maloof said querulously: "I felt as if I were hurtling through the air like a sack of chaff, all to no sensible purpose. But now I am tired and hungry."

Maloof served her a bowl of soup, an omelet, hot buttered scones, and a cream tart, then bedded her down in his own quarters, where she quickly fell asleep.

SIX

1

Once secure aboard the *Glicca*, Lady Maloof dismissed the *Maijaro* from her mind as if it had been a bad dream. Once again she became the grande dame of Traven society, with prestige so exalted as to insulate her from petty official annoyances.

Maloof patiently tried to explain the functioning of the Civil Authority. "The Agents interpret the Protocols rigidly; in their view you are a lawbreaker and subject to penalties of at least the second order."

Lady Maloof only shook her head and smiled. "Come now, Adair, they would not concern themselves over a trifling peccadillo, especially after they understand who I am."

"Who you are means nothing! They prosecute the act, not the person."

"Hmmf," sniffed Lady Maloof. "In my experience, all officials are flexible—especially if you show them a ten-sol certificate."

Maloof managed a painful grin. "The subject is moot, since you will not be leaving the *Glicca*."

Lady Maloof gave a gurgle of amusement. "Truly, Adair, you must cultivate a more sophisticated outlook; I do not intend to be immured as if I were a pariah! Be reasonable, Adair!"

"I plan to ship you back to Morlock at the first opportunity," said Maloof. "That is realism. Until that time, you must keep a low profile aboard the *Glicca*."

"This is quite impractical," said Lady Maloof haughtily. "I am planning to order a carriage and visit the O-Shar-Shan terrace, where I can enjoy the civilized intercourse to which I am entitled."

"I think not," said Maloof. "The Agents would pick you up before you left the spaceport."

Lady Maloof daubed at her brow with a handkerchief. "I cannot understand why you have to be so brutally dogmatic! As a boy, you were most gallant, at all times—the change is most unsettling!"

She rose to her feet and threw the handkerchief down to the deck. "You may take me to my stateroom."

2

An hour later, leaving Myron on guard, Maloof visited the passengers' lounge in the spaceport administration building, where he checked the posting of schedules for ships arriving at Coro-coro. He was delighted to find that the tourist packet *Farway Rambler* would depart Coro-coro at midnight and in due course would touch into Port Pallas on Tran, which served as a transfer depot for a dozen shipping lines and where a connection to Morlock could be arranged without difficulty.

Maloof departed the lounge and crossed the field to the great blue and silver packet. He went aboard and was conducted to the office of Captain Brevet Fane, with whom he had some previous acquaintance.

Maloof was cordially received and installed in a comfortable chair. After a few minutes of casual conversation, Maloof mentioned his mother, her difficulties, and his efforts to extricate her from own foolishness.

Fane listened sympathetically and assured Maloof that he need only bring his mother aboard the *Farway Rambler*; he and his staff would take care of any remaining problems. Maloof provided such information as was needed; then Fane pressed a button to summon his steward, who arrived carrying a tray on which rested a heavy bottle and two goblets.

Fane reverently lifted the bottle and poured three inches of a tawny liquor into each of the glasses, one of which he slid across to Maloof.

"In the ancient language, the word 'uisquebaugh' means 'water of life'," said Fane. "According to legend, the liquor is created from sunshine, rain, and soft turf smoke."

He raised his glass. "Slanche."

"Slanche," said Maloof.

3

Maloof returned to the *Glicca*, where he found Myron sitting alone at the galley table, reading a list of various cargoes awaiting transfer. Maloof looked into the saloon, which was empty. He asked: "Where is she?"

"Still in her cabin," said Myron. "She has not so much as stirred— I assume she is asleep."

Maloof went to the cabin which had been assigned to Lady Maloof. He knocked at the door and listened but heard nothing. He knocked again. This time Lady Maloof responded, in a fluting voice: "Who is it?"

Maloof pushed open the door and stepped into the cabin. He stopped short, eyebrows lofting in wonder.

Lady Maloof sat before the mirror of the dressing table, applying a mask of white cosmetic to her sagging features. She had accented her eye sockets with splotches of brown-purple pigment, so that she resembled an old white raccoon. Her hair, now dyed jet black, was drawn up into a tuft and was constrained by a binding of white beads. She wore a spectacular gown of lambent green, split down the legs to reveal a pale blue lining and glimpses of match-stick legs. She noticed Maloof's presence and turned upon him a glance of disapproval.

"Have you forgotten even the rudiments of decorum? You are intruding upon my privacy."

"Sorry," said Maloof. "I came to tell you that I have obtained passage for you back to Morlock. The ship leaves tonight, so pack your bags."

Lady Maloof turned her attention back to the mirror. "This arrangement must be postponed; it does not accord with my plans. I am ordering a carriage for the O-Shar-Shan. If I find the circumstances amusing, I may well book a suite for a week or two."

Maloof wasted neither time nor breath in recriminations. He called in Myron, and ignoring Lady Maloof's shrill protests, they crammed her belongings into her travel bags.

Maloof stepped down from the *Glicca* and surveyed the field, now obscured by the coming of dusk. Tourists in groups were returning to their ships. Maloof went back into the *Glicca*.

"Now is as good a time as any," he told his mother. "Are you ready?"

"Naturally not! This is a farrago of utter nonsense—it is tragic!"

"Very sad," said Maloof, bringing out a long black cloak which had been discarded by one of the pilgrims. "Your costume is a bit conspicuous; cover yourself in this cloak."

"What? It seethes with dirt!"

"Nevertheless, it must serve." Maloof wrapped the cloak about Lady Maloof's shrinking form and jammed a broad-brimmed hat down over her head. "We are as ready as we ever will be. Let's be away."

"This is a great fiasco," declared Lady Maloof. "I do not intend to walk a single step."

"Either you walk, or we take you in a wheelbarrow," said Maloof. "Are you ready?"

"It seems that I have no choice!" cried Lady Maloof piteously. "If I must, I must. I shall never forget this indignity." With Maloof at her side, she set forth, and at her best speed made for the *Farway Rambler* with Myron coming behind, carrying the bags.

Without incident they reached the comforting bulk of the packet. Mounting the embarcation ramp, they passed through a vestibule and entered the main saloon. The purser was not at hand; Myron went off to find him.

Maloof surveyed the chamber, which was panelled in golden-brown wood and carpeted with soft green plush, creating an ambience of understated elegance. He glanced sidewise at Lady Maloof, to find her looking about with a supercilious droop to her mouth.

"It seems comfortable enough," said Maloof cautiously. "You should have a pleasant voyage."

Lady Maloof gave a critical sniff. A group of passengers at a nearby table were drinking from frosted glasses and holding an animated conversation. They took note of Lady Maloof, and the conversation trailed off. A discreet chuckle or two could be heard, then the conversation resumed.

Lady Maloof made a hissing sound between her teeth. She wrenched her arms back and let the black cloak fall to the deck. For good measure she snatched the hat from her head and threw it aside.

Maloof watched gravely but made no attempt to interfere.

At that moment, Myron returned with the purser, who welcomed Lady Maloof aboard with punctilious formality. Using a rich baritone voice he exclaimed: "I admit to surprise! I had expected someone considerably older than yourself, and definitely lacking your evident panache!"

Lady Maloof muttered: "I feel that in many ways I am distinctly remarkable. I have never renounced my yearning to live by the precepts of romance!"

"A remarkable trait," declared the purser.

"Now I must conduct you to your cabin, where you will undoubtedly wish to rest before the gala following departure."

Maloof patted his mother's shoulder. "I am sure that you will enjoy your voyage. Soon you will be home."

"I shall do well enough, or so I suppose," said Lady Maloof distantly.

Myron also made his farewells, to which Lady Maloof vouchsafed

only a curt nod, then the purser led her away. A porter followed, carrying her bags.

Maloof and Myron waited until the purser returned. Maloof
asked: "I assume that you still depart at midnight?"

"There have been no changes; the ship will depart according to
schedule."

"I must warn you that my mother is often headstrong, if not unreasonable—even to her own detriment."

The purser smiled politely. "We accommodate passengers of many
temperaments. I doubt if Lady Maloof can show us anything novel."

"It is of utmost importance that she not be allowed to leave the
ship before departure. She has no legal papers, and the Civil Agents
will be sure to pick her up and subject her to the second order. If necessary, lock her in her stateroom, or even sedate her. Do not relax your
vigilance! She uses an animal cunning to get her own way."

"We will take special precautions," said the purser. "In fact, I will
go at once to lock her door. You need not concern yourselves, she will
not be allowed to leave the ship."

"Thank you, I am reassured," said Maloof. Taking their leave, the
two returned across the field to the *Glicca*.

Hours passed. Dusk deepened through evening into night, and the
Farway Rambler prepared for departure.

Midnight approached. Aboard the *Glicca*, Maloof and Myron went
out upon the small staging deck at the head of the gangway. At three
minutes to the hour the packet's embarcation ramp was drawn up into
the ship, and the entry port sealed; at midnight the farewell horn
sounded, rising from a mournful moan up the scale to an eerie soprano
wail, then dropping again to fade below the threshold of perception.

The *Farway Rambler* eased up from the field to an altitude of five
hundred feet, then slid off into the night, rising and gathering speed to
become a glimmer and disappear among the stars.

4

Aboard the *Glicca*, Maloof and Myron lingered in the dark, each with
his own thoughts. After a time Maloof went to the galley and returned
with a bottle of soft yellow wine.

He poured and they sat as before, although the wine, by some subtle process, had altered their mood.

Maloof spoke, half to himself. "The venture is over. There is
nothing more to do, and I feel empty. It is a most curious sensation;

what next? Perhaps nothing. Perhaps I shall try to rest; it is as if I have entered another phase of existence."

After a pause, Myron replied. "It seems natural enough, with so much less tension in your life. You might even ease into something like 'lurulu'."

Maloof laughed softly. "Lurulu is something different, and far more elusive. It cannot be precisely defined, but seems to come when yearnings are being gratified—not necessarily from the fact, which is too close to an inert tranquillity." He mused. "It seems that there is an active component of lurulu, which can be fragile."

Myron stared off into the night. "I doubt if I will ever chance upon such a state."

"How so?"

"My 'yearnings', if that is what they are, can never be reconciled; they pull in different directions. One involves a certain Tibbet Garwig, who lives at Duvray, on Alcydon. Second, my Aunt Hester has done me harm; she represents an itch I desperately want to scratch—call it a component of lurulu, if you like. Then there is the *Glicca;* I can not stay aboard the *Glicca* forever, and the prospect of any other life is dismal."

Maloof drained his glass. "For each of us, lurulu is in the nature of a far-off dream. But for now, it occurs to me that the night is still young, and that a short walk along Pomare Boulevard will bring us to the Pingis Tavern, where we might risk a Pooncho Number Two, or even a Number Three, depending upon the portents."

Myron was instantly on his feet. "The idea is constructive! As dauntless spacemen we may safely ignore portents, unless they take the form of Civil Agents—in which case we reconsider our plans."

The two descended the gangway, crossed the field, and set off up Pomare Boulevard toward the Pingis Tavern.

5

The sojourn of the *Glicca* at Coro-coro had reached its final days. Without enthusiasm, the crew began to prepare for departure.

One morning during a visit to the transshipment dock Myron provisionally accepted a parcel of cargo for a world somewhat to the side of the direct route to Blenkinsop, the next scheduled port of call.

Back aboard the *Glicca*, Myron reported the tentative transaction to Captain Maloof. "The parcel consists of thirty-two carboys of chemical—kasic, to be specific. It was shipped from Cax and off-loaded here for transshipment to Star Home."

"Star Home?"

"An obscure world on a dogleg off the direct run to Cax. I am told that the Port Director will pay charges of three hundred and twenty-five sols, which seems reasonable. The course is not impractical, and I accepted the parcel—subject to your approval, of course."

Maloof looked into *Handbook to the Planets*. He found 'Star Home' and read aloud.

" 'Star Home, second planet of the white dwarf Mireille, is a small, dense world with a breathable atmosphere, a congenial climate, and gravity close to Earth-normal. The sidereal day is twenty hours and twenty-three minutes. There are two continents: The smaller, to the north, is a dreary waste of stone and ice; the second is characterized by flat steppes overgrown with chest-high grass, with a few ranges of ancient hills and a minor upthrust of mountains in the far south.

" 'At first viewing, Star Home offers no great attraction either for the scholar or the casual traveler, though the sparse native population enlivens the scene. The "Ritters" are a patrician caste of uncompromising nomads, guided only by the unwritten doctrines of "Ritterway". They wander the seaside littoral, pausing as the mood strikes them, mingling with other groups, then separating into clan-like units. There are no settled communities of any description, and no formal social structure.

" 'The Ritters are versatile, and skilled at many small crafts, but are most notably expert in the fabrication of exquisite rugs, which they export off-world in return for needful articles beyond their ability to produce, such as tools, food synthesizers, and household utensils. Generally placid folk, they live without hostility and are indifferent to the presence of off-worlders. Crime is unknown, as is reprehensible behaviour—except for the antics of feckless young gallants, whose misdeeds are charitably ignored as "a sowing of wild oats". The single spaceport is Port Palactus, situated inconveniently in the center of the Great Mermaz Steppe. The facilities are meager: a pair of dilapidated warehouses and a structure serving as combination bank and port office. There is neither a machine shop nor tourist accommodations.

" 'Star Home flora is not abundant, but includes a dozen species of grass, among which is a lordly bamboo with black stalks and pale green leaves. Fauna, like the flora, is not various but includes the savagely ferocious "mereng", a predator which lives hidden in narrow tunnels under the grass. Merengs are supple, six-legged creatures with long fanged snouts, which may attain a length of twelve feet; they are dreaded by the Ritters but are occasionally hunted for meat and hides. Impressive and of mild disposition are the gigantic herbivores known as "wumps", ponderous creatures often forty or even fifty feet long and twenty feet high. Wumps walk on six heavy legs, ingesting grass by means of a sinuous snout, which brings grass to the maw. The Ritters domesticate wumps and build small residences called "trimbles" upon their broad backs. Some trimbles are quite picturesque, with peaked roofs; always at the rear is a workroom where rugs are produced.'"

Maloof frowned and looked up. "The article ends." He reread the section silently, fingers thrumming the table, then thrust the *Handbook* aside, in a mild show of vexation.

"The *Handbook* tells me less than I would like to know. Why is their spaceport located in the middle of a steppe? And there is little to suggest an explanation why the 'Ritters', as unconventional or peculiar as they are, might need thirty-two carboys of chemical."

Myron shook his head. "I cannot so much as guess."

Maloof waved the problem aside. "Still, it is none of our affair. More to the point, when we put down at Port Palactus, will anyone be there to receive the cargo? The Ritters might not trouble with such incidentals."

"The *Handbook* mentions a port office," said Myron dubiously. "That would seem to imply a Port Director."

"That is logic as seen from here," said Maloof. "Logic on Star Home might mean something else again. At out-of-the-way places like Port Palactus, the extraordinary is often the usual; the poor spaceman must look in all directions, and be ready for odd surprises."

Myron ventured a suggestion. "I can write a clause into the contract stipulating that if the cargo cannot be discharged within three days after our arrival, owing to absence of proper spaceport personnel, title to the cargo devolves upon the carrier—which is to say, the *Glicca*."

Maloof indicated approval. "A good idea. Write the provision into the contract, and we'll take our chances."

During the afternoon, thirty-two carboys were loaded aboard the *Glicca*, into the space previously occupied by the pilgrims.

6

The following morning, Moncrief and his troupe boarded the *Glicca* and took up their old quarters.

Moods varied; Flook, Pook, and Snook were disconsolate at the prospect of leaving Fluter, perhaps forever. Hunzel and Siglaf took themselves to a corner of the saloon and gruffly discussed secret plans. Hoping to elevate the morale of his company with good cheer, Moncrief beamed on one and all and went so far as to dance a jig.

Myron composed and sent off a letter to Miss Tibbet Garwig. Schwatzendale and Wingo consumed final Pooncho Punches at the Pingis Tavern but returned to the *Glicca* in good order during the early evening.

On the following morning, two hours after sunrise, the *Glicca* rose from the Coro-coro spaceport and set off on a course for Star Home.

SEVEN

1

Arriving from space, the *Glicca* descended upon the night side of Star Home, to land at Port Palactus by the light of the waning moon.

In the pilot-house, Captain Maloof disengaged the ship's dynamic systems and went to look from the observation window. The steppe, colorless in the pale moonlight, spread away under a blanket of grass past the edge of vision. Otherwise there was little to see. The old warehouses huddled dark and quiet; a few yards beyond and to the side stood a small square structure. Nothing stirred; in particular, no one appeared to register the arrival of the *Glicca*. The ship's crew composed itself to wait for dawn before venturing out upon the landscape.

After a time, a glimmer of gray appeared in the east, then a slow flush of yellow. The white sun rose from behind a bank of clouds, and wan light seeped across the steppe.

The *Glicca*'s entry port slid open, and the gangway dropped to the ground. One by one, the ship's company descended to the surface of Star Home, where they stood in silence, taking in the immensity of the landscape. In the immediate vicinity of the spaceport the grass had been cut short and compressed to create a mat of turf; elsewhere it grew in a uniform carpet four feet tall. After a moment the group discovered in the far distance several enormous gray hulks, moving slowly across the steppe. They trundled through the grass on six thick legs; with twin proboscises they cut grass and conveyed the forage to ventral maws.

Myron took it upon himself to explain the creatures to the passengers. "The local folk know them as 'wumps', though of course this is not proper nomenclature. It is hard to gauge their bulk from this distance, but they are of prodigious size: some forty or fifty feet long and twenty feet tall. According to the *Handbook*, their temperament is so mild that the Ritters domesticate them and build huts on their backs to live at ease while traveling beside the sea and across the steppe."

Moncrief spared the wumps a single dismissive glance. An encounter with Siglaf and Hunzel had left him in a testy mood, and Myron's display of knowledge was an added irritant. He pretended to search the surroundings.

"Are you sure of your facts? Star Home appears to be deserted; at least, I see no Ritters, nor anyone else! Might they be hiding under the grass?"

"The *Handbook* is quite definite," said Myron. "The Ritters are nomads who have rejected all technical adjuncts. For relaxation, they create rugs of high quality and attend banquets where they sing, dance, and vie in the high jump. They lack social cohesiveness but are ruled by an implicit system which seems to satisfy everyone. Some of their customs are quaint: for instance, if you admire a woman's rug, you must marry her. In any event, Ritters are not to be found hiding under the grass."

"The *Handbook* is wrong!" cried Flook, pointing with both forefingers. "Just now I saw a face, staring at me from under the grass!"

Snook asked with interest: "Was he handsome?"

"Not really; he had a shifty expression."

"Tschah," muttered Moncrief. "Sheer flapdoodle."

"No," declared Pook. "I saw him myself."

Moncrief could not conceal his impatience. "It is well known that girls of your age are subject to delusions, which are often unsettling! Restraint and wise counsel are of prime importance; I advise sober reflection."

"Exactly so," declared Pook. "I saw him clearly. What could be more sober than that?"

Once again, Myron was able to provide authoritative information. "What you saw was probably a 'mereng'—which is, according to the *Handbook*, a sinuous creature that may reach twelve feet long. It glides under the grass on six squat legs and is said to be extremely dangerous. So do not wander out into the grass hoping for romance."

"Bah!" muttered Moncrief, and turned away to study the steppe.

Meanwhile Maloof, looking past the warehouses, noticed a rock-melt structure, evidently the port office and bank mentioned in the *Handbook*. He moved away from the group and crossed the turf to the lonely structure. To the side he found the door: a slab of dark wood hanging on a pair of iron hinges.

He stepped back and turned to survey the landscape. Steppe extended to the horizon, with nothing in sight but wind-blown grass. He turned back to the door and rapped once, twice, three times, eliciting no response. He tried the latch; to his surprise the door eased open. For a moment Maloof hesitated; then he leaned forward and looked through the crack.

There was little to see. Three high windows admitted more gloom than light; in the dimness, Maloof glimpsed a couch, a table, chairs, and a desk on which rested dog-eared documents, scattered papers, and a somewhat battered communicator.

In the shadows along the back wall, the outline of a door indicated a rear chamber. Maloof turned away, reluctant to trespass upon private premises. Then, prompted by a troubling thought, he stopped short. Where was the Port Director? Might he be lying behind that door, ill, or otherwise incapacitated? Maloof put aside his scruples and entered the office.

The silence was complete. On the wall to his left, a hanging caught his attention: a rug, or section of a rug, about four feet on a side, framed in dark wood. He looked closely; the rug was clearly a work of high virtuosity. The craftsmanship was meticulous, and the patterns were worked with intricate shapes and unconventional colors: stinging blues, lime green, sulfurous reds, black, pomegranate, the bitter off-white of potash dye.

Reluctantly he turned away from the hanging and approached the door. He halted, stared at the panel, then raised his hand and knocked. He listened, but the silence was heavy. He knocked again, more vigorously; the silence was as before. But what was that? The ghost of a sound, no more than a whisper.

Emboldened, Maloof knocked again. From within came the tragic moan of a man aroused from a deep and beneficent slumber.

Again Maloof knocked, and now he heard the mutter of a thick voice: "Who pounds at my door? It is not yet daylight; have you no pity? I deserve my rest."

Maloof called: "Where is the Port Director? Why is he not on duty?"

"All in good time," came the grumbled response. "Allow me to collect my wits."

Maloof set himself to wait.

Time passed; Maloof became restive. He stood once again in front of the door and raised his hand to knock—but at that instant the door swung aside, to reveal a stocky man wearing a voluminous orange nightgown, which draped his portly physique from neck to ankle. He stood blinking at Maloof with a surly expression.

"I am Port Director Oswig. How do you explain your boisterous conduct?"

"I am Captain Maloof, of the ship *Glicca*. We arrived several hours ago; when you failed to appear, I came to make sure that you were not ill. We carry a cargo of thirty-two carboys for Port Palactus. All is ready for discharge, as soon as the freight is paid."

Oswig cried out in outrage. "What sort of fandangle is this? All freight is prepaid, at Cax on Blenkinsop!"

"Not in this case. These goods were taken aboard at Coro-coro as a cargo of opportunity. The bill of lading will make this clear."

Oswig held out his hand. "Show me the document, if you please."

Maloof tendered the paper, which Oswig scrutinized with care.

"Give special attention to the footnote," said Maloof politely. "You will notice that the freight charges must be paid within three days; if not, officers of the *Glicca* may confiscate the cargo and depart without formality."

"Bah!" muttered Oswig. "It is too early in the day for chaffering. Wait until I can deal with you on an official basis. Be seated and compose yourself." He stepped back; the door swung shut.

Instead of seating himself as Oswig had suggested, Maloof returned to study the wall hanging. The article exerted the same fascination as it had before; the craftsmanship seemed flawless, the colors were no less pungent, and the composition was even more clever and intricate than his first look had revealed.

The door slid aside; in the opening stood Oswig, now wearing his official regalia: a gray tunic, loose white breeches, and a white cap with a short black bill pulled down over dark ringlets. He advanced into the room and halted to inspect Maloof. He noticed Maloof's interest in the hanging, and his manner changed.

"That is an experimental panel created by my daughter Treblinka. She is twelve years old, but her work is of good quality."

"She would seem a prodigy," said Maloof.

"So it may be! But at this time I must see to business. There is reason for haste. Transport is my first concern; three wagons should suffice. I will call Dockerl at Farol Depot, and if he is brisk, the wagons will be here in three or four days. If the Lallankars are caught off guard, all will go well."

Oswig crossed the room to his desk and worked the controls of his communicator. At the tinkle of a chime he punched buttons, then sat back to wait.

Minutes passed. Oswig became impatient and drummed his fingers on the desk.

Finally, a gentle voice issued from the screen. "Wagon Master Dockerl here. Who calls, with such happy brio?"

Neither the wait nor Dockerl's flippant salute eased Oswig's disposition. Hunching forward, he issued a flood of instructions so energetically that Dockerl was unable to respond. Oswig stopped for breath and noticed that the screen had gone dead.

He leaned back in his chair, mouth drooping, then slowly swung around to face Maloof.

"Have you ever known the like? It is more than just a sorry joke." He came back across the room.

"When schmeer is scarce, the wagons cluster around the port like bugs on a corpse. When schmeer pots are full, with the rugmakers grinning from ear to ear, where are the wagons then? At Miskitter Marsh, or Blackwater Camp or Sluiceway Riverside, or off at the fringes of the steppe! At Palactus, we can only pray that they rumble their wumps and arrive within four days." Oswig gave his head an angry shake.

Maloof suggested, "Somehow you should enforce better service."

"We are Ritters; we enforce nothing! In the old days service went smartly. Wagons were assigned to the port. They took the cargo as soon as it was discharged; the Lallankars were helpless, and distribution was conducted properly. But the radio is a modern abomination! If the Lallankars pick up my signal, they trundle in from the steppe, preempt the carboys from under my nose, then ramble away, shouting slogans."

"Exasperating!" said Maloof.

Oswig nodded grimly.

After a pause Maloof ventured a cautious remark. "There is something here which I find mystifying. It would seem a true paradox."

Oswig showed little interest in Maloof's quandary. "You are an off-worlder; our way of life will baffle you."

"No doubt, but after making all allowances, the mystery remains. Perhaps you can throw some light on the matter."

"I am not a pundit," said Oswig brusquely. "Nor is there time for idle rumination."

"I will be brief. You might even be interested, since the matter touches upon yourself."

"Oh, very well," growled Oswig. "Let us hear this famous conundrum, and be done with it."

"Thank you. The situation is this: I have known you for only a short time, but already I can sense the broad outline of your character. In my opinion you are a strong, practical man, neither timid nor meek, and certainly not submissive."

Oswig gave a snort of dour amusement. "I will not try to refute you, but—more to the point—where is the mystery?"

Maloof held up his hand. "Oddly enough, at this moment I have come upon a reasonable explanation, and the mystery has dissolved."

Oswig eyed Maloof with suspicion. "That is good news, or so it seems, and now we can get on with our affairs. But what was the nature of this so-called 'mystery'?"

"It starts with the fact that I am a rational being; I could not understand why a man of your character should not defend his carboys to better effect. Then a new idea occurred to me, and the mystery dissolved. I realized that the Lallankars must be a reckless, ferocious race, whom Director Oswig—brave though he might be—was forced to allow to depredate and despoil as they chose, while he sought safety in a secret place. Am I right?"

"You are wrong!" thundered Oswig. "In every degree, respect and particular! The Lallankars are vermin, and I am a Ritter, of Star Home! I am self-guided, self-determined, and autonomous! On Star Home there are neither rules nor statutes. To even attempt to regulate the Lallankars would be to deny the Ritter franchise." Oswig made a sweeping gesture, to indicate that the topic had been exhausted. "Now then, let us look to the cargo. As I recall, there were thirty-two carboys of kasic, ready for discharge."

"Correct! By the way, what is kasic? I ask from sheer curiosity."

Oswig's response was tart. "Ask any way you like. The facts are immutable."

"Hm," said Maloof. "On a strange world, where paradoxes are rife, this is good news."

"Bah," muttered Oswig. "If I explained every detail, you would know no more than you do now."

Turning on his heel, Oswig marched through the doorway out into the pale light of morning, with Maloof following.

Oswig stopped short, as if at a sudden recollection. "Now it occurs to me! The warehousemen are not on duty—they have gone off to games at the Ballingay Traces. But there should be no real inconvenience; I expect that your crew will discharge the cargo for us, as a courtesy."

"Certainly," said Maloof. "We have done such work before, and we can do it again. Our fee will be the standard fifty sols."

Oswig cried out in shock. "Do my ears hear correctly? Did you truly mention the sum 'fifty sols'? Have you no morality whatever? How can a gentleman swindle with such aplomb?"

Maloof held up his hand. "I will answer your questions in the order they were asked. Yes, your ears are functioning properly. Yes; the price quoted was fifty sols. Yes, I use the morality of the working spaceman, which is compact but versatile. And I can explain the basis of our rates: often an official begs for a free service, as a courtesy, then puts the savings into his own pocket. Our schedule of fees is intended to curb this nuisance."

"Sheer bullypup!" stormed Oswig. "Save your excuses for ears more innocent than mine!" Swinging about, he re-entered the office and went to his desk. Opening a drawer, he snatched out a handful of pink and blue currency, oblivious to the notes which fluttered to the floor. He waved the notes in Maloof's face. "As you can see, your fee is secure!"

Maloof said: "I am interested less in security than in the money itself."

Oswig grimly paid over three hundred and seventy-five sols.

"Now then, your demands have been met. You may put your crew to work."

"Just as you say."

2

Maloof and Oswig stood to the side, watching as the work proceeded. In the cargo bay, Wingo operated the overhead hoist, shifting the carboys and lowering them to the turf, where Myron and Schwatzendale waited with power-dollies. Pursuant to Oswig's instructions they trucked the carboys into the far warehouse, which Oswig considered most secure from depredation. Moncrief strolled across the turf to join Maloof and Oswig.

Moncrief's romantic temperament disposed him to more or less innocent flights of fancy, which served to amuse him and relieve the tedium. On this occasion, he introduced himself to Oswig with flair: "I am Master Marcel Moncrief, roving polymath on the staff of the *Galactic Sentinel,* on open assignment."

Oswig inspected him without cordiality, while Maloof listened with raised eyebrows.

Moncrief enlarged upon his fabrication. "I have no explicit program for this planet, aside from my usual survey of a world and its culture. However, my references mention certain remote villages where ancient customs are preserved; if time permits, I would like to visit one or two of these villages to study their folk art, and perhaps record a few staves of their ceremonial chants."

Oswig gave a contemptuous snort. "You have been reading too many books. The Ritters are nomads. Villages are non-existent, and our most poignant music is the cries of woe heard when schmeer pots run dry."

"What is 'schmeer'?"

Oswig replied gracelessly: "Schmeer is the adhesive which binds our rugs. It is indispensable."

"Interesting. The carboys, then, contain schmeer?"

"Naturally not—the carboys contain kasic, a catalyst which is used to make schmeer."

Moncrief gave his head a smiling shake. "You are an artist with words, so much is clear, but you paint with too broad a brush. The pictorial scheme is striking, but the details are lost in a blur."

Oswig screwed up his eyebrows. "I confess to bafflement. Please clarify your remarks."

Moncrief considered. "Essentially, what I am asking is: what is 'kasic'?"

Oswig glowered, then decided to humor this unlikely savant.

"Kasic is a component of schmeer. When poured from the carboy, it is a semi-viscous, dark brown liquid, with a bad smell. For each forty gallons of schmeer, two gills of kasic are required."

"And who does the formulation? A special caste of adepts, I assume?"

"Not so! The Ritters are a single race. There are no castes, except, perhaps, for the Lallankars."

"Then who makes the schmeer?"

"Everyone! My daughter Treblinka is an expert."

"And what is her method?"

"The recipe is standard. Into a forty-gallon vat she pours twenty gallons of green grass gum, then adds ten gallons of barnacle slurry, ten pounds of mereng bladder-wax for unctuousness, three gallons of boiled red kelp, a jug of emalque extract, a gallon of fire oil for bite, and two gills of kasic. The vat is brought to a boil, simmered for two hours, strained, and allowed to rest. After a week the schmeer is ready."

"Most interesting!" Moncrief looked toward the *Glicca*, where the work of unloading was still under way. "With so much kasic, you will be inundated in schmeer! How can it all be put to use?"

"Curb your wonder!" Oswig told him. "Thirty-two carboys of kasic is barely adequate. The rugmaker's worst fear is that his pot will go dry."

Moncrief asked plaintively: "But where is the need for so many rugs? It seems that the rugmakers are driven by obsession. Surely these rampant energies could be put to better use."

"Indeed? What do you have in mind?"

Moncrief considered, tapping his chin with his forefinger. "First, a civilized town or two, with tourist hotels, cafes, and arcades where the best rugs could be put on display. This would seem a progressive program."

Oswig studied Moncrief for a long moment.

"Doubtless, you are a deep-dyed scholar, and a past master of poodle-de-doodle. Also, you have read several books. Still, your knowledge of Star Home is a muddle, and your theories are bunk."

Moncrief blinked but maintained his sangfroid. "I will give your comments careful study. They may well illuminate the unusual quirks of local custom."

"While you study, remember this," said Oswig. "We Ritters are nomads, wandering the steppe as the mood takes us, by the white light of day, through the pale moonlight by night. The vistas are never the same; the grass undulates in long swells, where it is moved by the wind. Sometimes rain sweeps down upon the trimbles—but the wumps amble on, taking no notice. Inside the trimbles, the rugs are worked on the racks. It is a placid life, so long as kasic is available on a timely basis. If Lallankars intercept the shipment, then rug-makers with short pots of schmeer become anxious."

Moncrief put a delicate question: "What, then, is a 'Lallankar'?"

Oswig spat on the ground. "The topic is tiresome; still, it cannot be ignored. Sometimes a youth with doting parents becomes an adolescent convinced of his own sublime importance. He daydreams, shirks his work, and joins the girls at play; he makes no effort to learn the way of the Ritters. No one interferes; they are Ritters, and each must pursue his own destiny! He has no friends but consorts with others of his own sort. They think of themselves as gallant bravos, entitled to the sweetest fruits on the tree of life! Their favorite ploy is to preempt a shipment of kasic, which becomes their property through the exigencies of the Ritter creed. Each Lallankar claims for himself a carboy of kasic; never in his life will he need more.

"The Lallankars make for an important camp, such as Blackwater Camp, and barter with the kasic. What is left is given over to a haphazard distribution—which is better than no distribution at all. The Lallankar now looks to his own affairs. He decorates his trimble with red satin cushions and sluices down his wump with floral water. He stocks his pantry with delicacies, flasks of brambleberry wine, and rare confections from the synthesizer. He ties a blue sash around his waist and sets off to find his favorite among the pretty girls, whom he invites up to his trimble. He seats her upon a cushion, then pours soft green wine into dainty cups of carved bamboo. Presently he serves a banquet of unusual viands, and the afternoon passes. At sunset, he displays a jug of kasic and asks if he might offer such a gift to signalize his fervent regard. The girl responds with joy and gratitude. Meanwhile the wump ambles across the steppe through the gathering dusk.

"And so it goes. Elsewhere the rugmakers scrape the bottoms of their schmeer-pots. Across the steppe, at every sweet-water pond, along every strand, on every hillock where the wumps encircle a camp, the rug-makers sing the same song, and it is a sad song indeed."

After a moment, Moncrief asked: "Could not the system be altered, so as to provide schmeer for these unfortunates whose pots have gone dry?"

Oswig was unmoved. "Thirty-two carboys of kasic yield a precise volume of schmeer. This is the basis for an orderly distribution of kasic."

"Aha!" cried Moncrief, his eyes bright with enthusiasm. "You have cited a problem to which I have the answer!"

Oswig had lost interest in the topic and turned to address Maloof, but Moncrief was not to be denied. "My concept is simple but elegant! I commend it to your attention."

Oswig heaved a patient sigh. "Very well! Explain this noble concept, if you will."

"With pleasure. You merely ship twice as many rugs to Cax; they will send back twice as much kasic. This cargo must be discharged at a site secure from the Lallankars, and that is the crux of the scheme. The kasic now is distributed with open-handed grandeur, and the song of the rugmakers will be heard no more."

Moncrief stepped back, in smiling anticipation of Oswig's plaudits.

"Startling!" Oswig admitted. "Particularly in view of its implicit purport."

"Oh?" said Moncrief, nonplussed, his smile fading. "How can this be?"

Oswig said: "Your scheme imputes to the Ritters a bewildered foolishness, from which they are rescued by the advice of a kindly off-world savant."

"Ahem," said Moncrief. "I fear that your meaning eludes me."

Oswig paid no heed. "The advice is spurious for several reasons. First, a flood of mediocre rugs would choke the repository. Second, doubling the amount of schmeer doubles the quantity of the other materials, which are tedious to collect. Third, even at this time, there are many who wish to limit the import of kasic to ten carboys. Fourth—

but perhaps you have heard enough. In essence, your scheme cannot be recommended."

Moncrief performed a stiff bow. "No further expatiation is necessary. And now, please excuse me; I have urgent business elsewhere." He swung about and marched off toward the *Glicca*, where the discharge of cargo had now been effected.

Oswig turned to Maloof. "What, may I ask, is your next destination?"

"We carry goods for Cax, which will be our next port of call."

"In that case, I can offer you a parcel of freight for Monomarche, at Cax, if you are interested."

"I am interested, certainly."

"The parcel consists of fourteen rugs, rolled into bundles about six feet long. They are now in the repository at Torqual Downs. I can order them out by wagon, which means a delay of two weeks, but there is a better way.

"Dockerl will arrive within three or four days, along with my assistant Zitzelman. As soon as Dockerl picks up the carboys of kasic, I suggest that you shift the *Glicca* to Torqual Downs, where the rugs can be loaded efficiently. The freight charges will be prepaid at the standard rate of one hundred and seventy-five sols."

Maloof considered. "As a matter of curiosity, what value is placed upon a single rug?"

Oswig glanced at Maloof with a flicker of suspicion; still, he responded without hesitation.

"There are several categories. The export grades command a price of three hundred sols. Occasionally, when we need a special item of machinery, such as a new food synthesizer or the like, we include in the shipment an extra rug, and the transaction is accomplished."

"And you sell only to Monomarche?"

"Correct. It is a long-standing arrangement."

3

Back aboard the *Glicca*, Captain Maloof told the ship's company of the altered schedule. "We will be delayed at Port Palactus for several days, until Director Oswig has cleared away his carboys. Then we move to Torqual Downs to take on freight for Cax. You may think of the period as a three-day vacation!"

Moncrief slapped the table and rose to his feet. "The layover comes at an opportune time. But for the Mouse-riders, it will not be a vacation. I have worked up several new routines, which I hope will play well at Cax. They differ from our usual entertainment and must be presented carefully, since the audiences at Cax are somewhat special."

Moncrief displayed a sheaf of papers. "These are my notes. I propose that we run through them now, and perhaps we will hold a scratch rehearsal later in the day. This way, if you please."

Moncrief set off across the saloon, with Flook, Pook, and Snook dancing and skittering at his heels. The Klutes sat watching silently with sardonic expressions; for a moment they muttered together, then lurched to their feet and sauntered across the saloon after the others. The girls, winsome and demure as always, settled upon a couch; the Klutes leaned contemptuously against the wall.

Moncrief placed his papers upon the table. "You might like to know that at Cax we will be performing at the Trevanian, which is an exceptionally large theater.

"The Trevanian is popular with ordinary Blenks and the upper classes as well. They come to relax and have a good time, and the audiences are boisterous; if they like the performance, the artists are rewarded, but if the audience is bored or displeased, the performers quickly learn of the fact, and even then must be gracious! The Trevanian will be an interesting experience for all of us. So: to work.

"These sequences are unlike our usual material, in view of the responsive audience. The first sequence is a tropical extravaganza. The girls wear costumes of green feathers and bird masks; they perch in the foliage of a lush jungle and produce fluting melodies based upon birdcalls. Suddenly, they mime terror and become silent. From off-stage comes a low, rumbling mutter—a sound felt rather than heard. The bird-girls hide in the foliage as best they can. The rumble becomes heavy, and slave-takers appear: massive creatures, wearing the iron armor of Bugasky warriors. They discover the bird-girls and set about their craft. The bird-girls are clever and use all manner of tricks to evade capture, and in the end the slave-takers are caught in their own snares and are hoisted high to hang by their heels. The green-feathered bird-girls cavort and dance gleefully. At last the slave-takers escape and chase the bird-girls into the jungle. From far away comes a horrid sound. Lavender murk slowly falls over the scene, and that is the first sequence." Moncrief looked from face to face, hoping for enthusiasm.

Hunzel muttered: "It sounds complicated, and I don't like hanging by my heels."

"It will please the audiences," said Moncrief cheerfully. "For the second sequence, I plan to use the old Zagazig routine, modified a bit, possibly. I wonder if we could lure enough daredevils from the audience. Hm. Perhaps not; the Blenks are somewhat self-conscious.

"In any case, for the third sequence I am inclined to try a truly innovative scheme, which is simple but which still should amuse the Blenks, who are always ready for a frolic." He chuckled. "They will remember the Mouse-riders to the end of their days!" He picked up his papers. "But now, and most urgently: the jungle sequence!"

Moncrief tendered papers to Flook, Pook, and Snook, but when he turned to the Klutes, they thrust the papers aside and stood with arms folded. "You may perform a private act with your papers," Hunzel told him.

Siglaf was less offensive but no less definite. "The sequences are irrelevant. We are here to collect our money, and for no other reason."

Hunzel added: "We want no evasions—chuckles and winks will no longer suffice! The money must be paid in full."

Moncrief sighed. "At the moment Mouse-rider finances are not robust, nor, for a fact, can I guess the extent of your demands. Can you draw up a detailed invoice?"

"That is unnecessary," said Hunzel. "We can calculate the total in this fashion: for Siglaf and myself, six sols per day each. For the girls: four sols per day. In all, the amount is twenty-four sols per day, or in fair estimate: one hundred twenty sols per week. We have served you for three years, which indicates a total of about eighteen thousand sols."

Moncrief's eyebrows rose high in shock. He started to speak, but Hunzel continued. "From this figure, we deduct a reasonable sum for layover times, moneys advanced to us, and miscellaneous items and arrive at a figure of fifteen thousand sols. That is our just demand."

Moncrief heaved a deep sigh. "This is astounding! You have plucked an inordinate figure out of the air and pretend that it is a logical demand. I dispute the accuracy of this figure, from one end to the other. If you want me to take you seriously, you must present a carefully detailed account. That will be the basis for negotiations."

"We want no negotiation," stormed Siglaf. "We want money! Do you intend to pay?"

"Your demands are preposterous! Prepare a careful invoice, and I will give it my attention, at the very least. As I have indicated, the Mouse-rider reserves are currently scant."

"That is not what we wanted to hear! We are listening for the crackle of financial certificates and the chink of sols!"

Moncrief tried to soothe the ruffled feelings. "Let us all be reasonable! We cannot allow a little tiff to spoil the game! I hope for great success at Cax, and you must be ready to share the acclaim!"

Siglaf produced a harsh grunt of what might have been laughter. "There will be no 'acclaim' if there are no Mouse-riders! Unless we are paid, we leave the ship at Cax."

Moncrief chided her: "That is sorry talk—if you leave the ship without funds, you will end up begging in the streets."

"Do not worry on our behalf!" Hunzel told him, leering. "We and the girls will quickly set up a profitable enterprise. We shall not lack funds."

Moncrief's jaw dropped as the implications of the program became clear to him. He spoke in a hushed voice: "You cannot be serious! The idea is unthinkable!"

"Not really," said Siglaf. "If you do not pay us our money, then we must rely upon what assets are under our control. You must accept the inevitable."

Moncrief had found his voice. "I accept nothing! The girls shall not leave the *Glicca*."

Siglaf produced her harsh laugh. "You are a foolish old man. You refuse to pay us our money, then you squeal at the consequences."

"The girls will go ashore with us at Cax," said Hunzel. "They have no choice—they are bound to us until their indentures are dissolved. The law will support our case."

Moncrief put on his most winning smile. "Truly, this talk is neither helpful nor progressive." He glanced across the saloon. "There is Captain Maloof—perhaps he can help us resolve our problem."

"Let him be," growled Siglaf. "This is none of his affair."

"Everything aboard the *Glicca* is his affair," Moncrief told her. He signaled to Maloof, who sauntered across the saloon.

Maloof looked from face to face. "No one seems happy. Are there difficulties?"

"Yes," said Moncrief. "We have reached an impasse. Your advice might be helpful."

"My opinions may please none of you. However, I will take the risk, if you will do the same."

Moncrief described the dispute, using as few words as possible and trying for objectivity. Siglaf and Hunzel made several more or less acerbic comments; then the three girls stated their points of view.

Maloof looked down at the table. "What papers are these?"

"Just my notes on Mouse-rider sequences," said Moncrief.

Maloof looked around. "Can any of you show documents to verify his or her demands?"

"We need no documents," growled Hunzel. "We base our claims on mathematical truths."

Maloof looked at Moncrief. "And what of you?"

"I can show only miscellaneous notes, a few receipts, perhaps a production ledger or two, also indexes and a few outlines for future Mouse-rider productions. They may cast a glimmer of light upon this miserable affair, or so I hope."

Siglaf snapped: "We want more than a glimmer of light. We want our money!"

Maloof rose to his feet. "My advice is this: each party should assemble all available documents, memoranda, contracts, notes, and anything else relevant, then prepare a careful schedule of claims, as detailed as possible. Then we can return to the negotiations whenever it becomes convenient."

Siglaf and Hunzel grimaced in dissatisfaction and stalked off to their quarters.

Moncrief said glumly: "I am a trained impresario, gifted with both creativity and wit. I have organized Mouse-rider pageants, and much else, but I am not a man for trifling detail."

"You must search your records with care," said Maloof. "One number is worth a dozen suppositions."

The deliberations Maloof had envisaged were forestalled by an unexpected event. During the night, unknown entities came in from the steppe, as furtive as ghosts. They halted behind the far warehouse and worked with silent efficiency. When they departed, the thirty-two carboys of kasic were in their possession.

4

Wingo, arising early, had gone for a morning stroll with his camera, hoping to surprise a mereng at one of its interesting activities. As he passed behind the far warehouse, he noticed evidence of the depredation, as well as confused tracks in the grass and a pair of ruts leading off into the northeast.

Wingo reported his findings to Maloof, who sent Myron to notify Director Oswig.

Myron found Oswig making a breakfast of porridge and tea. Neither tact nor delicacy was practical; he said: "Bad news, sir! The kasic has been stolen."

Oswig stared at him impassively, jaws moving as he ingested the last of his porridge. Then he turned to his radio.

Myron, standing by, heard Dockerl's cheerful call issuing from the mesh: "Dockerl here!"

Oswig's voice cracked with emotion. "You have not yet made instant departure for Port Palactus, as I instructed."

Dockerl made haste to explain. "We prepared to depart while dealing with a dozen emergencies! They are now defeated, and our departure is imminent!"

"Do not trouble yourself unduly," Oswig told him drily. "The Lallankars have preceded you. The kasic is gone. Allow me, if you will, to criticize your torpid activity—I ask only that you compare it with the Ritter's code of duty!"

When Dockerl finally was able to interpose a remark, he cried out: "Instead of taxing me for something, which is nothing, you should compliment my sagacity for avoiding a fruitless mad dash across the steppe! I avoided an exercise in futility and also saved you a howling embarrassment—have you no gratitude?"

Myron returned to the *Glicca*, to find Captain Maloof conferring with Wingo and Schwatzendale. He joined the group and listened with interest to the discussion.

"There should be no great risk, and the advantages are obvious," said Maloof. "Are there contrary opinions?"

"None at all," said Schwatzendale. "The scheme is sound."

"That is my personal feeling," said Maloof.

"Make your arrangements, and be on your way."

Schwatzendale, Wingo, and Myron lowered the ship's flitter to the turf. They boarded the craft and took it aloft; below, the steppe expanded far and wide, beyond the horizons, uniform but for a few slow waves where the wind touched the grass.

The twin tracks of the Lallankar wagons led away into the northeast. Flying at an altitude of a thousand feet the flitter followed the wagon trail, and after half an hour the quarry came into view, a column of five wumps, each carrying on its broad back a small cottage with a front and back deck. The high-pitched roofs were artfully concave, with quaint upturned eaves. The decks were vacant, the Lallankars apparently resting within after the night's work and subsequent carousing.

A long rope trailed from the last wump in the column, pulling a wagon loaded with carboys.

Aboard the flitter, Schwatzendale, Wingo, and Myron took counsel and agreed upon a strategy which seemed simple and direct.

Schwatzendale brought the flitter down until it skimmed the grass, then approached the column from the rear until the flitter almost nosed the last wagon. Myron jumped into one of the ruts where the grass had been smashed flat and ran to the front of the wagon; with a sharp knife he cut the rope, and it fell slack and trailed away through the grass after the receding wump.

Myron returned around the wagon to the flitter, before a mereng might emerge from the grass and seize his leg.

The column of wumps continued into the northeast, the Lallankars oblivious to the loss of their booty.

Schwatzendale made contact with the *Glicca* and reported events to Captain Maloof. "The Lallankars seem to all be asleep! Their wumps have made off into the distance, and all is serene. They will be surprised when they rouse themselves."

Fifteen minutes later the *Glicca* drifted down from the sky, to settle close beside the wagon.

The cargo doors were thrown open, and the carboys were transferred into the hold. The *Glicca* rose into the air and returned toward Port Palactus, to land in the grass a mile south of the spaceport.

"We are here for a purpose," Maloof told his crew. "Oswig is a complicated man, and he is also a Ritter. All in all, I would rather deal with him out here than in his own office."

Schwatzendale was skeptical. "Your theory is sound," he admitted, "but will Oswig come to the ship?"

"That remains to be seen. In any case, you may now approach him at his office and invite his presence aboard the *Glicca*."

Oswig was recalcitrant, as had been expected, but Schwatzendale finally prevailed upon him to board the flitter and fly out to the *Glicca*.

Maloof met Oswig at the port and ushered him aboard. The two sat at the conference table in the corner of the saloon. Wingo brought tea and cakes, which Oswig ignored.

"Why have you brought me out here, in the long grass?" Oswig demanded. "I prefer to deal with you in my official premises."

"Just so," said Maloof, "but I thought that we might be more comfortable out here."

"Whatever the case, it is immaterial. Be good enough to reveal the purpose of this meeting."

"First, I wish to commiserate with you upon the loss of your carboys."

Oswig shrugged. "Do not trouble yourself. As a Ritter, I take all with the same equanimity. The vector of my life is Ritterway."

"You are indifferent to the theft?"

Oswig scowled. "Your terms are curiously askew; naturally I prefer that the kasic should be distributed by the designated authority—

which is to say, myself. But as usual, the Lallankars have flouted propriety. They are rumbling their wumps across the steppe, to Maiden Water or some other notorious resort, and will convert the kasic into a grand poomsibah of sybaritical follies."

Maloof spoke. "Happily, I can now reveal that the Lallankars will enjoy excesses only of grief and anguish, for this reason: my crew followed the Lallankars and cut the carboys loose. They are now aboard the *Glicca*."

For a time Oswig sat in silence, mulling over this unsettling new situation. He spoke, straining to keep his voice civil. "What do you propose to do? I hope the kasic will revert into its proper custody."

"That is a possibility," said Maloof. "At the moment, we ourselves are the proper custodians, since we rescued the kasic from the irresponsible Lallankars. Still, under certain conditions, the kasic might well be transferred back to you."

Oswig asked in a frosty voice: "What are these conditions?"

"I shall be blunt," said Maloof. "You have told us that at Torqual Downs hundreds or even thousands of rugs are stored in the repository."

"I have said something to this effect," Oswig agreed tonelessly.

"Eventually these rugs will moulder and rot away—a great pity to waste these treasures, and their vibrant beauty, when they might be put to constructive use."

"Tragically, this is true."

Maloof nodded. "Fifty or sixty of these rugs could be put to very constructive use, and they will never be missed."

Oswig said cautiously: "Theoretical possibilities exist, provided that certain standards of—decorum—are recognized."

"That goes without saying!" declared Maloof. "We move to Torqual Downs in any event, to load the rugs for Monomarche. I suggest that the loading proceed quietly; the process can be accomplished expeditiously, with no one the wiser, if we do the loading ourselves."

"And the kasic?"

"The carboys will be relinquished into your care wherever you specify."

"That should be satisfactory," said Oswig.

Eight

1

An hour before sunset, the *Glicca* departed Star Home with sixty-two rugs bundled into the aft cargo bay. A parcel of fourteen rugs would be delivered to Monomarche at Cax; forty-eight rugs Director Oswig had transferred to Captain Maloof, in exchange for thirty-two carboys of kasic. Two of these rugs had been preempted by Myron Tany for his private purposes; the remaining forty-six would be marketed to best advantage by Captain Maloof, wherever conditions made such a transfer practical.

On the morning of the second day out, Captain Maloof and the Mouse-riders resumed the business which had been interrupted several days previously at Port Palactus.

The group gathered at the same table as before. Captain Maloof was first to arrive, followed by Moncrief and the three girls, and finally by the sullen Klutes. Maloof seated himself at the head of the table; the Klutes sat at the opposite end, Moncrief to the right, and the girls to the left.

Maloof surveyed the group but found no more bonhomie now than at the previous session. The Klutes muttered together, glaring at Moncrief from time to time. Moncrief sat with an expression of mild forbearance, hands clasped modestly on the table.

Maloof spoke, trying to project positivity. "Today we take up where we left off, and I hope that we can reach an accommodation which everyone will find tolerable, at the very least. I will act as an impartial arbiter. I am not a legal expert, but during my stint with the IPCC, I gained a working knowledge of Gaean law, which I have not forgotten. At our last meeting, I asked that you look through your papers and bring to the table whatever pertinent material you came upon. I hope that this has been done."

Siglaf said gruffly: "We found no papers of the sort you have in mind, but no such documents are needed, since we will prove our claim by the use of ordinary mathematics."

Maloof turned to Moncrief. "And what of you, Sir Mouse-rider? Have you anything you care to show us?"

Moncrief smiled, almost apologetically. "I have looked through my files and found a number of invoices, receipts, statements, and general memoranda, mostly items of little consequence. However, in the clutter I came upon a few documents which may be of interest." He reached into his pocket and brought out a brown folder, which he placed upon the table.

Maloof turned back to the Klutes. "What, exactly, is the substance of your claim?"

"It could not be more basic," stated Hunzel. "Moncrief owes us money. He can doodle and dodge no longer. Now he must pay."

Siglaf tilted her head and showed a grin which was almost a leer. "He will plead poverty, with tears in his eyes! But pay no heed—he carries a bundle of wealth among his effects."

Moncrief laughed sadly. "If only it were true. Here would be lurulu of the most exalted degree! I would never go mouse-riding again."

"Bah," muttered Hunzel. "Your mockery is in poor taste, and no one is amused. Instead of wasting our time with your foolishness, pay us our money."

"I was not aware that I owed you money."

The Klutes stared at him incredulously; then both uttered short sardonic laughs. "That is another of your jokes," said Hunzel. "No matter; we can prove our case. You have not a leg to stand on."

"If you please," said Maloof, "you may present the details of your case."

2

"Moncrief first saw us at Frippen, near the Bleary Hills on Numoy," Hunzel began. "We had come down from the hills to make our report to the Enders Valley Foundling Farm, where we had taken custody of the girls two years before.

"For some reason, Moncrief became interested in us. He spoke to us; then he spoke even longer with the girls. He said that he was head

of the famous Mouse-rider troupe, and at the moment there were va-
cancies that he was trying to fill. He asked if we would like to join the
troupe; he told us fine tales of exciting adventures and star travel, of
wonderful places we would visit, and the hundred kinds of strange people we would meet—and all the time we would be earning money.

"He saw that we were interested, and made offers of how we would
work. He spoke of this and that, and the various advantages of the
plans until we were quite confused. Then he wrote out the choices. We
chose the plan that seemed most advantageous, and so we became
Mouse-riders.

"For a time we toured the provinces of Numoy. Then a spaceship
took us to Lally Komar Town on the world Spangard. After that we
moved from here to there, and as Moncrief had promised, everywhere
was different—some good, some not so good.

"But whenever we wanted money, Moncrief went into a nervous
spasm—he would twitter, and chuckle, and dance from foot to foot,
then say that he must consult his books. Sometimes, his mouth pinched
up and his eyes went dim while he reached into his pocket, brought
forth a few sols, and passed them into our hands, one by one. So it
went until Siglaf finally calculated how much he owed us.

"He had contracted to pay Siglaf and me six sols each per day, and
the girls four sols each per day, all money payable to us—since the girls
are indentured and working under our supervision. They have never
attempted to amortize the indentures, which are four hundred sols
each."

Siglaf hunched forward. "Moncrief is subtly sly. At Frippen he
tried to confuse us, talking first out of one side of his mouth, then the
other! But we were too wise for him, and now he is distraught—he has
tried every trick to defraud us, but we are decided. If he fails to pay us,
we leave the Mouse-riders at Cax."

Maloof held up his hand. "You are going too far, too fast. How
much, by your calculations, does Moncrief owe you?"

"The figure is easily determined," said Hunzel. "We reckon five
days a week and fifty weeks a year. Siglaf and I earn six sols per day, or
thirty sols per week, to the sum of fifteen hundred sols per year. After
three years, each of us has earned forty-five hundred sols, to a total of
nine thousand sols. The girls earn one thousand sols per year, and for
the three of them for three years, a total of nine thousand sols, to a
grand total of eighteen thousand sols."

"Hm," said Maloof. "That is a substantial sum."

"So it is," said Siglaf. "From time to time Moncrief doled out a few
sols: five sols now, ten sols later, a few more dinkets when he felt mu-

nificent. Over the years, during his fits of guilt, he has given as much as
two hundred sols! On the other hand, we are large-handed; as a token
of our personal generosity, we will demand only fifteen thousand sols.
But this he must pay, or at Cax we leave the troupe, and Moncrief can
dance the kazatzka at the Trevanian while playing the flute."

Moncrief shook his head in wonder. "Never have I suspected the
Klutes of such extravagant imaginations. Their statements are, of
course, factitious."

Maloof sighed. "What, then, is your version of events?"

"I will explain with pleasure," Moncrief stated. "I first encountered
the Klutes and the three girls at Frippen on Numoy. They made a dramatic impact upon me. I was in the process of reorganizing the Mouse-
riders, and I was on the lookout for fresh personnel; I could see that the
Klutes, with their hulking bulks and ferocious faces—in striking contrast to the three girls, with their charm, innocence, and mischievous
precocity—could be valuable adjuncts to the Mouse-riders. I offered
them employment with the troupe, and all five accepted without
hesitation.

"The Klutes wanted to know how much they would earn. I explained that they could join the troupe and receive a share of the prof-
its after expenses, or they might choose a second option and work by
the hour, during performances, rehearsals, and whenever they might
be busy with troupe business, in which case they must pay their own
expenses.

"For the previous three months the troupe had been touring the
provinces of Fiametta, playing two performances a day. The Klutes
could see that under these conditions their earnings would be very
consequential, and they decided to work by the terms of the second
option.

"To make sure that they understood their choice, I prepared a paper detailing the terms of Option One and Option Two as clearly as
possible. I insisted that they indicate their choice of option and sign
their names, which was done. They explained that the girls were under
indenture and therefore need not sign, which I accepted."

"And you have retained this document?"

"Just so! Over the years I have learned the value of meticulous
records."

Moncrief opened his brown folder and removed a sheet of paper,
which he handed to Maloof. The Klutes watched with narrow-eyed
suspicion.

Maloof scanned the document. The second paragraph was endorsed by a pair of signatures, in handwriting so eccentric as to be al-

most illegible. He looked down the table to the Klutes. "I presume that
you recall signing this paper?"

The Klutes shrugged and looked at each other. Siglaf said: "That
happened three years ago. The paper is faded and old, and the writing
is obsolete. Put the paper aside, and let us deal with affairs as they are
now."

Maloof shook his head. "This may be the custom in the Bleary
Hills, but elsewhere in the Gaean Reach things go differently."

"No matter," said Siglaf. "Our figures cannot be faulted."

"They are fine figures indeed," said Maloof. "However, they lack
all connection with the business at hand."

The Klutes stared at him mulishly.

Maloof looked to Moncrief. "Do you have more records?"

Moncrief opened his folder again and drew out two notebooks. "In
the black notebook, I record details of all performances and associated
rehearsals. In the green notebook I keep a record of all expenses incurred by the troupe.

"I copy these into my information machine whenever it is convenient, which gives me access to all manner of purchases and payments—
for a fact, the machine provides more information than I need. I can
learn the time worked by both the Klutes and the girls, and the wages
they have earned.

"In the green book are recorded all expenses pursuant to Mouse-
rider operations. The figures include costs of food, shelter, and transportation incurred by the Klutes and the girls. I will point out that,
despite their contract, the Klutes have paid not one dinket of these expenses, which were not inconsiderable.

"Why have I allowed this delinquency to continue? Because I knew
the total of their earnings, and I saw that these two amounts were at all
times reasonably close. And whenever their earnings exceeded the expenses by any substantial sum, I paid over sufficient money to restore
the balance. I have receipts to prove that during the three years I have
paid over about nine hundred sols. There may be some small differen-
tial now; I have not checked recently."

Maloof turned to the Klutes. "You have heard Moncrief's explanation. Do you care to examine his books?"

Siglaf muttered: "To what purpose? We cannot decipher his
worm-tracks. We are confident only of our own figures, which represent three years of toil."

Hunzel said: "Moncrief must make a definite commitment, or we
leave the ship at Cax. That is our only recourse."

Moncrief held his arms wide, in a plea for moderation. "How can I pay money which I do not have? You ask the impossible!"

Siglaf uttered a coarse grunt. "We may have come down from the Bleary Hills, but we are not tumblewits. We know that you have a great bundle of sols hidden away among your things. We want our share."

Hunzel said, "The issues are clear—either you pay us, or the five of us will leave the ship at Cax."

Moncrief clicked his tongue in desperation. "You cannot take the girls! They belong with the troupe."

"Nevertheless, they go with us."

"This is merciless bluster! Cax is a dreary place; you would wander back and forth, cold and hungry. You can't subject the girls to such misery!"

"Give us credit for forethought!" said Siglaf. "We will set up an enterprise, and put the girls to work. With their endowments they will bring in a great deal of money, and we will keep our prices high. It will be a fine novelty for them."

Moncrief found his voice. "The idea is abominable! We will not allow the girls to leave the ship!"

Hunzel uttered a jeering laugh. "It is something you cannot avoid! We hold the indentures, and the girls are under our control. That is the law; defy it at your peril."

The girls looked back and forth between Moncrief and the Klutes. Flook asked: "What are you talking about? It seems to concern us; you must tell us what is going on!"

Moncrief spoke in a measured voice. "The Klutes intend to take you off the *Glicca* at Cax. They will bring men to look at you and will take money from whatever man wants to use you in his bed for the night, whether you like him or not. That will be your occupation."

The girls looked incredulously at the Klutes. "This cannot be true—would you do that to us?"

"It is a quick way to make money," said Siglaf. "On Cax we will need money, and you will quickly become accustomed to the work. It is better than being hungry and shivering in the rain."

"I do not want to be either hungry or shivering," said Flook. "But I don't think that I will care for that sort of work."

Pook said, "I prefer to stay aboard the *Glicca* and work with the Mouse-riders."

Snook said, "If Siglaf and Hunzel wish to take up that line of business they may do so, but we prefer to stay aboard the *Glicca*."

"Your preferences are not important!" snapped Siglaf. "You are indentured, and you must do as we say. That is the law, and you have no choice."

The girls sat silent and crestfallen.

Maloof rose to his feet. "I have heard statements from both parties, and in my opinion, Moncrief's records are convincing. My advice is that the Klutes carry on as before, but keep more careful records. If they would like to leave the ship at Cax, they may do so, but as for taking the girls with them, no tribunal in all the Reach would stretch the power of indenture to include such sordid purposes."

Maloof reflected a moment, then addressed the Klutes. "I would like to look over the certificates of indenture, if I may."

"You may not," snapped Hunzel. "They are private papers."

"Not necessarily," said Maloof. "The girls obviously have a right to examine them whenever they like."

Hunzel spoke to the girls. "You do not want to look at these papers now, or so I assume. Am I right?"

Flook said, "I am curious; I would like to look at the papers."

Pook said, "I am curious too. I want to see them."

Snook said: "And I as well."

Siglaf's eyes glinted. "Very well—you shall see them, when it is more private."

Flook asked: "Why not now? There is no one here but Moncrief and Captain Maloof—that is private enough."

The Klutes sat straight in their chairs, rigid as stone figures. After a moment Hunzel muttered, "It is not a convenient time to disturb our belongings for foolishness."

Maloof said: "One time is as good as another. Bring out the papers yourselves, now, or I must use my authority as master of the *Glicca* and locate them myself."

The Klutes looked at each other, then Siglaf heaved herself erect and strode off to the cabin she shared with Hunzel. After a moment she returned with a buff envelope, which she tossed upon the table in front of Maloof.

Maloof looked at the three girls. "Shall I open the envelope now?"

The girls nodded, sensing the possibility of imminent change in their lives.

Maloof opened the envelope and withdrew three sheets of heavy buff paper. He laid them on the table and began to read. After a time he smiled, then he chuckled.

Moncrief came to look over his shoulder. He spoke in a strange, emphatic language: "Ton-ton eskoy!"

"Exactly," said Maloof.

Pook asked anxiously: "What does that mean?"

Maloof spoke softly, as if he were reciting a fragment of lyric poetry. "The grotesque sometimes reaches such exalted levels that it becomes almost sublime." He glanced toward the Klutes; they gave back impersonal stares.

Maloof spoke to the girls. "The papers appear to be official forms, issued by the Enders Valley Foundling Farm, for Maundry Vale Province, at Frippen on the world Numoy. That is the heading at the top of the page." He turned to the papers and read: "'This paper grants custody of Prasilian Sklavo, age fourteen'—"

"That is me," said Flook.

"—'into the guardianship of Siglaf and Hunzel Podeska, of Cawterfel Farm of Tado Township in the Hills of Maundry Vale Province, subject to the following provisions: the guardians undertake to provide comfortable and secure lodgings for the ward, and to serve nutritious food of good quality to the ward's taste. The guardians must arrange for standard education for the ward, also medical and dental services when necessary, and try to provide a cheerful home atmosphere, along with normal recreational facilities. The ward is to be allowed leisure for appropriate social activity, but at the same time must be protected from unwholesome companions. The ward will not be required to perform labor other than minor household chores of an ordinary nature. The ward may not be asked to perform difficult, arduous, or dangerous work. The premises of the ward's residence will be regularly inspected by Institute personnel to ensure compliance with Institute regulations.'

"'The grant of custody is valid only within the province of Maundry Vale. The ward may not be removed from the province, or otherwise away from the authority of the Institute; if such transgression occurs, the grant of custody is revoked.'

"'If the guardians are put to extraordinary expense of legal and justifiable nature, the guardians may place an obligation or indenture not to exceed four hundred sols against the ward. This documentation will serve as authorization for such indenture so long as the debt is incurred, and discharged, inside Maundry Vale Province, and the Institute is notified.'

"'If the ward is removed from the province, any indenture is dissolved. Signatures of both parties will be appended below.'"

Maloof looked at the other two sheets. "The documents are all the same, except that one names Lulanie Sklavo, and the other Thalasso Sklavo, who I presume are Pook and Snook."

"That is quite right," said Pook excitedly. "Are we free of indenture, and need not obey the Klutes?"

"Precisely so."

Flook asked anxiously: "Are we to leave the ship at Cax?"

"No," said Maloof. "You owe nothing to the Klutes. They have no control over you. If you wish to become Mouse-riders and work with Moncrief, you are free to do so—and I think that he will agree to the arrangement."

"That would suit us very well," said Snook. "And the Klutes—what of them? Will they leave the ship at Cax and set up their enterprise?"

Hunzel and Siglaf sat stiffly. After a moment, Siglaf said off-handedly: "Perhaps we will stay with the Mouse-riders. We have nothing better to do."

Moncrief looked at the Klutes thoughtfully. "I will take the idea under advisement. I can't deny that you play a valuable role in many of the routines. Still, you could be replaced. We shall see."

After a pause, Maloof spoke. "The dispute which was initiated on Star Home has been resolved. I hope that all concerned will assure themselves that resolution was scrupulously just."

Siglaf and Hunzel, making no comment, rose to their feet and went to their quarters.

NINE

1

**Excerpt from *Handbook to the Planets*:
Blenkinsop, Moulder 17**

The orange star Moulder controls twenty-two far-flung planets, including a single habitable world to which the locator Abel Blenkinsop attached his own name. Now, three thousand years later, the world is home to a dour, dark-visaged race: the Blenks, who live in five great cities and work at the vast industrial yards which provide goods for half of the worlds in the local sector.

Neither the climate nor the geography of Blenkinsop can be considered congenial. More often than not, the sky is layered under a thin overcast through which the giant star Moulder shows as a dim orange disk. One season is much like another, though during the nominally winter months rain squalls and bitter winds more frequently range along the narrow city streets, driving pedestrians into their bungalows or underground into the subway system.

The polar continents to north and south are bitter wastes of glaciers between mountains of black gabbro. Of the six remaining continents, four are sodden marshes threaded by slow waterways. Two other continents have gentle terrain with rolling hills in the south, and here the Blenks have established their cities, for reasons lost to memory, each to the north of the hills, with the industrial yards still farther to the north.

Across the years, the population has created within itself three classes of citizenry, which have congealed into distinctive castes. The most prestigious are the relatively few Shimerati, who live along the ridges of the southern highlands in palaces behind exotic gardens. The next lower caste is the Hummers, comprising high-level financiers and mercantilists, legal, medical, and technical professionals, and general intelligentsia. Their mansions, situated along the slopes of the highlands, are notably more pretentious than the simple and elegant Shimerati palaces. The third caste encompasses the working classes of Blenkinsop, who live in solid little bungalows ranged side by side along the interminable streets of the cities.

There is little traffic along the narrow streets of the cities: drays and delivery vans, pushcarts operated by sturdy old women, and a few high-wheeled motorized rickshaws, which serve the Blenks as taxis. For general transportation, most Blenks ride the subway systems, which underlie the streets.

Despite occasional variation, the working Blenk is easily defined. He is of middle stature and stocky physique, usually a few pounds overweight—a fact to which he is indifferent, since he has little vanity. His clothes are chosen for durability rather than style, and if he chances to look into a mirror he accepts his image without reaction; this is himself in his singular individuality. His personal manner is abrupt and brusque, lacking both tact and grace, but to his credit he is loyal, generous, gentle with wife and children, and totally brave. At work he is competitive, since his basic goals are advancement in status and rank.

A typical Blenk visits the vast theater known as the 'Trevanian' often, sometimes with his family and sometimes alone. In the warm blur of the murmurous darkness, the stresses of his daily life ease away; he is at peace with himself and his surroundings. At the end of the evening he reluctantly rises from his seat and slowly leaves the hall, still lost in a semi-euphoric mood, to ride the subway home, where the children are asleep and his wife has a bowl of hot soup waiting for him.

The Trevanian is also patronized by the upper castes. The Shimerati occupy the high balcony, where they can be glimpsed by the players onstage should they trouble to look—though they would discover only a few pale oval blurs, devoid of animation. The Hummers on the balcony below are more conspicuous; they wear their most splendid costumes and conduct themselves in accordance with a ritualized etiquette. The ladies indulge themselves in monumental coiffures sparkling with small luminosities and streaming with colored ribbons. Their behavior is exaggerated for the occasion; they gesture with fluttering fingers, they simper, pout, and gaze toward the ceiling in mock-agony when their desires are inexcusably ignored. They beckon and chirrup to acquaintances and toss nosegays to their favorites, meanwhile enjoying the refreshments served by liveried attendants.

The same partiality for extravagance and exaggeration is apparent in Hummer architecture, dictating the unusual, bizarre, rococo, and fantastic. From hillside foundations, Hummer mansions loft three stories high, each with its complement of cupolas, bays, balconies, private decks, and pendant glass globes, furnished for the convenience of those who choose to take tea, and enjoy petits fours or frozen creams while swinging gently in the dim orange sunlight.

Far different are the palaces of the Shimerati, which are low, irregular, and deceptively simple, built to the terms of an understated elegance
using porphyry, moonstone, jet, and an occasional column of malachite.

2

From the pilot-house of the *Glicca*, the star Moulder first appeared as
an orange spark on a background of far dim constellations. As the
Glicca approached, the spark became an enormous orange disk, with a
retinue of twenty-two planets.

Captain Maloof directed the *Glicca* toward the seventeenth of
these worlds, which long ago the locator Abel Minger Blenkinsop had
registered, using his own name.

The world expanded below. Maloof made contact with the space-
control office at Cax and received landing instructions. The *Glicca*
dropped through overcast and down toward the early morning face of
Cax. Maloof located the landing field and guided the *Glicca* to its allo-
cated plat.

As soon as the exit port was slid open and the gangway lowered,
three uniformed officials left the port offices and trotted across the
field to the ship. They conferred a moment, then climbed the gangway
and entered the saloon. For half an hour they subjected the ship's company and the ship itself to standard entry formalities.

As soon as they issued clearances and departed, Myron crossed the
field to the long, low terminal building, where he expected to find the
office of the Port Director. He climbed a ramp to the cargo dock.

A few yards to the left, a corridor opened into the building. A sign
with a pointing arrow read:

To the Port Director

Myron turned into the corridor and almost at once came upon a
tall door, where another sign read:

Rico Yail
Director of the Port
Come at will

The door slid open to Myron's touch; he entered a large room
sparsely furnished with a desk, a few chairs, and a tall cabinet. The

walls displayed a single decoration: a poster printed in tones of black, gray, and mulberry, depicting twenty-five types of spaceship currently in operation.

At the back of the desk, a large man of indeterminate age, languidly handsome, sat at his ease. The desk bore neither documents, ledgers, nor files; the director, if this were he, seemed unoccupied and rather more casual than Myron had expected. He spoke courteously: "I am Rico Yail; please be seated and explain how I can help you."

Myron sat down and laid his sheaf of documents upon the desk. "I am Myron Tany, supercargo of the *Glicca*, which has just arrived. We carry a mixed cargo, including ten bales of skins from the world Madlock, some miscellaneous parcels from Fluter and elsewhere, and from Star Home a consignment of fourteen rugs for Monomarche, which I take to be a local merchandiser."

"In the broadest sense, you are correct," said Yail. "In each city of Blenkinsop, there are one or more great magazines similar to Monomarche, though on a lesser scale. These magazines purvey goods of every sort, both local and off-world. They deal with the ordinary Blenks and the upper castes as well. Monomarche is the most prestigious of the group and commands considerable influence. They will send a man for the rugs, so you may put them from your mind; also, I will send a crew to discharge the rest of the freight for Cax. Your responsibilities will be at an end."

Myron was puzzled. He indicated the documents he had placed on the desk. "Here are the applicable manifests, invoices, certificates, and a few forms which should be filled out immediately."

He started to pass them across the desk, but Yail raised his hand to forestall him. "A clerk is usually on hand to deal with such matters, but today he is away—so you may drop the papers into yonder trash basket, where they will do us no harm."

Myron's jaw dropped. "Are you serious?"

"Of course! A clerk will be here tomorrow; he can sort through the trash, if he likes—that is his prerogative. But we have more important things to do."

Without further demur, Myron obeyed the instructions.

"Good," said Yail, leaning back in his chair. "Now then: what are your next ports of call?"

"The schedule, so far as I know, is not yet definite," said Myron. "We have no outstanding commitments; we are at liberty to accept such cargoes as you might wish to move."

"Excellent. We can offer cargoes to a variety of ports, mostly, I must say, off the standard shipping routes—not necessarily a disadvantage, since non-conventional itineraries are often profitable! To compensate for exceptionally distant ports, a twenty percent adjustment in freight rates may be possible."

"That might well be an inducement," said Myron. "If you will give me a list of these cargoes and their destinations, and the projected freight charges, I will take it to Captain Maloof, and tonight we will work out some routings."

Yail turned to his information machine. He touched buttons; the screen glowed pink, with lines of bright blue-green text. Yail scanned the display, made a few changes, and pressed a button, and a sheet of paper issued from a slot. He gave the paper to Myron, who tucked it into his pocket.

"We will work on this tonight," Myron said. "If we have any success, I will let you know as soon as possible."

Myron prepared himself to leave, but hesitated. Yail looked inquiringly across the desk.

Myron spoke, half-apologetically: "If you have a minute or two to spare, I would be grateful for your advice."

"As of now, nothing presses," said Yail. "State your problem, then I can tell you whether my advice might be useful."

Myron arranged his thoughts. "The situation is this. On Star Home we shifted the *Glicca* from Port Palactus to the rug repository at Torqual Downs, where we would take aboard the rugs for Monomarche. At the repository we noticed hundreds of rugs in storage, the best of the best. A few days before, thieves had stolen thirty-two carboys of kasic from Port Palactus; we chased down the thieves and took back the carboys. The port director was anxious to recover the carboys, and so we traded forty-six rugs from the Torqual repository in exchange for the kasic. These rugs are now in our aft cargo bay, and we want to dispose of them to best advantage. But we do not know how to proceed."

Yail nodded thoughtfully. "You have correctly perceived the difficulties; as soon as you made a move, you would be wrapped up in a cocoon of red tape. But do not let me alarm you—proper tactics can circumvent these obstacles. After all, authorities cannot tax or regulate what is unknown to them; this is a universal law!

"Monomarche has achieved a virtual monopoly on the Star Home rugs, which it sells to the Shimerati—no doubt at a handsome profit. The other magazines would be happy to break this monopoly, I'm sure; perhaps they could be discreetly approached." He hitched himself forward. "What sort of price are you contemplating? For instance, would you accept three hundred sols per rug?"

"Hm," Myron mused. "Three hundred multiplied by forty-six equals thirteen thousand eight hundred, which is an impressive sum. But I must consult my colleagues before making a commitment."

Yail turned to look out the window, frowning in deep cogitation. At last he turned back to Myron. "The figure I mentioned is, of course, tentative. If you attempted to handle the business yourself, I imagine that the best offer you would hear might be a grudging two hundred sols. With my guidance, the price would be somewhat higher; however, I would expect a reasonable fee. I suggest that this might be twenty percent of any excess over three hundred sols per rug. For instance, if I sold a rug at four hundred sols, my fee would be twenty percent of one hundred sols, or twenty sols. You would be selling the rug for three hundred eighty sols. Would you accept such an arrangement?"

"It sounds better than two hundred sols per rug," said Myron. "Still, I can agree to nothing definite at this moment."

3

Myron returned to the *Glicca*, where he found Captain Maloof in the galley, along with Wingo and Schwatzendale.

Myron described his meeting with Yail. "He is a surprise—not the Blenk we have been led to expect. He is relaxed and easy; if he suffers nervous tensions, I saw no symptoms."

Maloof asked: "Does he have cargo for us?"

Myron produced the list which he had received from Yail. "There seem to be a number of parcels to ports somewhat off the usual shipping routes—I told him that we would look over the list, and try to work out a practical itinerary."

Maloof studied the list, with eyebrows raised. "I have never heard of most of these ports. I suspect these so-called 'parcels of cargo' are a collection of odd lots, which no other carrier will accept; they have been languishing in corners of Yail's warehouses like a band of lost waifs, waiting and hoping for a miracle." Maloof put the list down on the table. "Still, they seem to make up a proper cargo, which might turn us a profit, especially if we collect a twenty percent surcharge on the most inconvenient legs."

"And we might pick up a lot or two of cargo along the way," Myron theorized.

"That is always a possibility." Maloof picked up the list and scanned it again. "Hmf. These places are truly obscure, but I suppose they must exist, since Yail is sending them freight! Tonight we will use the Index to locate them on our charts, and sort out a route."

"For a fact, it will be something of a challenge," Myron mused.

"Yes, but perhaps by exercising our joint ingenuity, and throwing in a few zigzags, we may still produce a workable itinerary." He paused. "Even so, it is not good policy to travel a hundred light-years to deliver a sack of birdseed."

After a moment, Myron said: "I also mentioned our rugs to Yail, and asked how we could sell them to the best advantage. He warned me against trying to sell them ourselves, for fear of bureaucratic complications. He asked what price we had put on the rugs; I told him that our thinking had not gone so far, but he asked if we would be satisfied with three hundred sols per rug, or thirteen thousand eight hundred sols for the lot. I said that I would confer with my shipmates and get back to him as soon as possible.

"He went on to say that if we so chose, he would act as our agent, and that his commission would be twenty percent of the difference between three hundred and the final selling price; for instance, if he sold a rug for four hundred sols, he would earn twenty sols, while we would get three hundred eighty sols."

Schwatzendale wrote figures on a sheet of paper. "If we sold forty-six rugs, we would take seventeen thousand four hundred eighty sols, and Yail nine hundred twenty."

"Fair enough," said Maloof, "provided we are paid in cash at the time the rugs are delivered."

Myron returned to Yail's office. As before, he sat relaxed behind the desk.

Yail signaled Myron to a chair. "Do you have instructions for me?"

"I do. Your proposal is accepted, as long as payment is made in cash at the time that the rugs are delivered."

"The terms are accepted," said Yail.

"Now, to work. There are eleven magazines large enough to consider a transaction of this magnitude, including Monomarche. The trade is profitable, since the Shimerati control so much wealth that they ignore price and pay whatever is asked. But Monomarche has no need to be avaricious, and so far as I can gather the rugs are priced at about five hundred sols apiece.

"I will test the market. Come back later—I may have news for you."

4

During the early afternoon, the rain of the morning abated to a fine drizzle, then came to a halt altogether, and the orange disk of Moulder appeared behind the overcast.

An hour or two previously, the Klutes had wandered away from the *Glicca*, planning to explore the city on their own account. The circumstances were dismal; a light rain was falling, and the streets exhaled a sour odor. They marched along the narrow streets, rain-hoods pulled over their heads. At intervals, small, narrow-fronted shops overlooked the street, dark within, sometimes with the pale face of the proprietor half-seen peering through the grimy front panes. Otherwise, the Klutes saw little to interest them.

After a time, they returned to the space-port, grim and dissatisfied, striding through the rain and stamping through puddles to finally reach the *Glicca*.

They changed into dry clothes and went to the galley, where Wingo served them hot tea and scones.

"How did you find the city?" asked Wingo cheerfully.

"The streets were like dark passages, and smelled of dead dogs. The rain was incessant and coursed down our necks in a freshet. We tried to find a tea shop where we could refresh ourselves, but there was none to be found."

Siglaf added: "I believe that, despite its giddy foolishness, I prefer Fluter."

After a pause, Wingo asked delicately: "So then; are you staying with the Mouse-riders?"

Hunzel thought for a moment, then gave an ambiguous grunt. "We face some hard choices. We are in a state of flux."

Siglaf amplified the remark. "In effect, we are open to any propitious offers."

5

Meanwhile, Moncrief had embarked upon adventures of his own. After dressing with care, he had set off to find the Trevanian, where he hoped to secure favorable bookings for the Mouse-riders.

In front of the port offices he commanded the services of a motorized rickshaw, operated by a weedy, hollow-cheeked youth with long varnished mustachios. Before consenting to activate his vehicle, the operator looked Moncrief up and down, then asked: "What is your destination?"

Moncrief said grandly: "You may take me to the Trevanian, at best speed."

The operator nodded curtly, to indicate that he found the destination acceptable. "Climb aboard. The fare is ten dinkets; I will not move a man of your bulk for less."

Moncrief did not care for the operator's manner, which, so he thought, verged on the disrespectful—the more so when he found fault with Moncrief's method for climbing aboard the vehicle. "Briskly, now, Grandfather—the day is for jumping and running; sleep somewhere else if you are tired."

Moncrief, using all dignity, scrambled onto the narrow seat of the vehicle. The operator engaged gears, and the taxi set off across the field, careening dangerously through puddles while Moncrief held on for dear life.

The taxi trundled off the field to the street and presently arrived at the Trevanian. Moncrief alighted stiffly and for a moment gazed in awe at the great Blenk entertainment hall.

The operator tapped his hooter impatiently. "Come now, old toddler! Pay the ten dinkets at once, or I will charge a waiting supplement."

Moncrief hurriedly paid over the fare, which the operator accepted without comment. Cutting a final curvet through a puddle, the rickshaw departed.

Moncrief crossed to the Trevanian. A massive door of iron and glass slid aside at his approach; he passed through the opening into a short hall, which took him into a large octagonal foyer, notable for the corridors which led away from each of the wall-segments.

He stopped short; a multiplicity of choices confronted him. Which corridor led to the office of the Director of Production? On the opposite wall he noticed a long white panel printed with lines of informational text: a directory? He crossed the room and studied the panel.

The printed text was not immediately clear. Aha! A reference to Overman Murius Zank, Director of Production. Moncrief read the associated text and came upon the phrase: 'To reach the office, use the orange indicator.' Moncrief frowned; the words were cryptic indeed. What was an 'orange indicator'? Moncrief stood back and searched the chamber for indicators, of any color whatever, and was enlightened at once.

Each corridor exhibited a distinctive colored stripe along its centerline. Moncrief looked here and there and found a corridor marked by an orange stripe. The corridor and the stripe receded into the distance; without hesitation Moncrief set off into the bowels of the Trevanian.

At intervals, numbered doors appeared to right and left. Moncrief presently arrived at a pair of doors with a plaque reading:

OVERMAN MURIUS ZANK
DIRECTOR OF PRODUCTION

Moncrief touched the latch, and the doors swung aside. He entered a large, high-ceilinged room; a counter separated him from a business office, where a dozen clerks worked in attitudes of remarkable diligence. Moncrief advanced to the counter, where he assumed a posture of importance and waited for a clerk to approach and inquire his needs.

While he waited, Moncrief took occasion to assess the room. At the far end of the section where he stood, a carved wooden balustrade created what seemed to be a special waiting area, which was at the moment vacant. A door from the waiting area led into an inner office. Over the door a panel read:

OVERMAN MURIUS ZANK
DIRECTOR OF PRODUCTION
ENTER AT THE GREEN LIGHT

A red light now glowed above the door.

Moncrief turned his attention back to the office. He became impatient and thumped on the counter with his knuckles. The signal went unheeded.

The desk nearest the counter was occupied by a fresh-faced young man, a trifle plump, dressed in natty garments. A sign on his desk read: BAYARD DESOSSO. Like his colleagues, Bayard worked so diligently as to be oblivious to all else. Moncrief stared at him, trying to compel his attention by sheer force of will. He met no success; if anything, Bayard exerted himself even more energetically.

At this moment, a sudden tumult issued from the inner office; enraged voices, pounding and stamping, outcries and catcalls. Startled, Bayard looked up, and his gaze met Moncrief's insistent stare.

Moncrief instantly pointed his finger. "You there, Bayard! Come here at once!"

A sad expression crossed Bayard's face, altering at once to resolute courtesy.

"Certainly, sir! By all means!" Bayard strode to the counter. "How can I help you, sir?"

"I am Master Moncrief, director of the famous Mouse-rider troupe. I am here to see Director Zank; he will wish to fit the Mouse-riders into his schedule. Time is of the essence."

Bayard looked over his shoulder; the red light still glowed. Bayard said regretfully: "The Director may not be disturbed at this time."

Moncrief cocked his head to listen. "He is either rehearsing a very frolicsome act, or he is being soundly thrashed."

"Such a liberty would be unthinkable!" cried Bayard, but he turned an apprehensive look toward the inner office.

"I suggest," said Moncrief firmly, "that you at least announce that Master Moncrief of the famous Mouse-riders is on hand. It is important that he see me at once."

Bayard shook his head. "You propose an enormity." He paused, to hear the sound of stamping feet. "He is even now trying to quell the Futin Putos, and as you will note, they are emphatic."

Moncrief inquired: "Who are 'the Futin Putos'?"

"They are a troupe of acrobats from the Dark Forest," replied Bayard. "Overman Zank is disgusted with their brutish antics; still, they are popular with a certain segment of the audience, and he feels obliged to use them from time to time."

The sounds from Zank's office had subsided to a murmur of voices, which suddenly waxed in anger, then went quiet.

Moncrief drummed his fingers upon the counter. Suddenly, the rear door from Zank's office flew open, and out to the waiting area came a tumble of ten hairy men, jostling, shoving, struggling for places on the upholstered benches.

After squirming, elbowing, grumbling, and growling, the Futin Putos began to stare across the balustrade at the office clerks, with the curiosity of visitors to a zoo.

Moncrief looked with disfavor at what he considered the most uncouth group of individuals of his experience. They were of ordinary stature, but so burly as to seem squat; lank black hair hung down to join heavy black beards, cut off square under the chin. They wore leather vests and short leather pantaloons, dank with soil and grease.

"Not a savory group," said Moncrief with a sniff, and turned away.

"Don't show them overt disapproval!" Bayard warned quickly. "If they perceive an insult, they will take a vicious revenge. On the stage, they perform spectacular feats, but if someone makes a mistake, they knock him sprawling, then kick him until he crawls away in humiliation."

"In front of the audience?" asked Moncrief in disbelief.

"Definitely. Their audience eggs them on."

Moncrief studied Bayard without approval. "When I entered the office and came to the counter, you ignored me as if I were made of air. How do you explain this conduct?"

Bayard put on a stubborn face. "We must act according to our new regulations."

"Do I hear you aright?" asked Moncrief. "Is it your policy to ignore patrons? This would seem eccentric—to say the least!"

"That is not our affair. In the main, our regulations are not unreasonable."

Moncrief glanced across the room, but the green light was not yet visible. He turned back to Bayard. "Tell me of your new regulations."

Bayard responded mechanically. "Article One defines the need for punctuality and correlates a scale of penalties with degrees of tardiness. Article Two bans conversation, song, banter, gossip, and the like. Article Three establishes work quotas for all office personnel—these quotas are considered stringent! Article Four curtails an old custom; in the past, when a client arrived at the counter, four or five clerks might greet him, to inquire after the health of his family and to chat and learn the details of his business. After that the client might be sent to a new department, or advised as how best to conduct himself before Overman Zank. The new rule has changed this procedure. When a client appears, the first clerk to notice him must hurry to the counter and help the client alone, with crisp efficiency. Unfortunately, the clerk who helps clients will never make up his work quota! But we have found a solution to the dilemma. Nowhere is it specified that clerks are required to keep a vigilant watch on the counter; hence, if the clerk focuses upon his work, he cannot be faulted for neglect."

"Ingenious!" declared Moncrief.

Moncrief was distracted from further comment by the light over Zank's door, which had turned green.

"The green light has appeared," called Bayard. "Come, if you wish to see Zank!"

Adopting a stately posture, Moncrief pushed through the gate in the counter and followed Bayard toward another entrance to Zank's office, at the back of the room.

The Futin Putos suddenly became quiet, then crowded the balustrade, where they hooted and jeered.

"Hoy there, old tumper! Why do you trot so briskly?"

"Tell old Zank that our memories are long!"

"If you forget, we will pull your nose, or whatever it is that dangles between your legs."

Moncrief ignored the raillery and followed Bayard across the room.

Bayard stopped at the door. "I will go in first and announce you. After the Futin Putos, Director Zank's sangfroid may be frayed."

The Futin Putos continued to call advice; Moncrief waited with as much aplomb as he could muster.

A moment later, the door opened and Bayard stood in the opening. He spoke, somewhat self-importantly. "I have mentioned the Mouse-rider troupe to Overman Zank, and I gather that he is favorably impressed. You may now enter. Be polite, but not ebullient. Come, if you will."

Moncrief followed Bayard into a large chamber, sparsely furnished, and unoccupied except for a thin old man who sat motionless behind a massive semi-circular desk.

Bayard assumed a formal posture and performed introductions. To Moncrief he said: "You are in the presence of Overman Murius Zank, Director of Production." To Zank he said: "This gentleman is Professor Moncrief, master of the Mouse-rider troupe. He hopes to present one or more programs at the Trevanian, if circumstances permit."

Zank stared at Moncrief briefly, then dismissed Bayard with a flicker of his fingers. Bayard bowed with punctilio and left the chamber.

The men surveyed each other. Moncrief saw a small, gaunt man with a bald, bony head. Zank's eyes were round; his nose was a small rapacious hook; his mouth was thin and without color. If he ever felt emotion, his features gave no indication.

After a moment, Zank spoke. "If you wish to sit, you may do so."

Moncrief gingerly lowered himself onto a straight-backed chair of rather fragile appearance, which creaked under his weight.

"In regard to our programs, you come at an inconvenient time," said Zank. "The schedule for the week is booked solid, except for a few slots in the after-midnight 'graveyard'. There is a single slot the day after tomorrow, which the Futin Putos claim as their own, in a most raucous manner. But I do not agree with them, and this has been the source of some contention. My preference would be to send them hopping back to the Dark Forest. I hesitate only because they are popular with a segment of the audience which I cannot ignore."

"Hm," said Moncrief. "They seem a most intemperate group."

The ghost of a grim smile twitched Zank's thin mouth. "They hope to intimidate me, but it is a vain hope."

The Futin Putos had failed to fully close the door to the waiting area. Through the crack, a number of glittering eyes peered.

Moncrief and Zank continued their discussion, unaware of the inspection. Moncrief said, somewhat sententiously: "As a stranger at Cax, perhaps I should restrain my opinions; however, they seem to me a gang of sadistic thugs, lacking all charm."

"It is a fair appraisal," said Zank. "Now tell me something of the Mouse-riders."

"With pleasure! I need not explain that our programs contrast notably with the grotesque capers of the Futin Putos. The Mouse-riders are inspired by a different vision; our sequences combine gallant adventure, romance, and mystery. We are known for our creative imagery, so that every sequence is a mix of music, beauty, and the glamour of far places. I have in mind three sequences, joined by one means or another into a unity. If I may say so, the slot on the day after tomorrow would suit us well, since our stay at Cax will be brief."

"That is reasonable," said Zank, after a moment of consideration. "Especially since it accords with my own inclinations. The Futin Putos shall play the graveyard. If they protest, they may chase each other back to the Dark Forest."

The door slammed open, and the Futin Putos burst in a tumbling rush into Zank's office.

Zank muttered to Moncrief: "Stand behind me, and say nothing."

Moncrief obeyed with alacrity.

Zank spoke harshly: "What are you up to? Leave at once—you trespass my office."

The chief shuffled a step forward. "But you are to blame! You have called us 'stinking brutes' and mocked our artistry; you have schemed with that fat Mouse-rider and have given him our good slot; you have shifted us far and late past the midnight slot, to when the hall is empty! That is betrayal, and someone shall pay the price!"

Zank raised his hand and pointed his finger as if it were a weapon, bringing the Futin Putos to an uncertain halt.

"You are hysterical," he said in a low voice. "Take care, or it will be the worse for you."

Momentarily daunted, the Futin Putos stood crouching and glowering, ten feet from the desk.

Zank spoke again, his voice ringing with metallic overtones. "I am Director, and I arrange production as I see fit! Be happy with what I allow you, or take yourselves back to the Dark Forest! Go now!"

"Not just yet," said the chief. The Futin Putos began to inch forward, making guttural sounds, moaning, wheezing, and hissing.

Moncrief shrank back against the wall. The Futin Putos had closed their minds to reason! How sad, how strange, to die here in the Trevanian.

But Zank seemed unconcerned. "Are you going?" he asked.

"When we have taken our vengeance," replied the chief. "First we will give the Mouse-rider his due, and then we shall deal with you!"

Zank touched a button on his desk. The door into the office slid aside; Bayard stood in the opening.

"Yes, sir?"

"Clear away these intruders," Zank told him. "They are unwelcome."

Bayard faced the Futin Putos. "Clear the office! You heard the Director—you are unwelcome! Lively now; form a single file, if you please!"

The Futin Putos seized Bayard and tossed him back and forth like a large, sprawling bean-bag, ignoring his protests and threats. Finally, tiring of the game, they tossed him out through the door and turned back to Overman Zank. One step after another, they edged again toward the desk.

Without haste, Zank reached forward and touched another button. A heavy semi-circular glass panel lifted from a housing in the floor to create a barrier five feet tall around the desk.

Nonplussed, the Futin Putos paused again. Then the chief vented a contemptuous laugh. "What do you expect from that trifle? I can vault it using a single bound!"

The group howled with mockery.

Leaning back in his chair, Zank said lightly: "Do as you like. I recommend, however, that you leave the office at once, and in good order."

"Only after justice has been done," declared the chief.

"Justice is poised, and ready," said Zank.

The chief hunched his shoulders, crouched, then sprang to the top of the glass wall.

A dazzle of blue sparks ran up his arms and legs and caused all the hairs of his head and beard to expand and stiffen into the semblance of a great puff-ball, each hair crackling with sparks. He uttered a choking cry, then tumbled over into a backward somersault. Touching the floor, his feet spattered blue sparks, which gradually diminished as the chief danced and stepped high, his fellows looking on with slack-jawed wonder.

At this time, six Monitors in black and yellow uniforms filed quietly into the office. Without words they addressed themselves to the Futin Putos. After a brief scuffle, and a few taps with persuasion rods, the acrobats were shackled neck to neck along a chain and, at a signal, were marched unceremoniously from the office.

Moncrief sheepishly stepped from behind the desk. Resuming his place in the chair, he tried to act as if nothing in particular had occurred. After a moment he asked: "What will happen to them now?"

"Nothing very much," said Zank. "They ignore beatings, causing the Monitors to exert themselves to no avail. And incarceration only aggravates the Monitors, as the Futin Putos do nothing but sleep, waking only long enough to befoul their cells. If we send them north to Windy Isle, after a few months their audience raises a fearful protest. But if I write them into the midnight slot for three or four months, they will see the error of their ways, perhaps."

"Hm," mused Moncrief. "Are their threats to be taken seriously?"

Zank considered. "The best that I can tell you is that they are unpredictable. They are malevolent and vengeful without doubt, but whether the act depends upon opportunity, or whether they might be distracted by another exploit, it is hard to say. My advice to you is not to wander by night alone along dark streets." Zank straightened up in his tall chair. "But at this time you should consult Overman Skame to arrange for your stage sets." He touched one of the buttons on his desk.

Bayard limped into the room. "Yes, sir?"

Zank looked him over with raised eyebrows. "Bayard, you will please conduct Master Moncrief to the office of the stage manager."

"Yes, sir; at once!" spoke Bayard.

Zank inspected him coldly. "Then, before you resume your usual duties, step into the dressing room and freshen yourself. At the moment you cut a sorry figure. I insist that my staff take pride in a smart appearance."

"As you say, sir!" replied Bayard. He bowed stiffly, then turned to Moncrief.

"If you are ready, sir, I will take you to Overman Skame."

Moncrief expressed his gratitude to Overman Zank, then followed Bayard from the office.

6

By a cross-passage Bayard led Moncrief to a corridor with a blue stripe, which took them to a massive iron door decorated with a hundred silver rosettes. The plaque read:

OVERMAN LUCAN SKAME
DIRECTOR OF STAGE MANAGEMENT

Bayard spoke a few words of reassurance. "Overman Skame has an easy disposition and will always listen to your ideas. You may find him a bit startling at first, but pay no heed." He touched a pad, and the door slid aside. "I wish you luck."

Bayard bowed, then turned back along the corridor.

Moncrief stepped forward but was halted by the impact of what confronted him. Chaotic clutter appeared to occupy the entire volume of the office, except at the far end, where he saw Overman Skame sitting at an extraordinary desk, opposite a pair of clerks hunched over workstations.

Moncrief was unattended. He blinked and looked from right to left, up to the high ceiling, and down to the floor. The room was full of tables laden with contrivances of unknown purpose, as well as more familiar devices.

Moncrief moved slowly forward, appraising the concatenation of shape, color, and complication that lay around him. Cases displayed hundreds of animals, the denizens of as many worlds; dolls wearing characteristic costumes stood in groups or worked at typical tasks. Everywhere, in no perceptible order, stood modeled structures from many times and places. There were replicas of private dwellings; pavilions and palaces, odd little bungalows, and mountain lodges; there were towers, and tumbles of cones and spheres. From the ceiling on bronze chains hung lamps and lanterns of a hundred styles, some old, some archaic, others primitive, all aglow with appropriate sources of illumination. Interspersed were hundreds of mechanical and electrical devices of unknown purpose. Along the walls, completely encircling the room, shelves supported tracks along which moved vehicles of many descriptions, some emitting small hoots and whistles.

Moncrief gave up trying to assimilate the variety contained in the office. He came to Skame's desk, an object of eccentric design, at its basis a long table almost four feet wide, bent into a semi-circle with the director seated centrally, clasped by wings to right and left.

Skame's attention was fixed upon the pages of a large folio, depicting fashionable young women, not necessarily Blenk, bodies and limbs twisted into odd postures, wearing garments of extreme style. So intent was his interest that he seemed oblivious to Moncrief, who had come to a halt in front of the desk.

Moncrief studied Overman Skame. Here, he thought, was a man of undoubtedly distinctive character. Like Zank, and perhaps Bayard, he appeared to differ from the typical Blenk stock, as if there might be an admixture of another blood-line. Shimerati? Moncrief wondered. Skame was tall and gaunt, with narrow shoulders and thin arms. His face was long, pale, and narrow, with a thin nose, pale green eyes under near-invisible eyebrows, and a wide crooked mouth. He wore a loose robe striped dark blue and green, with a globular opal, two inches in diameter, dangling from his neck on a fine iron chain; on his head was a flat-crowned hat of heavy tan stuff with an extremely wide brim, worn rakishly aslant.

Overman Skame at last became aware of Moncrief. Closing the folio, he swung around in his chair. "Sir, you must excuse me; I became absorbed in thought. I was, so it appears, oblivious to all else. In any case, you now have my full attention; how can I help you? But first— please be seated! Remove the cloak of angel feathers from yonder chair, and use it properly; then we shall see to your business."

Moncrief followed the instructions, then introduced himself. "I am Marcel Moncrief, master of the Mouse-rider troupe. We have been scheduled into a slot on the day after tomorrow; Overman Zank has advised me to consult you at once in regard to such stage properties as I may require."

"Yes; just so. What is the nature of your program?"

"We shall present a medley of three sequences, each different from the others. I hope that this will not tax your resources."

Skame smiled and shook his head, setting the wide brim of his hat into flexible motion. "That is unlikely. At the Trevanian, we can provide almost any scenic effect, interior or exterior. For certain extravagant effects, such as naval battles, or the destruction of grand cities, or struggles between grotesque monsters of stupendous size, or astronomical spectacles such as collisions between black holes, sunspots, or other galactic convulsions, we use holographic projection. In short, we can produce whatever stage set you can stipulate in a very short time."

Moncrief spoke in awe: "That is most impressive!"

Skame laughed, almost waggishly. "So it must seem—still, our basic system is quite simple. If you like, I will explain it to you."

"I am indeed interested!"

Skame straightened in his chair. "The Trevanian stage is oblate, with a wall across the central diameter. While the half facing the audience is in use, the stagehands arrange the concealed half, using any of the thousands of components in our warehouses. At the end of the scene, the curtain falls and the stage rotates, so that when the curtain rises again, a new setting is revealed. Now, if you will supply me information regarding your troupe and your sequences, also the sets you have in mind, I will put the processes into motion."

Moncrief did as requested. When he had finished, Skame ruminated for a time, then said, "The sequences, for the most part, are ingenious. The contrast of mood between the first and second sequences is effective. The first exerts a strange force; events move with the ponderous momentum of fate itself."

"I am pleased to hear your favorable opinion," said Moncrief modestly.

Skame inclined his head, causing his hat to undulate. "The second sequence uses a different mood, as gay and happy as a frolic among white and yellow flowers! The concept of the three girls each trying to bring life to the marble statue, with its erotic intimations, is fascinating. The final scene, where the girls dance off across the glade, and the statue—at last aroused—struggles to follow, but can only totter and fall among the reeds, while the girls dance away, will pull at many a heartstring."

Moncrief gave a shrug of deprecation. "I am fortunate in the quality of my troupe."

Skame pursed his lips judiciously. "No doubt! In regard to the final sequence, I confess to puzzlement. This piece, for all its graceful attributes, seems a bit avant-garde for a Blenk audience."

Moncrief laughed indulgently. "Absurd! It is intended as a coda, to unify the entire program."

Skame was dubious. "A 'coda'? Few Blenks will recognize the word, much less your intent—even should astonishment allow them to think."

"No great matter," replied Moncrief. "The effect will be the same; after a blink or two, happy laughter will be heard, along with shouts of applause."

Skame brooded a moment, then gave a slight shrug. "Possibly so. I suspect that in any event no great harm will be done, except perhaps a premature birth or two. But the Blenks would certainly prefer a trained animal actor, or an erotic little farce."

"Not possible! My animals, and the girls, are intensely puritanical. They would never show so much as their bare bottoms, unless they were jumping from a window to escape a fire in their bedroom. As for our other concerns, I hope that everything is within your competence?"

"For the first two sequences, there is no great problem. Each has a few difficulties, which our technicians can solve without trouble. As for the third sequence, we have problems of another kind, but again they are all soluble. We shall bring out paraphernalia from our medieval warfare collections. The equipment is both massive and impressive."

"Excellent!" said Moncrief. "Now then, what of costumerie?"

"It shall be as you specify. You may inspect my folios, if you like. You will find an adequate range of choices."

After a pleasant half hour of exploration among Skame's folios,

Moncrief settled upon costumes which he considered optimum for his purposes.

"Very good," said Skame. "You choose with a sensitive eye. If you will bring in your personnel tomorrow morning for a fitting, the costumes will be ready by early afternoon."

"I appreciate your assistance," Moncrief told him. "It has been more than invaluable. The Trevanian must be the grandest theater in the Reach, certainly within the scope of my experience!"

"Thank you," said Skame. "I value your opinions."

"One small point," said Moncrief. "For the evening's performance, the troupe and the crew of the *Glicca* will arrive at the Trevanian aboard the ship's flitter. Where can they most expeditiously land?"

Skame answered without hesitation. "There is a landing plat at the northern wall of the Trevanian, on the second level, which could not be more convenient. It is designed for those Shimerati who choose to arrive for the performance by personal air-car, but it is never fully occupied. A hall leads from the plat to a parlor of sorts, adjacent to the stage. Elevators lead to the upper balconies, but these are seldom in use. A bank of seats provides an intimate view of the stage; I recommend that the crew use this facility."

Moncrief again expressed his thanks, and took his leave.

7

The next morning, Myron crossed to the office of the Port Director. He found Rico Yail as before, lounging behind his massive desk.

Yail gave Myron a casual nod and indicated a chair. "Seat yourself, and show me the papers you are carrying so carefully."

Myron settled into the chair and slid his charts across the desk. Yail sat forward and studied the itinerary with interest. At last he looked up to Myron.

"So far as I can tell, without a calculator, the routing seems as efficient as it can be. What are these red marks here, by Glame on Sussea, and again at Croy on New Hope?"

"The explanation is a bit complicated," said Myron. "After leaving First Camp on Welters, we travel to Glame, with the next halt at Croy. But if you refer to your chart you will notice that Fluter is not too far off the route. At Coro-coro a band of pilgrims is awaiting transit to Impy's Landing on Kyril; it would be convenient for us to detour to Fluter, pick up the pilgrims, then continue to Croy—especially if you could find us a parcel of cargo for Fluter."

"That can be done, easily enough."

"After Kyril, we proceed to Ocean City on Lavendry, which is the last stop on the list. After Lavendry, we veer off toward Naharius, where we have some small private business."

"Naharius?" Yail became pensive. "I have heard rumors regarding Naharius—not necessarily credible, but certainly provocative."

Myron smiled sadly. "My aunt went to Naharius, to learn the secrets of youth and beauty. I wonder what she found."

Yail looked off through the window with a musing half-smile. "Rumors flit along the spaceways like fireflies in the deep woods. Sometimes they are fascinating. No doubt quiet tales are told even of Blenkinsop, the five cities, the Shimerati, even the outcasts of the Dark Forest."

Yail squared himself to his desk. "Now then, the rugs. You can expect a profitable transaction. I have put quiet inquiries to five important magazines in the four outer cities; the response was immediate. I received offers ranging from four hundred sols per rug to four hundred and twenty-five, subject to inspection, which I tentatively accepted. Subject to your approval, the inspector will be arriving shortly, along with a dray."

"I approve. It seems a good price."

"I think so myself. As soon as the rugs are discharged, my warehousemen will begin to load cargo. You should be buttoned up before midnight, and ready for departure in the morning."

"We will be on hand one more day," said Myron. "Moncrief and his troupe play the Trevanian tomorrow evening. We will leave the morning after next."

The telephone at Yail's elbow chimed; he picked up the unit. "Director Yail here; how can I help you?"

The response prompted Yail to change his manner to an even, impersonal formality.

"No, sir; that is not the way of it. What you suggest was far from our intent." Yail listened, then said: "I am acting as an informal adviser in the case. The principal is a young off-worlder, of good character, but unaccustomed to Blenk trade practices. He is quite willing to deal with Monomarche, all else being equal." After listening again, Yail responded: "There are forty-six rugs, of prime export quality, direct from Star Home. The asking price is five hundred sols per rug. So far, our high offer has been four hundred and twenty-five."

The conversation continued. Finally Yail said, "I will submit your offer to the principal, who is now here in my office. A moment, if you please." He turned to Myron. "Monomarche offers four hundred and thirty-five sols per rug, subject to inspection. Shall I accept?"

"By all means!" said Myron.

Yail followed Myron's instructions, then put down the handpiece. He told Myron: "The deed is done. There will be no delay; the dray and the inspector will be here within the hour."

"They will bring the money?"

"Of course! Money is the life-blood of commerce." Yail calculated. "After my commission, you will net eighteen thousand seven hundred and sixty-eight sols. Does that accord with your figures?"

"Exactly."

"It has been a profitable transaction," said Yail. "I wish for many more of such happy occurrences."

"I as well!"

"One detail remains," said Yail. "I must terminate the tentative arrangement initiated with Overman Garloc of the Parre magazine."

Yail spoke into the telephone with Overman Garloc and made his apologies, which Garloc received with formal decorum. Yail put the telephone aside with relief.

Myron said: "As soon as the rugs are discharged, the warehousemen may start loading the cargo. With appropriate bills of lading, the *Glicca* will be ready for departure."

TEN

1

At the end of the day, close upon dusk, Schwatzendale unshipped the flitter from its bay and flew the Mouse-riders, along with Captain Maloof, Wingo, and Myron, to the landing plat on the northern wall of the Trevanian.

The group entered the great hall. The Mouse-riders went to the dressing rooms to prepare for the first scene while the crew of the *Glicca* located the parlor recommended by Overman Skame, where they found seats with an unobstructed view of the stage.

The hall began to fill with early arrivals hoping to secure favorite seats. Some had stopped at the stalls which lined the main corridor for bags of delicacies: fried clams, sweet sausages, tripe-sticks and the like, to fortify them during the performance. Others had made purchases of another sort; dead fish, packets of carrion, rotting fruit, and buckets of slime and ordure, which they would use to rebuke an inept performer. A warehouse under the theater maintained an inventory of such commodities, in volume.

Time passed. The lights flickered and dimmed; from high speakers issued a music of brass horns, gongs, and drums, in march-time cadence. A heavy gong sounded three clangorous tones, and the music ended.

A voice spoke, filling the hall. "The Trevanian tonight presents a program of unusual excellence! First, the Silurians undertake a remarkable exercise, which they call 'Sinuosities', and which you will call 'incredible'!"

From the audience came a spatter of applause.

The voice continued: "Then, Pooder Boy explains how he copes with his conniving mother. Po-po's wits are taxed to the utmost. Is his conduct proper?"

From the audience came enthusiastic applause.

"Next we present an off-world troupe of wide reputation. Master Moncrief and the Mouse-riders will bring us three sequences from their vast repertory!"

The applause was perfunctory, and punctuated by a few dispirited yelps.

The announcer went on to list the remaining events, then added: "Owing to administrative technicalities, the Futin Putos will not appear on tonight's program, nor at any time in the near future."

A chorus of hoots and hisses greeted the announcement.

The voice continued, unheeding: "And now, the Silurians, and their astonishing 'Sinuosities'!"

The curtains drew aside, revealing a scaffold constructed of a dozen poles eight feet high, standing six feet apart in a double row and joined at the tops by bars and cross-bars.

From the left side of the stage, six round gray bundles rolled out on the stage, each halting beside a pole. Each of the bundles unrolled, to become a long shape sheathed head to foot in gray fabric. At some signal, imperceptible to the audience, the six shapes reached for the poles and slid up to the cross-bars. They formed themselves into a pattern, which persisted for ten heartbeats, then broke apart, and so the first phase of the 'Sinuosities' began.

The gray shapes moved back and forth, over and under, veering and twisting, creating patterns past comprehension, returning finally to the original stasis. They held for a time; then they separated, and the second phase began. Now they moved at a ponderous tempo, with fateful decision, as if imparting an awesome secret; then quietly the shapes returned again to stasis.

For twenty seconds the shapes remained still; then they broke into the third phase. Now the permutations were deliberate, and baffling to the onlookers; sometimes only four undulated across the bars, sometimes there seemed to be eight. Over time the patterns evolved and collapsed through unlikely resolutions, conveying emotions without name. Finally, the shapes quietly slid down the poles and rolled off the stage, and the curtains closed.

For a time the audience sat blinking, then gradually rendered a tentative applause, as if not sure what they might be applauding.

The lights brightened, permitting the audience to recover their aplomb. Time was allowed for those wishing refreshment to visit the stalls; then the lights once more were extinguished.

From the high speakers came the announcer's voice. "The Silurians are gone, leaving us with our eyes pointed different directions. But no matter, somewhere nearby is Po-po the Pooder Boy, who always has his tragic woe, and an occasional triumph—as when he was asked to bring a gift of pooders to his dying grandfather! More often, his tales are tragic. Pooder is near at hand—listen!"

The audience went silent, straining for the first inkling of Po-po the Pooder Boy. An area of soft illumination remained at the center of the stage. Something appeared through the crack where the curtains came together—a nubbin so small that it escaped notice. The object thrust farther out over the stage, and now a faint rasping noise, like a rat gnawing at wainscoting, could be heard growing louder: "Crunch, Crunch, Crunch!"

The audience at last identified the protruding object as a nose, and gasped in delighted recognition. The curtain twitched; through the gap peered a moony face, with pink cheeks, lank snuff-brown hair, and a snub button of a nose. Po-po was gnawing on something he held to his mouth; he swallowed the last morsel. Then, with a sly smirk for the audience, he drew back, and the curtain swung shut.

"Po-po! Po-po! Po-po!" cried the audience, stamping their feet. Someone shouted: "Pooders by the score! Come for your pooders!"

The curtain parted, and out upon the stage capered Po-po, wearing a loose brown blouse and russet pantaloons flaring below the knees. He was notably plump and an inch or two shorter than ordinary. A saucy red cap constrained his hair; his eyes were round and set wide of his nose. For a moment he performed an odd little jig, then he halted, and began to chant in a reedy singsong voice.

"Oh, I am the Pooder Boy! I eat them where I find them. They try to rob me of my precious pooders, but I sniff them out and have a feast! My pooders were in a pot, but when I lifted the lid, a rat looked up, the last of my pooders in his whiskers; my mother thought to make her feast, but I took the pooders and put the boiled rat on her plate! I ate my private dinner."

Po-po took a small pooder from his pocket and tossed it high into the air, then ran below and caught it in his mouth.

"Yesterday a black dog committed an offense; he stole my choice pooder! I tracked him through the bushes, then seized my cudgel and beat him with proper zest. At this time, another black dog walked past, holding my choice pooder in his jaws! I had been beating the wrong dog! No matter, the mistake was soon mended, and once more I owned my pooder!" Po-po performed a few steps of his eccentric jig.

"Oh, I am the Pooder Boy; I spy them out; I sniff them down from their aroma; I steal them from my avaricious mother! I spank the baby and take his pooder! Oh, I am the Pooder Boy!"

Po-po continued the saga of his woes and triumphs, singing praises of the sublime tuber, interspersing his chant with capers and jigs. He attempted a somersault, which he failed to execute; for a time, he struggled with his broad bottom in the air, pooders tumbling from his pockets. At last he completed the revolution and began a frantic search for the truant pooders. With pooders retrieved, and to full applause, he disappeared through the curtains.

The applause continued; Po-po returned to the stage and cut a caper, eliciting whistling, stamping, and howling approval, then once again was gone.

The lights came on, permitting patronage of the stalls.

The hall returned to darkness. From the high speakers came the announcer's voice: "Po-po has left us for a time; he is anxious for his supper, which I suspect will be a fine dish of pooders—possibly furnished by his mother. No doubt he will return before too long with the latest news. But at this moment, Master Moncrief and the remarkable Mouse-riders are on hand; they bring us a program of three exotic adventures, in a wonderful land of magic and beauty! I now introduce Master Moncrief, for your approval!"

After Po-po's homely foolishness, the audience had no ready welcome for off-world interlopers and accorded the introduction only minimal enthusiasm.

Moncrief stepped out upon the stage, and his suave appearance did nothing to excite the sympathy of the audience. He wore an elegant suit of black velvet and a gray cape embroidered at the hem with a tracery of hermetic signs. Several whinnies and yelps greeted him as he smilingly surveyed the audience.

Still smiling, Moncrief inclined his head to left and right, by way of a polite salute. Then he spoke, his amplified voice sounding from the high speakers.

"Denizens of the city Cax, with its noble heights and hinterlands! I have little to tell you, except that it is a privilege to play the Trevanian—surely one of the premier theaters of the Gaean Reach! I suggest that you are about to discover a unique experience, which is to say, a presentation by the remarkable Mouse-riders! Nothing more! I will detain you no longer!" Moncrief performed a stately salute and left the stage.

The audience, a trifle mollified, gave a spatter of applause, then sat back to judge the marvels at which Moncrief had hinted.

The curtains parted to reveal a tropical jungle, with a range of purple mountains created by holographic projection looming across the background.

The sequence was played out to its macabre last moments, and the curtains closed upon the stage. The audience sat silent for a space, evidently uncertain as to how they felt about so strange a production, but finally reacted with cautious applause.

The curtains parted again, now upon an arcadian landscape. The sequence started with dancing nymphs in short white kirtles and developed along its fateful progression to the final pathos, the statue submerged in the reeds.

The curtains closed upon the desolate meadow. The applause was moderate, as if the audience were puzzled as to what should be the proper response to these unusual sequences. Once again, Moncrief stepped out on the stage in front of the curtains. He held up his hands, as if graciously calming tumultuous applause.

"We have presented two sequences for your apperception; I am pleased to find such keen awareness of our creative purposes. 'Art' is the transmission of emotion through the use of mutually recognizable symbols—clearly the Blenks of Cax are strongly receptive to the same impulses which propel our esthetic purposes!

"In appreciation of this receptivity, instead of a third sequence, which might come as an anticlimax, we will now produce what amounts to a coda to our first two pieces—by which we can best express our truest sentiments toward the Blenks and the fascinating Blenk civilization! We have visited many worlds; we have observed many distinctive cultures, but none has made quite the impression as has the culture of the Blenks!

"In sum, we are anxious to express our gratitude for your hospitality and your generous appreciation of our program. Our hope is to surprise and delight you—so now, we will finish our performance in a way you will long remember!"

Moncrief turned to look off-stage and made a signal. The entire Mouse-rider troupe appeared, now wearing ordinary clothes. "Aha!" cried Moncrief. "Here is our full complement." He spoke to the troupe. "You may take your posts, with dispatch and precision."

The six members of the troupe jumped down upon the shelf which bordered the stage. At intervals along the shelf were six pairs of massive shapes concealed under tarpaulins.

"Now then," said Moncrief. "Assume your positions." The three girls and the two Klutes each went to stand behind one of the shrouded shapes, while Moncrief stepped down to post himself behind the remaining brace of objects.

"Attention! I will count. You must act with full precision. Now, ready: One!"

All bent forward and pulled the tarpaulins loose, and dropped them to the floor. Revealed were twelve massive howitzers, their orifices covered with tinsel and rosettes of pink ribbons.

"Two!" called Moncrief. All put their hands to red buttons, left and right.

"Three!"

Twelve buttons were touched, creating twelve horrendous blasts of sound, and a great volume of stuffs spewed out over the audience. But instead of the sweetmeats, trinkets, fruit jellies, and perfumed confetti which Moncrief had installed, the audience was pelted with dead fish, ordure, shredded intestines, decaying fruit, and a dozen other stuffs. Some of the material ranged up into the second balcony, causing the Hummers to call out in surprise; only the Shimerati escaped outrage, and many congratulated themselves upon being present this remarkable evening.

For a brief period, a peculiar silence held the hall. Then a slow rumble of infinite menace arose, swelling into a wild reckless roar. The audience began to move toward the stage.

Moncrief reacted instantly. "Up!" he cried to the troupe. "Up, and out!"

The troupe needed no instruction. They jumped up from the shelf and ran to the off-stage parlor, with Moncrief close behind. Already the first wave of maddened Blenks was clambering up the shelf. In the wings at the far end of the stage, Moncrief saw several Futin Putos punching their fists into the air, showing white teeth in glee. "The revenge of the Futin Putos is pitiless," Moncrief told himself.

The troupe, Moncrief, and the crew of the *Glicca* ran out upon the plat and flung themselves aboard the flitter. Schwatzendale took the craft aloft just as the Blenks came racing out to crowd upon the landing, staring and shouting in thwarted passion after the departing craft.

Back at the spaceport, Schwatzendale and Myron hoisted the flitter into its bay, then boarded the ship, which promptly raised from the field.

Cax dwindled below. Up through the overcast rose the *Glicca*, then slanted away into the sky, leaving Blenkinsop behind.

Eleven

1

Departing Blenkinsop, the *Glicca* set off along an itinerary which after traversing remote regions of the Reach would eventually bring it back to Coro-coro on Fluter.

As time passed, shipboard routines were gradually resumed, but with differences. Moncrief had become morose; owing to his haste in taking leave of the Trevanian, he had neglected to collect his fee—a lapse which galled him to the quick. He spent hours planning reprisal against the Trevanian bursars, meanwhile neglecting his work with the Mouse-riders.

The Klutes had become more surly than ever and sat hunched in a corner of the saloon, glowering and muttering to each other. The girls had been altered in a more subtle fashion. The final moments at the Trevanian had intimidated them; never before had they been awed by events, and they had lost something of their careless innocence.

The first port of call was Falziel on the world Mirsten. The single habitable continent was dominated by a central mountain massif, with the lands along the littoral overgrown by forests where off-world species grew on equal terms with indigenous varieties. The population diligently exploited the resources of the forests, exporting precious wood to Cax and elsewhere.

At Falziel were the offices of the Institute; originally the Dendrological Institute, now the governing organization which exercised both executive and judicial authority over all of Mirsten.

Excerpt from *Handbook to the Planets:* Falziel

The traveler may wander far and wide across the Reach, but never will he find a city comparable in sheer bravura to Falziel.

The component structures occupy a site less than a mile on a side. The boundaries are strict, there are no annexes or subordinate communities; the city is an organic unit. The magnificent structures occupy sites along the avenues, some reaching seven stories high, others less. All are built to exactly the same specifications, differing only in size, and all show the same facade, which through some magic of proportion achieves an indefinable elegance. Each is surmounted by a dome of glossy red-brown mahogany, with a slender finial rising from the apex.

The inhabitants of Mirsten are a practical folk, but with a paradoxical dread of ghosts and other unnatural beings to be found in dark lonely places. Beliefs are most common in remote mountain villages, where on dark stormy nights the folk huddle around their firesides and impart the eerie lore to their fascinated children.

In due course, the *Glicca* descended upon the Falziel spaceport. The slanting light of late afternoon exhibited the fabulous city, with its hundreds of burnished mahogany domes, to dramatic advantage.

Immediately after arrival, Maloof and Myron crossed to the administration building to arrange for discharge of cargo. They found an office with a sign reading:

PORT DIRECTOR
ARMAN ROUFT
ENTER

The two pushed open the door and stepped into an office panelled in pale brown wood. Behind a counter stood a middle-aged man of moderate stature, inclined to a modest portliness which indicated a penchant for easy living. His face was round and cheerful, under a ruff of thick white hair. As Maloof and Myron approached, he put aside the earthenware demijohn which he had been inspecting, and spoke with a jovial lilt: "Gentlemen, if you are looking for the Port Director, you have found him. I am Arman Rouft, at your service."

Maloof introduced himself and Myron. "We are officers of the *Glicca*, which has just arrived, as you no doubt have noticed. We carry cargo for Falziel, which was put aboard at Cax. We are ready to discharge this cargo at your convenience."

"The cargo must wait for tomorrow, since the warehousemen have gone for the day."

"Quite all right," said Maloof. "We will have the opportunity to explore your remarkable city."

Rouft chuckled and shook his head. "If you are like the typical spacemen on the loose in a strange city, you may be disappointed. There are no resorts, nor any social parlors, where folk revel without restraint. We are, on the whole, a staid people."

Maloof laughed incredulously. "It was not a staid people who built this audacious city!"

"The notions do not intermesh," said Rouft. "It is probably this very trait which allowed Falziel its existence." He looked from Maloof to Myron. "You are puzzled?"

Maloof acknowledged as much. "Perhaps you will explain this paradox."

"Certainly. The tale is not overlong, but talking is dry work; luckily, a remedy is at hand."

He placed three goblets on the counter and, lifting the demijohn, poured tots of a tawny liquor into each. He slid two of the goblets across the counter to Maloof and Myron. "This is our prime plum brandy. Neophytes are warned to treat it with respect!"

Maloof and Myron took up their goblets and saw that they were carved with grace and finesse from cylinders of dense black wood.

Rouft raised his goblet and intoned a toast: "To tall trees, and fruitful women." He tossed the contents of the goblet down his throat, and swallowed at a gulp.

Maloof and Myron tested the liquor more cautiously, finding it heady, volatile, and intense. In the end, they followed the example set by Rouft and threw the tot against the back of their throats, where it exploded into pungent vapor.

Rouft asked solicitously: "Are you ready for a second tot? A man can hop only so far on one leg."

"Not just yet," said Maloof in a thick voice. "Of course, I cannot speak for Myron."

"Perhaps in a moment," said Myron.

Rouft, however, poured himself a second tot, and as before swallowed it at a gulp.

"Aha!" he said. "We can now proceed. I revert to a time six hundred years ago, when the old port city Skolpnes was destroyed in a great flood. Despite the flood, this was a time of prosperity, and the factors of the Dendrological Institute proposed to rebuild the city— but in a way to best represent the commercial consequence of Mirsten.

"An architectural genius named Riyban Trill resided then on Mirsten. Trill had worked far and wide across the Reach, achieving a remarkable reputation for superlative creativity and technical excellence, and had settled on Mirsten to live in semiretirement. From the first, the factors were resolved that Trill should be associated with the grand new project, though he was well past his first youth, and not in the best of health.

"A formal proposal was put to Trill soliciting his creative talents. Trill considered the proposal for a week, then responded with a document specifying the conditions under which he would accept the commission. In effect, he required total control over every phase of the project, without the possibility of interference of any sort. He allowed the factors only two options: they could either accept or reject his requirements. Flexibility or compromise was not offered.

"Grudgingly, the factors accepted Trill's conditions. The contract was signed and embossed with the seal of the Dendrological Institute, and Trill immediately went to work. The site was surveyed, a grid of avenues delineated, and a pilot building erected on a site beside the central plaza. When completed, the structure stood seven stories high; it was built completely of rich, red-brown mahogany, and was surmounted by a dome of ravishing rotundity. Ultimately the building would house the offices of the Dendrological Institute.

"The building met with universal approval; even Trill's detractors were silenced. But at this precise moment, with Trill's career at its zenith, his health deserted him; he suffered a debilitating stroke which enfeebled him, curtailing most of his physical functions.

"Trill realized that he could not complete the city as he had planned, but at almost the same instant he arrived at a scheme which obviated all his difficulties; with one stroke of the pen, he ordained that every building of the city should be constructed to the same specification as the pilot building, varying only in size.

"His boldness astonished everyone. From the factors came a storm of protest—along with the opinion that, since Trill's ploy was clearly the irresponsible whim of a madman, it must be invalidated forthwith. But the idea stimulated unease in the public. I mentioned that we are a staid race; the trait includes an ingrained regard for individual responsibility, and the sanctity of a formal contract. Eventually, the factors' suggestion that Trill's contract be violated aroused such outrage that the factors abandoned their plan.

"And so the new city came into being, and almost immediately was considered a work of ultimate genius. Trill was honored as never before; he was granted a patent of nobility and made a full Fellow of the Institute, which awarded him a gold coruscation to wear on his shoulder.

"So there you have it: Falziel, a tribute both to Trill's reckless creativity, and the steadfast faith of the population." Rouft indicated the demijohn. "Shall we try another dram or two, to memorialize the occasion?"

Maloof looked toward Myron, who gave a fatalistic shrug. "Perhaps, then, just a taste."

Rouft tilted the demijohn with a loose wrist, replenishing the goblets to their former level, then proposed another toast: "To tall women, and fruitful trees!"

The goblets were dealt with as before; the ardent fluid was consumed in appropriate style.

When Maloof found his voice, he asked, somewhat haltingly: "Can you recommend a tavern where we can sample the local ale?"

"Easily. The 'Court of King Gambrinus' instantly comes to mind; it is a place where I myself am a frequent visitor. The Darkling Stout is somewhat heavy for my taste, but the Bitter Silurian is beyond reproach. The tavern is convenient to hand; proceed along yonder boulevard to the first intersection, then turn left. Fifty yards ahead you will notice an arched portico supporting an effigy representing the demigod Atlas, carrying the globe of Old Earth on his shoulders. This effigy, by custom, marks every tavern of Falziel."

"Interesting!" said Maloof. "The information might be invaluable, if we had more time to explore the town."

Rouft sighed. "I often wish that I could drink in two taverns at the same instant. It would save much wasted energy, wandering to and fro."

Myron muttered, half to himself: "If anyone were capable of such a feat, it would be our engineer, Fay Schwatzendale."

Shortly after sunset, Captain Maloof and his crew sauntered forth from the spaceport; Moncrief and the Mouse-riders elected to remain aboard the *Glicca*. The men proceeded up the boulevard, turned at the intersection, and presently came upon the Court of King Gambrinus. Entering the tavern, the four men found themselves in a long, narrow, dimly lit chamber with a vaulted ceiling, and walls panelled with polished planks of wood the color of dark honey. Tables were scattered along the length of the chamber, with a bar flanking the wall to the right.

Business was slack. At a table far to the rear, a pair of old men sat hunched over a chessboard, with tankards at their elbows. On the wall behind them an artist of long ago had painted King Gambrinus, sitting in state on a majestic golden throne; in one hand he held a scepter, in the other a tankard of foaming brew. His expression as he surveyed the chamber was at once stern, yet benign.

Behind the bar stood a fat bartender, wearing a white smock and small white cap. He took note of the newcomers, displaying minimal interest, and spoke in a ripe, rolling baritone. "Good evening, gentlemen; you come at a late hour. Still, we will take pains to accommodate your thirst." He flourished his hand toward the tables. "You may sit where you notice your correct hermetic sign. Or if you prefer, I can advise you."

"That might be wise," said Maloof. "The signs are somewhat arcane."

"True," said the bartender. He reflected a moment, then pointed. "Yonder is a congenial table. It is dependable and has supported thousands of tankards with only rare spillage. It seems to induce kindness and liberality, even among strangers. There has never been a glottal congestion at this table, nor has anyone ever failed to pay his score."

The four seated themselves at the recommended table. The bartender asked: "What can I serve you?"

"Describe our choices," said Maloof.

"Very well. Our beers and ales are excellent. We serve Darkling Stout, Dankwel's Special, Wyvern, Old Spiteful, Pale Gothic, and Bitter Silurian Ale."

Maloof opted for the Bitter Silurian Ale, as did his companions.

The ale was served in tankards turned from billets of a dense dark wood. Maloof studied his tankard at length, turning it this way and that. He asked the bartender: "Does this black wood have a name?"

"Of course! It is swamp-gnarl, a tree which grows half-submerged in the swamp, never more than nine feet tall and four feet wide. The tree cannot be cut in place and must be pulled up entire by a floating derrick. The trunk is trimmed, cut into baulks, and seasoned for five years; then it is sliced into billets, and turned in a special lathe to become unfinished vessels known as 'blanks.' These are boiled in a special oil for three days, then shaped, carved, and finished by hand. Now they are tankards, no two alike! They cannot be broken, and last forever."

Maloof held up the heavy black tankard. "It has an extraordinary appeal, and seems to complement the ale. Are they available for purchase, and if so, where?"

The bartender looked at the clock upon the wall behind him, then said: "My information is both good and bad." He pointed through the window, toward a shop on the opposite side of the street with a green starburst over the door. "Yonder shop is directed by a true galardinet named Dame Florice. She sells curios, objects of vertu, and miscellaneous oddments to tourists, spacemen, and local folk alike, making no distinction so long as they can pay. She keeps an adequate supply of tankards, which she sells at reasonable prices. That is the good news. In five minutes, she turns off the lights and closes her shop with inexorable determination—that is the bad news."

Maloof stared up at the clock. "Five minutes?"

"Ten seconds less. You have time to finish your ale, pay the score, and dash across the street, with about two minutes and thirty seconds remaining to make your purchases—if Dame Florice sympathizes with your plight. I myself close at the same instant."

The four men drained their tankards. Between gulps, Myron gestured toward the chess players, one of whom had just made a move.

"What of them?"

The bartender shrugged. "They will continue their game by candle-light, and I shall find them here in the morning."

Maloof paid the score and, departing the Court of King Gambrinus, the four men hastened across the street to the shop under the green starburst.

Dame Florice was a tall woman with a long bony nose; she eyed the last-minute customers with disfavor. "You are overly casual; the shop is about to close. Business is done for the day."

"Not quite," declared Maloof. "There is time for you to sell me six swamp-gnarl tankards."

Myron added, "While you are serving Captain Maloof, it will save time if you will bring me six tankards, as well."

Dame Florice spoke sharply: "By the time I bring your orders from the stock-room, it will be time to turn out the lights. Do you propose to pay in the dark?"

"It might be more expedient if you would extend your business hours by another minute, or perhaps a minute and a half," Maloof suggested. "But you must do as you think best."

Dame Florice turned on her heel and strode off to her stock-room.

The four men took advantage of the delay to look about the shop. Myron came upon a small effigy of Atlas on his knees, supporting Old Earth on his shoulders. The figure was about six inches tall and was carved from a dense white wood. Ever the romantic, Myron was charmed; here was an amusing souvenir of Falziel and its taverns. He added the item to his purchases. A moment later, he discovered a rack from which hung a number of delicate chains about five feet long. Looking closely, Myron saw that the chains were carved with exquisite nicety from long wands of pale wood.

By this time Dame Florice had returned from the stock-room with the tankards, and had reconciled herself to the unprecedented experience of working after the close of regulation business hours. In response to Myron's questions, she explained that the chains were carved by a coterie of old women in an isolated mountain village, and that these women were held to be witches by local folk.

"Sheer nonsense, of course," she added with a frosty smile. "The chains are carved from long shoots of mountain hazel, and the work is uncannily precise, but witchery? Bah—rank superstition!"

Myron noted that despite her words, Dame Florice made a surreptitious sign with the fingers of her left hand. He selected two of the chains, to be used as necklaces to delight a certain Tibbet at Duvray on Alcydon.

The spacemen settled their accounts and, seven minutes after the ordinary closing hour, returned to the spaceport.

The next morning, warehousemen appeared and the cargo was off-loaded.

At noon the *Glicca* lifted from the spaceport; the burnished mahogany domes dwindled below, and the *Glicca* slanted away toward the next port of call.

2

After Falziel, the next two stops were Chancelade on Avente, then Organon on Archimbal.

Despite many similarities, the populations of the two worlds differed significantly in social philosophy. The folk of Avente were tolerant, sensitive to aesthetic subtlety, and intensely aware of themselves as individuals; the people of Archimbal, while of equivalent culture, were gregarious and most comfortable when working in communal groups, guided by precepts of progressivity and comprehensive altruism.

Even before the cargo had been fully discharged, the Port Director of Chancelade offered Myron a parcel of onward cargo on terms so advantageous that Myron immediately agreed to the transaction, though there would be a delay of three or four days before the cargo could be made ready. The layover was welcomed by everyone aboard the *Glicca*, since Chancelade was a pleasant city of many charms; picturesque, romantic, and casually elegant.

The city occupied a parkland at the confluence of three rivers, which were joined by a dozen lazy canals. Along the banks of both rivers and canals were shops, salons, cafes, restaurants, conservatories, and music halls, rendezvous for masked harlequins, gamins, dryads, and nymphs, venues dedicated to the unexpected and the preposterous.

East of the city rose massive mountains with crags and gorges, upland lakes and forests, and dozens of wilderness resorts, some rustic, others refined and luxurious.

Immediately upon arrival, the crew went off to explore the city and test its potentialities. Moncrief went off to solicit employment for the Mouse-riders.

Time passed quickly. Early on the day of departure, the cargo arrived at the spaceport and was loaded aboard the *Glicca*. The crew opted for a final afternoon and evening out, visiting their favorite haunts about the city.

During the afternoon, with the crew absent, the Mouse-riders boarded the ship, collected their belongings, and departed, never so much as looking back. When the crew returned to the *Glicca*, Maloof discovered a note on the galley table along with a sum of money.

Maloof read the letter aloud: " 'To the esteemed Captain Maloof and others of the crew: by a happy circumstance, we have been offered long-term employment among the mountain resorts. Contracts are lucrative, and we must of necessity accept. Our best wishes to everyone aboard the *Glicca*; you will not soon be forgotten. I enclose funds sufficient to settle our outstanding accounts. With best respect: Marcel Moncrief and the Mouse-riders.' "

Maloof tossed the note down upon the galley table. "So. They are gone." He stared down at the note. "All taken with all, their style of departure is commendable, or so it seems to me."

Wingo spoke, his expression bleak. "The ship will seem very quiet without them."

Schwatzendale leaned back in his chair and stared up at the ceiling. "For a fact, their going was opportune, for everyone. The atmosphere aboard had gone stale; Moncrief was a derelict, his magic fading; the Klutes were like lumps of rancid meat in the shadows. And the girls were feckless creatures from a lost land—they danced their own dances and sang their own songs; they knew nothing of responsibility and distracted us all. They leave behind only bittersweet memories."

Smiling wanly, Maloof said: "That is a moving testimonial."

"It is more like an epitaph," growled Wingo.

"They leave a gap," Myron agreed. "Still, life will be simpler without them."

"Bah!" said Wingo emphatically. "What good is simplicity? Even their foolishness was an event. With the Mouse-riders, anything was possible."

Myron nodded somberly. "Including the possibility that they might never leave the *Glicca*, but remain aboard forever."

Maloof winced. "The idea is alarming."

Myron apologized, and the conversation came to an end.

Early the next morning, the *Glicca* departed Chancelade, and set off toward Archimbal. The ship seemed unnaturally quiet; the corner of the saloon where the Klutes had brooded and muttered seemed curiously naked. Wingo abruptly halted his production of novel pastries. But as time passed, memories of the Mouse-riders became less vivid, and the new reality gradually submerged the old.

3

The *Glicca* arrived at the Organon spaceport halfway through the local morning. Cargo was expeditiously discharged, and the crew set off to explore the city. If, along the way, they chanced to discover a hospitable tavern where they could test the quality of the beer, so much the better.

An omnibus conveyed the four men along a scenic boulevard to the central plaza: an immaculate area paved with slabs of polished granite. At the center, fountains played around the base of a heroic statue celebrating the legendary locator Hans van der Veeke, who had first set foot upon the world Archimbal. He was depicted wearing a black frock coat and a flat black hat; his pose was portentous, with one great arm raised on high, saluting generations of the future. Ranked around the periphery of the plaza were narrow-fronted buildings of a spare, almost gaunt architecture, generally five or six stories high. At the ground level, shops of understated elegance relieved the austerity of the structures in which they were housed. Most sold goods of discreet luxury. There were also restaurants in evidence, as well as a number of agencies and salons.

Upon alighting from the omnibus, the four off-worlders paused to take stock of their surroundings. Inhabitants of the city strolled about the plaza. Men and women alike wore garments of formal cut and excellent quality, as if it were not reputable to appear in public wearing clothes which might not be considered genteel. As they passed, they gave the spacemen quick side-glances, then immediately looked away to avoid any imputation of undignified curiosity.

The four men from the *Glicca* turned their attention to shops around the square, noting restaurants and cafes, but nowhere any establishment suggesting the presence of a tavern. Myron theorized that such premises might be relegated to the back streets, or even a separate district of the city; Wingo agreed that the theory was as plausible as any, and that the mystery in good time would be resolved.

The four men set off around the plaza and soon came to an establishment, apparently a cafe, identified by an ornamental sign as 'The Blue Urn'. Windows under three wide arches afforded a view of persons sitting at tables, taking refreshment of various sorts. At a table nearby, four middle-aged gentlemen of obvious status drank from glass tankards containing amber liquid, under a notable collar of white foam. With one accord the four spacemen entered the Blue Urn and seated themselves at a vacant table.

A tall, gray-haired waiter of stately demeanor, wearing formal garments of impeccable cut, approached the table. He bowed slightly, as if to acknowledge their status as off-worlders, thereby entitled to sympathetic understanding. He spoke in a nicely modulated voice: "Gentlemen, may I enquire your wishes?"

"You may indeed," said Maloof. "We have worked up a thirst—you may bring us your premium bitter ale, in large tankards."

The waiter smilingly shook his head. "We offer no libation of this sort, sir."

"Oh?" demanded Maloof. "What are the gentlemen yonder drinking, with such gusto?"

The waiter politely turned to look. "Of course! They are enjoying our premium Mark Twelve Special, which for a fact is my own favorite."

"In that case," said Maloof, "you may bring me a tankard of the Mark Twelve Special."

The others gave the same instruction, and the waiter departed to fill the orders. He presently returned with four tankards, deftly served them around the table, then withdrew.

Maloof took up his tankard. "For want of a better toast, I salute the ten thousand generations of brewmasters who, through their unflagging genius, have in effect made this moment possible!"

"A noble toast," cried Wingo. "Allow me to add an epilogue. At the last moments of the universe, with eternal darkness converging from all sides, surely someone will arise and cry out: 'Hold back the end for a final moment, while I pay tribute to the gallant brewmasters who have provided us a pathway of golden glory down the fading corridors of time!' And then, is it not possible that a bright gap will appear in the dark, through which the brewmasters are allowed to proceed, to build a finer universe?"

"It is as reasonable as any other conjecture," said Schwatzendale. "But now." The four saluted each other, tilted their tankards, and drank deep draughts.

At this instant Maloof felt that bewildering shock of surprise which would never vanish from his memory. He slowly raised his head and stared at the waiter, who came inquiringly forward. "Sir?"

In a low, passionless voice, Maloof asked: "What is this liquid you have served us, when we called for beer?"

The waiter spoke feelingly: "Sirs, you were served our best barley-water!"

"Barley-water?" cried Maloof huskily.

"Exactly so. I did you a kindness! Alcohol is highly toxic; its use is interdicted on Archimbal."

Schwatzendale asked in a hushed voice: "There is neither beer nor ale to be had in Organon?"

"None at all."

The spacemen glumly paid the score and returned to the space-port. An hour later the *Glicca* departed Organon and set off for the next port of call.

4

The *Glicca* continued along its eccentric course, finally returning to Coro-coro on Fluter.

Immediately upon arrival, the pilgrims converged upon the *Glicca*. Maloof met with Perrumpter Kalash and Cooner, who had become coadjucator; he assured them that the previous commitments remained valid and that the next port of call would be Impy's Landing. Kalash and Cooner expressed satisfaction, then, citing their religious affiliation, argued for a discount from the fares previously quoted. Maloof explained that religion was known to be prevalent on certain over-populated worlds, but was conspicuously absent in space; for this reason, among others, no discounts would be allowed. Grumbling and disgruntled, the pilgrims boarded the *Glicca*, along with their chests of sanctified soil. And so the *Glicca* departed Coro-coro and set off for Impy's Landing on Kyril.

During the voyage Wingo became acquainted with a certain Efraim Cuireg, a peripatetic savant associated with the Institute of Transcendental Metaphysics, at Bantry's Bog on the world Montroy. Cuireg was a gentleman of obvious distinction. His stature was moderate, or a trifle less; his physique was trim, and his habits were fastidious. Under a cap of white hair Cuireg's features were crisp, his gaze cool, his expression austere and somewhat ironic; he carried himself with the erect posture of a patrician.

Cuireg travelled alone, and kept himself aloof from the pilgrims. The pilgrims, in turn, thought him condescending and supercilious. Nevertheless, the Perrumpter tried to include him into the company, and invited him to join the morning colloquies; but Cuireg declined participation. Cooner had evolved an abstruse theory postulating an infinite regression of ever more complex godheads, each subservient to the entity looming behind, with the Gaean race abjectly at the forefront; he deployed his theory before Cuireg, only to encounter a stare so blank and incurious that the confident smile froze on his plump pink cheeks. Cooner recalled urgent business elsewhere.

Wingo found Cuireg's presence an enigma, which gnawed at his curiosity. One day he invited Cuireg to a mid-afternoon collation of tea, scones, and fancy pastries. Cuireg, a dedicated epicure, readily accepted the invitation and appeared precisely upon the appointed hour. He surveyed the delicacies gracing the table with approval, and seated himself at Wingo's direction.

For a time the conversation was general, then at an appropriate moment Wingo put a casual question. "In all candor, I cannot understand why a scholar of your credentials should be travelling to Kyril, like one of the pilgrims, and presumably planning to join the march around the continent. Can you explain?"

"Naturally," said Cuireg with a cool smile. "However, I do not propose to do so, since you would surely find the ideas abstract, and probably beyond your comprehension."

Wingo raised his eyebrows, somewhat taken aback. A singular remark, indeed, and not one calculated to elevate his self-esteem. He sought for a suitable response, and finally said: "Naturally, you have a right to your assumptions, although from my point of view they are far too pessimistic."

Cuireg showed little interest in Wingo's opinion. "Indeed?" He selected a lemon tart from the platter and ingested half of it with a quick snap of small white teeth. "Ah well, no great matter."

"Except that, as we sit here, apparently at our ease, communication has been disrupted."

"Oh?" Cuireg's attention was caught. "You have left me behind."

"Just so!" said Wingo. "If folk want to exchange information, clarity is essential. If they want to confuse each other, various methods exist. They can use glossolalia, or a primitive language of clicks and grunts, or, as a last resort, the esoteric jargon of the Institute."

Cuireg was only mildly interested. "A pungent analysis. To what is it relevant?"

Wingo leaned back in his chair. "In regard to your visit to Kyril, you felt that your remarks would only confuse me. I suspect, however, that if you spoke in the ordinary Gaean idiom, using standard syntax, I should be able to capture the gist of your remarks."

Cuireg was sardonically amused. "Take care, Wingo! The epistemological jungle is dark and deep! There are pitfalls and strange byways, and monsters lurk in the shadows. An intrepid traveller such as yourself, however, should manage to discover at least the basic dogma, which is starkly simple, and germane to our discussion; it asserts that between individuals, exact communication is never possible." He inspected Wingo. "You doubt the proposition? You need only refer to the physical laws of uncertainty—ignoring, of course, the mischievous corollary which states that the laws themselves are laughably uncertain! The lemon tarts, incidentally, are excellent."

Wingo pondered a moment, then shrugged. "This is all very well, but it would seem that you do not concede the reality of 'Truth', at any level whatever."

"'Truth'?" Cuireg made an indolent gesture. "'Truth' is a refuge for weak minds—why concern yourself? It is a nonfunctional notion, like the square root of negative infinity or, if you prefer, a mare's nest. The good Baron Bodissey issued a definitive dictum: 'Truth is a barnacle on the arse of progress.'" He took the last lemon tart from the platter.

Wingo sighed and rose to his feet. He replenished the platter and resumed his place at the table. "I suggest that you try the rainberry creamcakes. The frosted eclairs are also quite good."

"Thank you," said Cuireg. "I shall do so at once. Is there still tea in the pot?"

Wingo refilled Cuireg's cup.

"Now," said Cuireg, "if you are still interested, I will tell you why I am travelling to Kyril."

"Just as you like," said Wingo, rather stiffly. "I do not care to intrude, even slightly, upon your privacy. My curiosity, such as it is, is only casual."

"In that case, I can satisfy this concern in five seconds or less." Cuireg took a rainberry creamcake from the platter. "I am visiting Kyril to verify the recollections of my first visit."

Wingo stared in surprise.

Cuireg went on pensively. "All this happened a long time ago, during the romantic phase of my life. The visit to Kyril seemed a gallant adventure, and so it was." His voice fell, and he seemed to reflect. He said presently: "There are too many memories. They come in a welter: images; voices, colors, faces, landscapes. Thousands of episodes; large tragedies, small triumphs." He watched silently as Wingo refilled his teacup, then went on.

"Kyril is not a kindly world. The pilgrim's way leads across arid wastes, dunes, bogs and moors, and rolling savannahs where nothing grows but thorn trees and canker bush. The weather is unpredictable; there are morning mists and afternoon thunderstorms. At night three dim moons drift across the sky.

"There are occasional inns and shelters along the wayside, where one may sit and watch the pilgrims pass by in never-ending diversity: young and old, men and women, often children. Sometimes they sing as they march past; sometimes they chant mantras. At times a madman rushes past, dancing and leaping, cursing the sky. His cries fade into the distance, and all is as before.

"In the far west is the Holy Mountain, a dying volcano with a crater at the summit where red-hot lava bubbles and seethes. The way up the mountain is hard and steep; some of the pilgrims are forced to crawl to the top."

Wingo was perturbed to hear of such shocking hardships. "What happens to these poor unfortunates?"

Cuireg shrugged, not over-interested in the topic. "They drag themselves up to the rim, where they rest and mend themselves. Eventually they rejoin the others.

"The way around the lip of the crater is, in effect, the focus of the pilgrimage. Halfway around, a look-out platform projects over the void, providing a spectacular view of the crater and the glowing magma below. Most of the pilgrims avoid the platform for fear of vertigo. However, at times someone succumbs to an attack of religious frenzy and runs out on the platform and throws himself into space, plunging down to disappear into the lava. Occasionally he seizes up his child—or someone else's child, for that matter—and hurls it out into the void. Most often, though, he is restrained by other pilgrims, and the child is dragged back to safety—often followed by the father, who has decided not to jump after all."

Wingo shook his head in wonder. "The pilgrimage is intense and dramatic beyond all expectations. I begin to understand the motive which urges you back to Kyril."

Cuireg, ignoring Wingo's comment, tested a frosted eclair. "In any case, the pilgrims finally return to Impy's Landing. They set off to the west, they return from the east; it is a moment of supreme exaltation! They laugh, they cry, they drop to their knees and kiss the ground; never have they known triumph so intense. The memory of this instant will be with them always."

"All this is clear, and dramatic," said Wingo. "To complete the pilgrimage is an act of personal vindication. But why do they come to Kyril in the first place?"

"There are as many reasons as there are pilgrims," said Cuireg. "Some want to appease their divinity; others want to mollify an ancestral ghost. Many are hermetics who want to mortify their flesh. Some hope to atone for forbidden acts; others want to evade an irascible spouse."

Wingo asked, half-facetiously: "And where on this list is your motive for undertaking the pilgrimage?"

Cuireg responded to the question without rancor. "There is no simple answer. Originally the pilgrimage was a challenge to my self-esteem, which I felt obliged to meet. Then, after three or four days along the way, my attitude insensibly began to change. The challenge lost its thrust, and faded from my mind. I found myself watching, and listening, and feeling with ever more intensity. I felt ever more aware of details and textures and nuances. One morning knowledge came to me in a burst of insight. I saw a black lump of rock thrusting up between bushes at the side of the road; I stopped short and said: 'Rock, I see you well enough, but you cannot see me. Why? Because I am sentient, but you are not! Why should this be? Simple enough! I am animate, and you are an inert lump.'"

"Remarkable," said Wingo. "There are inspirational elements here—although it seems rather pointless to taunt the rock."

"It did no great harm." Cuireg rose to his feet. "Thank you for the pleasant occasion. The pastries were beyond reproach." He nodded courteously, and left the galley.

Wingo remained at the table, drinking tea and brooding upon what he had learned.

5

The voyage proceeded without untoward incident. The pilgrims occupied themselves with study, doctrinal discussions and a few low-key games of Cagliostro, from which Schwatzendale was excluded, his past successes still rankling among the defeated players. Cuireg remained as aloof as ever, avoiding the morning colloquies and rebuffing all of Cooner's attempts to engage him in sectarian discourse.

The crew of the *Glicca* performed their usual duties, although Wingo now spent much time thinking over what he had learned of

Kyril, and the march around the great continent. By degrees he began to comprehend Cuireg's perception of the pilgrimage as a metaphor for an event of far larger significance. All very well, thought Wingo, but what of the pilgrims themselves? What compulsion induced them to undertake the hardships of the great march? The motives which Cuireg had facetiously suggested could not be taken seriously; what then? After deep reflection, Wingo thought to comprehend the impulse which prompted the pilgrims to undertake their great adventure—an urge superficially like that which sent the lemmings of Old Earth swarming out to sea. This, of course, was not the essential reason, thought Wingo; rather it was a real—if perhaps subconscious—assertion of vitality, and a rather desperate test of personal fortitude, physical and spiritual alike.

Wingo's preoccupation affected his ordinary conduct more than he realized. His cheerful ebullience became muted; his loquacity dwindled to absent-minded mutters. The change attracted the attention of his shipmates, and finally Schwatzendale, confronting him across the galley table, put an uncompromising question. Wingo gave an evasive answer, but Schwatzendale persisted, and in the end Wingo reported his conversation with Cuireg in full detail. He went on to say: "Despite his manner, which is hardly engaging, he is a most complicated man: a savant of high prestige, also an epicure, a cynic, and at the basis—almost incredibly—a romantic adventurer!"

"Peculiar!" said Schwatzendale. "He seems modest and retiring, with a rather sour disposition."

"That is an illusion," said Wingo. "He cultivates a manner of supercilious detachment to discourage excessive familiarity. The pose actually masks a keen perceptivity; when he chooses to speak, his views are most illuminating. I now understand the true nature of Kyril, and the conditions which the pilgrims encounter as they travel the great circuit. The march is not altogether sterile; there are surprises along the way—not always happy, but those who ultimately return to Impy's Landing find the triumph of their achievement an adequate requital for the hardships suffered along the way."

"Bah," growled Schwatzendale after a moment. "If this moment of relief is the only reward for so much toil, what is the point of the pilgrimage? It would seem a useless exercise, except for hermetics and flagellants."

"Not so," Wingo declared. "The pilgrimage has a subliminal purpose, which, admittedly, cannot easily be verbalized."

"I have no trouble," Schwatzendale stated. "It is an exercise in sheer futility, leading from nowhere to nowhere. It seems inexpressibly pointless."

Wingo managed a patient smile. "There are aspects to the pilgrimage which you do not understand! They are admittedly on a subliminal level, but still they are intensely important! The great march is a gauge by which a pilgrim can measure personal worth. When he returns to Impy's Landing from the east, he feels a personal vindication which must be close to exaltation!"

"Understandable," said Schwatzendale. "They are tired of walking."

Wingo, still smiling, shook his head. "Cuireg has already made the circuit. He has found imponderable aspects to the pilgrimage, which, in candor, I do not fully understand, but I am bound to take seriously."

"My dear fellow, you have been hypnotized," said Schwatzendale, rising to his feet. "I see that I must have a word with this redoubtable savant."

Wingo's smile became wry. "I wonder which of you will end up the more bewildered."

Schwatzendale said: "Despite his erudition, Cuireg still pulls on his trousers one leg at a time." He departed the galley, leaving Wingo first to sigh, then ponder.

Schwatzendale found the scholar in a relatively expansive mood. In amusement he described himself as not only a scholar, an epicure, and an adventurer, but also a creative financier who might undertake certain commercial developments at Impy's Landing. In response to Schwatzendale's questions, he provided information regarding the pilgrimage, some of which Schwatzendale found intriguing, some daunting, even macabre.

Time passed, and the voyage approached its termination. On the day that the cold white spark that was the star Rhys appeared ahead, Wingo entered the pilot-house, where Captain Maloof sat checking the entry on Kyril in *Handbook to the Planets*.

Wingo, distraught and half-desperate, came directly to the point. "Captain! After much turmoil, I have finally arrived at a decision!"

"Indeed," said Maloof, looking up and setting aside the *Handbook*. "In regard to what?"

Wingo came to stand before him. "Over the last few weeks I have taken stock of my life, and I find that it has arrived at a juncture. In one direction I continue as before, along an easy route. In the other direction there are challenges; the way is difficult and often bleak, but this route shows me to myself. After weighing both options, I have made my decision. At Impy's Landing I will resign my post aboard the *Glicca*;

I will then set off to the west, like any other pilgrim. In the end I will return from the east, inflated with pure triumph much like lurulu!" Wingo held up a clenched pink fist as a peroration to his remarks. "That is the gist of it. You have heard what I came to tell you. Our friendship persists!"

"Naturally," said Maloof. "Perhaps more than ever! But a thought occurs to me. Perhaps you will lose more than you gain."

Wingo grimaced. "I know what I am losing. It is a fellowship which I cherish beyond words! My dearest wish would be that we dock the *Glicca* at Impy's Landing and all four of us march off into the west, to return at last from the east, where we would share our triumph together, in the happiest moment of our lives!"

Maloof spoke dryly: "I am sure that we would all be glad to get back." He sighed. "Even in a dream, such a fantasy would seem bizarre."

"You must open your mind!" declared Wingo. "With dedication, the vision becomes real, and the triumph lives with us forever!"

Maloof sighed again, and leaned back in his chair. "Let us call in Schwatzendale, and test his reaction to the scheme."

Wingo said dubiously: "Fay is often indecisive; we must remind him of his bent for gallant adventure."

"Ha hm," said Maloof. He spoke into a mesh.

A moment later Schwatzendale appeared. He glanced from one to the other. "What is required of me?"

"We need your counsel," said Maloof. "We are faced with an unprecedented situation. Wingo intends to leave the ship at Impy's Landing, and set off pilgrim-style on a circuit of the continent."

"Truly?" Schwatzendale turned Wingo a grave inspection.

"That is not the whole of it. He wants the entire crew to join the venture—so that, when we return to Impy's Landing from the east, we shall celebrate the triumph together. Am I right, Wingo?"

"You have stated the matter concisely," said Wingo. "I might add that the feat is guided by a set of subliminal archetypes, which will transfigure the rest of our lives with grandeur."

"It is a novel idea," Schwatzendale admitted. "Startling, preposterous, and innocent! It would never have occurred to me—especially after my conversation with Cuireg. Apparently there are negative aspects to the pilgrimage, which are never publicized. For instance, only a modest percentage of those starting out from Impy's Landing to the west ever return from the east; many abandon the venture after a day or two. The way is especially hard on folk with sensitive feet, because of sharp flints in the road."

Wingo stared down at his own delicate feet. "This makes for poor hearing," he told himself. "Still, it cannot be ignored."

Schwatzendale went on to discuss more of what he had learned from Cuireg. "Many old persons with little vitality set out from Impy's Landing and die along the way from disease, hunger, dysentery, and physical abuse. Nights are especially dangerous; thugs come to steal boots—they use cudgels to smash knees and ankles at so much as a whimper!"

"That is inhuman!" gasped Wingo. "One should only travel with trusted companions!"

"The plan is attractive, but not always practical. You must pay a large sum to join a group. They march at a quick-step, and you must keep pace, sore feet and all; otherwise you will be left behind. If you pay out all your money, you will not have enough to buy food from the roadside shelters—should you choose to do so. Squeamish persons avoid the pale pink stew at all costs, and forage on tubers and seeds. But the worst is still ahead. Where the way crosses the hills it is paved with flints which cut your feet into bloody lumps; what then?"

Wingo considered the unpleasant possibility. "I have no choice! I must continue on hands and knees until the road is better."

"All very well," said Schwatzendale, "but the road is still only a tumble of shards and flints, and in the end your knees are a clutter of broken bones; what now?"

Wingo spoke in a taut thin voice: "I have not thought that far ahead, but I suppose that if I must, I will turn about and skooch along on my backside. It will be slow and painful, but better than sitting alone in the wilderness, at night under the light of the three dim moons. It is not a happy prospect."

"Even where the way leaves the hills, another enemy awaits you. The thorn trees hang overhead and drop thorns into the way. As you skooch along, these thorns will be driven into your bottom, so that every thorn will require a halt, a search, and a withdrawal before the next gallant surge forward. I suppose that a person in this condition might complete the circuit in ten years, to gain what? Glory? Triumph? More likely, a sickening grief for the tribulations which he has suffered for nothing."

Wingo sighed. "It has become clear—starkly so!—that I am not the man to test my fortitude in this fashion. It is troubling, certainly, but I must alter my resolve, and gladly."

Maloof asked with gentle solicitude: "Then you are not leaving the *Glicca* after all?"

Wingo sighed again. "Definitely not. The pilgrimage no longer carries a romantic association."

"You have arrived at a wise decision," said Maloof. "Do you not agree, Fay?"

"Totally, and in every respect," said Schwatzendale.

TWELVE

1

In due course the *Glicca* arrived at Impy's Landing. The pilgrims disembarked with graceless haste, led by the ineffable Cooner; Cuireg followed more deliberately, ignoring the others as if they had been strangers, and took himself to the most pretentious hostelry of the town where, if his statements were to be credited, he would prepare to transact the business which had brought him to Kyril.

As soon as the chests of sanctified soil had been discharged from the cargo bay, the *Glicca* prepared to set off for Port Tanjee on the world Taubry. Myron noticed that Naharius lay not far from the direct route to Port Tanjee. Prompted by a surge of old emotion, he felt a strong impulse to visit Naharius; if nothing else, he wanted to learn what transformation the fabulous local therapies had worked upon his great-aunt, Dame Hester Lajoie.

Captain Maloof was also curious, and made no difficulty about altering the ship's course so that the *Glicca* might put into Naharius.

2

Handbook to the Planets, for whatever reason, had little to say about Naharius. After citing geo-physical statistics, the text went on to state:

> The population of Naharius, for a variety of reasons, is relatively sparse and is concentrated in the neighborhood of Trajence, a partially urbanized settlement adjacent to the spaceport.
>
> A few miles east of Trajence an extinct volcano, Mount Maldoun,

rises from a line of low hills. Down the mountainside flow three streams, which, after seeping through wooded vales grown over with unique plants and mosses, become charged, according to local beliefs, with remarkable powers.

Even more potent are the waters from the sacred springs appearing at the base of the mountain. These waters, when used in conjunction with the therapies provided by local practitioners, reputedly neutralize the ravages of time and are said to restore at least the superficial aspects of youth. Such reports, whether or not accurate, attract ailing and aged persons from far and wide, hoping to participate in a miracle.

What is the truth regarding the therapies? Rigorous evidence is hard to come by. The *Handbook* advises caution.

3

The *Glicca* arrived at the Trajence spaceport. Other vessels were docked at the far end of the field; the *Glodwyn* was not among them.

Wingo and Schwatzendale rode an omnibus into town, while Maloof and Myron set off to learn what they could of Dame Hester Lajoie. They inquired first at the three principal clinics, then at less formal facilities.

During the afternoon of the second day they were referred to the Wayfarer's Hospice, a cheerless block of gray concrete on the outskirts of the settlement, which provided terminal shelter for the aged, the ailing, and the indigent. An orderly conducted them into a cavernous chamber, dim and ill-smelling, lined along the walls with narrow cots, at the moment only partially occupied. He indicated a cot at the far end of the chamber, then returned to his station and left them to their own devices.

Maloof and Myron approached the indicated cot. Under the sheet a thin and fragile shape barely created an outline. A gaunt head protruded, the skin drawn drum-taut around the contours of the skull. Arms brittle as twigs, terminating in bird-like claws, lay on the sheet beside the body.

Myron studied the bony wisp, controlling inner spasms of pity and horror, with an effort. A limp straggle of maroon hair, a long, pointed chin, and a twisted tendril of what once had been a rapacious nose identified a version of Dame Hester Lajoie.

A slight up-and-down shift of the sheet indicated that vitality was not yet exhausted. Peering into the dull eyes, Myron thought to see a flicker of recognition. Her lips twitched; her throat clenched; she produced a rasping sound. Myron leaned forward and thought to hear her say: "You have come at last." Her voice faded; then once again she managed to whisper: "It is very late. They took all my money, then they abused me, and cheated my hope, and put me here to take my wonderful life from me."

Myron could think of nothing to say.

As if driven by an obsession, gasping and wheezing, Dame Hester contrived to tell the bitter tale of what had befallen her. In the beginning, the practitioners, after receipt of their fees, had seemed to fall in with her requirements. They started her on a regimen of standard therapy, which she found overly stringent, but which they would not modify. There was arduous exercise; she was fed coarse black biscuits and a thin grassy soup. Daily she was rubbed with a few minims of water from one of the magic springs, and daily she ingested a gill of a secret ichor compounded from water of the three most potent streams.

As time went on, the practitioners took more of her money, but she discerned no significant changes in her personal attributes. The practitioners warned her against impatience and continued the regimen; but the metamorphosis into lissome new youth was slow in coming.

She complained, but the practitioners only demanded more money. At last Dame Hester dispensed with their services and embarked upon a therapy of her own devising, and instead of one regimen, she undertook three at the same time. Instead of careful lavations with a few minims of the miraculous water, she bathed daily in one or another of the springs, and imbibed gallons of the fabulous flow of the streams.

In the end she achieved nothing, and indeed became listless and ill; finally, her constitution gave way and she collapsed. The practitioners, when they found that she had no more money, refused to help her, stating that she had brought mortifaction upon herself and must now formulate her own solution to the problem. Eventually they sent her to the hospice.

Dame Hester sighed and gasped. "It has been a dreadful time." She paused, then, clenching and unclenching her clawlike fingers, spoke on. Now, she stated, all would be mended if Myron would whisk her back to Salou Sain, where she would surely recover her health, and all would be as before.

Myron asked cautiously: "What happened to Marko Fassig?"

The frail body quivered. The rasping whisper became hectic. "He was the worst traitor of all! He stole the *Glodwyn* and took it Beyond. There was news that pirates had killed him, which I will never regret, but the *Glodwyn* is gone forever. No matter; back at Salou Sain there will be another *Glodwyn*." She fell silent; her eyelids drooped. Then she spoke in a husky whisper: "I have done you a wrong; I am now filled with remorse. Once more at Salou Sain I will make amends." The whisper faded into silence, and again the eyelids drooped. She lay still, and signs of respiration were no longer evident.

Maloof said in a sepulchral voice: "She has gone into a coma."

Myron studied the still form. "No; there is still something going on."

A moment passed. The still figure gave a convulsive jerk; the eyelids lifted. She spoke in a guttural croak: "It is folly! There is nothing more—the doom is on me. I shall never breathe the sweet air of home again. I will do now what I must." She reached a trembling arm to the table beside the cot, took up a stylus, and scrawled hasty words and sentences upon a sheet of paper. When she had finished she dropped the pencil and let her arm sag upon the cot. She closed her eyes and lay still.

Myron took up the paper and read what Dame Hester had written. "It is a will," he told Maloof. "She leaves everything she owns to me."

Maloof scrutinized the document. "It appears to be valid, and I am a reputable witness."

Myron folded the document and tucked it into his pocket. For a time the two men watched the still figure. The eyes remained closed, and there was no further rise and fall of the sheet. Maloof said at last: "I think that she is dead."

"I think so, too," said Myron.

After another few moments Maloof stirred. "There is nothing to be gained by waiting."

"No," said Myron. "Nothing at all."

The two men left the chamber. In the front office they informed the orderly that the person whom they had come to visit was dead. The orderly showed neither surprise nor concern, but appraised the two spacemen sidelong. "You are evidently blood relatives of the deceased?"

"By no means," said Maloof. "We are here only to oblige a friend, who himself is indigent."

"A pity," said the orderly. "Still, for sixty sols I can arrange a fine funeral with pyrotechnics, a priest, athletic contests, and dancing children waving colored scarves to the music of a belp-horn."

Maloof said: "This sort of rite is unnecessary. The dead, during or after cremation, are indifferent to such a display; at least, this is my experience. A simple ceremony at minimum cost will suffice."

"Bah," muttered the orderly. "I can provide a simple ceremony for ten sols. There will be no dignitaries on hand, and the only music will be five recorded fanfares. For another sol, I will provide three sticks of incense."

Myron paid over ten sols. "You may omit the incense."

"As you like."

4

After a three-day layover at Port Tanjee, the *Glicca* was scheduled to continue onward to Salou Sain, where Myron now had important business to transact in connection with Dame Hester's estate. Captain Maloof agreed, however, to another detour; on this occasion, the *Glicca* would call at the city Duvray on the world Alcydon, site of the Pan-Arts Museum, and more importantly, the residence of Tibbet Garwig.

The *Glicca* landed at the Duvray spaceport. Myron gathered the parcels intended for Tibbet, departed the *Glicca*, and rode by taxicab through the elegant city into the fashionable Ranglin Heights district, to the Garwig residence: an imposing mansion at the back of a garden. Myron alighted and, after arranging for the cab to wait, set off along the path which led through the garden.

Almost immediately he was confronted by a pair of objects standing at either side of the path: statues twelve feet tall, apparently wrought by a mad genius in the avant-garde mode, as icons to represent his contempt for ordinary conventions of society. The objects were constructed of unusual materials, spars of metal, and twisted, pitted shapes contorted as if half-in half-out of another dimension. Gray-pink tubing looking unpleasantly like viscera wound in and out of the other materials. Myron stared at the objects in wonder; the Garwigs evidently were members of a clique where such demonstrations were fashionable. Odd, indeed!

He continued up the path to the front entrance, a massive door at the back of a short portico. The door lacked knob, latch, handle, or other such device; Myron looked in vain for a bell-push or knocker. Fixed to the door was a heavy demon-mask of antique copper, the features molded in high relief to express a leer of malignant triumph—or perhaps some other horrid emotion. The eyes bulged; the ears were distorted wads; a long black tongue dangled from the mouth. Myron gave his head a grim shake: here was another phase of avant-garde doctrine, where shock and novelty were accorded the highest priority. He wondered to what extent Tibbet had been infected; it was a depressing thought. He looked again for a bell-push, a toggle, or other signalling device, but as before found nothing. He pounded the door with his knuckles but produced only a muffled thump; he kicked the door with like result. Then, as a last resort, Myron pulled at the dangling tongue, and immediately from within came a peculiar fluting ululation, a quasi-musical sequence of discords lacking all charm, but which Myron nevertheless found intriguing; he pulled at the tongue a second time, eliciting a new, equally random set of discords. Strange! he thought. It was not music but the studious creation of non-music: another avant-garde demonstration! He reached to pull at the tongue a third time, but the door swung aside.

In the opening stood a tall woman wearing a house-maid's uniform, bearing an expression of annoyance. She swept Myron up and down with a severe gaze, then said: "What, sir, are your needs?"

Myron drew together the shreds of his dignity. "I am calling upon the Lady Tibbet. Be so good as to announce my presence."

The maid regarded him without sympathy. "That is beyond my ability, sir. The Lady is not on the premises."

"Oh? In that case, if you expect her back within a reasonable time, I will wait."

"That would not be practical, sir. Lady Tibbet and her husband are off-world, at the Palisades on Frantock, collecting shards for the Museum. Do you care to leave a message?"

"Yes," said Myron. "You may mention that Peter Birdsong called on a matter of no great importance."

"Very well, sir."

5

Myron returned to the cab and was conveyed back to the spaceport. Aboard the *Glicca*, Captain Maloof, Schwatzendale, and Wingo were in the galley, taking a mid-morning collation of tea and pastries. Myron went quietly to his quarters, stowed the parcels in a locker, changed into his ordinary clothes, then stood irresolute. At last he shrugged; there was nothing to be gained by delay. He drew a deep breath, squared his shoulders, and marched from his cabin, across the saloon, and into the galley. He seated himself, poured a cup of tea, and took a lemon tart from the tray.

His shipmates watched him with mild curiosity. Wingo at last spoke. "You are back early. How went the affair?"

Myron made a measured response. "All in all, the 'affair', as you put it, went smoothly, though in a negative direction." After a moment of rumination, he added: "If anyone is interested, I will mention that there is no longer any connection between Tibbet Garwig and myself."

"We are politely interested, of course," said Maloof. "I cannot help but notice that you seem quite definite in this regard."

"I could not be more so," said Myron. He sipped moodily from his cup.

Wingo at last spoke. "If you wish to explain in greater detail, we will listen with care."

Myron slumped back in his chair. "Very well; you shall have the facts in their full regalia. I rode by cab to the Garwig mansion without so much as an inkling of doom. I arranged for the cab to wait, then set off through the garden toward the house. Almost at once I was confronted by a pair of what I shall call 'statues'; they stood twelve feet tall and were fabricated in the avant-garde style. I found them not only lacking in charm, but actively offensive. I was disturbed; the Garwigs would never have chosen such a site for their statues had they not themselves been members of an avant-garde clique."

Myron went on to describe the massive front door, the copper demon-mask with its dangling black tongue, and the wailing discords produced when the tongue was pulled. He told of his encounter with the housemaid and her information regarding Tibbet. "I disguised my emotions and, returning to the cab, was conveyed back to the *Glicca*. At this time most of the emotions have subsided, and now I feel only gratitude to whatever agency is responsible for my narrow escape—destiny, lurulu, or blind stupid luck."

"Hm," said Wingo, smiling. "Myron uses the word 'luck', which, of course, is simple fatalism. But essentially he recognizes the presence of subliminal forces working at most delicate levels." He looked to Myron. "Am I right?"

Myron shrugged. "Better to say that I am confused."

Wingo spoke seriously. "The circumstances are mysterious. 'Destiny' is what happens; 'lurulu' is far more delicate, and in Myron's case, it exerts a protective influence—which, of course, is most interesting."

"Balderdash," said Schwatzendale, tilting his head and arching his eyebrows at different angles.

Myron said: "Tibbet will certainly be confused when she tries to identify 'Peter Birdsong'."

Captain Maloof rose to his feet. "Perhaps I alone am not confused, since for the moment I have become an unalloyed fatalist. I can see, without ambiguity, that the time has come for us to continue our voyage. On the alert—seal the ports; make ready for departure."

6

The *Glicca* arrived at the world Vermazen, and settled upon the space-port at Salou Sain. On the day after arrival, Myron visited the Municipal Conservancy, where Dame Hester's last will and testament was validated with a gratifying absence of formality. Myron found himself in possession of an unexpectedly large estate, which included the grand mansion Sarbiter House on Dingle Terrace.

Myron hired a domestic staff; then he and his shipmates took up residence among the luxurious precincts of the mansion, where they quickly developed an extremely agreeable pattern of existence. When the days were fine, they took long and languorous breakfasts in the garden. During the afternoons, they sometimes wandered into town, alone or as a group. Most often, though, they remained at the house lounging beside the pool, consuming fruit punches, and socializing with new acquaintances.

Dinners were formal, in the wood-panelled dining room, under a chandelier of a thousand glittering crystals. There were always seven, eight, or even nine courses, enhanced by dusty bottles brought up from the cellars.

After dinner, the four usually moved into the dim old library, where a fire burned in the stone fireplace, and chairs upholstered in soft leather awaited their coming. Decanters charged with spirits, essences, and distillations of notable marks were ready to hand. Conversation touched upon many topics and often continued into the late hours. Persons of recent acquaintance were discussed and their attributes analyzed; or the talk might wander to remote ports of call and the odd folk who dwelt in far places. Profundities sometimes entered the conversation, usually in response to Wingo's predilection for abstruse philosophy. Occasionally the word 'lurulu' was mentioned, and it developed that each of the four invested the word with a different significance.

During such discussions Maloof had little to say, and Myron even less, but Schwatzendale enlivened the discourse with fanciful conjectures, which Wingo felt compelled to qualify or refute before resuming his own remarks.

"If you recall, we were speaking of lurulu. At the risk of banality, I will point out that 'fate', 'destiny', and 'lurulu' are not synonymous. 'Fate' is dark and ponderous; 'destiny' is more like a beautiful sunset. In speaking of 'lurulu', however, language of this kind is not useful. Lurulu is personal; it is like hope, or a wistful longing, more real than a dream."

"Bah," grumbled Schwatzendale. "Wingo has become a poet; he

decorates the air with verbal finery, in the same way that he frosts his pastry with fine icing."

Wingo sighed. "My purposes are not ignoble; I believe the cosmos to be a thing of many complexities, most of which have no linkage with the words of our language, and can only be addressed through the use of allusion."

"Bah!" said Schwatzendale again. "Balderdash, of the purest stripe! The language serves us very well; why turn it inside-out to describe something which isn't there in the first place?"

Maloof poured wine from the decanter into his goblet. "Your motives are not under attack, but abstract language is not necessary to discuss lurulu, when sitting next to you, not a yard away, is the real thing—I refer to Myron, naturally. He is strong, personable, sound of wind; he has an easy disposition and a full head of hair. He lives in a palace; he has more wealth than he can count, and he wants for nothing. The girls find him appealing, and they cluster around him in a nimbus of charming vitality. If Myron needs someone to peel him a grape, or to scratch an inconvenient itch, he need only cock an eyebrow and the task is accomplished; Myron is the very embodiment of lurulu!"

Myron leaned back in his chair. "I don't know. If I look in the mirror, I see someone quite ordinary, only lucky enough to have Dame Hester Lajoie for an aunt."

Schwatzendale amended the statement: "Better to say, for a dead aunt."

Myron nodded. "Just so. In any case, it is not so easy as you might think. Half the time I feel guilty, as if I had been caught with my hand in the cookie jar." Myron looked from face to face. "You are laughing at me."

"Such qualms are hardly surprising," said Maloof. "I shouldn't worry about them overmuch."

Myron agreed. "But sometimes another mood comes on me. I feel nervous, or restless, and I have a dim intuition as to the cause." Myron leaned forward and stared into the fire. "I would feel more secure if the three of you were always to share this lurulu with me."

For a time the four sat in silence, gazing into the fire. Then Maloof said quietly: "Your intuition is correct. Transience cannot be altered. Your program, for all its idyllic qualities, never has been feasible. I am not a natural sybarite, content to live in an enchanted dream; I am restless, and possibly Wingo and Schwatzendale as well. The *Glicca* has been totally overhauled—it gleams with fresh enamel and new metal;

the galley flaunts some splendid new equipment. At the moment it sits at the side of the yard like an abandoned waif." Maloof laughed. "Could the *Glicca* be lonely? It is a point I must take up with Wingo—although I can see by his face that he has doubts."

"Not necessarily," declared Wingo. "It is a tantalizing thought."

Schwatzendale yawned and rose to his feet. "At this moment I still enjoy decadence, and I am trying to break several records in the field. The life of a full-fledged epicurean, dancing with flowers and smelling beautiful ladies, requires more strength of character than I can deploy at this time! I am off to bed—good night, all." He departed the library and was presently followed by Maloof and Wingo, and finally Myron, leaving the fire to flicker to a smoulder in the silent library.

7

On several occasions Myron visited his father and mother at the family home in Lilling. The visits were never wholly comfortable, since his parents had never abandoned the hope that Myron might be induced to remain at Lilling and take up a position at the Exchange, where he could work in association with his father. Such a step could be the basis for a most creditable career, and would certainly enhance Myron's reputation. Myron politely rejected these proposals, citing his commitments at Salou Sain.

Once Myron urged his parents to spend some time with him at Salou Sain. The invitation was accepted, and in due course the parents travelled to Salou Sain, to spend two days at Sarbiter House. During this time the elderly Tanys used the utmost propriety, and irreproachable good manners, but were secretly perturbed by the casual conduct of Myron and his companions. They thankfully returned to Lilling, convinced that Myron's friends were vagabonds, intent upon infecting him with their own deplorable standards.

Weeks passed, and departure from Salou Sain began to be openly discussed. Finally, during one dreary dinner a definite date was fixed upon, a date a week and a half hence.

The days now took on a different character, each with its distinctive identity. Captain Maloof, Wingo, and Schwatzendale visited the *Glicca* and were occasionally joined by Myron, but more often Myron remained alone at Sarbiter House, thinking dismal thoughts.

A day and a half before departure, Myron was galvanized by a sudden impulse. He visited his bank and his legal representative, made arrangements with an estate agent, dismissed the domestic staff, hired caretakers, and packed his personal gear. On the appointed day, at the specified hour, the *Glicca* departed the Salou Sain spaceport. Aboard were Captain Maloof, Schwatzendale, Wingo, and, to no one's surprise, Myron Tany.